Two for

Lindsey Davis was born in Birmingham but now lives in Greenwich. After an English degree at Oxford she joined the Civil Service but now writes full time.

Eight of her novels featuring Marcus Didius Falco are available in Arrow paperback. *Two for the Lions* won the first CWA Ellis Peters Historical Dagger.

ALSO BY LINDSEY DAVIS

The Course of Honour

TWO FOR THE LIONS

Lindsey Davis

ARROW

Published by Arrow Books in 1999

1 3 5 7 9 10 8 6 4 2

Copyright © Lindsey Davis 1998

Lindsey Davis has asserted her right under the Copyright, Designs and Patents Act, 1988 to be identified as the author of this work

First published in the United Kingdom in 1998 by Century

Arrow Books Limited
20 Vauxhall Bridge Road, London SW1V 2SA

Random House Australia (Pty) Limited
20 Alfred Street, Milsons Point, Sydney,
New South Wales 2061, Australia

Random House New Zealand Limited
18 Poland Road, Glenfield
Auckland 10, New Zealand

Random House South Africa (Pty) Limited
Endulini, 5a Jubilee Road, Parktown 2193, South Africa

Random House UK Limited Reg. No. 954009

A CIP catalogue record for this book
is available from the British Library

Papers used by Random House UK Limited
are natural, recyclable products made from wood grown in sustainable forests. The manufacturing processes conform to the environmental regulations of the country of origin

ISBN 0 09 979961 8

Typeset by Deltatype Limited, Birkenhead, Merseyside
Printed and bound in Germany by
Elsnerdruck, Berlin

*The tenth Falco novel is dedicated
with the author's affection and gratitude
to all the readers who have made this
continuing series possible*

PRINCIPAL CHARACTERS

Friends

M Didius Falco	Director of Falco & Partner, auditors to the Census
Anacrites	Temporary partner in Falco & Partner, a protégé
Ma	Permanent protector of Anacrites
Helena Justina	Permanent partner of Falco
Julia Junilla	Infant child of Falco and Helena
Pa (Geminus)	Ex-partner of, and in need of protection from Ma
Maia	Falco's youngest sister, looking for her chance
Famia	Maia's husband, looking for a drink
D Camillus Verus	A senator, father to Helena, looking for his son
Q Camillus Justinus	An idealist, looking for a plant
Claudia Rufina	An heiress disappointed in love
A Camillus Aelianus	A hopeful, disappointed in money
Lenia	Looking to let go of her husband
Smaractus	Looking to hang on to his wife's cash
Rodan & Asiacus	Deadbeats, regularly beaten and usually half-dead
Thalia	An exotic circus manager

Romans

Vespasian Augustus	Emperor and Censor, building the Flavian Amphitheatre
Antonia Caenis	Mistress and long-term partner to the Emperor
Claudius Laeta	Senior administrator at the Palace, a loner
Rutilius Gallicus	Special Envoy to Tripolitania
Romanus	An unknown
Scilla	A wild girl looking for a legal device

Pomponius Urtica	A praetor who never did anything illegal
Rumex	A celebrity graffiti
Buxus	An animal keeper
An elderly gooseboy	Just looking at birds all day

Tripolitanians

Saturninus	A gladiators' trainer, from Lepcis Magna
Euphrasia	His wife, who has promised to say nothing
Calliopus	A venatio specialist, from Oea
Artemisia	His wife, who can't say anything as she isn't there
Hanno	A man who can afford to pay his taxes, from Sabratha
Myrrha	Who may say something, but only in Punic
Iddibal	A far from beastly bestiarius
Fidelis	A faithful interpreter

Animals

Nux	A personable pup, commander of the Falco household
Leonidas	A friendly lion, who is due to make a killer dead meat
Draco	A very unfriendly lion
Anethum	A performer who brings lying doggo to perfection

Also featuring	Borago the bear, Ruta the alleged aurochs, Ostriches, Pigeons, Lions, Stone lions, A Leopardess

By Special Request	Jason the python
And Introducing	The Sacred Geese of Juno

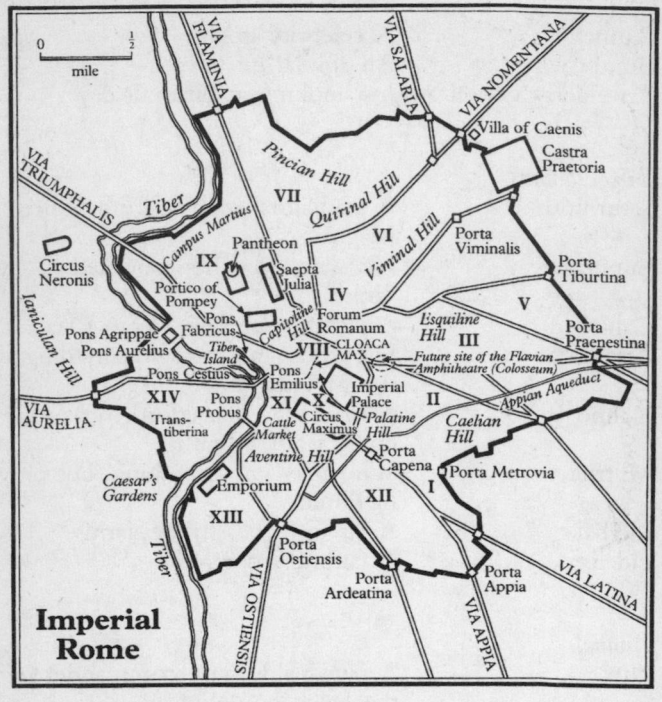

Jurisdictions of the Vigiles Cohorts in Rome:

Coh I	Regions VII & VIII (Via Lata, Forum Romanum)
Coh II	Regions III & V (Isis and Serapis, Esquiline)
Coh III	Regions IV & VI (Temple of Peace, Alta Semita)
Coh IV	Regions XII & XIII (Piscina Publica, Aventine)
Coh V	Regions I & II (Porta Capena, Caelimontium)
Coh VI	Regions X & XI (Palatine, Circus Maximus)
Coh VII	Regions IX & XIV (Circus Flaminius, Transtiberina)

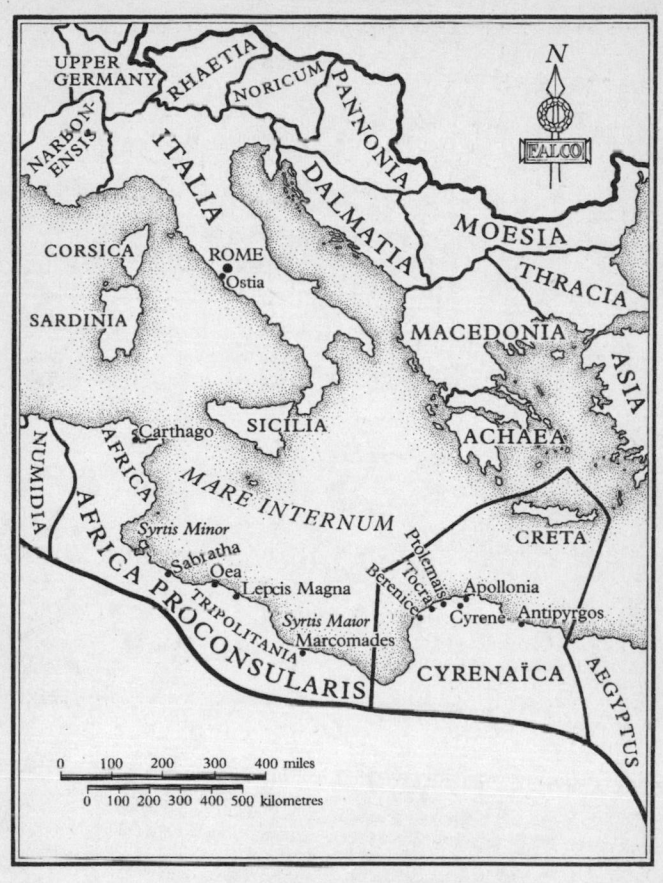

Tripolitania and Cyrenaïca

PART ONE

ROME: December, AD73 – April AD74

I

My partner and I had been well set up to earn our fortunes until we were told about the corpse.

Death, it has to be said, was ever-present in those surroundings. Anacrites and I were working among the suppliers of wild beasts and gladiators for the arena Games in Rome; every time we took our auditing note tablets on a site visit, we spent the day surrounded by those who were destined to die in the near future and those who would only escape being killed if they killed someone else first. Life, the victors' main prize, would be in most cases temporary.

But there amongst the fighters' barracks and the big cats' cages, death was commonplace. Our own victims, the fat businessmen whose financial affairs we were so delicately probing as part of our new career, were themselves looking forwards to long, comfortable lives – yet the formal description of their business was *Slaughter*. Their stock-in-trade was measured as units of mass murder; their success would depend upon those units satisfying the crowd in straightforward volume terms, and upon their devising ever more sophisticated ways to deliver the blood.

We knew there must be big money in it. The suppliers and trainers were free men – a prerequisite of engaging in commerce, however sordid – and so they had presented themselves with the rest of Roman society in the Great Census. This had been decreed by the Emperor on his accession, and it was not simply intended to count heads. When Vespasian assumed power in a bankrupt Empire after the chaos of Nero's reign, he famously declared that he would need four hundred million sesterces to restore the Roman world. Lacking a personal fortune, he set out to find funding in the way that seemed most attractive to a man with middle-class origins. He named himself and his elder son Titus as Censors, then called up the rest of us to give an account of ourselves and of everything we owned. Then we were swingeingly taxed on the latter, which was the real point of the exercise.

The shrewd amongst you will deduce that some heads of household found themselves excited by the challenge; foolish fellows tried to minimise the figures when declaring the value of their property. Only those who can afford extremely cute financial advisers ever get away with this, and since the Great Census was intended to rake in four hundred million it was madness to attempt a bluff. The target was too high; evasion would be tackled head-on – by an Emperor who had tax farmers in his recent family pedigree.

The machinery for extortion already existed. The Census traditionally used the first principle of fiscal administration: the Censors had the right to say: *we don't believe a word of what you're telling us*. Then they made their own assessment, and the victim had to pay up accordingly. There was no appeal.

No; that's a lie. Free men always have the right to petition the Emperor. And it's a perk of being Emperor that he can twitch his purple robe and augustly tell them to get lost.

While the Emperor and his son were acting as Censors, it would in any case be a waste of time to ask them to overrule themselves. But first they had to make the hard-hitting reassessments, and for that they needed help. To save Vespasian and Titus from being forced personally to measure the boundaries of estates, interrogate sweaty Forum bankers, or pore over ledgers with an abacus – given that they were simultaneously trying to run the tattered Empire after all – they were now employing my partner and me. The Censors needed to identify cases where they could clamp down. No emperor wants to be accused of cruelty. Somebody had to spot the cheats who could be reassessed without causing an outcry, so Falco & Partner had been hired — at my own suggestion and on an extremely attractive fee basis — to investigate low declarations.

We had hoped this would entail a cosy life scanning columns of neat sums on best quality parchment in rich men's luxurious studies: no such luck. I for one was known to be tough, and as an informer I was probably thought to have slightly grubby origins. So Vespasian and Titus had thwarted me by deciding that they wanted the best value for hiring Falco & Partner (the specific identity of my Partner had not been revealed, for good reasons). They ordered us to forget the easy life and to investigate the grey economy.

Hence the arena. It was thought that the trainers and suppliers were lying through their teeth — as they undoubtedly were, and so was everybody. Anyway their shifty looks had caught the attention of our imperial masters, and that was what we were probing on that seemingly ordinary morning, when we were unexpectedly invited to look at a corpse.

II

Working for the Censors had been my idea. A chance conversation with the senator Camillus Verus some weeks before had alerted me that tax reassessments were being imposed. I realised that this could be properly organised, with a dedicated audit team looking into suspect cases (a category into which Camillus himself did not fall; he was just a poor coot with an unlucky face who fell foul of an assessor and who could not afford the kind of smooth accountant who might have dug him out of it).

Putting myself forward to direct the enquiries proved tricky. There were always scores of bright sparks in their best togas running up to the Palace to suggest wonderful ruses that would be the salvation of the Empire. Court officials were adept at rejecting them. For one thing, even wonderful ideas were not always welcome to Vespasian, because he was a realist. It was said that when an engineer described how the huge new columns for the restored Temple of Jupiter could be hauled up the Capitol very cheaply by mechanical means, Vespasian rejected the idea because he preferred paying the lower classes to do the job and earn themselves money to eat. Certainly the old man knew how to avoid a riot.

I did go up to the Palatine with my suggestion. I sat in an imperial salon full of other hopefuls for half a morning, but I soon grew bored. It was no good, anyway. If I wanted to make money from the Census I had to start quickly. I dared not wait in a queue for months; the Census was only supposed to take a year.

There was another problem at the Palace: my current partner was an imperial employee already. I had not wanted Anacrites to attach himself to me, but after eight hard years as a solo informer I had bowed to pressure from everyone close to me and agreed that I needed a colleague. For a few weeks I worked in harness with my best friend Petronius Longus, who had been temporarily suspended from the vigiles. I'd like to say it had been a success, though in fact his approach had been opposite from mine on virtually everything. When Petro decided to clean up his private life and was reinstated by his tribune, it had been a relief to us both.

That left me with a meagre choice. Nobody wants to be an informer. Not many men have the necessary qualities of shrewdness and tenacity, or decent feet for slogging the pavements, or good contacts for supplying information – particularly information that by rights ought to be unobtainable. Among the few who qualified even fewer wanted my company, especially now Petro was trumpeting all around the Aventine that I was a picky swine to share an office with.

Anacrites and I had never been soul mates. I had disliked him on principle when he was Chief Spy at the court and I was a backstreet operator with only private clients; once I started hacking for Vespasian myself, my dislike was soon enhanced by first hand knowledge that Anacrites was incompetent, devious, and cheap. (All these accusations are levelled at informers too, but that's just slander.) When, during a mission to Nabataea, Anacrites tried to have me murdered I stopped pretending to be tolerant.

Fate took a hand after he was attacked by a would-be assassin. It was not me; I would have made a thorough job of it. Even he knew that. Instead, when he was found unconscious with a hole in his skull, I somehow ended up persuading my own mother to look after him. For weeks his life hung in the balance, but Ma dragged him back from the shore of the Lethe using sheer determination and vegetable broth. After she had saved him I came home from a trip to Baetica to find a bond between them that was as strong as if Ma had fostered an orphaned duck.

Anacrites' respect for my mother was only slightly less revolting than her reverence for him.

It was Ma's idea to foist him on to me. Believe me, the arrangement would only stay in place until I found someone else. In any case, Anacrites was officially on sick-leave from his old job. That was why I could hardly appear at the Palace listing him as half my partnership: the Palace was already paying him to do nothing on account of his terrible head wound, and his superiors must not find out he was moonlighting.

Just one of those additional complications that keep life sweet.

Strictly speaking I already had one partner. She shared my problems and laughed at my mistakes; I was assisted in doing my accounts, solving puzzles, and even sometimes conducting interviews by my live-in love, Helena. If nobody took her seriously as a business associate it was partly because women have no legal identity. Besides, Helena was a senator's daughter; most people still believed she would leave me one day. Even after three years of the closest kind of friendship, after travelling abroad with me, and bearing my child, Helena Justina was still expected to grow tired of me and flee back to her former life. Her illustrious father was the same Camillus Verus who gave me the idea of working for the Censors; her noble mother, Julia Justa, would be only too happy to send a chair to fetch Helena home.

We lived as subtenants in a dire first-floor apartment on the rough side of the Aventine. We had to wash the baby at the public baths and have our baking done at a pie shop. Our dog had brought us several rats as presents, which we reckoned she had caught pretty close to home. This was why I needed decent work, with healthy incomings. The senator would be delighted that his chance remarks had given me the idea for it. He would be even more proud if he ever found out that in the end it was Helena who obtained the work for me.

'Marcus, would you like Papa to ask Vespasian to offer you work with the Censors?'

'No,' I said.

'I thought not.'

'You mean I'm pigheaded?'

'You like to do things for yourself,' Helena replied calmly. She could be at her most insulting when she pretended to be fair.

She was a tall girl, with a strict expression and a searing glance. People who had expected me to find myself some bonny piece with lambswool where her brains should be were still surprised at my choice, but once I had met Helena Justina I reckoned on sticking with her for as long as she would have me. She was neat, scathing, intelligent, wondrously unpredictable. I still could not believe my luck that she had even noticed me, let alone that she lived in my apartment, was the mother of my baby daughter, and had taken charge of my disorganised life.

The gorgeous armful knew that she could run rings around me, and that I loved to let her do it. 'Well Marcus, darling, if you won't be going back to the Palace this afternoon, could you possibly assist me with an errand on the other side of the city?'

'Of course,' I agreed handsomely. Anything to put myself out of reach of Anacrites.

Helena's errand required us to take a hired carrying chair for a distance that made me wonder if the sparse coins in my armpurse would cover the fare. First she dragged us to a warehouse that my auctioneer father owned near the Emporium. He allowed us to use the back end to store things that we had picked up on our travels which were waiting for the day when we had a decent house. I had built a partition to keep Pa out of our section of the warehouse, since he was the sort of entrepreneur who would sell off our carefully chosen treasures for less than we paid for them, then think he had done us a favour.

On today's escapade I was just a passenger. Helena made

no attempt to explain. Various shapeless bales that were obviously none of my business were collected from store and piled on a donkey, then we skirted the Forum and headed over the Esquiline.

We travelled north for ages. Peering through the ragged modesty curtain of our conveyance I saw we were outside the old Servian Walls, apparently aiming for the Praetorian Camp. I made no comment. When people want to have secrets, I just let them get on with it.

'Yes, I've taken a lover in the Guards,' said Helena. Joking, presumably. Her idea of a rough entanglement was me: sensitive lover, loyal protector, sophisticated racon-teur, and would-be poet. Any Praetorian who thought to persuade her otherwise would get my boot up his arse.

We went right around the Camp, and came on to the Via Nomentana. Shortly afterwards we stopped and Helena jumped out. I followed, in surprise because I expected to find her among the winter brassicas in some out of season market garden. Instead, we were parked at a large villa just beyond the Nomentana Gate. It looked substantial, which was a puzzle. Nobody who had enough cash for a decent house would normally choose to live so far outside the city – let alone within spitting reach of the Praetorians. The occupants would be deafened when all those big bastards were drunk on pay day, and the incessant trumpets and tramping would drive most folk demented.

The location was neither city nor country. There was neither hilltop panorama nor river view. Yet we were looking at the kind of high, blank walls that normally surround luxurious amenities owned by people who don't want the public knowing what they own. In case we doubted it, the heavy front door with its antique dolphin knocker and well-tended urns of formally clipped bay, announced that somebody lived here who felt like quality (not always the same thing as actually being it, of course).

I still said nothing, and was allowed to stay helping to unload the bales, while my dearest skipped up to the forbidding portal and disappeared inside. Eventually I myself was led indoors by a silent slave in a firmly belted white tunic, then passed through a traditional short corridor to an atrium where I could hang about until required. I had been labelled a supernumerary who would wait for Helena as long as needed: true. Apart from the fact I never abandoned her amongst strangers, I was not going home yet. I wanted to know where I had come and what happened here. Left alone, I soon obeyed my itchy feet, and set off to explore.

It was nice. My word, it was. For once taste and money had combined successfully. Light-filled corridors headed in every direction to gracious rooms painted with decorous, slightly old-fashioned frescos. (The house seemed so quiet I brazenly opened doors and looked inside.) The scenes were architectural citiscapes or grottos with idyllic pastoral life. The rooms housed padded couches with footstools, side-tables positioned for convenience, elegant bronze candelabra; the occasional statuary included one or two busts of the old unnaturally handsome Julio–Claudian imperial family and a smiling head of Vespasian, apparently predating his accession as Emperor.

I reckoned the place had been built in my lifetime: that meant new money. The lack of painted battle scenes, trophies or phallic symbols, together with the preponderance of women's chairs, made me guess it could be a wealthy widow's house. Objects and furniture were expensive, though chosen for use rather than purely decorative. The owner had money, taste, and a practical outlook.

It was a quiet home. No children. No pets. No braziers against the winter coolness. Apparently almost unlived in. Nothing much going on today.

Then I caught a low murmur of female voices. Following the sound, I came to a colonnade of grey stone pillars forming an enclosed peristyle garden, so sheltered that the rampaging rose-bushes still bore occasional flowers even though it was December. Four rather dusty laurels marked the corners and a huge stone fountain bowl stood silent in the centre space.

Strolling out into the garden casually I came upon Helena Justina with another woman. I knew who she was; I had seen her before. She was just a freed slave, an ex-secretary from the Palace – yet potentially the most influential woman in the Empire today. I straightened up. If the rumours about how she used her position were true, then more power might be wielded on the sly in this isolated villa than in any other private house in Rome.

III

They had been laughing quietly, two straight-backed, civilised, unselfconscious women braving the weather as they discussed how the world worked. Helena had the animated look that meant she was truly enjoying herself. That was rare; she tended to be unsociable except with people she knew well.

Her companion was twice her age, an undeniably elderly woman with a slightly drawn expression. Her name was Antonia Caenis. Though a freedwoman, she was one of grand status: she once worked for the mother of the Emperor Claudius. That had given her long and close connections with the old discredited imperial family and she now possessed even more intimate links with the new one: she was the long-time mistress of Vespasian. As an ex-slave she could never marry him, but after his wife died they had lived openly together. Everyone had assumed that upon becoming Emperor he would shed her discreetly, but he took her with him to the Palace. At their age it was hardly a scandal. This villa presumably belonged to Caenis herself; if she still came here, it must be to transact business of an unofficial kind.

I had heard that it happened. Vespasian liked to appear too straight to permit backstage machinations – yet he must be happy to have somebody he trusted negotiate discreet deals while he kept his distance and apparently kept his hands clean.

The two women were seated on cushions on a low stone seat with lion's paw feet. At my approach both turned and broke off what they were saying. I glimpsed mutual annoyance at my interruption. I was a man. Whatever they had been debating was outside my sphere.

That did not mean it had been frivolous.

'Well, here you are then!' exclaimed Helena, making me nervous.

'I wondered what I was missing.'

Antonia Caenis inclined her head and greeted me without being introduced. 'Didius Falco.'

She was good; I had once stood aside for her when I was visiting Titus Caesar at the Palace, but it was some time ago and we had never met formally. I had already heard she was intelligent, and possessed a phenomenal memory. Apparently I had been well catalogued: but in which pigeon-hole?

'Antonia Caenis.'

I was standing, the traditional position for the servile element in the presence of the great. The ladies enjoyed treating me like a barbarian. I winked at Helena, who coloured slightly, afraid I might wink at Caenis too. I reckoned Vespasian's dame would have handled it, but I was a guest in her house. Besides, she was a woman with unknown Palace privileges. Before I risked annoying her I wanted to assess just how powerful she was.

'You have presented me with a most generous gift,' said Caenis. That was news. As it had been explained to me some months ago in Hispania, Helena Justina was proposing a private sale of some purple-dyed Baetican cloth that would be suitable for imperial uniforms. It was supposed to bring in goodwill, but had been intended as a commercial transaction. For a senator's daughter Helena possessed a surprising knack for bargaining; if she had now decided to waive payment, she must have a very good reason: something else was being brokered here today. I could guess what it was.

'I should think you are fairly showered with presents nowadays,' I commented daringly.

'Rather an irony,' returned Caenis, unperturbed. She had a cultured Palace voice, but with a permanent dry tone. I could imagine how she and Vespasian might always have mocked at the establishment; she at least probably still did so.

'People believe you can influence the Emperor.'

'That would be most improper.'

'I don't see why,' protested Helena Justina. 'Men in power always have their intimate circle of friends who advise them. Why should it not include the women they trust?'

'Of course I am free to say what I think!' smiled the Emperor's mistress.

'Forthright women are a joy,' I said. Helena and I had exchanged views on the crispness of cabbage in terms that still made my hair stand on end.

'I'm glad that you think so,' Helena commented.

'Vespasian always values sound opinions,' replied Caenis, speaking like an official court biographer, though I sensed domestic satire much like our own was lurking underneath.

'With his burden of work in rebuilding the Empire,' I suggested, 'Vespasian must also welcome a partner in his labours.'

'Titus is a great joy to him,' returned Caenis serenely. She knew how to misunderstand a tricky point. 'And I am sure he has hopes of Domitian.' Vespasian's elder son was virtually co-Emperor and although the younger had made a few gaffes, he still carried out formal duties. I had a deep-running feud with Domitian Caesar and fell silent, brooding on how he charged me with bile. Antonia Caenis finally waved me to a seat.

In the three years since Vespasian became Emperor popular suspicion had it that this lady was enjoying herself. It was believed that the highest posts — tribuneships and priesthoods — could be allocated at her word (in return for payment). Pardons were bought. Decisions were fixed. It was said that Vespasian encouraged this trade, which not only enriched and empowered his concubine but bought grateful friends for him. I wondered about their arrangement for sharing the financial profits. Was it divided by a strict percentage? On a sliding scale? Did Caenis make deductions for expenses and wear and tear?

'Falco, I am not in a position to sell you favours,' she declared, as if she read my thoughts. All her life people must have made up to her because of her closeness to the court. Her eyes were dark and watchful. In the mad, suspicious turbulence of the Claudian family, too many of her patrons and friends had died. Too many of her years had been lost to painful uncertainty. Whatever was for sale in this elegant villa would be handled with scrupulous attention, not least attention to its value.

'I am not in a position to buy,' I replied frankly.

'I cannot even make you promises.'

I disbelieved that.

Helena leant forwards to speak, so her blue stole slipped from her left shoulder and fell across her lap, its trim catching in one of the row of light bangles she wore to cover the scar from a scorpion bite. She shook the stole free impatiently. The gown below was white, a formal choice. I noticed she was wearing an old agate necklace that she had owned before I met her, subconsciously playing the senator's daughter again. Pulling rank seemed unlikely to work.

'Marcus Didius is far too proud to pay for privileges.' I loved Helena when she spoke so earnestly, especially when it was about me. 'He won't tell you himself, but he has been sorely disappointed – and after Vespasian had made him a direct offer of promotion to the middle rank.'

Caenis listened with an air of distaste, as if complaints were bad manners. She had undoubtedly heard the whole story of how I went to the Palace to claim my reward. Vespasian had promised me social advancement, but I chose to ask for it one night when Vespasian himself had been out of Rome and Domitian was handling pleas. Overconfident, I brazened it out with the princeling; for that I paid the penalty. I held evidence against Domitian on a very serious charge, and he knew it. He had never moved against me openly, but that night he took his revenge by turning me down.

Domitian was a brat. He was also dangerous, and I reckoned Caenis was shrewd enough to see it. Whether she would ever disturb the family peace by saying so was another matter. But if she *was* prepared to criticise him, would she speak up on my behalf?

Caenis must know what we wanted. Helena had made an appointment to come here, and as an ex-secretary to the court, Caenis would naturally have obtained full briefing material before confronting supplicants.

She made no answer, still pretending not to intervene in affairs of state.

'Disappointment has never made Marcus falter in his service to the Empire.' Helena spoke again, without bitterness though her expression was austere. 'His work has included several very dangerous provincial journeys, and you must be aware of what he achieved in Britain, Germany, Nabataea, and Spain. Now he wants to offer his services to the Census, as I outlined to you just now—'

This was received with a cool, noncommittal nod.

'It's an idea I conceived with Camillus Verus,' I explained. 'Helena's father is of course a good friend of the Emperor.'

Caenis graciously picked up the hint: 'Camillus is your patron?' Patronage was the weft of Roman society (where the warp was graft). 'So has the senator spoken to the Emperor on your behalf?'

'I was not brought up to be anybody's client.'

'Papa supports Marcus Didius fully,' interposed Helena. 'I am sure that he would do.'

'It seems to me,' Helena carried on, growing fiercer, 'Marcus has done as much for the Empire as he should do without formal recognition.'

'What do you think, Marcus Didius?' asked Caenis, ignoring Helena's anger.

'I would like to tackle this Census job. It poses a good challenge, and I don't deny it could be very lucrative.'

'I was not aware Vespasian paid you exorbitant fees!'

'He never has,' I grinned. 'But this would be different. I won't act on piecework rates. I want a percentage of whatever income I recover for the state.'

'Vespasian could never agree to that.' The lady was emphatic.

'Think about it.' I could be tough too.

'Why, what sort of amounts are we discussing?'

'If as many people as I suspect are attempting to fiddle their returns, the sums to be extracted from culprits will be enormous. The only limitation would be my personal stamina.'

'But you have a partner?' So she knew that.

'He's untried as yet, though I'm confident.'

'Who is he?'

'Just an out of work scrutineer my old mother took pity on.'

'Indeed.' I reckoned Antonia Caenis had discovered it was Anacrites. She might know him. She could dislike him as much as I did — or she could view him as Vespasian's servant and ally. I stared her out.

She smiled abruptly. It was frank, intelligent, and startlingly full of character. There was no recognition that she was an elderly woman who should feel ready to relinquish her place in the world. For a moment I glimpsed what Vespasian must always have seen in her. She must be well up to the old man's undoubted calibre. 'Your proposition sounds attractive, Marcus Didius. I shall certainly discuss it with Vespasian if an occasion arises.'

'I bet you keep a note tablet with a formal list of queries that you and he pore over at a set hour every day!'

'You have a peculiar notion of our daily routine.'

I smiled gently. 'No, I just thought you might pin down Titus Flavius Vespasianus in the same way that Helena tackles me.'

They both laughed. They were laughing at me. I could

bear it. I was a happy man. I knew Antonia Caenis was going to land me the job I wanted, and I had high hopes that she might do more than that.

'I suppose,' she said, still being direct, 'you want to explain to me what went wrong about promoting you?'

'I expect you know what went wrong, lady! Domitian was of the opinion that informers are sordid characters, none of whom is worthy of inclusion in the lists for the middle rank.'

'Is he correct?'

'Informers are far less sordid than some of the musty gargoyles with clammy ethics who people the upper rank lists.'

'No doubt,' said Caenis with the slightest suggestion of reproof, 'the Emperor will bear your strictures in mind when he reviews the lists.'

'I hope he does.'

'Your remarks could indicate, Marcus Didius, that you would not now wish to be aligned near the musty gargoyles.'

'I can't afford to feel superior.'

'But you can risk outspokenness?'

'It's one of the talents that will help me screw cash from Census cheats.'

She looked severe. 'If I were writing minutes of this meeting, Marcus Didius, I should rephrase that as "recovery of revenue".'

'Is there to be a formal record?' Helena asked her quietly.

Caenis looked even more stern. 'Only in my head.'

'So there is no guarantee that any reward promised to Marcus Didius will be acknowledged at a future date?' Helena never lost sight of her original aim.

I leant forwards abruptly. 'Don't worry. It could be safely written on twenty scrolls, yet if I lost favour they could all be lost in the archives by inattentive scribes. If Antonia Caenis is prepared to support me, her word is enough.'

Antonia Caenis was well used to being badgered for favours. 'I can only make recommendations. All matters of state are at the discretion of the Emperor.'

I bet! Vespasian had been listening to her since she was a girl, when he was just an impoverished young senator. I grinned at Helena. 'There you are. That's the best guarantee you could want.'

At the time I really thought it was.

IV

Half a day later I was called to the Palace. I saw neither Vespasian nor Titus. A silky administrator called Claudius Laeta pretended he was responsible for employing me. I knew Laeta. He was responsible only for chaos and grief.

'I don't seem to have the name of your new partner.' He was fumbling with scrolls to avoid my eye.

'How unusually casual. I'll send you in a chitty with his name and a full résumé.' Laeta could see I had no intention of doing it.

Acting pleasant (a certain sign that he had been leaned on hard by the Emperor) he then gave me the job I had asked for. We agreed my percentage of the profits. Numeracy must be Laeta's weak point. He knew everything about inventive drafting and greasy diplomacy, but could not spot an inflated tender. I came away feeling smug.

Our first subject to investigate was Calliopus, a semi-successful lanista from Tripolitania who trained and promoted gladiators, mainly the kind who fight wild beasts. When Calliopus produced his personnel list I had heard of none of them. He owned no top fighters in the glamour class. No women would throw themselves at his mediocre crew, and there were no gold victory crowns displayed in his office. But I did know the name of his lion: Leonidas.

The lion shared his praenomen with a great Spartan general; that hardly endeared him to Romans like me, who had been brought up from the crawling frame to be wary of Greeks in case we became infected with *louche* habits like wearing beards and discussing philosophy. But I loved this lion before I even met him. Leonidas was a man-eater, a trained one. At the next suitable Games he was going to execute a repulsive sexual killer called Thurius. Thurius had been preying on women for decades, then chopping them into pieces and dumping the remains; I myself had identified and brought him to court. The first thing I had done when Anacrites and I met Calliopus was to ask for a conducted tour of the cages, and once there, I made a beeline for the lion.

Addressing Leonidas like a trusted colleague, I explained very carefully the degree of ferocious savagery I expected from him on the day. 'I'm sorry we can't get it over with at the Saturnalia, but that's a festival of jollity, so the priests say doing away with criminals would pollute the event. Well this gives the bastard longer to dwell on his agony when you finally get to him. Rip him to shreds just as slowly as you can, Leo. Make him linger.'

'No use, Falco.' The keeper, Buxus, had listened. 'Lions are kind and polite killers. One pawswipe and you're out.'

'I'll make a note to ask for the big cats if I ever fall foul of the law!'

Leonidas was still young. He was fit and bright-eyed, though foul of breath from eating bloody meat. Not too much of it – they kept him starved so he would do his work efficiently. He lay at the far edge of his cage in the semi-darkness. The heavy twitch of his tail was filled with contemptuous menace. Distrustful golden eyes watched us.

'What I admire about you, Falco,' Anacrites commented, coming up behind me on stealthy feet, 'is your personal attention to the most obscure detail.'

It was better than hearing Petronius Longus constantly moaning that I became bogged down in trivia, but it meant the same: just like the old one, my new partner was telling me I wasted time.

'Leonidas,' I stated (wondering what the chances were of persuading the lion to devour my new partner), 'is entirely relevant. He cost a lot of money, didn't he, Buxus?'

'Naturally.' The keeper nodded. He was ignoring Anacrites; he preferred to deal with me. 'The problem is catching them alive. I've been over to Africa and seen it. They use a kid for bait. Getting beasts to pounce and fall into a pit is dodgy enough – then they have to extract the cats without damage, while they are roaring their heads off and trying to maul anyone who comes close. Calliopus uses an agent who sometimes snatches cubs for us – but he has to hunt and kill the mother first. And then there's the bother of rearing the cubs until they're a useful size for the Games.'

I grinned. 'No wonder the proverb says the first requirement for a successful politician is knowing a good source for tigers.'

'We don't have tigers,' said Buxus gravely. Satire was lost on him. Jokes about senators bribing the people with gory spectacles just bounced off his bald cranium. 'Tigers come from Asia, and that's why so few reach Rome. We only have links with North Africa, Falco. We get lions and leopards. Calliopus comes from Oea—'

'Right. He keeps the business in the family. Does Calliopus' agent rear his lion cubs over there?'

'No point wasting the expense of shipping them – that's a game in itself – not until they're big enough to be of some use.'

'So Calliopus owns a menagerie in Tripolitania as well as this one?'

'Yes.' That would be the establishment in Oea that Calliopus had sworn to the Censors was in his brother's name. Anacrites surreptitiously made a note on a tablet, finally aware what I was driving at. The beasts could be as valuable as they liked; it was land, whether in Italy or the provinces, that we were tracking down. We suspected that this Oean 'brother' of Calliopus was a fiction.

★

That had been enough for us to pursue on site the first day. We collected the menagerie records to add to a pile of scrolls about Calliopus' fighting tough men, then we slogged back with the documents to our new office.

This roost was another point of disagreement. All my career I had operated as an informer from a gruesome apartment in Fountain Court up on the Aventine. Complainants could traipse up the six flights of stairs and rouse me from bed to listen to their woes. Timewasters baulked at the climb. Bad fellows who wanted to dissuade me from my investigations by hitting me hard on the head could be heard coming.

When Helena and I had needed more spacious living accommodation we moved across the road, keeping my old place to work from. I had let Petronius move in after his wife threw him out for philandering, and even though we were no longer partners, he was still there. Anacrites insisted that we now required somewhere to stash the scrolls we amassed for the Census job, somewhere without Petro glowering at us disapprovingly. What we did not need, as I wasted my breath saying, was to install ourselves among the deadbeats at the Saepta Julia.

He fixed it up without consulting me. That was the kind of partner my mother had stuck me with.

The Saepta is a large enclosure next to the Pantheon and the Election Hall. Its internal arcades in those days – before the great clearances – were home to informers. The ones who lurked there were the slyest and grubbiest. The political creeps. Nero's old crawlers and grasses. No tact and no taste. No ethical standards. The glory of our profession. I wanted nothing to do with any of them, but Anacrites had plunged us right into the middle of their louse-ridden habitat.

The other low class of Saepta Julia wildlife was composed of goldsmiths and jewellers, a clique loosely formed around a group of auctioneers and antique-dealers. One of them being my father, from whom it was my habit to keep as far away as possible.

'Welcome to civilisation!' crowed Pa, bursting in within five minutes of us arriving back there.

'Get lost, Pa.'

'That's my boy.'

My father was a square, heavy man with untamed grey curls and what passed even among women of experience for a charming grin. He had a reputation as a shrewd businessman; that meant he would sooner lie than tell the truth. He had sold more fake Athenian blackware vases than any other auctioneer in Italy. A potter turned them out for him specially.

People said I was like my father, but if they noticed my reaction they only ever said it once.

I knew why he was happy. Every time I was deep in some complex job he would be interrupting with urgent demands that I pop down to his warehouse and help him shift some heavy piece of furniture. With me nearby he was hoping to lay off two porters and the lad who brewed borage tea. What was worse, Pa would make instant friends with every suspect I wanted to keep at a distance, then he would blab my business throughout Rome.

'This calls for drinks,' he cried, and rushed away to find some.

'You can tell Ma about this yourself,' I growled at Anacrites. That did make him go paler than ever. He must have gathered that my mother had not spoken to my father since the day he ran off with a redhead, leaving Ma to bring up his children. The idea of me working in Pa's vicinity would have her looking for somebody she could hang up by the heels on her smoked-meat hook. By moving into this office Anacrites could well have just terminated his lease at Ma's house, sacrificing some very palatable dinners and risking a far worse wounding than the one after which she saved his life. 'I hope you can run fast, Anacrites.'

'You're all heart, Falco. Why don't you thank me for finding us this fine billet?'

'I've seen bigger pens for pigs.'

It was a first-floor closet that had been abandoned for two years after the previous tenant died in it. When Anacrites made the landlord an offer, he couldn't believe his luck. Every time we moved we banged our elbows. The door didn't close, mice were refusing to give way to us, there was nowhere to pee, and the nearest foodstall was right the other side of the enclosure; it sold mouldy rolls that made us bilious.

I had established my own space at a small wooden counter where I could watch the world going by. Anacrites wound himself on to a stool in the darker rear area. His unobtrusive oyster tunic and oiled-back hair merged into the shadows, so only his smooth pale face stood out. He was looking worried, leaning back his head on the partition as if to hide the great cleft of his wound. Memory and logic were both playing tricks on him. All the same, he seemed to have brightened when he joined me in partnership; he gave the peculiar impression he was looking forward to his new active life.

'Don't tell Pa what we're doing for the Census, or the news will be everywhere by dinner time.'

'Well what can I tell him, Falco?' As a spy he had always lacked initiative.

'Internal audit.'

'Oh right! That usually makes people lose interest rapidly. What shall we say to suspects?'

'Have to be careful. We don't want them to realise our draconian powers.'

'No. They might respond by offering us bribes.'

'Which we are far too respectable to accept,' I said.

'Not unless the bribes are very handsome indeed,' replied Anacrites demurely.

'As with any luck they will be,' I chortled back.

'Here we are!' Pa reappeared, carrying an amphora. 'I told the vintner you'd call in later to pay for it.'

'Oh thanks!' Pa squashed in beside me, and gestured expectantly for the formal introductions he had brushed aside before. 'Anacrites, this is my father, the devious miser

Didius Favonius. Otherwise known as Geminus; he had to change his name because there were too many angry people after him.'

My new partner evidently thought I had introduced him to a fascinating character, some colourful and sought-after Saepta eccentric. Actually they had met before, when we were all involved in searching goods in a treason case. Neither seemed to remember it.

'You're the lodger,' exclaimed my father. Anacrites looked pleased by his local fame.

As Pa poured wine into metal cups, I could tell he was watching us together. I let him stare. Playing games was his idea of fun, not mine.

'So it's Falco & Partner again?'

I pressed out a tired smile. Anacrites sniffed; he had not wanted to be merely '& Partner', but I had insisted on continuity. I was, after all, hoping to ride on straight into a different partnership as soon as possible.

'Settling in?' Pa was pleased to sense an atmosphere.

'It's a bit tight, but we're expecting to be out and about so that shouldn't matter.' Anacrites seemed determined to annoy me by engaging Pa in chat. 'At least the price is reasonable. Apparently there hasn't been anyone renting for some time.'

Pa nodded. He liked to gossip. 'Old Potinus had it. Until he cut his throat.'

'If he worked here I can see why he did it,' I said.

Anacrites was looking around the Villa Potinus nervously, in case there were still bloodstains. Unrepentant, my father winked at me.

Then my partner gave a start. 'Internal audit's no good as a cover!' he complained to me in a huff. 'No one will believe that, Falco. The internal auditors are meant to examine mistakes in the Palace bureaucracy. They never go out among the public—' He realised I had put one over on him. I was pleased to see he was furious.

'Just testing,' I smirked.

'What's this about?' nudged Pa, hating to be left out.
'Confidential!' I answered crushingly.

V

The next day, having boned up on what Calliopus *said* he was worth, we went back to his training barracks to take his operation apart.

The man himself hardly looked as if he was engaged in the trade of death and cruelty. He was a tall, thin, neat fellow with a well-trimmed head of dark, crinkled hair, big ears, flared nostrils, and enough of a suntan to suggest foreign extraction though he blended in well. An immigrant from south of Carthage, if you closed your eyes he could have been Suburra-born. His Latin was colloquial, its accent pure Circus Maximus, unmarred by elocution training. He wore plain white tunics with just enough finger jewellery to imply he was humanly vain. A wide boy, one who had made good by hard work and who conducted himself with a decorous manner. The kind Rome loves to hate.

He was the right age to have worked his way up from anywhere. He could have learned all sorts of business practices along the way. He saw to us himself. It implied that he could only afford a small group of slaves, who all had their own work to do and could not be spared for us. Since I had seen his manpower schedules, I knew differently; he wanted to keep personal control over anything Anacrites and I were told. He seemed friendly and incurious. We knew what to make of that.

His establishment comprised a small palaestra where his men were trained, and a menagerie. Because of the animals, the aediles had made him stay out of Rome, on the Via Portuensis, way over the river. At least it was the right side of town for us, but in all other respects it was a damned nuisance. To avoid the Transtiberina rough quarter we had to persuade a skiffman to row us across from the Emporium to the Portuensis Gate. From there it was a short sprint past the Sanctuary of the Syrian Gods, which put us in an exotic mood, and then on past a Sanctuary of Hercules.

We had kept our first visit brief. Yesterday we met our subject, looked at his lion in a rather unsafely chewed wooden cage, then grabbed some documents to get to grips with. Today things would get tough.

Anacrites was supposed to be primed to conduct the initial interview. My own study of the records had told me Calliopus currently owned eleven gladiators. They were 'bestiarii' of the professional grade. By that I mean they were not simply criminals shoved into the ring in pairs to kill one another during the morning warm-up sessions, with the last survivor despatched by an attendant; these were eleven properly trained and armed animal fighters. Professionals like them give a good show but try to be 'sent back' – that is, returned to the tunnels alive after each bout. They have to fight again, but they hope one day the crowd will shout for them to receive a large reward and perhaps their freedom.

'Not many survive?' I asked Calliopus, putting him at ease as we settled in.

'Oh more than you think, especially among the bestiarii. You have to have survivors. The hope of money and fame is what keeps them coming up to join. For young lads from poor backgrounds it may be their one chance to succeed in life.'

'I expect you know, everyone thinks the fights are fixed.'

'So I believe,' said Calliopus noncommittally.

He probably also knew the other theory every self-respecting Roman mutters whenever the president of the Games waves his pesky white handkerchief to interfere with the action: the referee is blind.

One reason this lanista's gladiators were regarded as

feeble specimens was that he really specialised in mock hunts: the part of the Games which is called the venatio. He owned various large wild animals whom he would set free in the arena in staged settings, then his men pursued them either on horseback or on foot, killing as few as they could get away with while still pleasing the crowd. Sometimes the beasts fought each other, in unlikely combinations – elephants against bulls, or panthers against lions. Sometimes a man and a beast were pitted one to one. Bestiarii, however, were little more than expert hunters. The crowd despised them compared with the Thracians, myrmillons and retarii, the fighters of various types who were intended to end up dead on the sand themselves.

'Oh we lose the odd man, Falco. The hunts need to look dangerous.'

That did not square with events I had watched where reluctant animals had to be lured to their fate by banging shields loudly or waving fiery brands.

'So you like your four-footed stock to be ferocious. And you collect them in Tripolitania?'

'Mainly. My agents scour the whole of North Africa – Numidia, Cyrenaïca, even Egypt.'

'The animals cost a lot to find, house and feed?'

Calliopus gave me a narrow look. 'Where's this leading, Falco?'

We had announced that Anacrites would ask the first questions, but I was happy to start in like this myself; it unsettled Calliopus who felt unsure whether the interview had yet begun formally. It unsettled Anacrites too, come to that.

Time to be frank: 'The Censors have asked my partner and me to conduct what we call a lifestyle check.'

'A what?'

'Oh you know. They wonder how you can manage to own that pretty villa at Surrentum when you say your business is running at a loss.'

'I declared my Surrentum villa!' Calliopus protested.

That, of course, had been his mistake. Property on the Bay of Neapolis runs at a premium. Villas on the cliffs with sparkling views across the shimmering blue to Capreae are the mark of millionaires from consular families, ex-imperial slaves from the petitions bureau, and the more successful blackmailers.

'Very proper,' I soothed him. 'Of course Vespasian and Titus are sure you're not one of those evil bastards who plead piteously that they work in a field which has heavy overheads, while at the same time they are maintaining troops of thoroughbreds in the Circus of Nero and driving chariots with go-faster spokes and gilt finials. What wheels do you run, by the way?' I asked innocently.

'I have a family-style mule-drawn conveyance and a litter for the personal use of my wife,' said Calliopus in a hurt tone, obviously making rapid plans to sell his boy-racer quadriga and its quartet of zippy Spanish greys.

'Most frugal. But you know the sort of thing that causes excitement in the bureaucracy. Big carriages, as I said. Large gambling stakes. Flash tunics. Noisy confederates. Nights out entertaining girls who provide unusual services. Nothing you could ever be accused of, I realise.' The lanista blushed. I carried on blithely: 'Pentellic marble nudes. Mistresses of the type who can speak five languages and judge a cabochon-cut sapphire, who are kept in discreet penthouses up Saffron Street.'

He cleared his throat nervously. I made a note to discover the mistress. A job for Anacrites, perhaps; he seemed to have nothing to say for himself. The woman might only have mastered two or three lingos, one of them merely shopping-list Greek, but she was bound to have wheedled out of her lover a little apartment 'to keep mother in', and Calliopus would probably have his foolish name on the transfer deed.

What a great deal of mire there was to uncover in the course of our noble work. Dear gods, how deceitful my fellow citizens were (thought I, contentedly).

There was no sign yet that Calliopus intended to offer

us inducements to leave him alone. It suited Falco &
Partner at present. We were not yet that type of audit
team. We intended to nail him; it was his hard luck. We
wanted to start with a genuine high strike rate and a
matching income for the Treasury, in order to prove to
Vespasian and Titus that we were worth employing.

It would also alert the general population that being
investigated by us was dangerous, so people on our list
might like to reach an early settlement.

'So you own eleven gladiators,' Anacrites weighed in
finally. 'How do you acquire them, may I ask? Do you
purchase them?'

A rare look of anxiety crossed Calliopus' face as he
worked out that this question would precede one that
asked where the purchase money came from. 'Some.'

'Are they slaves?' continued Anacrites.

'Some.'

'Sold to you by their masters?'

'Yes.'

'In what circumstances?'

'They will normally be troublemakers who have
offended the master – or else he just thinks they look
tough and decides to convert them to cash.'

'You pay a lot for them?'

'Not often. But people always hope we will.'

'You also acquire foreign captives? Do you have to pay
for them?'

'Yes; they belong to the state originally.'

'Are they regularly available?'

'In times of war.'

'That market could dry up if our new Emperor installs a
glorious period of peace . . . Where will you look then?'

'Men come forward.'

'They *choose* this life?'

'Some people are desperate for money.'

'You pay them a lot?'

'I pay them nothing – only their bread.'

'Is that enough to hold them?'

'If they could not eat before. There is an initial enrolment fee paid to free men who volunteer.'

'How much?'

'Two thousand sesterces.'

Anacrites raised his eyebrows. 'That's not much more than the Emperor pays poets who recite a good ode at a concert! Is it reasonable for men signing their lives away?'

'It's more than most have ever seen.'

'Not a large figure, however, in return for slavery and death. And when they join, they have to sign a contract?'

'They bind themselves to me.'

'For how long?'

'For ever. Unless they win the wooden sword and are made free. But once they have been successful, even those who win the biggest prizes tend to grow restless and rejoin.'

'On the same terms?'

'No; the recommissioning fee is six times the original.'

'Twelve thousand?'

'And of course they expect to garner more prizes; they believe themselves winners.'

'Well that won't be for ever!'

Calliopus smiled quietly. 'No.'

Anacrites stretched himself, looking thoughtful. He conducted an unforced style of interview, making copious notes in a large, loose hand. His manner was calm, as if merely familiarising himself with the local scenery. It was not what I had expected. Still, to become Chief Spy he must have been successful once.

Calliopus, we had already decided, had been advised by his accountant to co-operate where it was unavoidable, but never to volunteer anything. Once Anacrites had started him talking, a drawn-out pause threw him. 'Of course I can see what you're after,' he burbled. 'You wonder how I can afford to make these purchases, when I told the Censors most of my outgoings were long-term ones with no immediate returns.'

'Training your gladiators,' Anacrites agreed, making no comment on the guilty gush of extra information.

'It takes years!'

'During which time you have to pay for their board?'

'And provide trainers, doctors, armourers—'

'Then they may die on their first public outing.'

'Mine is a high-risk enterprise, yes.'

I leant forwards, interrupting. 'I never met a business-man who didn't make that claim!'

Anacrites laughed, more with Calliopus than me, still winning his confidence. We were going to play this like nice fellows, implying that nothing the suspect said mattered. No tutting and head-shaking. Just smiles, pleasantries, sympathy with all his problems – then writing a report that would kick the poor victim to Hades.

'What do you do for capital?' I asked.

'I am paid for supplying men and beasts for the venatio. Plus, if we stage an actual fight, some prize money.'

'I thought the winning gladiator took the purse?'

'A lanista receives his own share.'

Much bigger than the fighter's, no doubt. 'Enough for a villa with views to Neapolis? Well, no doubt that represents years of work.' Calliopus wanted to speak but I carried on regardless. We had him on the run. 'Given that you have accrued your rewards over a long period, we did wonder whether when you prepared your return for the Census there might have been any other items of estate – outside Rome, perhaps, or properties which you have owned for so long they slipped your memory – which were inadvertently omitted from your tax declaration?'

I had made it sound as though we knew something. Calliopus managed not to gulp. 'I will look at the scrolls again to make quite sure—'

Falco & Partner were both nodding at Calliopus (and preparing to take down his confession) when he was given an unexpected reprieve.

A hot, tousled slave with dung on his boots rushed into the room. For a moment he squirmed in embarrassment, unwilling to speak to Calliopus in our presence. Anacrites and I politely put our heads together, pretending to discuss our next move, whilst in fact we listened in.

We caught some mumbled words about something terrible having happened, and an urgent request for Calliopus to attend the menagerie. He cursed angrily. Then he jumped to his feet. For a moment he stared at us, debating what to say.

'We have a death.' His tone was curt; clearly he was annoyed about it. The loss, I deduced, would be expensive. 'I need to investigate. You can come if you want.'

Anacrites, easily able to look off colour nowadays, said he would remain in the office; even a bad spy knows when to take a chance to search the premises. Then Calliopus informed me that whatever had happened had struck down his lion, Leonidas.

VI

The menagerie was a long, low, roofed area. A series of big cages, the size of slave cubicles, ran along one side; from these came odd rustling sounds and suddenly a deep grunt from another large animal of some kind, maybe a bear. Opposite the cages were smaller pens with lower bars, mainly empty. At one end four uncaged ostriches were ogling us while Buxus tried feebly to restrain their curiosity by offering them a bowl of grain. They were taller than him and determined to be nosy, like ghouls craning their necks when someone has been run over by a waggon.

Leonidas was lying in his cage, not far from where he had been when I saw him yesterday. This time his head was turned away from us.

'We need more light.'

Calliopus, sounding terse, called for torches. 'We keep it dim to pacify the beasts.'

'Can we go in?' I put a hand on one bar of the cage. It felt stronger than I expected from its gnawed appearance; the contraption was wooden, though reinforced with metal. A short length of chain kept the door fastened, secured by a closed padlock. Apparently the keys were kept in the office; Calliopus yelled to a slave to run for them.

Buxus abandoned his nursemaiding task and joined us, still jostled by the long-legged birds.

'You can go in. He's safe. He's dead, definitely.' He nodded to a flyblown carcass inside the cage. 'He's never touched his breakfast!'

'You fed him that meat this morning?'

'Just a titbit to keep him going.' It looked like a whole goat. 'I called him; he was lying just like that. I just thought he was asleep. Poor thing must already have gone and I never realised.'

'So you left him to finish his snooze, as you thought?'

'That's right. When I came back later to bring some corn for the daft birds here, I thought he seemed quiet. When I checked I knew he hadn't moved. There were flies all over him, and not even a twitch of his tail. I even poked him with a long stick. Then I said to myself, *he's gone all right.*'

The torches and keys arrived together. Calliopus roused himself and jingled the keys on a huge ring, with difficulty sorting out the right one. He shook his head. 'Once you take them from their natural habitat these creatures are vulnerable. Now you can see what I'm up against, Falco. People like you' – he meant people who queried his financial probity – 'don't realise how delicate this business is. The animals can pop off overnight, and we never know why.'

'I can see you kept him in the best possible conditions.' I entered rather carefully. Like all cages it had become sordid, but the straw bedding was thick. There was a large trough of water, and the goat carcass, though Buxus was already towing that off for some other beast's snack, shoving aside the ostriches who had followed him, then closing the cage door to keep them out.

The unkind thought struck me that Leonidas was now heading for the same fate as the goat who had been intended for his breakfast. As soon as interest in him waned, he too would be served up to some cannibalistic crony.

Close up he was bigger than I had realised. His coat was brown, his untidy mane black. His powerful back legs were tucked neatly either side of him, his front paws stretched out like a sphinx, his fat tail curled like a domestic cat's with its black tassel neatly aligned with his body. His great head was nose down against the back of the cage. The smell of dead lion had not yet supplanted the smells he accrued in his living quarters when alive. Those were pretty strong.

Buxus offered to open the lion's huge mouth and exhibit his teeth for me. Since this was closer than I ever wanted to be to a live lion, I agreed politely. I always welcome new experiences. Calliopus stood watching, frowning over his loss as he reckoned up what replacing Leonidas would cost him. The keeper bent over the prone animal. I heard him mutter some only half-ironic endearment. Gripping the rough mane with both hands, Buxus heaved hard to turn the lion over towards us.

Then he let out a cry of real disgust. Calliopus and I took a moment to respond, then we stepped closer to look. We smelt the powerful reek of lion. We saw blood, on the straw and in the matted fur. Then we noticed something else: from the great beast's chest protruded the splintered handle of a broken spear.

'Somebody's done for him!' raged Buxus. 'Some bastard's gone and murdered Leonidas!'

VII

'Just promise,' cajoled Anacrites, back in the lanista's office. 'Tell me you won't let yourself be sidetracked by this, Falco.'

'Mind your own business.'

'That's exactly what I am doing. My business and yours at present is to earn sesterces by pinpointing bastards for the Censors. We don't have time to worry about mysterious killings of Circus lions.'

But this was not any old Circus creature. This was Leonidas, the lion who was due to eat Thurius. 'Leonidas despatched criminals. He was the Empire's official executioner. Anacrites, that lion was as much a state employee as you and me.'

'I shall not object then,' said my partner, a man of sour and wizened ethics, 'if you put up a plaque in his name denoting the Emperor's gratitude, and then make a frugal one-off payment to whoever runs his funeral club.'

I told him he could object or not object to anything, so long as he left me alone. I was perfectly able to wind up our audit here with one hand tied behind my back in the time it took Anacrites to remember how to write the date on our report in administration Greek. While I was doing my share, I would also discover who killed Leonidas.

Anacrites never knew when to leave a het up man to settle down. 'Isn't what has happened a matter for his owner now?'

It was. And I already knew what his owner was planning to do about it: nothing.

When he first saw the wound and the spear butt, Calliopus had gone a funny colour, then he looked as if he was regretting having invited me to view the corpse. I noticed him frown at Buxus, obviously warning him to keep quiet. The lanista assured me the death was nothing sinister, and said he would soon sort it out by talking to his slaves. It was perfectly clear to a seasoned informer that Calliopus was fobbing me off. He intended some kind of cover up.

Well he had reckoned without me.

★

I told Anacrites he looked as if he needed a rest. In fact he looked the same as usual, but I needed to patronise him to cheer myself up. Leaving him in the lanista's office trying to reconcile figures (perhaps not the best cure for a man with a bad head), I walked outside to the area of hard ground where five or six of the gladiators had been practising for most of the morning. It was a bleak rectangle at the heart of the complex, with the menagerie on one side rather unsuitably sited next to the fighters' refectory; barracks with sleeping quarters lay at the back end behind a half-hearted colonnade, which came round to an equipment store with the office over it. The office had its own balcony from which Calliopus could watch his men practise, and an exterior staircase. A crude statue of Mercury at the far end of the yard was supposed to inspire the men as they exercised. Even he looked depressed.

The nerve-racking clatter of the exercise swords and the aggressive shouting had finally ceased. The bestiarii were now in a curious huddle near the doorway to the menagerie. In the silence as I approached them I could make out harsh grunts and roars from the animals.

These bestiarii were not huge muscle-bound fellows, though strong enough to hurt you if you stared at them longer than they wanted. They all wore loincloths, some favoured various leather binding straps on their sturdy arms, and for verisimilitude one or two were even in helmets, though plainer shapes than the finely crafted casques worn by fighters in the arena. More wiry and

41

quicker on their feet than most professionals, these men also looked younger and brighter than average. I soon discovered that did not mean they would handle questions meekly.

'Any of you notice anything suspicious last night or today?'

'No.'

'The name's Falco.'

'Shove off then, Falco.'

As one man they turned away and pointedly resumed their exercises, doing gymnastic backflips and battering at each other's swords. It was dangerous to get in their way, and far too noisy for questions. I didn't fancy bawling. I gave them a mock salute and took my leave. Somebody had gagged them. I wondered why.

Outside the main gate to the complex lay a throwing range; four more of the group were measuring its length with spears. Anacrites and I had noticed them when we arrived. Now I strolled out there, to find them still at work, presumably not having heard about Leonidas' fate. The nearest, a young, fit, dark-skinned lad with a fine bare torso, strong legs and a keen eye, completed a magnificent throw. Applauding, I waved to him and when he came over politely I told him about the lion's death. His companions all joined us, apparently in a different, more helpful mood than those in the palaestra. I repeated my question about whether any of them had seen anything.

The first fellow introduced himself as Iddibal and told me they avoided close contact with the animals. 'If we get to know them, it becomes hard to chase them down in the mock hunts.'

'I noticed your keeper, Buxus, treated Leonidas as more of a friend, almost a pet.'

'He could afford to get fond of him; Leonidas was meant to come home from the arena every time.'

'Sent back standing,' another agreed, using the gladiators' term for reprieve.

'Yes, Leonidas was different!' Grins were being exchanged.

'What am I missing?' I asked.

After a few seconds looking embarrassed, Iddibal said, 'Calliopus bought him by mistake. The lion was passed off to him as a brand-new import, fresh from North Africa, but then as soon as the money had changed hands someone whispered to Calliopus that Leonidas had been specially trained. It made him useless for the hunts. Calliopus was furious. He tried to pass him on to Saturninus — he's in the same business — but Saturninus found out in time and backed out of the deal.'

'Specially trained? You mean, to eat men? Why was Calliopus furious? Is a trained lion less valuable?'

'Calliopus has to house and feed him but he only receives the standard state fee every time the lion is used against criminals.'

'Not a very big fee?'

'You know the government.'

'I do!' They paid me. They tried to keep the fees for that as small as possible too.

'For the hunts he stages,' Iddibal explained, 'Calliopus puts in a tender, based on the spectacles he can offer at the time. He's in competition with the other lanistae, and the outcome depends on who promises the best show. With a good full grown lion as the centrepiece, his bid for the venatio would have been very attractive.' I noticed Iddibal was talking with quite an air of authority. 'The crowd loves seeing us go after a decent big cat and Calliopus doesn't often have one. He uses a lousy agent.'

'To catch his beasts?'

Iddibal nodded, then fell silent as if he felt he had gone too far.

'Do you have much to do with the procurement side?' I asked him.

The others were prodding him teasingly; maybe they thought he had sounded off too much like an expert. 'Oh

I'm just one of the boys who spears them,' he smiled. 'We go after whatever we're given.'

I looked around the group. 'I suppose nobody's been indulging in a spot of off duty target practice using Leonidas?'

'Oh no,' they said, with the kind of assurance that never quite rings true.

I did not seriously suppose they would risk annoying Calliopus by damaging the lion. Even if Leonidas only brought in official fees, a working executioner was still better than a dead one, at least until the lanista had recouped his original purchase price. Anyway there must be cachet for Calliopus in owning the beast who destroyed the most notorious criminals. The forthcoming punishment of Thurius, the murderer, was attracting much public interest. And Calliopus did seem genuinely upset to lose Leonidas; that was why I felt so troubled that he was pretending the death was unexceptional.

Whatever else I might have extracted from these gladiators was forestalled. Calliopus himself arrived, presumably to tell the men to button up, just as he had obviously told their colleagues in the palaestra. Rather than have a confrontation at that point, I nodded to him and left, casually taking with me one of the training spears.

I made my way swiftly back to the cage where the lion lay. Since the door still stood open, I went straight inside. Using my knife to widen the wound in the lion's ribcage, I managed to withdraw the protruding spearhead. Then I laid it side by side with the one I was carrying: they did not match. The one that killed the lion had a longer, narrower head and was attached to its shaft with a different length of metal. I'm no expert, but it was clearly forged on a different anvil by a smith with a different style.

Buxus came in.

'Does Calliopus use a particular armourer?'

'Can't afford it.'

'So where does he obtain his spears?'

'Wherever they're on discount that week.'

Why do I always take on jobs involving cheapskates? 'Buxus, tell me: did Leonidas have any enemies?'

The keeper looked at me. He was a slave, with the usual slave's unhealthy pallor, wearing a dirty brown tunic and rough, oversized sandals. Between the thongs his lumpen feet were badly scratched by the straw he spent his days in. Fleas and flies, of which there were all kinds in his working environment, had feasted on his legs and arms. Neither as underweight as he might have been nor as downtrodden either, he had a cautious face with pouchy eyes. His gaze seemed more open than I expected; that probably meant Buxus had been selected by Calliopus to convey whatever rubbish his master hoped to palm off on me.

'Enemies? I don't expect the men he was due to eat liked him, Falco.'

'But they're in chains. Thurius can hardly have taken a night off from the condemned cell and nipped here to get in first.' I wondered whether Buxus himself might be involved in the killing; this death, like most murders, could well have a domestic cause. But his affection for the great creature and his anger when he discovered his lion's murder both seemed genuine. 'Were you the last person to see Leonidas alive?'

'I topped up his water last night. He was a bit peckish but all right then.'

'Still moving about?'

'Yes, he had a bit of a prowl. Like most big cats he hates – hated – being caged. It makes them pace around restlessly. I don't like seeing them get that way. They go mad, just the same as you or I would do if we were locked up.'

'Did you go inside the cage last night?'

'No, I couldn't be bothered to fetch the key to open up so I just sloshed his drink through the bars with a pannikin and whispered a sweet goodnight.'

'Did he answer?'

'Bloody big roar. I told you he was hungry.'

'Why didn't you feed him then?'

'We keep him short.'

'Why? He's not due for the arena yet. What's the reason for starving him?'

'Lions don't have to have meat every day. They enjoy it more with an appetite.'

'You sound like my girlfriend! All right; you sloshed in a jug or two, then what? Do you sleep nearby?'

'Loft next door.'

'What's the nightly routine? How is the menagerie kept secure?'

'All the cages are locked all the time. We often have members of the public coming to look at the animals.'

'They get up to all sorts?'

'We don't take chances.'

'Were any strangers around last night?'

'Not that I saw. People don't usually trek out here after dark.'

I returned to security arrangements. 'I gather the keys are kept in the office? What happens when you need to muck out and at feeding time? Are you allowed to use the keys yourself?'

'Oh yes.' I had rightly deduced that the keeper enjoyed a position of some trust here.

'And at night?'

'The whole menagerie is locked up. The boss sees to it himself. The keys go into the office and the office is locked when Calliopus goes home. He has a house in town of course—'

'Yes, I know.' Plus several others; that was why Calliopus had been favoured by a visit from Anacrites and me. 'I expect you close up fairly early in the evening. Calliopus will want to go to the baths before dinner. A man of his standing is bound to be dining formally most nights, I suppose?'

'I dare say.' The slave had little idea of social life among free citizens apparently.

'His wife's demanding?'

'Artemisia has to take him as he is.'

'Girlfriends?'

'I've no idea,' declared Buxus, obviously lying. 'He doesn't often stay late here anyway. He gets whacked out drilling the men all day; he wants his rest.'

'Well that leaves you to your own devices.' Buxus said nothing as I changed tack, assuming that I was now being critical of himself. 'But what would happen, Buxus, if one of the beasts were ill in the night, or if you had a fire? Presumably you don't have to run all the way into Rome to ask your master for the keys? If you have no access to the menagerie he could lose everything in an emergency.'

Buxus paused, then admitted, 'We have an arrangement.'

'And what's that?'

'Never you mind.'

I let it pass. Probably there was a duplicate key hanging on a nail somewhere really obvious. I could find out the details when I knew for sure it was relevant. If my guess was right, any competent burglar who cased the joint could have found that nail.

'So did everything go smoothly last night, Buxus?'

'Yes.'

'No sick beasts needing the farrier's attention? No alarms?'

'No, Falco. All quiet.'

'Did you have a girl in? A gambling mate?'

He jumped. 'What are you accusing me of?'

'Just a man's right to company. So did you?'

'No.'

He was probably lying again, this time on his own behalf. He realised I was on to him. But he was a slave; Calliopus was unlikely to tolerate open socialising of any kind, so Buxus would understandably want to keep his habits to himself. I could extract details if I needed to. It was too soon in the game to start heavy-handed questioning.

I sighed. With a cold corpse at your feet, it's all the

same. That this one was a lion did not change how I felt. The same old dreary depression at life being wasted for some barely credible motive and probably by some lowlife who just thought he could get away with it. The same anger and indignation. Then the same questions to ask: *Who saw him last? How did he spend his last evening? Who were his associates? What did he eat last? Whom did he eat, in fact?*

'Were you the only person who had dealings with the lion, Buxus?'

'Him and me were like brothers.'

When you investigate murders, that claim often turns out to be untrue. 'Oh yes?'

'Well he was used to me, and I was used to him – as far as I wanted to be. I never turned my back on him.'

The keeper was still facing Leonidas now. With his eyes as much on the lion as if it were still liable to spring and maul him, Buxus crouched down to where I had set the spear and the bloody spearhead alongside one another. Calliopus might be trying to hush this up, but I had a feeling Buxus wanted to know who had killed his powerful pal. 'Falco—' His voice was low as he gestured to the snapped–off spike. 'Where's the shaft off the one that did for him?'

'Have you looked around, Buxus?'

'No sign of it here.'

'The man who stuck it in probably carried off what was left. Do you think it could have been one of the bestiarii?'

'It was someone who could fight,' Buxus reckoned. 'Leonidas wouldn't just roll over and let any killer tickle his tum with a weapon.'

'Had any of the lads been showing an interest in Leonidas?'

'Iddibal had a chat to me about him.'

I raised an eyebrow. 'What was he asking?'

'Oh just general talk. He knows a lot about the business.'

'How's that, Buxus?'

'Don't know. He just takes an interest.'

'Nothing suspicious?'

'No, Iddibal was just homesick for Africa.'

'He comes from Oea like Calliopus?'

'No, Sabratha. He doesn't talk about his old life. None of them do.'

'All right.' This seemed to be going nowhere. 'We need to know what happened last night, Buxus. Let's start with whether Leonidas was killed in his cage.'

The keeper looked surprised. 'Must have been. You saw this morning. It was locked.'

I laughed. 'Oldest trick there is. "*The body was in a locked room: nobody could have got in there*". Usually it's meant to look like suicide. Don't even try to tell me this lion killed himself!'

'No call to,' joked his keeper darkly. 'Leonidas had too good a life. Me to hunt for him and talk to him all day – then every few months we put ribbons in his mane and sprinkled him with real gold dust to make him look pretty, and sent him to run free after criminals.'

'So he wasn't depressed?'

'Of course he was!' the keeper snapped, changing mood suddenly. 'Falco, he was turning into a cage-pacer. He wanted to be running after gazelles back in Africa, with lionesses available. All lions can be solitary if they have to – but for preference they love to fornicate.'

'He was fretting, and you were very fond of him. So was it you who put him out of his misery?' I asked sternly.

'No.' Buxus' voice was miserable. 'He was just restless. I've seen worse. I'm going to miss the old beast. I never wanted to lose him.'

'All right. Well that puts us back with the mystery. A locked cage isn't a closed room though; it's accessible. Could he have been speared through the bars?'

Buxus shook his head. 'Not easily.'

I was outside the cage by then, trying it out with the long spear. 'No, there's not much space—' With hardly room to draw back my arm, it was a short, awkward throw. 'It would take someone extremely accurate to loose off a shot through the bars. The bestiarii are good, but they don't hunt indoors. I suppose they could have just poked him—'

'Leonidas would have tried to avoid the spear, Falco. And he would have roared. I was only next door. I'd have heard him.'

'That's a good point. It was some spear thrust that killed him anyway. From close quarters, and with space to manoeuvre.' I knelt beside the corpse, checking it over again. There were no other wounds on the body. The lion was definitely killed by one terrific blow – with the weapon hand-held, I reckoned, not a throw – impaling the beast from straight in front. It was extremely professional. The situation must have been damned dangerous. The spear itself would have been a heavy one, and withstanding the onrush of the lion would have taken courage and power. Then I guessed Leonidas had fallen immediately, right where he was killed.

'Maybe he was killed near the front of the cage, the spear broke, then he crawled away.' Buxus lacked my expertise in working out the processes. He had a slave's habit of self-contradiction too – unless he were deliberately trying to confuse me.

'We said killing him through the bars wouldn't work.' Even so, to cover the possibility, I led Buxus to the front of the cage and examined the straw. 'Look – no blood. You haven't mucked him out today, have you? If he was alive and crawling, he would have bled.' I walked the keeper back to where the lion lay. Seizing the beast by its massive paws I braced myself and dragged him sideways to examine the straw under his belly. Buxus lent a hand. 'Some blood, but not enough.'

'What's it mean, Falco?'

'He was not killed through the bars, and I doubt if anyone came inside the cage. It would be far too risky and there isn't enough space to wield the spear.'

'So what happened to Leonidas?'

'He was killed somewhere else. Then his body was moved in here after he died.'

VIII

If Leonidas was taken elsewhere, let's look for signs of what happened—'

'Falco, nobody could have got him away from here!'

'It will do no harm to look.'

Buxus was looking nervous now, as if he had remembered that Calliopus wanted him to mislead me. I needed to search for evidence quickly, before some slave came along with a flat-headed broom and either accidentally or purposely swept away clues.

Outside in the exercise area the gladiators had stirred up so much dust there was no longer any chance that tracks from last night would show. I wondered if this was deliberate, but the fighters had to train, and this was where they normally did it. They had gone back to their exercises and kept up their racket, leaping around me with horrible yells as I crouched looking for pawprints on the hard dry ground. Their aggression made me feel tense. It was supposed to be practice, but they were big enough and moving fast enough to do serious damage if we collided. Occasionally one of the sparring men crashed so close I was forced to scramble aside. They ignored what I was trying to do. That in itself was unnatural. People are normally more curious.

'There's no hope of prints or spots of blood. We're too late—' I stood up. Time for a new tack. 'Buxus, if you had been moving Leonidas to the arena, how would you have done it? I presume you don't take the big growlers out for walkies on dog leads?'

The slave looked shifty for some reason. 'We have travelling cages.'

'Where are they kept?'

Controlling his reluctance he led me slowly around the back of the barracks to a row of lean-to stores. Impassively he watched as I glanced into most of them, finding bales of straw and tools – buckets, long poles for controlling angry animals, straw figures to distract the wild beasts in the arena, and finally under an open-sided shed three or four compact cages on wheels, neat enough to be squeezed between the cages of the menagerie, and just large enough to transport a lion or leopard from place to place.

'How do you get the beasts inside one of these?'

'It's quite a game!'

'But you're well practised?'

Buxus squirmed in his rough tunic; he was embarrassed, though pleased, by my praising his skill.

I examined the nearest cage closely. There was nothing suspicious. I was walking away when intuition drew me back.

Empty, the wheeled cages were easy to manipulate. I managed to pull out the one I had examined single-handed; Buxus stood by, glaring. He said nothing and made no attempt to stop me, but nor did he weigh in to help. Perhaps he knew, or guessed, what I would find: the next cage did provide evidence. Kneeling down inside it, I soon discovered traces of blood.

I jumped out and dragged the second cage into the light. 'Someone has made a very crude attempt to hide this, simply pulling out another cage and parking the significant one at the back.'

'Oh really?' said Buxus.

'Pathetic!' I showed him the blood. 'Seen that before?'

'I might have done. It's just an old stain.'

'That stain is not too old, my friend. And it looks as if somebody tried to wash it away – the kind of useless scrubber my mother would refuse to have working on her kitchen floor.' The watery run-off had been absorbed far along the grain of the wooden floor of the cage, but the original splashes of blood could still be seen as darker, more concentrated marks. 'Not much effort went into it — or else there wasn't enough time to do a good job.'

'You think Leonidas was taken somewhere in this cart, Falco?'

'I bet he was.'

'That's terrible.'

I gave Buxus a sharp look. He seemed deeply unhappy, though I could not tell whether he was simply grieving for his lost big cat, or whether he was uncomfortable with my discovery and line of questioning. 'He was taken away — and then brought back dead, Buxus. What's puzzling me, is how anyone could have extracted him from his normal cage without you hearing the commotion?'

'It's a real puzzle,' the keeper said sorrowfully.

I kept my eyes boring into him. 'He would have been quiet enough when he came back with the spear in him, but whoever delivered the corpse may well have been panicking. I doubt if they were able to stop themselves making some noise.'

'I just can't understand it,' Buxus agreed. A barefaced lie.

'I don't think you're trying.' He feigned not to notice my dangerously low tone.

I left the wheeled cage where it was. Someone else in this deceitful establishment could put it away again. Then something caught my eye, against the side wall of the shed. I pulled up what seemed to be a bundle of straw. What had attracted my attention were twined strands binding it into a definite form. 'This is a straw man — or what's left of him.' The crude shape had been savaged and torn. The ties at the tops of its legs were still in place but the shoulder bindings were broken. One of the arms and the head had been ripped off altogether. Half the straw of the body had been pulled away and the rest was all over the place. As I held the pathetic remains, they fell into two pieces. 'Poor fellow's been thoroughly ravaged! You use these as decoys, don't you?'

'In the ring,' said Buxus, still playing the unhelpful misery.

'You throw them in to draw the beasts' attention, and sometimes to madden them?'

'Yes, Falco.'

Some extremely maddened creature had torn at the manikin I was holding. 'What's this wrecked one doing here?'

'Must be just an old one,' said Buxus, managing to find the innocent expression I had no faith in.

I looked around. Everywhere was neat. This was a yard where items were routinely stacked, counted, inventoried and put away. Anything that was broken would be replaced or repaired. The straw men were kept on ceiling hooks in the same shack as the safety poles. All the used decoys that currently dangled there had been rebound to a reasonable shape.

I tucked the two halves of the dismembered figure under my arm, making a big point of confiscating the evidence. 'On two occasions last night there must have been quite a commotion near Leonidas' cage – when he was fetched, and when he was brought home. You claim you missed all of it. So are you now going to tell me, Buxus, where you really were that evening?'

'I was here in bed,' he repeated. 'I was here and I heard nothing.'

I was a good Roman citizen. No matter how brazenly he was defying me, I knew better than to beat up another citizen's slave.

IX

When we returned to the main area Buxus pointedly involved himself in his work while I took a last look around the cages. He surrounded himself with the four ostriches, who nuzzled close, lifting their feet with the exaggerated delicacy of any farmyard fowls. 'Watch yourself, Falco; they can give a hefty kick.'

Kicking was not their only talent; one of them took a fancy to the wavy-edged braid around the neck of my tunic and kept leaning over my shoulder to give it a peck. The keeper made no attempt to control the pestilential things, and I soon gave up my sleuthing, which was undoubtedly what he had hoped.

I walked back to the office, still holding the scraps of the straw man. Anacrites was talking to Calliopus. They both eyed my trophy. I propped up the pieces on a stool and said nothing about it.

'Calliopus, your lion was taken out on an excursion last night, and not – presumably – because his doctor had recommended fresh air carriage trips.'

'That's impossible,' the lanista assured me. When I described the evidence he merely scowled.

'You did not sanction the trip?'

'Of course not, Falco. Don't be ridiculous.'

'Does it cause you concern that somebody made Leonidas their plaything on an illicit night out?'

'Of course it does.'

'Any idea who might have done it?'

'None at all.'

'It must have been someone who felt confident about handling lions.'

'Mindless thieves.'

'Yet thoughtful enough to bring Leonidas back.'

'Madness,' moaned Calliopus, burying any real feelings in a show of theatrical woe. 'It's incomprehensible!'

'Had it ever happened before to your knowledge?'

'Certainly not. And it won't happen again.'

'Well not now Leonidas is dead!' provided Anacrites. His sense of humour was infantile.

I tried ignoring my partner, which was always the safest way to deal with him except when he was actually hiring hitmen and had been seen writing my name on a scroll. Then I watched him very closely indeed.

'Buxus has not been very helpful, Calliopus. I wanted him to give me some clues as to how the lion could have been pinched – and, indeed, put back in his cage afterwards – without anybody noticing.'

'I'll speak to Buxus,' Calliopus fussed. 'Please leave this business to me, Falco. I really don't see why you have to involve yourself.' Behind his back, Anacrites nodded agreement vigorously.

I gave Calliopus my threatening auditor's sneer. 'Oh we always take a keen interest in anything peculiar that happens while we are carrying out a lifestyle check!'

'Whether it seems relevant or not,' added Anacrites, pleasantly aiming to strike fear into the interviewee. He was a good civil servant after all.

Calliopus shot us a filthy look and bustled off.

I seated myself quietly and began making memos for myself about the lion's death. I held my tablet up at an angle so Anacrites had to guess what my scratchings were about.

He had worked alone for too long. He had been a man who kept his own council with perverted secrecy. Once he joined me he had braced himself to be companionable, but he then found it unbearable to share an office with someone who refused to talk to him. 'Are you intending to carry on with the Censor's enquiry, Falco?' It was like doing your school homework with a fidgety younger brother. 'Or are you giving up our paid assignment for this silly Circus interlude?'

'May as well do both.'

I kept my eyes down. When I finished the notes that I actually wanted, I fooled him by drawing stickmen with busy scratches of my stylus. I completed three different sets of gladiators in combat, together with gesticulating lanistae urging on their efforts. My thinking time ended. I drew a sharp breath, as if I had reached some great conclusion. Then I squashed out the doodles with the flat end of my stylus, which was a shame because some had artistic merit.

I spun around to a pile of scrolls we were supposed to have scrutinised already, and spent the whole afternoon unwinding and rewinding them though never taking notes. Anacrites managed to stop himself asking what I was up to. Without even trying I managed to keep it to myself.

In fact I was re-examining the dockets and price lists for the animals Calliopus imported. We had previously looked at what he paid for them individually, and his overall cashflow for the menagerie account. All that had been aimed at deciding his true personal worth. Now I wanted to acquire a more general understanding of how the importation business worked. Where the beasts came from. In what numbers and what condition. And what it might mean to Calliopus first to buy a lion with the wrong pedigree for the venatio – and then to have him mysteriously killed.

Most of his animals came via his home town of Oea in the province of Tripolitania. They were delivered by one regular shipper, who was probably his third cousin. All the shipments were put together over there at the menagerie which Anacrites and I had doubts about, the one which allegedly belonged to Calliopus' 'brother', the 'brother' whose existence we thought might be faked. We had certainly failed to find any scribbled notes from him saying, '*What are the women like in Rome?*' or '*Mother had another bad turn last week*' – let alone that old family favourite '*Please send more money*'. If he was real, he seemed strangely unfraternal in making a nuisance of himself.

Occasional entries recorded other purchases. Calliopus had bought a bear, five leopards and a rhinoceros (who promptly died on him) from a senator whose private collection was being broken up. Iddibal was right; he rarely acquired big cats, although two years ago he had shared with a fellow lanista called Saturninus a huge purchase from a defunct arena supplier's estate. Going solo again, Calliopus then made a rare acquisition of crocodiles direct from Egypt, but they suffered badly on the voyage and proved unsatisfactory in the arena, where audiences had come to regard exotics from the Nile as less than spectacular unless they had a provenance all the way from Cleopatra's own fishpools. He had accepted a stray python that had been captured in a market by the vigiles.

After a long search I finally turned up the records for Leonidas. Calliopus had bought him last year, through a factor in Puteoli named as Cotys. The original entry merged almost boringly into a hundred others, neatly lettered by Calliopus' accountant, who had been taught enough calligraphy to write a hand so tidy it was illegible; luckily his figures were cruder and easier to read. I was immediately intrigued by what looked like a later note, added alongside the original entry with blotchier ink in a wilder hand. After 'bought from Cotys' someone had scrawled angrily 'Acting for Saturninus, that bastard!'

Well. Whatever the man's legal parentage, I had just unearthed the third reference to this Saturninus today. First Iddibal had told me that when Calliopus discovered he had bought a trained man-eater by mistake, he had tried to sell Leonidas to another lanista who bore that name. Now it transpired that Saturninus had been the *seller* all along – so presumably Calliopus was really trying to make the agent take the lion back to the man who had tricked him. This followed a partnership they had joined in the previous year – which in my experience of partnerships was likely to have ended in at least an awkward parting, if not a blazing row.

Rivalry, eh?

X

At leaving time I managed to shed Anacrites. We walked out through the barracks portico together and started up the road, then I lost him with a simple lie about having left my stylus behind. While he went on to cross the Tiber alone, I wasted time at the Temple of Hercules, trying to squeeze some gossip out of a slightly tipsy priest. He had no idea who his neighbours were. He had not even noticed lions constantly roaring just down the highway, and if any of the bestiarii ever came to the sanctuary to make offerings for favourable treatment from the gods, they had wasted their sacrifices. This charlatan was only interested in scrutinising entrails if they came in a bowl with bacon and celery, nicely doused in a wine sauce.

I left the temple. Anacrites had safely vanished. By the time I returned to the Calliopus establishment, the exercise grounds had both emptied. All gladiators love the feeding trough.

I walked in looking innocent, then since no one was about I managed to station myself in the shadow at the base of the rough and ready statue of Mercury. Huddling in my cloak against the chill, I prepared to wait. With the short winter hours the light had faded already. I could hear the hum of the fighters at their meal indoors. Occasionally a slave brought a bucket to or from the menagerie. Then someone came out from one of the rooms below the office.

Whoever was that?

It proved to be two people. Hanging back a bit was a sturdy young fellow who looked like Iddibal, the most helpful of the fighters I had talked to that morning. He was trailing after a woman. She looked distinctly classy — in the confident, expensive sense. Well, that's another thing all gladiators are supposed to like.

It was too dark to make out her face, though I could see the flash of jewellery on her well-padded chest. She was lurking in a veil, probably with good reason; rich women are renowned for hanging around gladiators' schools — but we still all pretend it's a scandal when they do. There was a flounce on her gown and another in her gait. She carried herself like one of those heavy, extremely senior Greek goddesses who bear on their heads walled cities instead of topknots and ribbons. Although neither was speaking, I gained the impression strong words had been exchanged between Iddibal and this personage before they made their exit, and that there was still much to be said, on her side at least.

Just then Calliopus came out from his office, which was on an upper storey. He looked down over the balcony without comment. The woman saw him, then stalked away out of the complex with immense dignity — a complete phoney if she had just been here for the illicit thrill of throwing herself at a young stud. I glimpsed a slave waiting for her just beyond the main gate.

No lanista encourages sordid goings-on. Well, not openly. Pragmatists will appreciate that presents from rich women help keep their fighters optimistic, though they don't actually hold the door open. For one thing, the wealthy dames love a hint of secrecy. Whatever the rules were here officially, Iddibal (if he it was) ducked his head without acknowledging his master, then quickly scuttled across to the main building where his cronies were scoffing their meal.

Calliopus watched with his arms folded. He came down the staircase and crossed the open ground to the animal house, walking at a brisk pace. I noticed he had a long cloak folded on over one shoulder; it was hometime for the man in charge. That was good; I had been prepared to squat here in the cold half the night.

He stayed inside just a short while, then came out again with Buxus and a couple of other attendants. Calliopus dismissed the slaves who scampered off in the direction of the barracks, no doubt hoping the gladiators had left them a few morsels to eat. Calliopus locked the menagerie. Then he and Buxus walked together back up to the office, which was solemnly secured as well. The lanista hung the big keyring on his belt. Instead of departing through the outer entrance gate as I expected, Calliopus then gave me a nasty shock: he and Buxus returned to ground level and came marching straight towards me.

I had slid behind the plinth when the lanista first appeared. Now I pulled in my head, and waited for what seemed like inevitable discovery. There was a colonnade behind me, in front of the row of cells where the bestiarii slept, but if I scampered back to take cover I would be making myself visible. Escaping detection seemed impossible. As soon as the two men drew level with me, I would be like a virgin caught out with a melon-seller. I prepared to jump up and make some feeble excuse for still being on the premises. Even so, the measured pace at which the two men were walking made me pause. I flattened myself against the rough-cast plinth and held my breath.

They were on me. Only the statue remained between us. A couple of footsteps scuffed: boot leather on wood instead of baked earth. A quiet clink of metal and a soft little knocking sound. Two more steps. Then to my astonishment, I heard Calliopus and Buxus walking away again. Once my heart had stopped beating, I ventured to peep out. This time they had their backs to me, going straight to the portico. By now I could see a big carriage drawn up and waiting in the roadway outside. Calliopus said something casual, then he left. Buxus went whistling off for his evening meal.

I sat tight until my confidence returned. I crept around the statue base and stood thoughtfully in front of the calm-eyed Mercury in his winged sandals and ill-chosen December nudity. He stared over my head, no doubt trying to pretend that he did not feel like an idiot showing his all to the local sparrows and wearing a wreath perched on top of his travelling hat. A couple of wooden steps in front of his plinth provided access for whoever renewed his laurel leaves.

I trod silently up the steps. With a whispered 'excuse me' I fumbled under the wreath. As I suspected, some hard-hearted pervert had knocked a nail into Mercury's head, just behind his left ear. What a way to treat a man – let alone the messenger of the gods. Hanging on the nail was a single large key. I left it there. Now I knew where they kept their emergency spare. So did half of Rome, probably.

Like Calliopus I went home. Unlike him, my earnings were moderate. I had no carriage to come and collect me; I just walked. For informers this is an ideal way to think.

Of our girlfriends and our dinner, usually.

XI

My apartment was full of people. Most had come to annoy me, but it's the duty of a good Roman to make himself available at home to those who wish to fawn on him. Naturally I wanted my daughter to grow up with an appreciation of the sociable customs that had applied in our great city since Republican times. On the other hand, since Julia Junilla was little over six months old, her only current interest was in applying her crawling skills to heading out to the landing as fast as she could and flinging herself off into the street ten feet below. I scooped her up just as she reached the edge, let myself be charmed by her sudden beaming smile of recognition, and went indoors to tell the rest of them firmly that they could clear out.

It got me nowhere as usual.

My sister Maia, who was on very friendly terms with Helena, had come to visit; on my entry she groaned loudly then grabbed her cloak and pushed out past me, implying that my arrival had spoiled the happy atmosphere. Maia had a family; she must also have had things to do. I was fond of her, and she could usually make a pretence of tolerating me. Behind her as she barged past I had glimpsed a small, scowling figure, robed in five sensible layers of long woollen tunic and looking at me the way the Medusa sized up passers-by before turning them to stone: our mama. I guessed she would be accompanied by Anacrites.

Helena, whose face revealed a previous moment of panic on realising that Julia had escaped again, noted that I had now recaptured our offspring. Recovering from her alarm, she made a cutting remark about Cato the Elder always being home from the Senate in time to see the baby bathed. I congratulated myself on having cornered a woman who could flay me with literary allusions rather than having picked up some dumb pudding with a big bust and no sense of historical niceties. Then I said, if ever I was made a member of the Senate I would ensure that I followed Cato's sterling example but while I remained on the rougher side of the Sacred Way I might have to spend time earning fees instead.

'Talking of earning,' my mother started in, 'I'm pleased to see you settling down to working with Anacrites. He's just the person to set you straight.'

'No one can touch Anacrites for talent, Ma.' He was a weevil, but I wanted my dinner not an argument. He always had been a weevil, and now he was littering up my domestic life as well. In fact he was sitting on my particular stool. Not for long, I vowed. 'What are you doing here, partner? You look like some snotty-nosed infant that's been parked all day with his auntie and now has to wait until Mother comes to take him back home!'

'I lost you somewhere, Falco.'

'That's right; you let me give you the slip,' I grinned, annoying him by making a joke of it.

'We were all just discussing wherever you could have got to,' glared Ma. 'Anacrites told us you had already finished your work.' She clearly believed I had dumped him in order to waste time and money in a winebar, though she was too tactful to say so in front of Helena. In fact Helena was perfectly capable of reaching the same conclusion, and requiring an oath on the altar of Zeus at Olympus (yes, the full round trip to Greece) before she would change her mind.

'If Anacrites said that, I'm sure it's what he sincerely believed.' Still carrying the baby, I waved my free hand airily. 'There was a detail I wanted to investigate.'

'Oh!' Ever alert to me keeping secrets from him, Anacrites started up in indignation. 'What was that, Falco?'

I glanced around the room, tapped my nose, and

whispered, 'State business. Tell you tomorrow.' He knew I was intending to forget.

'You don't need any secrets here,' scoffed my mother.

I said I would be the judge of that, and she aimed a swipe at me with a colander.

The reason she had the implement (which I dodged) was that Ma deemed Helena Justina too noble to prepare cabbages. Don't get me wrong; she *approved* of Helena. But if Ma was there, Ma shredded the greens.

Anacrites, as her lodger, obviously supposed this meant that they would both be staying to dine with us. I let him dream.

Now I was home, in what passed for my place as the master of the household, Ma quickly completed her work and gathered herself together to leave. She took the baby from me with the air of saving Julia from the talons of a bird of ill omen, kissed her goodbye, and handed her to Helena for safe keeping. We had offered Ma a meal, but as usual she decided that we would rather be left on our own for romantic reasons (though of course being given permission crushed any romance there might have been). I hooked a hand under Anacrites' elbow, and without actually letting it seem like rudeness, propelled him to his feet. 'Thanks for escorting my mother home, old fellow.'

'It's no trouble,' he squeezed out. 'Look, have you been taking that lion business further on your own?'

'Never entered my head,' I lied.

As soon as I had waved off Ma, I closed the door firmly. Helena, more tolerant than Ma, waited for me to explain in my own time where I had been. She allowed me to reassert my authority with a few moments of lewd assault, followed by tickling the baby until Julia was hysterical, then looking round for titbits to nibble until I was provided with proper sustenance.

Anacrites had made sure he gave Helena his opinion of our progress on the Census job, adding a warped description of what I had been up to regarding Leonidas. I now told her the parts I had not told him. 'There's a smell of something nasty. It's quite clear the lanista is trying to stop me poking my nose in—'

Helena laughed. 'Little does he realise that's a certain way to ensure you take an interest!'

'You know me.'

'On the whole.' She shrugged, taking a bowl of nuts away from me, ostensibly to stop me filling myself up before supper, then tucked into it herself. It always gave me a thrill to see this girl who looked so prim revealing her healthy appetites. As she guessed what I was thinking, her huge eyes gazed back at me serenely; she smoothed her skirt over her knees with a very precise, stiff-fingered gesture – then she cracked open another pistachio.

'Am I being stubborn over this, sweetheart?' I reached for the nut bowl but she swung around on her stool and avoided me. 'There is a lion that has been somehow spirited away from his cage, apparently without a roar – or if he did roar, without anybody hearing him even though his devoted keeper and a gaggle of gladiators were just strides away. He's been killed somewhere else – why? – then returned to his billet and locked in.'

'To make it look as if he never left?'

'Seems so. Doesn't it make you curious?'

'Certainly, Marcus.'

'The keeper is lying, and has probably been ordered to do so.'

'That's odd too.'

'And the gladiators have clammed up.'

Helena was watching me, her dark brown eyes as thoughtful about the mystery as they were about evaluating what it meant to me. 'This is troubling you, my darling.'

'I hate secrets.'

'And?' She could tell there was more to it.

'Well, perhaps I'm getting overexcited.'

'You!' She was teasing. 'How, Marcus?'

'I wonder whether it is pure coincidence that this happened when I'm conducting enquiries there.'

'What could be behind it?' prompted Helena levelly.

'The dead lion is the one who had been booked to execute Thurius. Since it was me who apprehended Thurius—' I told her my real suspicion; it was one I could never mention to Anacrites: 'I wondered whether somebody may have it in for me.'

Helena could well have laughed or scoffed. I would not have blamed her. Instead, she listened calmly and as I expected she made no attempt to patronise me. She simply told me that I was an idiot, and on reflection I agreed.

'Can we have some dinner now?'

'Later,' she said firmly. 'First, you're going to be a good Roman like Cato the Elder, and you're going to see the baby bathed.'

XII

We had no domestic water supply. Like most of Rome we inhabited an apartment where the nearest fountain was around a corner in another street. For our daily ablutions we went to the public baths. They were plentiful, sociable, and in many cases free. The more luxurious parts of the Aventine boasted large detached mansions with their own private bathhouses, but in our slum we had a long walk with our strigil and oil-flask. Our street was called Fountain Court, but that was an administrative joke.

Across the road, in the huge gloomy block where I had once lived myself, stood Lenia's laundry, which did possess a deep, rather fitful well. Its murky water was usually available in winter, and big cauldrons were always on the fires in the back yard. Because I was supposed to be helping Lenia arrange her divorce I felt able to cadge what remained of her warm water after the laundry closed for the night. She had been married a whole year now – having lived with her husband for all of a fortnight – so in accordance with local custom it was well time she shed her spouse.

Lenia was married to Smaractus, the most stinking, greedy, heartless and degenerate Aventine landlord. Their union, which all her friends had been denouncing from the moment she proposed it, had been cobbled together out of their mutual hopes of defrauding each other of property. The wedding night had ended with the nuptial bed on fire, the husband in jail accused of arson, Lenia in acrimonious hysterics, and everyone else drunk out of their minds. An occasion to remember – as the wedding guests now insisted on reminding the unhappy pair. They did not thank us for it.

Their curious start should have provided years of nostalgic stories to retell happily around the fire at Saturnalia. Well, perhaps not around the *fire*, since Smaractus had been rather badly frightened by his adventure in the flaming bed. Around a festive table, with the lampwicks all trimmed neatly, perhaps. But from their night being rescued by the vigiles they had descended into a hell from which nobody could save them. Smaractus came home from jail in a foul temper; Lenia pretended she had had no idea he was so violent and unpleasant; he accused her of setting fire to the bed deliberately with a view to grabbing a big inheritance if she killed him; she said she wished she had done it, even if there was no inheritance. Smaractus made a few feeble attempts to claim rights in the laundry (the one freehold he had omitted to acquire in our district), then he stole what he could carry and fled back to his own grimy apartment. Now they were getting divorced. They had been talking about it for the past twelve months without any progress, but that was typical of the Aventine.

Lenia had been in her office where black winter mould, encouraged by the laundry steam, had encased the walls in a sinister patina. Hearing us, she swayed to the door. She seemed subdued, which meant either she had not yet drunk enough to liven her up this evening, or she had tippled so much she had poisoned herself. Her unusual red hair, product of violent substances unknown to most cosmetics vendors, hung either side of her white, bleary-eyed face in frizzled hanks as she dithered at the doorway.

While Helena slipped past me to avail herself of the still-warm tubs, I planted myself in Lenia's path with a well-placed verbal tackle. 'Hello! I see your hot-blooded lover's here.'

'Falco, when the bastard comes down, trip him up and make him talk about my settlement.'

'Call me when you hear him coming, and I'll make another attempt to reason with him.'

'Reason? Don't make me laugh, Falco! Just you put a noose around his throat and pull it tight; I'll hold the agreement so he can sign it. Then you can finish strangling him.'

She meant it too.

Smaractus must be collecting rent from his hapless tenants. We could tell that from the angry shouting upstairs and also because the two dwindling stars of his back-up team, Rodan and Asiacus, were flat out with a wineskin in Lenia's front portico. Smaractus ran what he called a gladiators' school, and these punch-drunk specimens were part of it. He took them around for protection; I mean, to protect the rest of the populace from what these idiots might get up to if Smaractus left them unattended. There was no need to drag Rodan and Asiacus up all the six storeys of leasehold hovels, because Smaractus himself was perfectly capable of forcing his debtors to turn out their purses if he caught them in.

He didn't scare me though. Nor did his thugs.

Giving Julia her bath was my job (hence the jibes about Cato the Elder and the late hour I had slunk home).

'I want her to grow up knowing who her father is,' said Helena.

'Is that to ensure she will be rude and defiant to the right person?'

'Yes. And so you will know it is all your own fault. I don't want you ever to say "Her mother brought her up and ruined her"!'

'She's a bright child. She should manage to ruin herself.'

It took me at least twice as long to clean up the baby as it took Helena to rinse out her little tunics in another cauldron. Helena disappeared, perhaps to console Lenia, though I hoped she had gone to prepare my dinner back at home. I was left to make my usual failed attempt to interest Julia in the floating ship I had whittled for her, while she played instead with her favourite toy, the cheesegrater. We had to bring it or there was screaming. She had perfected how to smack it down on the water apparently aimlessly, though with a true knack of soaking her papa.

The cheesegrater had a curious history. I had swiped it at Pa's warehouse, thinking it looked like an ordinary product of a house clearance. When Pa noticed it at our apartment one day, he told me it had in fact come from an Etruscan tomb. Whether he was himself the tomb robber remained vague, as usual. He reckoned it might be five hundred years old. Still, it worked all right.

By the time I had dried Julia and dressed her, then dried myself, I felt exhausted but there was to be no peaceful relaxation because when I clutched the wriggling baby under my cloak and gathered up all her accessories I found Helena Justina, my supposedly refined girlfriend, leaning on one of the crooked pillars in the outside portico, rewinding her stole around her shoulders and risking serious assault by actually talking to Rodan and Asiacus.

The ugly pair shifted nervously. They were ill-fed, unhealthy specimens, kept on short rations by Smaractus' meanness. He had owned them for years. They were slaves, of course, pallid bruisers in leather skirts and with their arms wrapped in grimy bandages to make them look tough. Smaractus still made a pretence of exercising them at his seedy training barracks, but the place was just a cover and he could never dare risk them in the arena; for one thing, they fought even more dirtily than the Roman crowd liked.

There were no graffiti from lovelorn manicure girls scrawled on the walls of that particular gladiators' barracks, and no gold-laden ladies stopped their litters surreptitiously around the corner while they slipped inside with presents for the hulk of the month. So Rodan and Asiacus must have been startled when they found themselves accosted by Helena Justina, who was well-known in these parts as Didius Falco's snooty piece, the girl who had stepped down two ranks to live with me. Most people on the rough side of the Aventine were still trying to fathom where I could have bought the powerful love potion to bewitch her. Sometimes at the dead of night, I woke up in a sweat and wondered that myself.

'So how is the world of gladiating?' she had just asked, quite as calmly as if she were enquiring of a Praetorian friend of her father's how his latest court case was progressing at the Basilica Julia.

It took the clapped-out wrecks a few minutes to interpret her cultured vowels, though not long to compose replies. 'It stinks.'

'It bloody stinks.' From them that was sophisticated repartee.

'Ah!' Helena responded wisely. The fact that she seemed unafraid of them was giving them the jitters. It was not doing much for me. 'You both work for Smaractus, don't you?'

She could not yet have seen me lurking in the shadows, anguishing how I could possibly protect her if the rancid pair heaved themselves upright and got lively. They were trouble. They always had been. They had beaten me up several times in the past, trying to make me pay my rent; I had been younger then, and not normally impeded by carrying a baby as I was now.

'He treats us worse than dogs,' grumbled Rodan. He was the one with the broken nose. A tenant had hit him in the face with a mallet when Rodan tried to forestall a moonlit flit. Any desperate tenant who had finally glimpsed escape from Smaractus was likely to fight for it fiercely.

'You poor things.'

'Still it's better than being an informer!' giggled Asiacus, the rude one with the pustular skin complaint.

'Most things are,' Helena smiled.

'What are you doing shacked up with one?' They were bursting with curiosity.

'Falco spun me some fables; you know how he talks. He makes me laugh.'

'Oh he's a clown, all right!'

'I like looking after him. Besides, we have a baby now.'

'We all thought he was after your money.'

'I expect that's it.' Maybe by this time Helena had guessed I was listening in. She was an evil tease. 'Speaking of money, I suppose Smaractus is hoping to make some out of the Emperor's new project?'

'That big place?'

'Yes, the arena that they are building at the end of the Forum, where Nero had his lake. The Flavian Amphitheatre, they are calling it. Won't it provide good opportunities when it opens? I should imagine there will be a big ceremony, probably lasting weeks, with regular gladiatorial shows – and probably animals.'

'You're talking real spectacle,' replied Asiacus, trying to impress her with size.

'That should be healthy for people in your line.'

'Oh Smaractus thinks he'll be rolling – but he'll be lucky!' sneered Asiacus. 'They'll be wanting class acts there. Besides, the big operators will have all the contracts well sewn up long before.'

'Are they manoeuvring already?'

'You bet.'

'Will there be a lot of competition?'

'Sharp as knives.'

'Who are the big operators?'

'Saturninus, Hanno – *not* Smaractus. No chance!'

'Still, there should be plenty of profit to go round – or do you think things might turn nasty?'

'Bound to,' said Rodan.

'Is that a well-educated guess, or do you know for sure?'

'We know it.'

Helena sounded in awe of their inside knowledge: 'Has trouble started?'

'Plenty,' Rodan said, boasting like a Celtic beer-swiller. 'It's not so bad among the fighters' lanistae. Supplying men can be fixed without much trouble – though of course they have to be trained,' he remembered to say, as if he and his filthy partner were talented experts not simple brutes. 'But the word is that there's going to be a huge venatio – as many big cats as the organisers can get hold of, and they are promising thousands. That's got the beast importers shitting bricks.'

Helena ignored the obscenity without flinching. 'It's going to be a wonderful building, so I suppose they will inaugurate it with appropriately lavish shows. Are the beast importers afraid they cannot meet the demand?'

'More like, each one is afraid the others *will* meet it and he'll lose out! They all want to make a killing!' Rodan collapsed, laughing hoarsely, overcome by his wit. 'Make a killing, see—'

Asiacus put on a show of greater intelligence, bashing Rodan sideways in disgust at the terrible pun. They sprawled over even more of the pavement while Helena politely stepped back to make more room for them.

'So what are the importers up to at the moment?' she asked, still as if she were simply gossiping. 'Have you heard any stories?'

'Oh there's plenty of *stories*!' Asiacus assured her (which meant he had heard absolutely nothing definite).

'Blackening each other's character,' suggested Rodan.

'Dirty tricks,' added Asiacus.

'Oh you mean like stealing each other's animals?' Helena asked them innocently.

'Well, I bet they would if they thought of it,' Rodan decreed. 'Most of 'em are too thick to have the idea. Besides,' he went on, 'nobody's going to tangle with a great big roaring lion, are they?'

'Falco saw something very peculiar today,' Helena decided to confess. 'He thinks some dirty trick with a lion may have happened.'

'That Falco's an idiot.'

I decided it was time to step forward and show myself before Helena Justina heard something else a well-brought-up senator's daughter should not be told.

XIII

Helena took the baby from me demurely while the two heavies sat up and jeered. '*Io*, Falco! Watch out; Smaractus is looking for you.'

They had immediately become perky now that I had appeared to put myself in line for thumping.

'Forget it,' I said, giving Helena a glare to keep her in some sort of order. 'Smaractus has stopped harassing me. He promised me a year's free rent when I saved his life in the wedding fire.'

'Get up to date,' chortled Rodan. 'The wedding was over a year ago. Smaractus has just realised you owe him for the past two months!'

I sighed.

Helena sent me a look that said she would talk to me at home about which part of our tight budget the money would come from. Since the rent in question was owed for my old apartment, currently occupied by my disreputable friend Petronius, she would reckon he should contribute. His life was such a mess at present, I preferred not to bother him. I winked at Helena, which nowhere near fooled her, then I encouraged her to go ahead and start putting pans on our cooking bench.

'Don't fry the fish; I'll do that,' I ordered, asserting my rights as the cook.

'Don't stay too long gossiping then; I'm hungry,' she retaliated, as if the delay in dinner was all my fault. I watched her cross the road, a figure that made the two gladiators salivate, and walking with more confidence than she ought to show. Then I saw the scampering shape of

Nux our dog shoot out from the shadows at the foot of the stairs and accompany her safely home.

I had no intention of pressing Rodan and Asiacus for more information, but I had promised to tackle Smaractus about Lenia's divorce. He was on his way down. That became obvious, as the shrieks of abuse from his tenants grew louder. His bodyguards hid their wineskin to stop him pinching it, and shambled to their feet.

I yelled up to Smaractus. As I expected, the pleasure of telling me my period of free rent had ended brought him rushing down the staircase. A lolloping figure with a belted-in winegut, he stumbled badly as he reached ground level.

'You want to watch that,' I advised in a nasty tone. 'Those treads are crumbling badly. The landlord's heading for a huge compensation claim when someone breaks their neck.'

'I hope it's you, Falco. I'll pay the claim; it would be worth it.'

'Glad to see relations between us are as amicable as ever – by the way, I'm surprised you haven't been asking for rent again; it's very good of you to extend my free-gift period—'

Smaractus went a horrid shade of purple, outraged by my cheek. He clutched at a heavy gold torque he had taken to wearing; he had always been prone to insulting his tenants by flashing large chunks of ugly jewellery. It seemed to act as a talisman and he hit back straightaway: 'That big bastard from the vigiles who you've planted in my apartment on the sixth, Falco – I want him out. I never allow sub-letting.'

'No; you prefer that when folk go on holiday you can stick in filthy subtenants of your own and charge twice – Petro's all right. He's part of the family. He's just staying with me for a short term while he sorts out some personal business. And speaking of women, I want to talk to you about Lenia.'

'You keep out of that.'

'Now settle down. You can't go on like this. You both need your freedom; the mess you've put yourselves in needs to be untangled, and the only way is to face the situation.'

'I've spelt out my terms.'

'Your terms stink. Lenia's told you what she wants. I dare say she's been rather over-demanding too. I'm offering to arbitrate. Let's try and arrange a sensible compromise.'

'Stuff you, Falco.'

'You're so refined! Smaractus, this is the kind of stubbornness that dragged out the Trojan War to a decade of misery. Think about what I've said.'

'No, I'll just think about the day I can lose you off my tenants' list.'

I beamed at him. 'Well, we're at one there!'

Rodan and Asiacus were growing bored, so they made their usual offer to Smaractus of rolling me out like a pastry and making a human fruit tart. Before he decided which of his pet bullies was to hold me down and which to jump on me, I put myself in the street with room to sprint for home, then asked him casually, 'Is Calliopus, the lanista, a colleague of yours?'

'Never heard of him,' growled Smaractus. As an informant he measured up to his filthy qualities as a landlord: he was as welcome as root rot.

'Rodan and Asiacus have been telling me about the ructions in your business. I gather the big new amphitheatre heralds an unparalleled era of happiness among the high-living venatio boys. Calliopus is one of them; I'm surprised a man of the world like you doesn't know him. What about Saturninus then?'

'Don't know him, and wouldn't tell you if I did.'

'Generous as ever.' At least that made him look worried that his truculence had in some subtle way shed light for me. 'So you didn't know the arena suppliers are all hoping to make their fortunes when the new place officially opens?'

Smaractus merely looked furtive, so I grinned and waved goodbye. I arrived home just in time to wrench the fish skillet from Helena before she let the whitebait stick.

She was waiting for me to rebuke her for chatting to dangerous characters. I deplore arguments, unless there is a good chance of me winning. So we avoided that. We ate the fish, none of which were much bigger than my eyebrow though they were all equipped with spiky skeletons; there was also a small white cabbage and a few bread rolls.

'As soon as I start getting paid for the Census job we're going to indulge in some fat tunny steaks.'

'The cabbage is nice, Marcus.'

'If you like cabbage.'

'I remember my grandmother's cook used to do it with a pinch of silphium.'

'Real silphium is a thing of the past. That was in the good old days when girls stayed virgins till they married, and we all believed the sun was a rather warm god's chariot.'

'Yes, everyone nowadays complains that the silphium you can buy is nothing like it used to be.' Helena Justina had an insatiable appetite for information, though she usually answered her own questions by raiding her father's library. I stared at her warily. She seemed to be playing innocent over something. 'Is there a reason for this, Marcus?'

'I'm no expert. Silphium was always the prerogative of the rich.'

'It's some kind of herb, isn't it? Imported in ground up form,' Helena mused. 'Is it not brought here from Africa?'

'Not any more.' I leant on my elbows and stared at her. 'What's the wrinkle about silphium?' She seemed determined not to tell me, but I knew her well enough to reckon this was more than a general knowledge forum. I racked my brains to get it straight, then declared: 'Silphium, known to those who can't afford it as Stinking Goat's Breath—'

'You made that up!'

'As I recall, it does smell. Silphium used to come from Cyrenaïca; the Cyrenians protected their monopoly jealously—'

'You can see it on coins from Cyrene when you get one palmed in your change at market?'

'Looks like a bunch of grotesque onions.'

'The Greeks always loved it?'

'Yes. We Romans for once allowed ourselves to copy them, since it involved our stomachs which always overrule our national pride. It was powerful stuff, but the ill-advised rural locals where it used to grow let their flocks overgraze the land until the precious crop disappeared. Presumably that causes much grief to their urban relations who used to run the silphium monopoly. Cyrene must be a dead town. The last known shoot was sent to Nero. You can guess what he did with it.'

Helena's eyes widened. 'Do I dare?'

'He ate it. Why, lady; were you imagining some imperial obscenity with the highly prized herbage?'

'Certainly not – go on.'

'What's to add? New sprouts failed to appear. Cyrene declined. Roman cooks mourn. Now we import an inferior strain of silphium from the East, and gourmets at banquets moan about the lost Golden Age when stinking herbs really stank.'

Helena considered what I had just said, filtering out the exaggerations for herself. 'I suppose if anybody rediscovered the Cyrenian species, they could make their fortune?'

'The man who found it would be regarded as the saviour of civilisation.'

'Really, Marcus?' Helena looked enthusiastic. My heart sank.

'Darling, you are not, I hope, suggesting that I should leap on a ship and sail to North Africa with a trowel and a trug? I really would much rather enjoy myself persecuting tax dodgers, even in partnership with Anacrites. Anyway, the Census is more of a certainty.'

81

'Sweetheart, you carry on squeezing defaulters.' Helena was decidedly preoccupied; she had allowed me to pick up the cabbage dish and drink the coriander sauce. 'My parents have had a letter from young Quintus at last. And so have I.'

I replaced the dish on the table as unobtrusively as possible. Quintus Camillus Justinus was the younger of her brothers. He was currently missing, along with a Baetican heiress who had been his elder brother's intended bride. Justinus, who had once possessed the Emperor's personal interest and a promise of a spectacular public career, was now just any disgraced senatorial sprig with no money (the heiress had presumably been disinherited by her thwarted grandparents the moment they arrived in Rome for the wedding that was never to be).

It was still unclear whether Helena's favourite brother had run off with Claudia Rufina out of true love. If not, he was truly stuck. In retrospect – as soon as they vanished – we had all realised she had adored him; unlike her stodgy betrothed Aelianus, Justinus was a handsome young dog with a wicked expression and winsome ways. What he felt for Claudia I was in two minds about. Still, even if he returned her devotion, he had eloped into disgrace. He had thrown away his hopes of entering the Senate, offending his parents and jumping into what was bound to be a lifelong feud with his brother, whose vindictive reaction nobody could blame. As for me, I had once been his keen supporter, but even my enthusiasm was tempered, and for the soundest of reasons: when Justinus bunked off with his brother's rich bride, everyone blamed me.

'So how is the errant Quintus?' I enquired of his sister. 'Or should I say, *where* is he?'

Helena gazed at me peacefully. Justinus had always been dear to her. It seemed to me, the adventurous streak which had made her come to live with me also made her respond to her brother's shocking behaviour with less outrage than she ought to show. She was going to let him off. I bet he always knew she would.

'Quintus has apparently gone to Africa, my darling. Searching for the silphium is an idea he has had.'

If he did find it, he would make himself so much money he would certainly rehabilitate himself. Indeed, he would become so rich he need not care what anyone in the Empire thought of him – including the Emperor. On the other hand, though he was a well-educated senator's son and supposedly intelligent, I had never seen any indication that Justinus knew the first thing about plants.

'My brother has asked,' said Helena, gazing now at her foodbowl with a subdued expression that suggested to me she was on the verge of laughing, 'whether you – with your market-gardening family background and your well-known horticultural expertise – could possibly send him a description of what he is looking for?'

XIV

Something's happened and I can't decide whether to tell you or not,' said Anacrites next morning.

'Suit yourself.'

Petronius Longus had also loved keeping things to himself, though at least he usually kept quiet until I noticed the signs and forced him to come clean. Why could none of my partners be honest, open types like me?

That day Anacrites and I had both reached the Calliopus barracks at roughly the same time, and at once took up our station pouring over the lanista's scrolls like dutiful taxation screws. I could learn to like this life. Knowing that every discrepancy we identified meant more aureae for rebuilding the state made me, as a patriotic citizen, simper with piety. Knowing that I took my percentage from every gold coin kept a big grin on my face too.

Anacrites opted to remain coy. Secrets were his dirty heritage as a spy. I kept working until it was obvious he chose to play the shy maiden, then I rose from my stool quietly and went out of the office. As soon as our profits topped a reasonable figure, I would chain up my partner, smear him with my mother's damson jelly, and place him on a very hot sun terrace that was known to be undermined by biting ants. Could I endure him until summer, though?

Breathing slowly to control my wrath, I walked to the menagerie. Slaves were mucking out the cages but they seemed to assume I had right of entry. Trying not to impede their work, I elbowed through the tall-necked crowd of inanely curious ostriches, then set about taking a full inventory of the beasts. In one stall a sleepy-eyed bull dribbled gloomily; he was labelled 'Aurochs' and named 'Ruta', but having once fought a wild aurochs on a riverbank way outside the bounds of civilisation, I knew this was just some domesticated cud-chewer. Ruta was big, nonetheless. So was the bear, 'Borago', chained by one back leg to a post which he was slyly gnawing his way through. Each of them could be matched against an elephant and it would be a balanced fight.

I helped a man to unload a bale of straw. He spread it around in the bear's stall, keeping well out of arm and snout's reach, then stirred the prongs of his fork in a ground-level feeding-trough. It was falling to pieces after what must have been a very violent life. 'What happened to the manger?'

'We had a croc once.' Apparently that explained it all.

'You sound as if you didn't like him.'

'I hated him. We all did. Laurus looked after him, thank the gods. Poor old Laurus disappeared — gone without a trace — and we reckoned he had ended up inside the snapper.'

'If the croc got Laurus, who got the croc?'

'Iddibal and the others, in the Augustan Games venatio.'

I grinned. 'Iddibal's the one who knows what to do with his spear?'

'Pardon, Falco?'

'Sorry; that was lewd. Doesn't he have some fancy dame chasing after him?'

'I wouldn't know.' It sounded genuine. But then lies always do. The fellow seemed to think about it, with a rather scathing expression, then he added in an oblique tone, 'Who knows anything about the mysterious Iddibal?'

I let it pass, but noted what he said.

They had braziers lit today, keeping the animals warm; the fug made the smells almost unbearable. I felt unsettled by the stink, the heat, the growls and occasional shuffling noises. I noticed there was an open door that I had never explored at the end of the building. Nobody stopped me, so I mooched along and looked in. I found an unconvincingly small pen labelled 'Rhinoceros' and a slabbed area with damp edges labelled 'Sea lion'; both were empty. A sad eagle was chewing out his feathers on a perch. And letting out a hard, terrifying roar was a huge black-maned lion.

For some reason, with Leonidas dead, the last thing I had expected to see was another great cat. He was caged up, thank Jupiter. I stood my ground, regretting the show of bravado. He was more than two strides long. The muscles of his long, straight back rippled effortlessly as he paced around. I could not imagine how anyone had ever captured him. He looked younger than Leonidas, and far more unhappy at being confined. A board leaning outside the bars said his name was 'Draco'. At my entrance he had rushed forwards and with a huge roar let me know what he would do to me, given the chance. When I faced up to him he prowled angrily, searching for a way to break free and attack.

I backed out of the room. The lion's roar had attracted attention from the slaves. They let out appreciative whistles at how he had made me go white. 'Draco looks a handful.'

'He's new; just off a boat from Carthage. He's going in the next hunt.'

'Something tells me you haven't fed him yet. In fact he looks as hungry as if he hasn't been fed since he left Africa.'

The slaves all grinned. I said I hoped the cage was strong. 'Oh we'll be moving him later. He belongs in here normally.'

'Why has he been in solitary? Is he the bad boy of the class?'

'Oh . . .' Vagueness set in suddenly. 'All the beasts get shifted to and fro a lot.'

There was nothing to query in what they had told me, yet I felt a distinct doubt. Instead of creating a fuss, I merely asked, 'Did Leonidas have a name board? If no one else wants it, could I have it for a souvenir?'

'All yours, Falco.' They seemed relieved I had changed the subject. One of them went for the board, which I noticed he had to fetch from the inner room. I was trying to remember whether Leonidas had had his official cognomen on his cage on previous occasions. I could not recall it, and when the board was brought out and displayed for me, I failed to recognise the uneven red lettering. I decided this was the first time I had seen it.

'Why were you keeping it in there instead of on his cage?'

'It must have been on the cage when he was in it.'

'Sure?' They didn't answer. 'All your animals have names, don't they?'

'We're a friendly group.'

'And the crowd like something to yell out as the creatures go to their deaths?'

'Right.'

'What's happened to Leonidas, now he's dead?'

They knew I had a particular interest, because of Thurius. They must have guessed I had worked out for myself that the dead lion's carcass would become cheap fodder for some other animal. 'Don't ask, Falco!'

I was not intending to stick my neck out here. Not in a place where even a keeper could completely vanish without trace. I had heard that crocodiles chew you up boots, belt and all. A hungry lion would probably clean his plate nicely too.

I wondered how many casualties had there been at this barracks? And had any of the victims ever died other than accidentally? This would be a good place to dispose of an unwanted corpse. Was Leonidas simply the latest in a line? And if so, why?

Feeling gloomy, I returned to the office where Anacrites had undergone one of his unpredictable mood swings and was now eager to please. To get my own back I pretended not to notice his welcoming smile, but wrote steadily on my tablet until he could bear it no longer and jumped up to see what I was doing. 'That's poetry!'

'I'm a poet.' It was an old ode I was scribbling to annoy him, but he assumed I had just composed it at speed while he watched. He was so easy to fool it was hardly worth the effort.

'You're a man of many parts, Falco.'

'Thanks.' I wanted to hold a formal reading of my work one day, but I was not telling him that. There would be enough hecklers if I invited my family and real friends.

'You wrote all those lines just now?'

'I can handle words.'

'No one will argue with that, Falco.'

'Sounds like an insult.'

'You talk too much.'

'So everyone tells me. Now talk yourself: earlier you mentioned some new information. If we are to stand a chance in partnership we have to share. Are you going to cough?'

Anacrites wanted to look like the serious, responsible partner, so he felt forced to come clean: 'Last night, someone brought a letter to your mother's house which purports to say who killed your friend Leonidas.'

I noted the cautious administrator's way he insisted it was only 'purported' information. He was so mealy-mouthed I could kick him. 'And who does the purporter allege that to be?'

'It said "Rumex did for that lion." Interesting, eh?'

'Interesting, if true. It's too much to hope we know who Rumex is?'

'Never heard of him.' Chief Spies never know anything. Or anyone.

'Who brought the note?' He looked at me, wanting for some perverted reason to be difficult. 'Anacrites, I'm well aware my mother pretends to be deaf when it suits her, but if any stranger is crazy enough to approach her door – especially after dark on a murky evening in winter – she pops out and grabs them before they can blink. So whose ear lobe did she twist off last night?'

'It was a slave who said a stranger had paid him a copper to bring the tablet.'

'I suppose he swore it was a man he never saw in his life before?'

'Yes, that old line.'

'Did you get the slave's name?'

'Fidelis.'

'Oh a "trusty fellow"! Sounds too good to be true.'

'A pseudonym, I thought,' mused Anacrites. He liked to be suspicious of everything.

'Description?'

'Slim build, under-average height, very dark colouring, stubbly jaw, off-white tunic.'

'No dead eye, or his name tattooed in woad? Rome is full of identical slaves. Could be any one of a million.'

'Could be,' replied Anacrites. 'But it isn't. I was Chief Spy remember: I followed him home.'

Surprised at his initiative, I made out I was unimpressed. 'No more than you should have done. So where did the mysterious trail take you, sleuth?'

My partner gave me a knowing look. 'Straight back here,' he said.

XV

With one accord we rose to our feet and went out to search the establishment. We found plenty of slaves, mostly smelling of stables, but none Anacrites could identify.

'Do we demand that Calliopus should produce him, Falco?'

'You're not a Palace torturer now. Leave it. He'll say he doesn't recognise your description as any slave he owns. And he'll imply you're a romancer.'

Anacrites looked offended. Typical of a spy. We informers may be reviled by everyone but at least we have the guts to acknowledge how our reputation stinks. Some of us even occasionally admit that the profession has asked for it.

'How long did you wait outside after he got here?' I asked.

'Wait?' Anacrites looked puzzled.

'Forget it.' He was a typical spy all right – absolutely amateur.

The messenger belonged elsewhere. Still, if he had turned up here once to contact somebody, he might come again.

'So what now, Falco? We need to interview this Rumex.'

'Sorry to be logical, but we need to find him first.'

'Aren't you anxious we'll lose the lead?'

'Somebody assumes we know who he is. So he'll probably come crawling out from under his stone if we just carry on as normal. Anyway, you were the one who said we were not to be sidetracked. If somebody's trying to give us something else to think about we don't have to comply like lambs. Let's go back to the office and concentrate on our tax report.'

As we turned away to do just that, we ran into the bestiarius called Iddibal.

'Who is your fabulous lady admirer?' I chaffed him.

The young bastard looked me straight in the eye and claimed that the woman was his auntie. I looked straight back at him like an informer who had supposed *that* antique story went out with the Punic Wars.

'Know anyone called Rumex?' Anacrites then asked him casually.

'Why, who's he? Your bathhouse back-scratcher?' Iddibal sneered and went on his way.

I noticed a change in Iddibal. He seemed harder, and as if he were harbouring some new streak of bitterness. As he walked off in the direction of the throwing range Calliopus emerged from a side-room and said something to him in a very sharp voice. Maybe that explained it. Maybe Calliopus had pulled Iddibal up for the affair with his so-called aunt.

We waited for Calliopus to join us, then asked him the Rumex question. 'Not one of my boys,' he answered, as if he assumed it was a gladiator. He should have known we knew it was not one of his troop, or the man's name would have been on the list of personnel he had given us – assuming the version he was offering to the Censors was accurate. He drew himself up for what looked like a prepared speech. 'About Leonidas – you've no need to involve yourselves. I've looked into what happened. Some of the lads were playing up that night and the lion was let out for a bit of a lark. He turned troublesome, and they had to put him down. Naturally nobody wanted to own up. They knew I would be furious. That's all. It's an internal matter. Iddibal was the ringleader, and I'll be getting rid of him.'

Anacrites gazed at him. For once I could imagine how it had felt in Nero's day to be interrogated by the Praetorian

Guards in the bowels of the Palace with the notorious Quaestionarii in attendance, bringing their imaginative range of torture implements. 'Internal? That's odd,' Anacrites commented frostily. 'We have received further information about the death of Leonidas, which doesn't square with that. He was killed by this man Rumex, apparently – though now you tell us Rumex is not one of your boys!'

'Save him having to be got rid of as you're planning for Iddibal,' I said. Proposing a dubious fate for Rumex was, as it turned out later, a poignant piece of augury.

The lanista huffed and puffed for a moment, then thought of something urgent he had to run off and do.

Anacrites waited until we were back in the office and had the place to ourselves.

'So that's that, Falco. We may not have heard the whole story, but the lion's death need not trouble us any more.'

'Whatever you want,' I answered, with the smile I keep for butchers who sell last week's meat as fresh. 'Still, it was good of you to defend my viewpoint when Calliopus was so obviously fibbing.'

'Partners stick together,' Anacrites assured me glibly. 'Now let's finish taking the cheat apart for his financial misdemeanours, shall we?'

I stuck with the audit report like a good boy until lunchtime. As soon as my partner had sunk his jaws into one of my mother's homecooked rissoles and was preoccupied with mopping the squidged gravy from the front of his tunic, I let out a curse and pretended Helena had forgotten to give me any fish-pickle to sauce up my cold sausage, so I would have to go and scrounge some . . . If Anacrites was only half a spy he must have guessed I was bunking off to interview someone else about the lion.

I really did mean to go back to auditing later. Unfortunately one or two little adventures got in the way.

XVI

My brother-in-law Famia worked – if you can call it that – at the chariot-horse stables used by the Green team. We had nothing in common; I supported the Blues. Once, many years back, Famia had actually done something sensible; that was when he married Maia. She was the best of my sisters, whose one aberration had been her alliance with him. Jove knows how he persuaded her. Famia had made Maia a drudge, fathered four children just to prove he knew what his plunger was for, then gave up the struggle and set himself the easy target of an early death from drink. He must be pretty close to his goal now.

He was a short, fat, squint-eyed, florid-faced, devious drone whose profession was administering linctus to racehorses: the kind of disaster only the Greens could rely on. Even the knock-kneed nags who pulled their cranky carriagework knew how to avoid Famia's ministrations. They kicked so hard when they saw him approaching he was lucky never to have been castrated with his own equine ball-snipper. When I found him, a mean-looking grey was rearing up and savagely lashing out with his hooves in response to a sesame sweetie that Famia was coaxing him to take; it was no doubt dosed with jollop from a sinister black pottery bottle that had already been kicked over in the fray.

Seeing me, Famia promptly gave up. The horse whinneyed sneeringly.

'Need some help?'

'Push off, Falco!'

Well that saved me from having my fingers bitten off while pretending I could whisper sweet nothings in a stallion's ear. Bluff would be wasted on Famia anyway. If I did make the grey swallow his medicine, Famia would take the credit himself.

'I want some information, Famia.'

'And I want a drink.' I had come prepared to bribe him. 'Oh thanks, Marcus!'

'You ought to level off.'

'I will – when I've had this one.'

Talking to Famia was like trying to clean your ear with a very bulky sponge. You told yourself the procedure would work, but you could waste hours screwing up your fist without managing to poke anything down the hole.

'You sound like Petronius,' I scolded.

'Good lad – he always liked a drop.'

'But he knows when to stop.'

'Maybe he knows, Falco – yet from what I hear nowadays he's not doing it.'

'Well, his wife's left him and taken his children, and he almost lost his job.'

'Plus he's living in your old disgusting apartment, his girlfriend went back to her husband, and his promotion prospects are a joke!' cackled my brother-in-law, his slit-like eyes becoming almost invisible. 'And you're his best pal. You're right. Poor dog. No wonder he prefers oblivion.'

'Have you finished, Famia?'

'I haven't started yet.'

'Nice rhetoric.' I had to pretend to be tolerant. 'Listen, you're the fountain of knowledge about the entertainment world. Will you give me the benefit?' Famia was too busy guzzling my flagon to refuse. 'What's the word about a beast importers' feud? Someone told me all the lanistae are wetting their loincloths; they all hope the new amphitheatre in the Forum will mean rows of gold winecoolers on their side-tables.'

'Greed's all they know.' That was rich, from him.

'Is their rivalry hotting up? Is there a trainers' war looming?'

'They are always at it, Falco.' Some dregs of intelligence had been warmed up by the wine. He was almost capable of holding a useful conversation. 'But yes, they do reckon the new arena means really big shows in the offing. That's good news for us all. There has been no word about how it will be organised though.'

'What do you think?'

I had sensed rightly that Famia was bursting with a pet theory: 'I reckon the damned lanistae with their carefully guarded sources for wild animals and their private cliques of fighters will be in for a big shock. If you ask me – oh of course you *did* ask me—'

'Enjoy your joke.'

'Well, I bet everything gets taken over and run by the state.'

'Vespasian's an organiser,' I agreed. 'He's presenting the Flavian Amphitheatre as his gift to the populace: the benign Emperor affectionately saluting the Senate and People of Rome. We all know what that entails. SPQR stands for official catastrophe. Public slaves, committees, consular control.'

'Vespasian has two sons, both young men,' Famia said, stabbing the air with his thumb for emphasis. 'He's the first Emperor in living memory to possess that advantage – he comes equipped with his own Games committee. He'll be giving the world a magnificent show – and you mark my words: the whole affair will be run from an office in the Golden House, headed up by Titus and Domitian.'

'A Palace scheme?' I was thinking that if nobody had yet formulated this plan, I might do myself some good by suggesting it to Vespasian. Better still, I would suggest it to Titus Caesar, so he had a chance to propose it formally, getting ahead of his younger brother before Domitian knew what was happening. Titus was the main heir, the coming man. His gratitude was something I liked to cultivate. 'You could be right, Famia.'

'I know I'm right. They're going to take everything out of the hands of the private lanistae, on the grounds that the new amphitheatre is too important to be left to unregulated private enterprise.'

'And once the state organisation is in place, you reckon it will become permanent?'

'A right cock-up.' Famia's idea of political commentary tended to follow routine lines. The four charioteering factions were funded by private sponsorship, but there was always talk of them being state run; it might never happen but Famia and all his colleagues had developed fixed prejudices in advance.

'Imperial control: beasts caught by the legions and shipped by the national fleets; gladiators trained in army-style barracks; Palace clerks running it. All the glory to the Emperor. And everything paid for from the Treasury of Saturn,' I foolishly mused.

'That means paid for by the hard-earned silver I had to cough up for the bloody Census tax.' With luck, Famia had not yet heard how I was currently employed.

My brother-in-law was reaching the point where he wanted to confide to me the troubles of his private life. I reckoned they were all his fault; anyway, I was on my sister's side. I interrupted his moans to ask if he could tell me anything about Calliopus, or better still about Saturninus, the rival who seemed to feature rather large in my suspect's business life. Famia claimed the beast importers and gladiatorial bashers were strangers to all in his more refined racetrack sphere. I managed not to choke with laughter.

By chance I happened to mention the Tripolitanian connection. Then he did take an interest. Apparently some of the best horses came from Africa.

'Numidia – Libya – they're all that way, aren't they?'

'Roughly. But I thought good steeds came from Spain, Famia?'

'The best of all come from bloody Parthia, actually. This huge fellow' – indicating the grey who had spurned his medicine – 'is from Cappadocia; he'll have Parthian or

Median ancestors in his bloodline. Gives him the power to drag a chariot round the bends on the outside of the team. You're the best, aren't you, boy?' The grey showed his teeth ferociously; Famia decided against patting him. So much for being good with animals. 'After that, Spain and Africa rank about equal. Libyan horses are famous for toughness and endurance. That's good in a race. You don't want a pretty four that prances up to the starting gate but can only manage a quick sprint. You need a team that can hang on solidly for seven laps.'

'Right.' I managed not to tease him by suggesting, *you mean like the Blues have?* 'I suppose the horse shippers are probably the same lot who bring in big cats and other exotics for the venatio?'

'Reckon so, Falco. Which may mean that I know a supplier who can tell you what you want to find out. Whatever that may be.'

I let him jeer. That's what you expect from family. As usual I myself felt rather vague about what I was really looking for, but I spared Famia my uncertainty and just thanked him for offering to introduce me to his hypothetical pal. He would probably forget all about it, so I did not trouble to be too effusive.

'By the way, have you ever heard of a character called Rumex?'

Famia looked at me as if I was mad. 'Where have you been, Falco?'

He obviously knew more than I did but before he could tell me, he was stopped by a slave, wild-eyed with excitement, who rushed into the stables, saw Famia, and shrieked, 'You've got to come at once and bring a rope!'

'What's up?'

'An escaped leopard's up on the roof of the Saepta Julia!'

XVII

Famia did not bother finding a rope. Like most chronic drinkers, his intake hardly affected him. He was alert enough to know this was not the same as catching horses. Apprehending a leopard would involve rather more than approaching in a sly manner holding out a carrot, while hiding a bridle behind your back. We were both running fast to the Saepta, but I knew without asking that Famia had come simply for the show. That did leave me wondering who in Rome might be thought appropriate to deal with this situation. Not me, I knew that. I was going for the show too.

When we got there, and saw the size and menace of the beast — a leopardess, in fact — I was damned sure I didn't want to be involved. She was lying on the roof with her fat tail dangling like a Greek epsilon, occasionally snarling when the crowd below annoyed her. In the true manner of a Roman street crowd, that was what they were trying very hard to do. Forgetting that they had seen leopards in the arena biting human necks then casually tearing human flesh, the locals were waving, growling, allowing their children to prance nearby grimacing, and even offering up broom handles to see if they were long enough to poke the cat.

Someone was going to get killed. One glance at the leopardess's narrow eyes told me she had decided it would not be her.

She was a beautiful animal. Sometimes the long sea voyage across the Internal Sea, not to mention the stress of captivity, leaves arena cats looking the worse for wear. This one was as healthy as she was finely marked. Her spotted fur was thick and her muscle tone at its peak. She was lithe, bonny, and powerful. When Famia and I arrived outside the Saepta she was lying motionless. Her head came up, watching the crowd like potential prey on the savannah. Not a scratched ear or sniff escaped her.

It was safest to leave her alone in full view. The Sacpta Julia enclosure was only two stories high. However she got up there, she could as easily get down again and be away. Everyone should have stood well back, keeping quiet, while some wild beast expert with equipment was fetched.

Instead, the vigiles had taken charge. They ought to have cleared the streets and contained the situation. Instead they were like boys who had found a snake curled up under a portico and were wondering what they could make it do. To my horror, they dragged up their syphon engine and prepared to squirt a cold douche at the leopardess to frighten her down. They were the Seventh Cohort. Idiots. They patrolled the Transtiberina, which was crammed with foreigners and itinerants. They were only adept at beating up frightened immigrants, many of whom did not even know Latin and took to their heels rather than discuss life and fate with the vigiles. The Seventh had never learned to think.

The centurion in charge was a ridiculous oaf who could not see that if the leopardess was forced down to ground level they were in big trouble. She could run amock. Worse, they could lose her for days among the massive temples, theatres, and art-filled porticos in the Field of Mars. The area was too crowded to hunt her safely, and yet too exposed to stand much hope of cornering her. There were people milling everywhere; some had not even noticed they had wandered into an incident.

Before I could offer these helpful thoughts, the rumpled troops of the Seventh started playing with their toy.

'Stupid bastards,' commented Famia.

The fire engine was a gigantic tank of water pulled on a waggon. It had two cylinder pistons which were operated by a large rocker arm. As the vigiles worked the arm up and down – something they did with gusto when a crowd was watching – the pistons forced a jet of water up and out through a central nozzle. It had a flexible joint that could be turned through three hundred and sixty degrees.

With more skill than they ever applied to house fires or burning granaries, the Seventh projected their water spray straight at the leopardess. She was knocked sideways, more by surprise than by the initial impact. Now angry and unpredictable, she started to slide, but recovered and scrambled to get a grip on the roof tiles with her extended claws. The Seventh followed her with the fine arc of the waterjet.

'I'm getting out of here!' Famia muttered. Many of the crowd lost their nerve too and surged off in different directions. Above us the troubled leopardess tried to walk along the roof-tree. The vigiles swung their nozzle to intercept her. She decided to escape downwards and moved tentatively lower on the pantiles a couple of steps, coming down on the street side rather than the internal Saepta enclosure. She was nervous of the roof's slope. It took the Seventh a fraction longer to adjust to the new direction; once they caught her in the spray again she made up her mind to leap.

People scattered. I should have done the same. Instead I reached for a stool, abandoned on the street by a flower-seller. I freed my knife from my boot and moved towards where the cat was intending to land. She was aiming for the narrow street half-way along Agrippa's Pantheon.

'Shift your arse out!' shouted the centurion, spotting a hero who might show him up.

'Shut up and do something useful!' I snarled back. 'Get your lads sorted. Make a line. When she jumps we can try to guide her inside the Saepta. If we lock all the doors at least she'll be confined, then we can get specialist help—'

She leapt. I was ten strides away. Nearer folk scrambled for safety, screaming. Street-sellers ran with their trays. Parents grabbed infants. Youths jumped behind statues. The leopardess looked around, sizing up the situation.

'Everyone stand still! Turn off that bloody water!' yelled the centurion, as if pumping it had never been his own idea.

The scene quietened. The leopardess yawned. But her eyes never ceased watching; her head never failed to turn towards any hint of movement.

'Everyone keep calm!' shouted the centurion, sweating badly. 'Leave it to us. It's all under control—'

The leopardess decided he was annoying her and adopted a low crouch, fixing him with those dangerous dark eyes.

'Oh great gawds,' muttered one of the troopers in a low voice. 'She's stalking Piperita!'

One of the others laughed a bit, then advised in an unhelpful tone, 'Better stand still, sir!'

I felt myself grin involuntarily: still one of the ranks, still hoping any officer would come unstuck. The centurion now had his own worries, so I took charge myself. 'Avoid sudden movements, Piperita. She's probably more scared than we are—' That old lie. 'Famia,' I called quietly. 'Nip round the back and get into the Saepta. Tell everyone to lock the other doors and stay inside their booths. Some of you lads run around the Pantheon to the other side of her so we can make a phalanx and guide her indoors—'

The Seventh responded at once. They were so unused to leadership that they had never developed healthy rebellion against it.

The silent leopardess was still observing the centurion as if he was the most interesting prey she had seen for weeks. Rightly or wrongly Piperita tried to inch further away from her without appearing to react. This aroused her hunting instincts even more. We could see her tense.

A small group of vigiles appeared from behind the Baths of Agrippa, on the far side of her, now sensibly holding esparto mats in front of them. The grass mats hardly offered much protection, but gave the impression of a solid barrier across the street and might help them steer the beast. They would be steering her towards me and the others, but we had to put up with that. I told the men in my row to take off their cloaks to use for a similar barrier. Not many were wearing them; even in December such luxuries were never part of their uniform. All the vigiles were unarmed too. A couple of nervous ones hid behind the syphon waggon. Holding my stool in front of me, I steered the others forwards slowly.

It was going well. It had been a good idea. The leopardess saw us advancing. She tried a feinting run towards our group, but we stamped our feet and made off-putting gestures; she turned tail. Piperita scampered amongst us and lost himself from her view. Threatened, the leopardess was looking for somewhere to escape. We had two lines of men walking towards her, closing in to make a V-shape at the Pantheon side. It left her a wide space the other way, inviting her to retreat through one of the grand side entrances to the Saepta. I heard Famia call down from one of the upper storeys, confirming that the other doors were closed. This was going to work.

Then disaster intervened. Just as the leopardess was approaching the open archway, a familiar voice boomed from inside: 'Marcus! What's going on out there, Marcus? What in Hades are you playing at?'

I could hardly believe this nightmare: the short, wide-bodied shape of my father had popped out of the Saepta. Face to face with the cat, he stood plumb in the middle of the entrance: grey curls, startled brown eyes, delinquent scowl, no damned sense. Famia must have told him to stay under cover – so the fool had to come straight out here to see why.

He must have thought about running. Then, being Pa, he clapped his hands smartly as if he were shooing cattle. 'Hep! Hep! Get out of it, puss!'

Brilliant.

The leopardess took one look, decided Geminus was too scary to tackle, and bounded for freedom at full stretch, straight towards the hapless row of men opposite me.

They stood their ground in horror, then leapt aside. We

saw the big cat pounding through the gap, muscles rippling all along its back, paws pounding, tail up, backside in the air in that distinctive leopardine style.

'She's away!'

She was – but not far enough. She made a beeline for what may have looked like a place to hide: the Agrippan Baths.

'Come on!' I set off after the cat, urging the vigiles to follow me. As I passed Pa, I shot him a disgusted look.

'You harbouring a death wish, boy?' he greeted me. I was too good a Roman to tell my own father to jump into a quaking bog, without a plank or ropes. Well, there was no time to phrase it rudely enough. 'I'll get Petronius,' he called after me. 'He likes cats!'

Petro wouldn't like this one. Anyway, it was marauding in the Seventh's jurisdiction: not his problem. I, though, had somehow involved myself. So who was stupid?

We tried telling the attendants to close the doors behind us. No use. Too many frightened people were rushing out through the monumental entrance. The attendants simply decided to run away with them. Everyone was shrieking in panic. When we ran inside, the leopardess had disappeared. The noise died down after the first exodus of naked men. We started to search the place.

I ran through the apodyterium, snatching at clothes on the pegs to check that the cat was not hidden under togas and cloaks. The Baths of Agrippa had been planned to impress; together with the Pantheon they formed the most dramatic building complex in the large output of Augustus' organising son-in-law, his visible monument after he realised that despite decades of service he would never himself get to be Emperor. These baths had been free to the public since Agrippa died, a gracious gesture in his will. They were elegant, lofty, marble-clad, and supremely functional. Every time we pushed open the door to the next chamber we were slapped back by a wall of ever hotter, steamier air. Every step forward became more slippery and dangerous.

Out here in the Field of Mars was a long way to come for most folk, but even so the baths were generally well patronised. The leopardess had almost cleared them. The pickpockets and snack-salesmen had been first out. The fat women who took money for guarding clothes and supplying equipment had knocked us sideways as they ran for cover. A solitary slave now cowered in the unguent room, too frightened even to flee. For once the Spartan dry heat room and steamy tepidarium lay eerily empty. I kept going, accompanied by a few of the vigiles, our studded boots scraping and sliding on the tiled floors. When we staggered through the heavy self-closing door to the hot room, our clothes instantly stuck to us. Unprepared by normal warming-up procedures, we found the wet heat utterly draining. Our hair dripped. Our hearts pounded unnaturally. Through the stifling steam we could make out naked shapes, the shiny raspberry flesh of soporific bathers all apparently undismayed by the chaos outside — oblivious in fact. These men had not been recently inspected by a loose leopard.

'She can't have come this way!' The great door would have stopped her. It was cantilevered so it swung easily to the touch, but the cat would have seen it as a fixed obstacle.

We fell back with relief. Curious bathers tried to follow us. 'Stay inside. Keep the door shut!' One of the vigiles had sense, but he was wasting his breath with advice. He was sweating so much he had lost all authority. People wanted to know what was happening. We had to find the cat. Then we could organise proper security around the area where she was.

These baths were unfamiliar to me. There seemed to be corridors everywhere. They had private pools, latrines, cubby holes, attendants' quarters . . . A thought struck. 'Oh Jove! We have to make sure she doesn't get into the hypocaust.'

A vigilis swore. Under the suspended floors of the baths lay the heating chambers, fuelled by huge furnaces. He realised as I had done that crawling through stacked brick piers in the baking hot cavity in search of the leopard would be ghastly. The space was hardly big enough to squeeze through and the heat would be unbearable. It would be dangerous to breathe the fumes. An attendant wandered through a doorway holding an armful of towels, thin things that were hardly fit to blow your nose on. Piperita grabbed him, threw the towels away, and shoved him down one of the access points, with a large trooper standing guard.

'Search round all the columns. Shout if you see anything moving—' The man on guard grinned at me as Piperita gave his orders; even he looked a bit rueful. 'Well, it's a start!'

'He'll collapse.' I was curt. It was stupidity. A big cat looking for a refuge just might slink between the hot pillars below, but for a man it was no joke.

'I'll send someone else in to get him if he does.'

Without further comment I ran back towards the cold room. I met another attendant whom I sent running to warn the furnace master. 'Where can I find the manager?'

'He's still at lunch probably.' Typical.

Luckily the vigiles had hauled out an under-manager from some nook. He had been chewing a filled roll, but the cheese was rather ripe and he seemed glad to abandon it. We persuaded him to organise his staff in a methodical search. Every time we checked a room we left a man in it to warn us if the leopardess prowled in there later. Slaves started persuading the rest of the public to leave, grumbling but fairly orderly.

The heat and steam were exhausting us. Fully dressed, we were overheating, losing our will to continue. Wild rumours of sightings were being exchanged. As the building finally emptied, the echoes of running feet and the vigiles' shouts made the atmosphere even wilder. I dragged my arm across my forehead, desperate to clear the perspiration. An overweight vigilis was emerging from a hypocaust vent but had stuck. His joshing mates rubbed his red face with towels as he gasped and swore. 'Someone said they saw her go down – I went to look around, but it's hopeless. The space is only about three feet high and there's a forest of columns. If you met her nose to nose you'd be dead.' With a last effort he wrenched his body out through the manhole. 'Phew! It's hot as stink and the air's foul!'

Temporarily done for, he fell full length against the corridor wall, recovering from the effects of humidity and hot gases.

'Best to seal up the underfloor area,' I suggested. 'If she is in there either she'll expire or she'll come out of her own accord later. When we're sure she's nowhere else we can deal with that.'

We left him, and the rest of us dragged ourselves back to the search. Soon we reckoned we had checked everywhere. Maybe the leopardess was outside the baths altogether by now, causing a panic somewhere else while we wasted our time. The vigiles were ready to give up.

I was finished myself but I did a final check through the building. Everyone else had gone out. Finding myself alone I glanced through a wedged open door to the hot steam room. Much of the heat had escaped now. I walked to the great marble bowl of standing water and leaned over to splash my face. It was tepid, and had no effect. As I straightened up, I heard something that made all the hairs on my neck stand up.

The huge establishment was virtually silent. But I had caught the scratch of claws on marble – very close.

XVIII

Very gently I made myself turn around. The leopardess was eyeing me. She had stationed herself on one of the wallseats, sitting up like a sweating bather – between me and the open door.

'Good girl—' She growled. It was terrifying. Fair enough. My luck with the feminine element had never been good.

I kept still. There was no way out. I had my knife but was otherwise unarmed. Even my cloak lay on the flat marble seat beyond the leopardess. The floor was slippery, worsened by a large slick of spilled bathing oil. Its perfume was vine blossom. The one I hate most, more fishy than festive. Needle-sharp shards of the broken alabastron that once contained it lay in wait amongst the oil too.

I sensed failure already. Expecting the worst makes it happen. If only success was as simple.

I felt exhausted by the humidity. This was not for me. I had never been a hunting man. Still, I knew nobody who had any experience would try to tackle a big, fit leopard with only a small hand-knife.

The spotted cat licked her whiskers. She seemed perfectly relaxed.

Noises surprised me: low voices and hurried footsteps approaching in the outer corridor. The leopardess twitched her ears and growled ominously. My throat became too dry to call for help – a bad idea anyway. Very slowly I adopted a crouch, hoping the cat would have learned to recognise a human threat posture. A boot sole skidded on the oily floor. The sickly scent of the spilled *oenanthinum* caught in my windpipe. The leopardess also moved and also slipped, one great paw dangling off the seat. Replacing it fastidiously, she looked annoyed. A low, harsh rumble came from her throat again. We were now watching each other, though I tried to feign disinterest, not offering a challenge. She still had room to escape. She could hop down, turn, and stalk away. At least she could until the voices we had heard came yet nearer; then both she and I knew she was about to be trapped.

It was a spaciously designed chamber. High walls. Vaulted roof. Room for a whole guild of augurs to come here from the Temple of Minerva in the Saepta and lounge in the steam without knocking elbows. To a man hemmed in by a carnivorous wild cat, it suddenly seemed pretty confined.

The voices reached the door. 'Stay out!' I called. People came in anyway.

The leopardess decided that the men now behind her represented danger. I must have just looked pitiful. She stood up and paced along the seat towards me, alert to the disturbance yet twitchingly aware of me. I backed against the stone bowl; then I started ducking round it sideways. The mighty basin was shoulder high and might offer some protection. I never made it far enough. Whether the cat decided to spring up on to the bowl or whether I was her target, she came flying towards me. I shouted and got my knife up, though I stood no chance.

Then one of her pounding paws must have caught in a drainage cover – one of the small square grids with flower-shaped patterns that allowed condensed steam to soak away. Splay-legged, she scrabbled for balance. Either the grid or a shard of glass from the broken alabastron must have hurt her; she bit angrily at a claw, where blood streamed. I kept yelling, trying to drive her off.

Someone broke through the knot of men in the doorway. A dark shape whirled through the air, briefly opened like a sail, then closed around the leopardess. She ended up writhing in a bundle, snarling and spitting, partially held in the folds of a net. It was not enough. One great spotted leg worked free, desperately striking out. The scrabbling bundle of fur and claws still came at me.

My arm flew up to protect my neck. Then I was knocked askew. The powerful weight, all wet pelt, teeth and snarls, belted me sideways. Smelling carnivore, I gasped. I hit the wall. I must have crash-landed right by one of the internal flues; at first I didn't feel it, then I knew my bare arm had been burned from the wrist to the hem of my sleeve.

People raced to the leopard, brisk figures who skated on the wet tiling but who knew what they were doing. Another net arched, spread and fell. Men held the beast down with long iron-shod poles. Sharp commands rang out – then soothing noises for the animal. A cage was slid in and swiftly dragged across to the writhing cat. She was still angry and terrified, but she knew these were the people in control. So, with relief, did I.

'Come out of the way, Falco!' A harsh order came from the tall, shapely female who had flung the first net and saved me. Not a voice to argue with. Not a woman to cross. I had had some dealings with her, though the last time I saw her seemed an age ago and we had been in Syria. Her name was Thalia. 'Make some room for the experts—'

She grabbed my burned arm. Pain kicked in; I shrieked involuntarily. She let go, but took a firmer grip on my shoulders, bunching handfuls of tunic. I let myself be hauled outside the sweating room like a drunk being expelled by a particularly adept bouncer, then I leaned on the wall of the corridor, sweat pouring off in rivulets, holding my right arm away from my body. Breathing seemed something I might never do in comfort again.

My rescuer turned back to see the leopardess successfully caged. 'She's in – you could have waited, darling. Trust a bloody man to want to do everything himself!' The inference was lewd. It seemed best to accept the criticism, both topical and sexual. She had always made suggestive remarks, and I had always pretended not to have heard them. I told myself I was safe because the lady was extremely fond of Helena. If she did decide to grope me, I was not in a state to protect myself.

I had known Thalia some years now. We were supposed to be friends. I treated her with nervous respect. She worked in the Circus, usually with snakes. A woman who could be described as 'statuesque' – *not* meaning a sculpture of some delicate nymph with a sweet smile and virginal properties – and she had a large character to match. I thought I liked her. It seemed the best attitude to take.

As usual Thalia was bursting out of a minimal stage costume that was deliberately designed to cause offence to prudes. To augment the outfit she wore platform boots that had her tottering and arm bracelets like warship anchor chains. Her hair was piled in a towering concoction that she must have kept in place for weeks without dismantling. I swear I glimpsed a stuffed finch among its mass of combs and knob-headed pins.

She dragged me to the cold room, made me kneel beside the dipping pool, and plunged my arm under water, up to the shoulder, to draw out some of the heat from the burn. 'Lie still.'

'I bet you say that to all the men you get hold of—' It was a terrifying thought. Thalia knew it too.

'Take my advice or you'll be in a fever tomorrow, and scarred for life. I'll give you a salve, Falco.'

'I'd rather have a chat.'

'You'll get what's good for you.'

'Whatever you say, princess.'

Eventually she let me up. As she was leading me meekly out through the baths we met a man carrying a whip and a long-legged stool. 'Ooh look!' she shouted sarcastically. 'Here's a little boy who wants to grow up to be a lion-tamer!' He looked suitably embarrassed.

Thalia had accosted a tall, wide, dark-skinned, crinkle-haired man, built like a fighter, puffed nose and all, though unexpectedly well-dressed. He wore a tunic with rich blue and gold braid, carried a full cloak of fine wool with Celtic silver toggles, and flaunted an expensive belt with a buckle that looked as if it had once cinched in Achilles when he was in a party mood. A group of men, obviously his slaves, followed him along the corridor, some bringing ropes and long hooked staves.

'I caught her for you,' Thalia called back over one shoulder as our paths crossed. Apparently he owned the leopardess. 'Come and see me when you've got her home, and we'll talk about the salvage fee.'

The man grinned back weakly, trying to persuade himself she wasn't serious. I thought she was. So did he really.

Thalia kept walking. I limped along after her. 'Who was that?'

'Idiot called Saturninus.'

'Saturninus! You know him, Thalia?'

'Same business, sort of.'

'Well that's a bit of luck.' She looked surprised. Then I promised that I would accept having my arm lathered with ointment, if she would tell me what she knew about the men who imported beasts for the venatio.

'Saturninus, in particular?'

'Both Saturninus and Calliopus, please.'

'Calliopus?' Thalia's eyes narrowed. She must have heard he was being audited for the Census. 'Oh bugger it, Falco! Don't tell me you're the bastard who is doing the lifestyle checks? I suppose I'll be next?'

'Thalia,' I promised, 'whatever lies you have chosen to tell the Censors, believe me, you are perfectly safe. I would never dare investigate your lifestyle — let alone your finances!'

XIX

Thalia had always lurked outside the city, near the Circus of Nero. When I first knew her she was a down-at-heel exotic dancer. Now she had become a manager – of slinky banquet dancing girls, lovable donkeys who could perform feats of memory, extremely expensive musicians, one-legged fortune-tellers who had been born with eagles' beaks, and dwarves who could stand on their heads on a pile of ten vertical amphorae. Her own act featured close contact with a python, an electric combination with the kind of pornographic sleaze you normally don't see outside of the nightmare bordellos dreamed up by high life villains.

Her business had been inherited from an entrepreneur (of whom she spoke disparagingly, as she did of most men); he had experienced a fatal mishap with a panther (of whom she still seemed rather fond). Under Thalia's new strong management things appeared to be flourishing, though she still lived in a tattered tent. Inside it were new silken cushions and oriental metalwork. They vied for space with battered old baskets, some of which I knew probably housed untrustworthy snakes.

'Here's Jason! Say hello to him, Falco.' He was never stuffed in a basket. Jason was not her dancing partner, just a smaller pet, the fast-expanding python whom Thalia had always tried to persuade me was a soft touch who loved company. She knew he despised me and I was scared to death of him. That just made her try harder to throw us together; a typical matchmaker. 'He looks a bit rough at the moment and he's feeling low. You're sloughing another skin, aren't you, darling?'

'Better leave him in peace then,' I countered, feeling

feeble for saying it. 'So how long have you been back in Rome, Thalia?'

'Since last summer.' She handed me a cup of water and waited while I drank deeply. I knew how to be a good patient if the nurse was truly forceful. 'I looked you up; you and Helena were in Spain. More spying on innocent businessmen?'

'Family trip.' I never liked to make too much of the work I had done for the Emperor. I finished my drink. When I put down the beaker on an ivory tray, Jason wove his way to it and licked the dregs. 'How are things, Thalia? Davos still with you?'

'Oh he's around somewhere.'

Davos was an actor whom Thalia had plucked from his peaceful life playing moth-eaten stage gods by persuading him he should revitalise his existence yoked to her. Their relationship was presumably personal, though I avoided asking. Davos was a private man; I respected that. Thalia herself was likely to make me blush with ribald details, stressing measurements.

She was busying herself in a carved wooden chest, from which she extracted a small leather bag where I knew she kept medicaments. She had saved Helena's life once with an exquisite Parthian pick-me-up called mithridatium. Our eyes met, both remembering. I owed her a lot. No need to mention it. Under no circumstances would Thalia be audited by the Falco partnership, and if anyone else bothered her they would have to deal with me. 'Did you bring home the little water-organist and her boyfriend as well?'

'I shed the doe-eyed lad.' She had found what she wanted and applied a big dollop of waxy, strong smelling ointment to my hot arm.

'Oh I thought you would – Ow!'

'Sophrona's here. She plays nicely and she looks good; I make a mint with her. But she's still a dopey little cow, always mooning after unsuitable men instead of thinking about her career.'

'You owe me a finder's fee.' It was a joke.

'Better send me a bill then.' Even more frivolous.

'And you're also still importing exotic beasts?'

Thalia said nothing, eyeing me. If she thought the question was official, this could be where our friendship ended. Only what was good for her business would ever really count. Her life had been too hard. She had no room to lower her standards; she would never grow soft.

'Thalia, I've no quarrel with you. I'll ensure the Census takes no interest in your outfit, if you'll tell me about the men on my enquiry list.'

'Better be quick,' Thalia then agreed quite readily. She relaxed, fixing the lid back on her pot of salve and then wiping her finger clean on her few inches of tassled skirt. 'You don't want Saturninus to walk in while we're dissecting him.'

'Will he come? He didn't look too keen when you mentioned salvage money.'

'Oh he'll be here. He knows what's good for him. How's your burn?'

I waggled my arm. 'Cooling. Thanks.' Saturninus had already seen me with Thalia but if I could leave before he showed up here, he might not remember that. I was undecided how I intended to tackle him, and preferred not to let him see I had Circus friends.

Enquiry soon ascertained that Thalia's own purchasing contacts were still mainly in the East. That let me exclude her from my audit on geographical grounds. 'Don't worry. Falco & Partner are heroes with an abacus but we can't do everything. We're working on Tripolitania.'

'Good. You hammer those bastards so they leave some room for me!'

'Rivalry? I thought your field was speciality acts, not the venatio?'

'Why should I stand back when there are good times coming?' So here was yet another entrepreneur who saw the opening of the new Flavian Amphitheatre as a date with destiny. Well, I would rather Thalia made her fortune out of it than anyone else. She had a heart and she was a lively character. Whatever she offered the crowds would be good quality.

I grinned at her. 'I take it you don't stoop to any funny business to annoy the other managers?' Thalia gave me a hilarious round-eyed stare. If she trifled with them, she was not saying. I did not expect her to. In fact, I preferred not to know. 'But is there serious trouble among the lanistae?'

'Plenty. Look at today, Falco.'

'Today?'

'Why, I could have sworn I met you entertaining a leopardess in the Agrippan Baths earlier, Marcus Didius – is that an everyday occurrence?'

'I assumed she had just escaped.'

'Maybe she did.' Thalia screwed up her mouth. 'Maybe she had help. Nobody will ever prove it – but I saw a whole bunch of Calliopus' bestiarii up by the Portico of Octavia, all leaning on statues laughing their little heads off while Saturninus ran rings around himself looking for his lost animal.'

'Bestiarii? Weren't they training back at the barracks? How could they have known there was a rumpus here? Calliopus has his place way out past the Transtiberina—'

Thalia shrugged. 'It looked peculiar. That doesn't mean I was surprised. Saturninus saw them too – so that's bad news. If he thinks Calliopus freed the leopardess to stir up trouble, he'll do something really evil in return.'

'A dirty tricks war? Has this been going on long?'

'Never quite so serious.'

'There's bad feeling, though? Can you tell me about it?'

'They're vying for the same contracts all the time,' Thalia commented matter-of-factly. 'Both for gladiatorial combats and for the hunts. Then they are men. You can't expect them to be civilised. Oh, and I heard once that they come from rival towns that have some frightful feud.'

'In Tripolitania?'

'Wherever.'

'Calliopus is from Oea. What about Saturninus?'
'Is there a town called Lepcis?'
'Believe so.'
'Right. You know what these potty little neighbour-hoods are like in the provinces, Falco. Any excuse for an annual punch-up, if possible with one or two killed. That gives them all a reason to keep the fight going. If they can tie it to a festival, they can drag religion into it and blame the gods—'
'Is this real?'
'The principle's right.'
I asked her if she had heard about the time when, according to the records that I'd seen, Calliopus and Saturninus briefly went into partnership. 'Yes, they were trying to gang up and squeeze out anyone else from Tripolitania. Not that it worked – the other main player's Hannobalus; he's far too big to take on.' She was of my opinion that when two men shared a business it was doomed to end in a squabble. 'Well, you should know, Falco – I heard you've been playing a disastrous game of soldiers with that mate of yours.'
I tried to make light of it. 'Lucius Petronius was merely going through a bad patch in his personal life—'
'So you two old pals were struck by the thought you would love to work together. I suppose that turned out to be a nasty surprise when it failed?'
'Close.'
Thalia roared with raucous laughter. 'Grow up, Falco. More friendships have died that way than I've had fools in bed. You're lucky Petronius didn't seduce your best clients and embezzle all your funds. You'd stand more chance working with a sworn enemy!'
I smiled bravely. 'I'm trying that now.'
She calmed down. 'You never know when to give up.'
'Doggedness is part of my charm.'
'Helena may think that.'
'Helena just thinks I'm wonderful.'
'Olympus! How'd you swing that? She can't be after

116

your money. You must be a nippy performer – at something, eh, Jason?'

I drew myself up sternly and decided it was time to leave. It meant stepping over the python, unfortunately. Jason liked to curl up right in the exit to the tent where he could look up people's tunic skirts. He wasn't even pretending to be asleep. He was staring right at me, daring me to approach. 'Helena Justina is a fine judge. I'm a sensitive poet, a dedicated father, and I cook a mean chicken wing.'

'Oh that explains it,' simpered Thalia.

I took a big step, nervously. Astride Jason, I remembered something. 'This feud between Saturninus and Calliopus – it's already well warmed-up. Calliopus had a lion—'

'Big new Libyan called Draco,' Thalia reported unperturbedly. 'I was after him myself; Calliopus beat me by going to Puteoli and nabbing him straight off the boat. And I heard he also owns a trained executioner.'

'He did. Leonidas. Saturninus had sold it to him under false colours.'

'Cheeky sod.'

'Worse than that. Leonidas has just been found dead, in very suspicious circumstances.'

'Jupiter!' The lion's murder aroused her fiercest feelings. Other wild beasts were brought to Rome purely to be hunted in the arena, but Leonidas had had work to do in the Circus. He ranked with her own animals and reptiles: a professional. 'That's terrible. Who would do that? And why, Falco?'

'I presume he had enemies – though everyone claims he was the sweetest lion you could meet. A benefactor even to the convicts he tore to pieces and ate, apparently. I'm working on the usual theories for a murder case: that the corpse probably slept around, amassed huge debts, caused fights when drunk, owned a slave with a grudge, was rude to his mother, and had been heard insulting the Emperor.

One of those always turns out right—' I finally plucked up the nerve to finish stepping over the python.

'Anyway,' said Thalia, 'Calliopus and bloody Saturninus may make all the noise, but they aren't the only people chasing after the beast contracts.'

'You mentioned one other big supplier? Also from Tripolitania?'

'Hannobalus. He thinks he'll clean up.'

'Any other names?'

'Oh go on, Falco! Don't tell me you haven't got a list on a nice official scroll.'

'I can make my own list. What about this other Tripolitanian gilthead, Hannobalus?'

'You don't miss much, Falco.'

'We've got one from Oea, one from Lepcis – I suppose there had to be a Third Man, from the Third Town.'

'Neat,' Thalia agreed noncommittally, like a woman who thought nothing involving the male sex was ever tidy.

'Sabratha, isn't it? Very Punic, so I'm told.'

'They can keep that then.'

Thalia's opinion suited me too. I was a Roman. As the poet said, my mission was bringing civilised pursuits to the known world. In the face of tenacious opposition, I believed you whacked them, taxed them, absorbed them, patronised them, then proscribed human sacrifice, dressed them in togas and discouraged them from openly insulting Rome. That done, you put in a strong governor, and left them to get on with it.

We beat Hannibal, didn't we? We razed the city and sowed the fields with salt. We had nothing to prove. That would explain why my hackles rose at the mention of anything Carthaginian.

'Is the man from Sabratha Punic, Thalia?'

'Don't ask me. Who are you going to hammer over that poor lion?'

'A certain Rumex did it, according to my sources.'

Thalia shook her head sadly. 'He's an idiot. Calliopus will fix him good.'

'Calliopus is trying to cover it up.'

'Keeping it in the family.'

'He denies even knowing Rumex.'

'Pizzle.'

'Oh?'

Thalia must finally have realised I had no trace on the fingered Rumex and that I was hoping she could give me a lead. She eyed me askance. I looked shamefaced; she roared with mocking laughter, but then while I wriggled with embarrassment she explained who the great Rumex was.

I must have been the only man in Rome who had never heard of him.

Well, me and Anacrites. That only made it worse.

XX

Once you know, the evidence leaps out at you from every wall:

OUR MONEY'S ON RUMEX:
THE TANNERS OF DOGSTAR STREET
WE LOVE RUMEX – GALLA AND HERMIONE
RUMEX CAN HAVE APPOLLONIA ANY TIME HE WANTS
HE HAD HER LAST WEEK!
HE'S DEAD IF I CATCH HIM – APPOLLONIA'S MOTHER
RUMEX IS HERCULES
RUMEX IS STRONGER THAN HERCULES
AND HIS [DOODLE] IS BIGGER TOO

I even spotted in rather shy, small letters on a temple column an impassioned mutter of:

Rumex stinks!!!

I knew who he was now all right. The man who had been named as the slayer of Leonidas was this year's most idolised gladiator from the Games. His fighting role was as a Samnite, not normally a popular category. But Rumex was a real favourite. He must have been around for years, and was probably lousy, but he had now achieved the fame that only comes to a few. Even if he was only half as good as his reputation, he was not a man to tangle with.

There were graffiti on bakeries and bathhouses, and a poem nailed to a wooden Herm at a crossroads. Outside the Saturninus Gladiators' School stood a small but obviously permanent group of young female admirers waiting for a chance to scream adulation if ever Rumex appeared; a slave walked out with a shopping basket so to keep in good voice they screamed at him. Apparently used to it, he went over and cashed in by chatting them up. They were so hot for Rumex that in his absence they were fair game for anyone.

Inside the barracks gate lurked a porter who was assembling his pension fund from bribes for taking in letters, bouquets, seal rings, Greek sweetmeats, addresses, and intimate items of womenswear for Rumex. This was bad. To a civilised male it was positively embarrassing. Lest I should doubt that women who ought to know better were throwing themselves at this overdeveloped mongrel, two fine and fancy ladies were approaching the gate just as I arrived. They had jumped out of a hired chair together, brazenly showing flashes of leg through slit sideseams in their modest gowns. Their hair was curled. They flaunted shameless stacks of jewellery, advertising the fact that they came from well-off, supposedly respectable homes. But there was no doubt why they were here today; they had already proffered the door porter a tip to admit them. Cursing, I recognised them both.

I would lose them unless I did something about it. I raced up to the barracks angrily. They looked annoyed: these two hussies cruising for a hunk were Helena Justina, my supposedly chaste darling, and my irresponsible youngest sister Maia. Maia muttered something that I lip-read as an obscenity.

'Ah, Marcus!' exclaimed Helena, without batting an eyelid. I noticed that her eyelids were brilliant with antimonised paste. 'At last you have caught up with us — carry my basket now.' She thrust it into my hands.

Dear gods, they were pretending I was some domestic slave. I was not having that. 'I want a word with you—'

'I want a word with *you*!' hissed Maia, in genuine wrath. 'I hear you've been giving drink to my husband — I shall beat you if it happens again!'

'We're just going in here,' Helena announced, with the

peremptory high-class disdain that had once flummoxed me into falling for her. 'We want to see someone. You can either follow us quietly or wait for us outside.'

Apparently their tip had been a huge one. The porter not only allowed them in, but bowed so low he nearly scraped his nostrils on the ground. He gave them directions. They swept past me, ignoring my glares. Whistling started up as soon as they were spotted by the riff-raff inside, so I bit back my indignation and hurried after them.

The Saturninus barracks put Calliopus and his measly hutments in the shade. We passed a forge alongside an armoury, then a whole suite of offices. The timberwork was sharp, the shutters were painted, the paths were neat and swept. The slaves skipping about all wore livery. One large courtyard was simply for show: perfectly raked golden sand, with cool white statues of naked Greek hoplites positioned ostentatiously between well-watered stone urns of dark green topiary. There was enough outdoor art to grace a national portico. The shrubs were manicured into boxtree peacocks and obelisks.

Beyond lay the palaestra, again huge and smart. The peace of the first courtyard gave way to highly organised bustle: more trainers' voices yelling than at the Calliopus establishment. More thumps and whacks of punchbags, weights, and wooden swords on dummy targets. In one corner rose the distinctive arched roofs of a private bathhouse.

My two womenfolk stopped, not as I hoped to apologise, but to pin their necklines more revealingly. As they threw their stoles over their shoulders with more of a swagger and pegged back their little slips of modesty veils, I made a last attempt to reason with them. 'I'm horrified. This is scandalous.'

'Shut up,' said Maia.

I rounded on Helena. 'While you're shaming yourself at a school for killers, where, may I ask, is our child?'

'Gaius is looking after Julia at my house,' snapped Maia.

Helena condescended to explain swiftly, 'Your mother told us about that note Anacrites received. We're using our initiative. Now, please don't interfere.'

'You're visiting a damned gladiator? You're doing it openly? You have come without a chaperone or a bodyguard — and without telling me?'

'We are just intending to talk to the man,' Helena cooed.

'Necessitating four bangles apiece and your Saturnalia necklaces? He may have killed a lion.'

'Ooh lovely!' minced Maia. 'Well he won't kill us. We're just two admirers who want to swoon over him and feel the length of his sword.'

'You're disgusting.'

'That,' Helena assured me quite calmly, 'is the general effect we were aiming for.'

I could see they were both really enjoying themselves. They must have spent hours getting ready. They had raided their jewellery boxes for an eye-catching selection — then piled on everything. Dressed up as cheap bits with too much money, they were throwing themselves into it. I started to panic. Apart from any danger in this ludicrous situation, I had the awful feeling that my sensible sister and my scrupulous girlfriend might happily turn into flirting harridans, given the money and the chance. Helena, come to think of it, already possessed her own money. Maia, married to a determined soak who never bothered what she got up to, might well decide to seize the chance.

Rumex was minded by four world-weary slaves. As a slave himself he could not actually own them, but Saturninus had ensured that his prize fighter was pampered with a generous back-up team. Perhaps female admirers paid for it.

'He's resting. No one can see him.' Resting after what the spokesman did not say. I imagined the unsavoury possibilities.

'We just wanted to tell him how much we adore him.' Maia flashed the slaves a brilliant smile. The spokesman surveyed her. Maia had always been a looker. Despite four children she had kept her figure. She combed her dark, tight curls in a neat frame to her round face. Her eyes were intelligent, merry and adventurous.

She was not pressing the slaves. She knew how to get what she wanted, and what Maia wanted tended to be a tad different. My youngest sister sometimes failed to follow the rules. She still had hopes. She disliked compromise. I worried over Maia.

'Leave whatever you've brought. I'll see that he gets it.' The response was offhand.

Helena adjusted the gold collar at her throat; she was playing the nervous one, the one who was afraid they would be named in the scandal column of the *Daily Gazette*. 'He won't know who sent it!' *He won't care*, I reckoned.

'Oh I'll tell him.' The minder had given the brush-off to plenty before them.

Helena Justina smiled at him. It was a smile that said these two were not the same as all the others. If he chose to believe it, the message could be perilous – not least for Helena and Maia. I was in despair. 'It's all right,' Helena assured the man, with all the confidence of a senator's daughter who was up to no good. Her refined accent announced that Rumex had acquired himself a delicate devotee. 'We didn't expect special treatment. He must have lots of people who are desperate to meet him. He's so famous. It would be such a privilege.' I could see the men thinking this one was really innocent. I was wondering how I had ever hitched myself to a girlfriend who was actually so much *less* innocent than the rude tightrope-walking acrobats I had hankered for first. 'It must be hard work for you,' she commiserated. 'Dealing with people who have no idea of allowing him any privacy. Do they get hysterical?'

'We've had our moments!' the spokesman had allowed himself to be lured into a chat.

'People throw themselves at him,' Maia sneered knowingly. 'I hate that. It's disgusting, isn't it?'

'All right if you can get it,' laughed one of the slaves.

'But you have to keep a sense of proportion. Now my friend and me—' She and Helena exchanged the cloying glances of dedicated followers talking about their hero. 'We follow all his fights. We know all his history.' She listed it off: 'Seventeen wins: three draws: twice down but the crowd spared his jugular and sent him back. The bout with the Thracian last spring had our hearts in our mouths. He was robbed there—'

'The referee!' Helena leant forwards, stabbing her finger angrily. This was some old controversy, apparently.

'Rumex was tripped.' I was impressed by their research. 'He was winning, no question, then his boot let him down. He'd had three hits, including that tricky one when he did the cartwheel and cut up under the other man's arm. He ought to have been given the fight.'

'Yes, but accidents don't count,' put in one of the slaves.

'That bastard the old Emperor Claudius used to have their throats cut if they fell by accident,' someone else said.

'That was in case they were fixing it,' said Helena.

'No way. The crowd would spot that.'

'The crowd only sees what it wants to see,' suggested Maia. Her interest seemed genuinely passionate. It looked as if the finer points of the Rumex loss against the Thracian would be haggled over for the next three hours. This was worse than overhearing a row between two half-drunk bargees on pay night.

My sister stopped. She beamed at the minders, as if pleased to have shared with them her knowledge and expertise. 'Can't you let us in just for a few moments?'

'Normally,' explained the spokesman carefully. 'Normally there wouldn't be a problem, girls.' So what was abnormal today?

'We have money,' Helena proposed bluntly. 'We want

to give him a present – but we thought it would be nicer if we could just see him, to ask him what he really wants.'

The man shook his head.

Helena clutched her hand to her mouth. 'He's not ill?'

Over-indulgence, I thought to myself. In what, it seemed best not to speculate.

'Has he been hurt in practice?' gasped Maia, with real distress.

'He's resting,' said the spokesman for the second time.

I let myself speculate after all. Everyone knows what top gladiators are like. I could imagine the scene indoors. An uneducated thug, provided with indecent luxury. Gorging on sweated suckling pig, dousing it in lashings of cheap fish-pickle sauce. Reeking of impossibly scented pomades. Swilling undiluted Falernian like water, then leaving half-empty amphorae unstoppered for the wineflies. Playing endless repetitive games of Latrunculi with his sycophantic hangers-on. Pausing for three-in-a-bed orgies with teen-age acolytes even dafter than the two rash women who were debasing themselves outside his quarters now . . .

'He's resting,' said Maia to Helena.

'Just resting,' Helena answered her. Then she turned to the group of minders and exclaimed, with innocent lack of tact, 'That's such a relief. We were afraid of what might have happened to him – after what people are saying about that lion.'

There was a small pause.

'What lion?' asked the spokesman in a patronising voice. He stood up. He and the others adopted a well-practised shepherding technique. 'We don't know anything about no lion, ladies. Now, excuse me, but I'll have to ask you to be moving on. Rumex is very particular about his training régime. He has to have absolute quiet all around him. I'm sorry, but I can't allow any members of the public to hang about when there's a risk of disturbing him—'

'You don't know about it, then?' Helena persisted. 'It's just that there is a terrible rumour running round the

Forum that Rumex has killed a lion that belonged to Calliopus. His name was Leonidas. It's all over Rome—'

'And I'm a gryphon with three legs,' asserted the chief minder, evicting Helena and my sister from the barracks area ruthlessly.

Outside in the street again, Maia swore.

I said nothing. I know when to carry a basket with my head down. I walked quietly behind them as they stalked away from the gate, making sure I looked like a particularly meek boudoir slave.

'You can stop playing the know-all,' scoffed Maia to me grumpily. 'It was a good try.'

I straightened up. 'I'm just agog at your encyclopedic knowledge of the Games. You both sounded true arena bores. Who fed you the gladiatorial lore?'

'Petronius Longus. We wasted time on it for nothing, though.'

Helena Justina had always been shrewd. 'No, it's all right,' she told my sister in a satisfied voice. 'We didn't manage to see Rumex, but the way those men made us leave so rapidly when we mentioned Leonidas says it all. My guess is that Rumex has been deliberately quarantined. Whatever happened when the lion was killed, Rumex was definitely involved.'

XXI

It was all set to play the heavy-handed paterfamilias, berating them.

'We could have got in if we had really tried,' interrupted Maia.

'At what price?'

My sister smiled at me wickedly.

I made the mistake of commenting that I had once been glad that Helena had found a friend amongst the Didius family, but I had not expected to see her being led astray so shamelessly by Maia. The two of them groaned and raised their eyes to the heavens. Then I realised Helena's air of studied neutrality meant that their coming here had been her idea.

Luckily for those disreputable scamps, that was when the lanista Saturninus returned home with his troupe of animal keepers, dragging a cart containing the escaped leopardess. It had taken them time to arrive here because the curfew on wheeled vehicles meant they had to manhandle the cage and the beast. They were sweating over the task but obviously wanted to replace her safely on their own premises before there were any more accidents.

I bundled my outrageous womenfolk into their conveyance, from which they peered out unrepentantly.

'I suggest that you pair of Messalinas take yourself home and knit bootsocks like proper domestic matrons – the best of wives, whom Famia and I won't mind mentioning on our tombstones one day.' Maia and Helena laughed. It sounded as if they were intending to outlive Famia and me, then take unsuitable lovers and throw away their children's inheritance at some tawdry leisure spa. 'I would escort you but I have urgent business. I,' said I haughtily, 'will go in and attempt to see Rumex – now you two beauties have queered my pitch!'

The door porter failed to recognise me. Without my basket and bossy womenfolk I was a citizen; slaves, of course, are invisible. It was a dodge I had used before when I wanted to stay anonymous.

I asked to see Saturninus. The porter told me the master was not at home. I pointed out that I had just seen the master entering, so the lag answered that whoever I was and whatever I had seen, Saturninus was not at home to *me*.

I could have tried charm, or simple persistence. But with Helena and Maia watching, I took out my official pass as a Palace auditor, held it half a digit from the porter's face. Then I declaimed like a little schoolboy orator that unless his master wanted to be denounced for obstructing the Census, the elusive Saturninus had better see me at once. A slave was summoned to show me the way.

Almost before the door closed behind the slave who took my message in to Saturninus, the chief of Rumex' minders came out of the room. I stood quietly with downcast eyes. He disappeared, also apparently without spotting that I was the 'slave' who had come with Helena and Maia – whose interest in Leonidas he had almost certainly just been reporting. Then I was called in. There was no fuss over it.

The lanista was standing in the centre of a modest room while one slave poured what looked to be water into a beaker he held ready, and another crouched at his feet removing his outdoor boots. He met my gaze, neither hostile nor particularly curious, though I noticed a slight frown as if he was wondering where he had seen me before. I let him puzzle it out.

Now I had a chance to look at him properly. He must have been some sort of fighter himself once. He was middle-aged and solid – but the muscles in his arms and legs told their own story. Whereas my first quarry Calliopus looked more like a cushion-seller than a gladiators' manager, this one was every inch the part, still with the scars and the bearing of his own fighting past. He looked as if when he didn't like his dinner he might kick the legs right off the table – and then kick the legs off the cook too. I could imagine how he egged on his men in the arena. As a trainer, he would know the job from personal experience. There are lanistae who, when they accompany their fighters, jump around so excitedly they expend even more energy than their myrmillons and retarii. Saturninus, I reckoned, would be the calm sort, who circled quietly, just putting in well-placed words of encouragement.

He had surrounded himself with tokens of his low trade. In his spare, functional office, he had weapons and ceremonial helmets hung on wall-pegs; a set of the staves lanistae carry in the arena stood on a large urn in one corner; an elaborately enamelled breastplate was displayed on a wooden rack. There were winner's crowns and padded purses – perhaps ones he had won in the old days himself.

His gaze was intelligent; that went with success in the arena. No man survived to earn his freedom without a cunning streak. I expected him to seem watchful, but he was quiet, friendly – suspiciously friendly, perhaps – and untroubled by my visit.

I said who I was, what I was doing for Vespasian, and that auditing Calliopus was the first stage in a wider review of the Circus world. He made no comment. Word had certainly gone round. I did not suggest he would be my next victim, though he must have deduced it.

'Arising from my enquiries there is a loose end to tie up. Calliopus has had a lion kidnapped and destroyed. I have received information that one of your troupe was responsible. So I would like to interview Rumex, please.'

'Thank you,' said Saturninus, 'for contacting me about it first.'

'A natural courtesy.'

'I appreciate your formality.' His slaves had previously left us. He went to the door and spoke to somebody outside. This place was unexpectedly polite. Something had to be wrong. 'Rumex is coming.'

That was annoying. I had to interview him with Saturninus present. Still, I decided not to insist on privacy. There was no doubt I was about to be spun a yarn here. Might as well go along with what they wanted until I worked out their angle and could apply pressure where it would hurt. I was certainly not intending to grab a prize gladiator by the tunic seams and hurl him against a wall with the idea of beating the truth out of him. This would call for greater subtlety.

I busied myself looking at the trophies and armour. Saturninus stood beside me recounting what they all were. When he described an old fight he was good on theory. He could tell an interesting tale too. The waiting time passed harmlessly.

There was a small knock on the door, then a slave opened it for Rumex. I knew as soon as I saw him that I might as well not have bothered.

He had probably been stupid before fighting made him worse. He was tall, lithe on his feet, beautifully honed in the body, hideously ugly in the features, and as dense as a wharfside pile. He could probably string two words together – if they were 'where's mine?', 'get lost', or 'kill him'. That was his limit. He walked into his master's room as if he were afraid of knocking over furniture, yet the dance in his feet that must make him the envy of his opponents was obvious even here. He was definitely powerful and looked as if he could be fearless too.

There was a rather silly fringe on his tunic skirt, and he wore a gold necklace that must have cost a fortune though its design was of astounding trashiness. Jewellers in the Saepta Julia make them up especially for men of his type. The chunks of linked gold had his name on a square tag. That must have helped when he forgot who he was.

'Greetings, Rumex. I'm honoured to meet you. My name's Falco; I have a few questions to ask.'

'That's all right.' He looked at me so honestly I knew at once that Rumex had been tutored for this. Besides, he agreed to help me far too willingly. Most people who are innocent are puzzled why you should approach them. No need for that here. Rumex knew. He knew the answers too: both the ones I was looking for and the lies he had been told to say instead.

'I am investigating the suspicious death of the man-eating lion, Leonidas. Do you know anything about it, please?'

'No, sir.'

'He was taken from his quarters at night, speared, and mysteriously returned.'

'No, sir,' repeated Rumex, though my last remark had been a statement not a question. If he had been this slow at following on in the arena he would have been a one-fight phenomenon.

'I have been told that Leonidas was killed by you. Is that correct?'

'No, sir.'

'Had you ever actually seen him?'

'No, sir.'

'Can you remember where you were and what you were doing the night before last?'

Rumex wanted to give me his usual answer but realised that would sound damning. His eyes tried to look at his trainer for advice, but he managed to keep his gaze fixed 'honestly' on me.

'I can answer that, Falco,' Saturninus intervened. Rumex looked grateful. 'Rumex was with me all night.' I thought that did startle Rumex; perhaps then it was true. 'I took him to a small dinner party at the house of an ex-praetor.' If I was supposed to be impressed by rank, it failed.

'Showing him off?' I asked, implying that Saturninus was too delicate to say so.

He smiled, acknowledging us both as men of the world. 'People are always eager to meet Rumex.'

I turned to Rumex, who had been thinking he was safe from further questioning. 'And did you give the ex-praetor a private demonstration of your fabulous prowess?'

I had been making conversation but this time he looked horrified.

His trainer inserted smoothly, 'A few standing press-ups and feints with a practice sword always go down well.'

I glanced at each in turn. I had hit a nerve, clearly. I absorbed the implications. Could Leonidas have been murdered in a senior magistrate's house? Was Saturninus present at the time? 'I'm sorry, Saturninus; I'll have to insist on a name for your host that night.'

'Of course, Falco. I'd like to send word to the man before I mention him to a stranger. Just a courtesy.' Neat.

'I can insist that you don't alert him.'

'With a man of his rank, surely there can be no objection?' Saturninus was already making one of his little trips to the door to give murmured orders to a runner.

I let him win. I was not confident that I could withstand a formal complaint of harassment from a praetor. Vespasian would take it amiss even if I had evidence against the man – and I had none. Well, not at this stage. His rank didn't daunt me, but I would have to be certain first.

It was an interesting development. One minute I was checking dodgy ledgers amongst society's dregs, the next I wanted to view the social diary of somebody one step down from consul – and what's more, he was being rather obviously warned about my interest.

'Who else was present at your dinner with the mystery man?' I asked, keeping it casual.

The lanista matched my tone: 'Oh it was quite informal.'

'Friends?'

I felt he was trying not to tell me, though he was skilled enough to give way when there was no alternative. 'Me and my wife – with just the praetor and a ladyfriend.'

Dinners at big men's houses tended to be nearer the classic number of nine sitting down. This foursome was oddly cosy, if true.

'You're moving in enviable circles. I'm dying to ask you how it came about.'

'A business connection.' Saturninus knew how to make anything sound natural.

I pretended to be more amateur than I was: 'I thought senators were rather limited in their freedom to engage in commerce?' They were forbidden to do it, in fact. However they could engage their freedmen as go-betweens, and many did.

'Oh it's nothing commercial,' Saturninus was quick to respond. 'We met when he was organising the Games.' That was a formal responsibility of the praetors in their year as magistrates. To end up friendly with one particular lanista could look like an abuse of patronage – but some members of government do assume that abusing their position is the whole purpose of holding high office. Proving that money had changed hands illegally would be next to impossible – and even if I discovered it had happened, most praetors would genuinely fail to understand my complaint.

'Wonderful to think you have maintained such good relationships after his term of office,' I said. Saturninus gave me a bland smile. 'So – your messenger must have had time to purvey the politenesses by now. Can I have the ex-praetor's name?'

'Pomponius Urtica,' said Saturninus, as if he really loved assisting me. I made a point of taking out a note tablet and writing it down. Unphased, Saturninus volunteered spellings. Equally calmly I pressed him to give the ex-praetor's home address.

It was understood I had reached the limits of this interview. Without consulting me, the lanista dismissed Rumex. The big gladiator slipped from the room.

'Thank you for your help,' I said to Saturninus. This was all a nice game.

'I have enjoyed our talk,' he replied, as if it had been just a tight set of draughts. Then he startled me by adding, 'You seem an interesting character. My wife is very keen on entertaining. Perhaps you would accept an invitation to dine with us tomorrow night? With your guest of choice,' he suggested, in a very civilised manner leaving me free to bring a wife, a prostitute, or a bug-eyed little boy masseur from the baths.

It was folly for a state auditor to fraternise with the subjects of his current investigation. Naturally I said yes.

XXII

Pomponius Urtica lived on the Pincian. His mansion lay up on the high ground to the east of the Via Flaminia, way out past the Mausoleum of Augustus. Nice district. Patrician open spaces, with panoramic views that were interrupted only by tall, elderly pine trees where doves cooed. Beautiful sunsets over the Tiber. Miles from the racket of the Forum. Clean air, peaceful atmosphere, stunning property, gracious neighbours: wonderful for the smart élite who inhabited that fine district – and miserably inconvenient for the rest of us if we came visiting.

Urtica himself had it easy. When he needed to travel down to conduct public business he would be carried in a big litter borne by well-matched, well-tempered slaves with unfaltering steps. He never had to get his boots dirty in the dust and donkey droppings, and he could while away the hour the journey took each way with a little light reading as he reclined on downy cushions. He may have been equipped with a hip-flask and a packet of sweet toast. For added entertainment no doubt he sometimes squashed in some flirty flutegirl with a big bust.

I walked. I had nothing and no one to sustain me. Winter had turned the dust in the roads to mud, and the donkey droppings had mingled with the mud, leaving loose lumps among the slurry like half-stirred polenta in a caupona that the aediles were about to close down.

I found the lush praetorian abode. It took some time since all the ostentatious Pincian spreads were pretty much identical and all were sited up extremely long approach roads too. At Urtica's I was told by the door porter that his master was away from home. This was no surprise. The slave did not say, though I readily deduced, that even had his master been there (which was perfectly possible) I would not have been allowed in. My fine informer's intuition told me that an order had been given to reject any tired lag who called himself Didius Falco. I did not cause offence at that elegant mansion by proffering my Palace pass. It had been a long hard day already. I spared myself the embarrassment.

I walked all the way back into town. I bought myself a hot pancake and a cup of flavoured wine, but on that nippy winter's afternoon companionship was hard to find. All the flirty flutegirls seemed to be visiting their aunties in Ostia.

XXIII

Well, back to reality. I went to the baths, got warm again, was insulted by my trainer, met a friend, took him home for a bite.

You know how it is when you have moved into a new apartment and invite an important guest home with you. If you don't own a slave to send on ahead, you arrive, playing suave, and just hoping not to be greeted by an embarrassing scene. That evening I brought home a senator – an infrequent occurrence, I have to say. Naturally we found something extremely embarrassing as soon as we walked in: my wife, as I now forced myself to call her, was painting a door.

'Hello!' exclaimed the senator. 'What's going on, Falco?'

'Helena Justina, daughter of the illustrious Camillus, is painting a door,' I replied courteously.

He gave me a sideways glance. 'Is that because you cannot afford a painter,' he mused anxiously. 'Or because she likes doing it?' The second suggestion seemed worse than the first.

'She likes it,' I admitted. Helena went on painting as if neither of us were there.

'Why do you allow this, Falco?'

'Senator, I have not yet discovered how to stop Helena doing what she likes. Also,' I said proudly, 'she does it much better than any hired painter would.'

This was why she had not spoken to us. Helena paints her doors with great concentration. She was sitting cross-legged on the floor, with a pannikin of evil dark red liquid beside her, slowly laying off the paint with relaxed, regular strokes, leaving a perfect even finish. It was one of my life's great pleasures to watch this. I explained that to the senator and when I pulled up a stool he did the same.

'Notice,' I murmured, 'that she starts at the bottom. Most painters start at the top; half an hour after they walk away, spare paint oozes down and forms a line of sticky drips all along the lower edge. They set hard before you notice. Then you never get rid of them. However, Helena Justina leaves no drips.'

In fact, it was not the way I would have done it, but Helena made her method effective, and the senator looked impressed. 'Yet what do your people think, Falco?'

'Oh they are horrified, of course. She was a respectable girl from a very good background. My mother is particularly shocked. She thinks Helena has suffered enough through living with me.' Helena, who had just risen to her knees as she worked upwards, paused in the action of reloading her paintbrush to look around at me thoughtfully. 'She is allowed to tell people that I make her do it.'

'And what do you say, Falco?'

'I blame the people who brought her up.'

Helena at last spoke: 'Hello, Father,' she said.

The lead in the paint was affecting her, so she sniffed. I winked at her, knowing that when she was painting she normally wiped her nose on her sleeve.

The senator Camillus Verus, her father, my dinner guest, offered politely, 'I could pay for a painter, Marcus, if you're pushed.'

I deferred to my wife. I was a good Roman. Well, I knew what was good for me.

'Don't waste your money, dear Papa.' Helena had reached the level of the door handle which I had previously removed for her, at which point she stood up so she could reach the upper half of the door. Camillus and I moved our stools back slightly, giving her more room. 'Thanks,' she commented.

'She does make a good job of it,' her father remarked to

me. He seemed uneasy speaking directly to his single-minded child.

'I taught her,' I said. He gave me a look.

'I made him, of course,' Helena added. He turned the look on her. Where I had deemed it good-mannered to appear rather diffident, Helena carried on, ignoring him. 'What is there to eat for our guest, Marcus?'

Her father accused me roundly, 'Now I suppose you will make her prepare our dinner too?'

'No,' I told him very gently. 'I am the cook here.'

Having reached the door's top rail, Helena stepped back and consented to kiss her father, albeit rather distantly for she was busy inspecting her work for snibs of dust. The light was too poor for her. December was the wrong time for such work, but household maintenance has to be done when the mood strikes. She drew her brush over some minute bubbles near the top, frowning. I smiled. After a moment her father smiled too. She turned around to look at us, both still sitting on our stools and both still smiling because we loved to see her happy in her life. Suspicious of our motives, Helena suddenly gave us her full attention, defiantly smiling back at us.

'She hates cleaning the paintbrush,' I said to her noble papa. 'So do I.' Nonetheless I took it from her, kissing her hand (avoiding the paint splodges). 'Cleaning up is one of the small tasks I undertake for her.' I gazed into her eyes. 'In return for the many generosities she gives to me.'

It would have been unseemly to add that on occasions when her father was not present I liked to enjoy myself rather wickedly cleaning up the painter too. Helena's one fault was that she tended to get paint on herself *everywhere*.

Luckily the senator was easily sidetracked; we sent him into another room to play with his granddaughter, leaving us to snatch some fun.

Later, when I had fed everyone, our illustrious visitor confided the reason why he had so keenly accepted my invitation to our tiny apartment when he could have been dining on richer cuisine and in comfort at his own home. It was some time since we had walked over the Aventine to the slightly run-down Camillus mansion near the Capena Gate to visit Helena's family. We had never been formally debarred, but since Justinus absconded with the girl that we two had introduced as a suitable (that is, rich) bride for his elder brother, there had been a cool atmosphere. Nobody blamed Helena for the family troubles. On the other hand, I made a good target. The jilted Aelianus had been particularly ribald.

'What's this?' demanded the senator; he had found a parchment on which I had drawn a large onion-like plant.

'A botanical sketch of a silphium plant,' I said neutrally.

Helena, who had been feeding the baby, handed Julia to me. This meant I could occupy my attention with patting up the baby's wind. Helena herself was keeping her eyes down, refixing her dress brooches.

'So you've heard from my son too!' Camillus looked from one to another of us. He could read the omens from a skyful of rooks.

While we admitted it shiftily, pretending we had of course been planning to mention it, the senator laid aside my botany and brought out a map. I realised that meeting him at Glaucus' baths had been no coincidence; he had come prepared. He must have been intending to discuss the missing couple with us. Although I believed that his relationship with his wife Julia Justa was as open and confiding as it traditionally ought to be, a disloyal thought did cross my mind that her husband might not yet have told her that Justinus had written home. Julia Justa had taken the elopement pretty hard. For one thing, the missing girl's elderly grandparents had arrived in Rome all the way from Spain only two days afterwards, intending to celebrate Claudia's betrothal and marriage; Julia Justa had had to endure a tricky period with the furious old couple as house guests before they left in a huff.

'He's got as far as Carthage.' The senator spread the

mapskin from his home library. 'Clearly has no idea of geography.'

'I expect they fled on the first boat going south.' Acting the peace-keeper was not my natural style. 'Carthage is a short hop from Sicily.'

'Well, now he knows,' said Camillus, placing one forefinger on Carthage and the other virtually at arm's length away on Cyrene, 'that he's in the wrong province, with a ships' graveyard between him and his purported goal.'

Yes. There was Carthage, Rome's ancient enemy, west of Sicily, high on the tip of the proconsular sector of the province of Roman Africa. Right around the double curves of the dangerous Syrtes, eastwards past the Tripolitanian sector of Africa, into Cyrenaïca, and almost as far as Egypt in fact, lay the town of Cyrene which had once been the resplendent entrepôt for the sought-after silphium. The troubled waters of the great bays Syrtis Minor and Syrtis Major, across which our traveller would now have to transport himself on his mad quest, had sunk quite a few ships.

'Could he travel by land?' asked Helena, in an unusually meek voice.

'It's about a thousand miles,' I mentioned. She knew what that meant.

'Much of it desert. Check with Sallust,' her father said crisply. 'Sallust is *very* good on the burning wind that rises in the desert and swirls sandstorms that fill your eyes and mouth with dust.'

'We need a nice plan to keep him in Carthage then,' suggested Helena.

'I want him home!' snapped her papa. 'Did he tell you what they are doing for money?'

Helena cleared her throat. 'I believe they may have sold some of Claudia's jewellery.' Claudia Rufina was an heiress of the best quality; she had possessed a great many jewels. That was why we had thought she was such a catch for the elder son of the family. Aelianus had hoped to boost his standing in the Senate elections with this financially adept marriage; instead, shamed by the scandal, he had now stood down altogether and was loafing at home with no career for another year. Meanwhile Claudia's dowry was being spent by his brother on Carthaginian hospitality.

'Well, they won't have to sell themselves into slavery as camel-drovers then.'

'Afraid they might have to, sir,' I admitted. 'Justinus tells us they accidentally left the main jewellery chest behind.'

'In the excitement, no doubt!' Camillus senior gave me a sharp look. 'So, Marcus; you're the horticulture expert—' I refrained from protesting that my only connection was one grandfather who ran a market garden where I had sometimes stayed in childhood. 'I've been told the crazy story about looking for silphium. What chance is there that Justinus will actually rediscover this magic herb?'

'Slim, sir.'

'Thought so. I gather it was all grazed out years ago. I shouldn't imagine the shepherds who have let the silphium be eaten will welcome an offer to reclaim their grazing fields and turn them back into a big herb garden ... I don't suppose you fancy a trip across the Internal Sea?'

I looked sorrowful. 'I'm rather too busy tied up with my Census work, I'm afraid. As you know, it's very important that I do well and establish myself.'

He held my gaze rather longer than I found comfortable but then his expression changed to a more indulgent one. He rolled up the mapskin briskly. 'Well! I expect it will be sorted out.'

'Leave the map,' Helena offered. 'I'll make a copy and send it to Quintus when we write. At least he'll know where he is then.'

'He knows where he is,' her father quipped bitterly. 'In deep trouble. I can't help him; it would be insulting to his brother. Perhaps I should send my gardener to look after him. When Claudia's emeralds run out he's going to have to be damned quick with his search for the precious herb cuttings.'

To change the subject, I introduced the story of Leonidas. Helena wanted to know whether I had succeeded in meeting Rumex after she and Maia were turned away.

'Turned away?' asked her father.

I rushed into how I had met Saturninus and his prize fighter, hoping to avoid worrying the senator with his daughter's scandalous attempt to meet a gladiator. 'Rumex is a typical hulk: immaculate body and brain like an ox, but he speaks slowly and carefully, as if he thinks himself a philosopher. The trainer, Saturninus, is a more interesting character—' I decided not to mention that Helena and I were to dine with the lanista the next day. 'Incidentally, sir, Saturninus has given an alibi for Rumex by saying that when Leonidas was killed they were together at the house of an ex-praetor called Pomponius Urtica. Have you come across the man?'

Camillus smiled. 'His name is in the news these days.'

'Anything I should know?'

'He is being touted as the man to organise the opening of the new amphitheatre.'

I sucked my teeth. 'Convenient!'

'Improper for him to favour a particular lanista, though.'

'When did impropriety stop a praetor jumping in? Do you know what kind of man he is?'

'Keen on the Games,' said Camillus, adding in his dry way, 'within respectable limits, naturally! In his year of office there were no complaints about his magistracy, nor about how he ran the shows he organised. His private life is only slightly soiled,' he said, as if we assumed that most senators were famous for rampant debauchery. 'He's been married a couple of times, I believe; some time ago perhaps, because his children are grown up. At present he leads a single life.'

'Meaning? Women? Boys?'

'Well, one of the other reasons his name features

publicly is that he hooked himself up recently with a girl who has a rather wild reputation.'

'You're a demon for gossip, Papa!' marvelled Helena.

Her father looked endearingly pleased with himself. 'I can even tell you she's called Scilla.'

I grinned. 'And what form is Scilla's wildness supposed to take?'

This time Camillus Verus reddened a little. 'Whatever form is usual, no doubt. I'm afraid I lead too quiet a life to know.'

He was a lovely man.

After her father had gone Helena Justina unrolled his map again.

'Look!' she said, pointing part way between Carthage and Cyrene, to a spot on the Tripolitanian coastline. 'Here's Oea and here's Lepcis Magna.' She gazed at me disingenuously. 'Aren't they the two towns where Saturninus and Calliopus have their roots?'

'How lucky for me,' I commented, 'that neither of them lives there any longer, so I can pursue my enquiries in comfort, here in Rome!'

XXIV

Two problems had to be dealt with the next morning: finding a clean tunic without too many moth-holes for my dinner engagement, and responding to the whines of my dear business partner Anacrites about where I had vanished to the previous day. They were about equal in difficulty.

I wanted to wear my old favourite green tunic, until I held it up by the shoulders and had an honest look. It was neither so thick in the nap as I thought, nor so smart. There was a long run from the corner of the neckline, where the threads always give out if you lead an active life. And it was sized for a younger, leaner man. No alternative: the new thing that Helena had been trying to introduce to my wardrobe would have to be tried on. It was russet. I hate that colour. The tunic was warm, well designed, a good fit, the right length, and ornamented with two long stripes of braid. Dear gods, I hated it.

'Very nice,' I lied.

'That's you sorted then,' she said.

I managed to drop it on the floor where Nux could use it all day as a dog basket. That should give it some character.

Nux took one sniff, then turned away in disgust. She wouldn't stay in the house with it. She came out with me.

Anacrites took longer to pacify. We were in Calliopus' upstairs office at the barracks. 'Falco, where did you get to—?'

'Be quiet, and I'll tell you.'

'Is that your dog?'

'Yes.' Nux, who could tell who ranked with squirrels

and cats, growled as if she was about to fly at Anacrites with her teeth bared. 'Just being friendly,' I assured him unfeelingly.

I did him the honour of telling him everything of my adventure yesterday. Famia's theory. The escaped leopard. Thalia's theory. Saturninus. And Rumex.

I held back on Urtica, and his nymph Scilla. Anacrites was a Palace spy. Unless I kept him on a tight rein, he was liable to rush off screaming treachery to a bank of scribes with poison in their inkwells. No point in libelling an ex-praetor in triplicate until I was certain he deserved it. And no point in confusing my partner with too much of the truth.

'None of this gets you anywhere,' Anacrites decided. 'So a gladiator can't remember where he was one night – what's new? Some of the lanistae dislike each other – well, we could have guessed that. There's no harm in honest rivalry; competition encourages quality.'

'Next you'll be saying that Leonidas is just a tragic victim of circumstance who was in the wrong cage at the wrong time, and that in business you have to allow for sustainable loss.'

'Very true,' he remarked.

'Anacrites, a man who has had his head bashed in once, should learn not to make people angry—' I gave up. 'Did you get any further with the figures on Calliopus? Where is the bastard, anyway? He usually sites himself three inches behind us to overhear what we may say.'

Calliopus had so far failed to put in an appearance that day. Anacrites, who had arrived there before me and asked about it, said piously, 'There is a rumour he is stuck at home, having a bust-up with his wife.'

'So we were right to suspect a mistress!'

'Saccarina,' replied Anacrites. 'I wormed it out of that keeper called Buxus. Her boudoir appears to be by an inn called the Octopus, in Borealis Street. Should be easy to discover whose name is on the tenancy agreement. Then we've got him. But we were right to suspect he was hiding more than the mistress, Falco.' He produced a schedule from a satchel he carried about with him. It was the list of discrepancies between what Calliopus had declared to the Censors, and extra properties we had identified. 'He's in shit,' Anacrites gloated, ever the fair-minded investigator. 'The only thing we ought to find out before we shop him, is whether the so-called brother in Tripolitania really exists. If not, and if the family outlet for beasts at Oea really belongs to Calliopus himself, I reckon there will be a five digit sum in this for us.'

I ran my eyes down the figures. It looked good even without the Oean element – but if that could be included, this was a first-class bust. We could be very proud of ourselves.

'I have an idea how we can run a check,' I said thoughtfully. 'A contact of mine is in Carthage at present. I'm due to write to him. It would be worth the investment for us to guarantee his fare, so he could look into the Oean landholding for us.'

'Who is it? Is he trustworthy?' Anacrites seemed to know the kind of contacts I generally used.

'He's a gem,' I reassured my partner. 'And more importantly, his word will carry weight with Vespasian.'

'Let's do it then.'

One thing to be said for Anacrites was that since his head wound had made him erratic he could take a decision to spend large sums of our so far unearned money without turning a hair. Of course tomorrow the same erratic behaviour would make him change his mind – but by then I would have sent off a banker's order to Justinus and it would be too late.

'Alternatively,' Anacrites suggested (always alert to a chance of thwarting some private plan of mine), 'I could go out to Oea myself.'

'Good idea.' I liked to disappoint him when he was playing me up. 'Of course it's December so it won't be easy getting there. You'll have to take short hop sailings –

Ostia–Puteoli, Puteoli–Buxentum–Rhegium, Rhegium–
–Sicily just to start. You should get a lift out from Syracusa
to the island of Melita quite readily, but it could become
tricky after that—'

'All right, Falco.'

'No, no; it's good of you to volunteer.'

We left it in the air, though I was planning to write to
Justinus anyway.

We talked about what to do next. The documents on
Calliopus could now be set aside until we finalised the
issues of the mistress's house and the overseas property.
We needed to move on to another victim, either
Saturninus or one of the other lanistae. I was sorry that this
meant we ought to leave Calliopus' training barracks with
the Leonidas question unanswered. But we had no choice.
The Census was supposed to be over within twelve
months of its inception. In theory we could drag out the
disputes for years if we chose to, but Vespasian was in a
hurry for the state revenue – and we were hungry for our
fees.

I mentioned that I would be dining with Saturninus. I
said I would try to gauge whether he looked a likely
prospect for auditing. Anacrites seemed quite happy for me
to fraternise. If it was useful he could share in the credit; if
it went wrong he could denounce me to Vespasian for
corrupt practices. Nice to have a partner I could trust.

'It's acceptable,' I joked, 'so long as I don't enjoy
myself.'

'Watch out for poison in the food,' he warned in a
friendly voice, as if he were thinking of supplying some
best quality aconite to my host. It was the poison in our
partnership that was bothering me.

I was feeling low. I seemed to have caught a chill during
my exploits at the Agrippan Baths yesterday.

Restless, I mooched out on to the balcony that ran
around this part of the barracks. Nux gave a last growl at
Anacrites and came to sit on my feet. While I stood there
attempting to clear my raw throat, I noticed Buxus come

out from the building opposite where the animals were kept, carrying one of the ostriches. I had seen him do it before. It was the easiest way to transport them: tucking them under one arm, gripping their wings with his elbow, while dodging their long necks and prying beaks.

This one was different. The big bird had lost all its curiosity. Its legs dangled limply, its wings hung quite still, and its bare neck was down so its tiny head dangled almost in the dust. I knew at once that it was dead.

I called down: 'What's up with him, Buxus?'

The keeper, always tender-hearted, appeared to be snivelling. 'Something disagreed with him.'

Nux noticed the corpse and leapt down the stairs to investigate. I called her back; she stopped and turned to look at me, puzzled that I was spoiling her fun. I went after her, down to the yard.

Some of the bestiarii had been exercising with weights; they came up to see what was going on. We all gazed at the dead bird. I recognised it as the largest male, the one that had been nearly eight feet high, once resplendent in black and white feathers but now reduced to a selection of fan dancer's costumery. 'Poor thing,' I said. 'The birds are a damned nuisance if they can get at you and bite your tunic to shreds, but it's sad to see one dead. Are you sure he hasn't been off colour? Maybe the Roman winter disagrees with ostriches.'

'He was fine an hour ago,' moaned Buxus. He laid his burden on the hard ground of the exercise yard, then squatted on his haunches with his head in his hands. I gripped Nux by the collar as she struggled to get at the bird and worry it. 'Who's going to be next?' moaned the keeper, in great distress. 'This is all getting too much—'

The bestiarii glanced at each other. Some shuffled away, not wanting to be involved. Some patted Buxus on the shoulder firmly, as if to shut him up. Gripping Nux under my arm, I went down on one knee to examine the ostrich. It had definitely stopped breathing, but I'm no ornithologist. It was just a lump of limp poultry to me.

'What happened exactly?' I asked quietly.

Buxus had taken the hint from the others. Now his reply was neutral, just like when he was putting off my interest in Leonidas. 'He stood still, then sort of folded up. He lay down in a heap and put his head on the ground, as if he had gone off to sleep.'

Someone had come up behind me; I glanced round and saw Calliopus. He must have just arrived for the day. Still in his outdoor cloak, he pushed past me, lifted the bird's head, dropped it, and swore. Buxus kept his own head down, looking cowed.

'That bastard!' Calliopus must be referring to Saturninus. Furious, apparently he did not care what I overheard. He strode inside the menagerie. Buxus then leapt up and followed him. The bestiarii hung back, but I was hard on the keeper's heels.

'It's the grain, I think,' I heard Buxus mutter in an undertone. 'The new load. That's where I found him foraging. Before I could shoo the silly brat away, it was too late. The sack split when they delivered it—'

Calliopus brushed him off, rampaging past the cages and on into the second area. Borago the bear growled at the commotion, so did the new lion Draco who was now in the cage where his predecessor died. He prowled about, but seemed quieter, no doubt calmed by a few choice cuts of Leonidas.

The second room with the sea lion's pit was empty now that Draco had been moved out. Even the eagle was gone from his perch. Beyond it again lay a short corridor which led to a store. There stood a modest grain bin − with a wooden cover on it − and on the ground in front of that lay a hempen sack. It had burst open at one seam, spilling corn on to the ground. Calliopus took a cursory look round, then seized a scoop. He caught up a good panful of the grain from the broken sack, then shoved out past us again. Buxus and I trotted after him like children playing hide and seek. In the yard, Calliopus spread the grain in a patch on the ground. He whistled. 'Watch the pigeons!' he commanded. Without a word more to Buxus he marched off to his office. I might as well have been invisible.

Buxus looked up to the roof, where one or two scrawny pigeons were always making a nuisance of themselves. He went and squatted in the shade of the building, waiting to see if any of the flying vermin would come down and commit suicide. Still carrying Nux to keep her out of harm's way, I walked up to him.

'When was that sack delivered?' I assumed it was recently. This place was well-run. The spilt grain would normally have been cleared up fairly soon after the accident happened.

'This morning,' Buxus consented to tell me in a mournful voice.

I had seen a cart unloading when I walked in. 'Half an hour ago?' He nodded. 'So there wasn't much chance it was tampered with here? And where is it supplied from?'

He looked furtive. 'I don't know about that. You'll have to ask the boss.'

'But you have a regular arrangement?' Buxus still looked guarded, but he said yes. 'And how often do they make a delivery?'

'Once a week.'

Crouching on his haunches, he put his head down on his arms. It was either a good imitation of a very depressed man, or a strong hint for me to move along.

I went back inside the menagerie and took another look at the grain sack. Where it was slit two long ends of the seam binding were dangling; their ends looked neatly cut rather than frayed. Tampered with, apparently. I heaved up one end of the sack and peered at the underside. It was labelled with abbreviations that said it had come from Africa Proconsularis, the grainbasket of the Empire nowadays. I nearly left it at that, but luckily I turned up the other end too. That carried in red lettering '*Horrea Galbana*', which would have been where it had been stored in Rome, plus the peculiar label '*ARX: ANS*'. Nux was straining to get at the spilled grain, so I gripped her more firmly and let her lick my neck while I tried to decipher the abbreviated note. It looked like an address. Not the address of the barracks here.

I returned to the office, churning over the possibilities.

'Calliopus, am I right that you suspect your grain has been poisoned by Saturninus as part of your feud?'

'I have nothing to say,' said Calliopus coldly.

'You ought to have,' commented Anacrites. I could at least rely on him to back me up if it meant annoying someone else.

'Who supplies your corn?' I croaked, as my sore throat gave out on me.

'Oh . . . one of the big granaries. I'll have to look up the requisition—'

'Don't bother,' I rasped. 'I think you'll find it's the Granary of the Galbae.'

Judging by his frown, I had managed to annoy Calliopus myself. If 'ARX: ANS' meant what I suspected, I knew exactly why.

I tipped the wink to Anacrites. Rather to my surprise he said nothing, but simply rose from his stool, collected our equipment, and told Calliopus we were finished here; he would hear either from us or from the Censors' Office in due course. As we hopped down the outer stairs with Nux happily scampering ahead of us, two pigeons made a feeble attempt to flutter up from the grainy bait laid in the yard, but collapsed into tattered grey clumps with their beaks in the dirt. I called the dog to heel. A few flies were already inspecting the dead ostrich as we walked out through the gate.

XXV

Once we reached the road, Anacrites expected me to tell him what was on my mind and began annoying me with his usual questions. I said he could do something useful by finding out about the house Calliopus had bought for his mistress. I would meet him later at our office in the Saepta. First, it would do no harm for me to visit the Granary of the Galbae. I only had to cross the Tiber and I was there.

He looked suspicious, thinking that was the last he would see of me. It had not escaped him that the Granary of the Galbae lay at the back of the Emporium and the Porticus Aemilia, just below the Lavernal Gate. From there it was just a short, steep hike up to the crest of the Aventine — and a long lunch at home with Helena. I reassured him that since I was going out to dinner I would not be needing lunch. Feeling evil, I made it sound as unconvincing as I could.

The *Horrea Galbana* was a whole palace of commerce. By the time I had struggled from the river wharf through the battling crush of stevedores and porters who were unloading barges and boats for the Emporium I was in no mood to be lightly impressed. It grated to enter this monstrous establishment, built by a rich family as the short cut to even greater wealth. The rental potential had always been enormous, even though the Sulpicii Galbae were probably unwilling to come down here themselves and haggle over grain prices. They had been persons of great status since Republican times; one of them became Emperor. He only stuck it for six months, but that must have been long enough to bring the Granary under state control.

I had to admit this was an astonishing place. It contained several great courtyards, each with hundreds of rooms on more than one floor, run by military-style cohorts of staff. At least that gave me half a chance of finding out what I was after. There was bound to be documentation for everything, if I could find the relevant scribe before he bunked off for the local caupona. Anacrites was right; it was mid-morning: dangerously near the time when skivers had their lunch.

Not only grain was stored and sold here. Space was rented out for everything from wine cellars to strong-rooms. Some of the single booths were leased to working tradesmen: woven goods, expensive architectural stoneware, even fish. But mostly the buildings were specially constructed cornstores. They had raised tiled floors, set on dwarf walls with ventilated thresholds to allow good air circulation through the tunnels underneath. They were plaster-lined, with only a louvred vent at the back for light. The great quadrangles were lined with rows of these dim, cool rooms, sealed with tight doors against dampness, vermin and theft, the triple enemies of stored grain. Most of the staircases turned into ramps after a few steps, to facilitate life for the porters as they struggled around with the heavy sacks on their backs; many of them were permanently bent in the spine and bow-legged. Cats were allowed to run everywhere as a countermeasure to rats and mice. Fire buckets stood at frequent intervals. Maybe it was my cold, but to me that day the air seemed thick with annoying dust.

I found the administrative office easily. An hour later I had wormed my way up the queue to see a slinky-hipped clerk with long eyelashes. He might eventually spare time from telling coarse jokes to his neighbour, the rent-clerk, and might discuss the dockets I needed to know about. Once I reached him, he buffed his nails on the shoulder of his tunic and prepared to fob me off.

We had a long wrangle about whether he was empowered to let me see despatching details, followed by a fierce set-to over his claim that there was no customer called Calliopus.

I borrowed a tablet from the rent-clerk, who had been observing my problems with a supercilious smirk. On it I wrote clearly: '*ARX: ANS*'.

'Mean anything?'

'Oh that!' mouthed the beauteous king of the dockets. 'Well, that's not a private customer.'

'So who is this public one?'

'Confidential.' I had thought it would be. 'SPQR.'

I stood on his foot, letting my boot studs press between his sandal straps, grabbed handfuls of his pristine tunic, and pushed his chest until he was squealing and leaning backwards.

'Spare me the secret passwords,' I growled. 'You may be the prettiest scribe at the snootiest old granary on the Embankment, but any tough nut with an ounce of good sweetbreads in his cranium can decipher that logo once he associates the words "grain" and "once a week". Adding "S" and "P" and "Q" and "R" just shows you know some of the alphabet. Now listen to me, petal. The corn you supplied this week is poisoning birds. Think about that very carefully. Then consider how you will explain to the Senate and People of Rome why you refused to help me find who tampered with the corn.'

I stepped back suddenly, loosening my grip on his tunic.

'It goes to the Arx,' confessed the scribe in a terrified whisper.

'And the rest stands for "*Anseres Sacri*",' I told him, though he knew it well enough.

He was right to be anxious. The sack of corn that had poisoned the ostrich had been intended for the famous Sacred Geese.

XXVI

'Down, nuxie!'

For a moment there seemed a good chance my scruff would end up in custody for goose-worrying. A priest of the Temple of Juno Moneta peered out from the sanctum suspiciously. Casual visitors were discouraged up here; the Citadel was no place to walk your dog.

Juno Moneta had in ancient times assumed responsibility for the Mint and for the patronage of Roman commerce – an early instance of the female sex taking over the housekeeping purse. Jupiter might be the Best and Greatest, but his celestial wife had grabbed the cash. I sympathised. Still, as Helena said so sensibly, it was useful for one person to control the home budget.

'Oh *please*, don't set them off!' The custodian of Juno's sacred guard-birds seemed cheerful and relaxed. If Nux retrieved one of his charges for my cooking pot it would simply pose awkward problems of bureaucracy. 'I have to call out the Praetorians if they decide to have a honk – not to mention filing an incident report as long as your arm. You're no marauding Gaul, I hope?'

'Certainly not. Even my dog has Roman citizenship.'

'What a relief.'

Ever since a monstrous army of Celts once raided Italy and actually sacked Rome, a permanent gaggle of geese had been given privileged status on the Arx, in honour of their feathered forebears who had raised the alarm and saved the Capitol. I had imagined that the big white birds led a pampered life. This lot looked a bit wormy, to tell the truth.

The geese were taking an aggressive interest in Nux.

She barked once, then shrank back against my legs. I wasn't too confident I could save the little coward. As I bent to pat her reassuringly, I noticed I had stepped in some of the slimy green droppings that lay in wait all over the hillside at the top of the steps past the Mamertine.

Across the dip on the Capitol, the twin peak to the Arx, the restored Temple of Jupiter had begun to rise slowly. Destroyed by a catastrophic fire at the end of the civil war that brought Vespasian to power, the Temple was now being rebuilt in due magnificence as a sign of the Flavian Emperors' triumph over their rivals. Or as they would no doubt put it, as a gesture of piety and the renewal of Rome. Fine white dust drifted towards us on the misty rain, through which there was no diminution in the sound of stonemasons chipping at marble; they were, of course, secure in the knowledge that the Census property tax would be paying for their materials and labour at top rates. Once they had built the new Temple of Capitoline Jove, they would be moving on profitably to the Flavian Amphitheatre, the new stage for the Theatre of Marcellus, restoring the Temple of the Divine Claudius, then creating the Forum of Vespasian, complete with two libraries and a Temple of Peace.

An area near Juno's outdoor altar had been turned into a tiny garden for the Sacred Geese. They had a fine view over the roof of the Mamertine prison to the Forum, though their enclosure was rather rocky and inhospitable.

The custodian was a slight, elderly public slave with a whispy beard and bandy legs, clearly not chosen for his love of winged creatures. Every time a goose wandered too close to him he jeered, 'Foxes!'

'It's a terrible place for them,' he confirmed, noticing my polite concern. He sheltered in a hut under a stunted pine tree. For a man with easy access to goose egg omelettes, not to mention the occasional roast drumstick no doubt, he was oddly underweight. He matched his thin charges, though. 'They ought to have a pond or a stream, with growing herbage to tear up. If I take my eyes off them, they wander off in search of better pasture. I go down and round them up with my stave—' He shook it in a listless manner. It was a splintered stick I wouldn't throw for the dog. 'Sometimes they come home with a few feathers plucked, but normally nobody bothers them.'

'Out of respect for their sanctity?'

'No. They can peck very nastily.'

I noticed that although there was loose corn sprinkled on a bare patch of ground, the geese were foraging in a heap of faded grass clippings. Interesting. I cleaned my boot on some of the greenery that had been supplied to the hissing guard-poultry. 'I have to talk to you about your corn supply.'

The custodian groaned. 'Nothing to do with me!'

'The weekly sacks of grain?'

'I keep telling them we don't want so much.'

'Who do you tell?'

'The drivers.'

'And what do they do with the surplus?'

'Take it back to the granary, I guess.'

'The geese don't eat corn?'

'Oh if I scatter some for them they toss it about a bit. But they prefer greens.'

'Where do you get their green feed then?'

'The men at Caesar's Gardens; they bring me their clippings. It eases the load, given that they have to cart their rubbish outside the city. And some of the herbalists who have market stalls bring me unsold bundles when they're getting limp, rather than carry them home again.'

This was classic bureaucracy. Some clerk believed that the Sacred Geese required a large supply of grain because his predecessors had left him a brief saying so. Nobody ever asked the keeper of the poultry yard to confirm what was needed. He probably did complain to the drivers, but the drivers didn't want to know. No chance they would report back to the suppliers at the Granary of the Galbae. The suppliers were being paid by the Treasury so they kept on posting out the sacks. If you could find the original order clerk it could be put right; but nobody ever did find him.

'What's the rationale for the corn then?'

'If the poor can have a corn dole, so can Juno's geese. They saved Rome. The city shows its gratitude.'

'What; a hundred thousand skivers receive their vouchers for free corn – and one of the dockets is routinely made out to the Sacred Honkers? I suppose they get best white loaf wheat too?'

'No, no,' soothed their elderly gooseboy, who was slow to appreciate irony.

'This has been going on for five hundred years?'

'All my time,' nodded the custodian self-righteously.

'Is it possible,' I asked, wearily because my cold was getting the better of me now, 'that the drivers take your rejects away and sell off the sacks cheap?'

'Oh gods, don't ask me,' scoffed the custodian. 'I'm just stuck here talking to birds all day.'

I told him I did not want to worry him, but he really ought to think about it seriously since today's sacks must have been tampered with. He could have ended up in charge of a pile of pillow feathers. When I mentioned the dead ostrich, he did finally react.

'Ostriches!' It had brought forth real contempt. 'Those bastards will eat anything, you know. They like to swallow stones.' He seemed fonder of his geese now, by comparison.

'The ostriches don't object to corn, and it looks as if they get it,' I said shortly. 'Look, this is serious. First we had better collect up what you've put down today, and then don't give the geese any more unless you've tested that sack on some bird who's not sacred.'

It took a bit of persuasion, but the threat of losing his charges worked in the end. I tied Nux to a tree – where the geese came and pretended to mob her – then the custodian and I spent half an hour on our knees, carefully picking up every speck of corn we could see.

160

'So what's this about?' he asked me when we finally stood up and stretched our aching backs.

'It's part of a war to the death between the keepers of the wild beast menageries that supply the arena. If their stupidity has brought them too close to the Sacred Geese, it needs to be stopped right now. I have to find out how and when the sack that did for the ostrich found its way off the granary cart—'

'Oh I can tell you that.'

'How come?'

'The drivers always stop at the caupona at the bottom of the hill and have a warming drink before they toddle off again. In winter they have their beaker indoors. Anyone who knows their habits could come and have a quiet word about any spare sacks on the cart. Of course it would be risky – the sacks are labelled for the geese. What's just happened must have been a one-off.'

'Reckon so?'

I thought Calliopus' ostriches had probably been fed cheaply on the sacred grain for longer than the custodian wanted me to think. It was possible – and indeed it was the most plausible solution – that this cheery old fellow took a cut from the grainsack scam. Doing so was probably the traditional perk of his job. I could land him in big trouble if I reported it – but I wasn't after him.

'Thanks for your help.'

'I'll have to put in a report about my geese being nearly poisoned today.'

'Oh don't do that, or we'll all have to waste a great deal of time over it.'

'What's your name?' he insisted.

'Didius Falco. I work for the Palace. Trust me; I'll deal with this. I'm intending to interrogate the man behind the poisoning. It shouldn't happen again – but take my advice: if you don't want all the corn sacks, ask your superiors to reduce the official order. Otherwise, one day some interfering auditor with less good manners than me is going to raise a stink.'

There must have been unwanted corn coming up to the Capitol since records began. I could have just ended one of the Empire's most historic supply rackets. Vespasian would be proud of me. On the other hand, there were going to be some pretty skinny ostriches entertaining the crowds. Our new Emperor wanted to be popular; he might prefer me to ignore the stolen sacks and keep the exotics big and fit.

I picked up Nux for her own safety. As I left, the custodian was still muttering about his duty to inform various officials that disaster had been levelled at the precious geese. I reckoned it was all for show. He must know it was best to keep quiet.

Once he realised that I had stopped listening, he returned to his normal tasks. Walking down the hill towards the corner of the Forum, I heard him teasing the sacred birds with an affectionate cry of 'Roasted in Green Sauce!'

It was about then I realised that while I had taken my eyes off her, Nux must have been rolling in the unpleasant goose droppings.

XXVII

Helena Justina placed a deliciously cool hand on my forehead, then told me I was certainly not going out again. She carried the baby off to another room, and set herself to look after me. This could be fun. She had seen me battered by villains plenty of times, but in the three years I had known her I had probably not had a streaming cold.

'I keep telling you to dry your hair properly before you leave the baths.'

'It's nothing to do with wet hair.'

'And your arm's so horribly burned. You're probably feverish.'

'I'll need nursing then,' I suggested hopefully.

'Bedrest?' asked Helena, in a rather mocking tone. Her eyes had the glint of a girl who knows her loved one is sinking, and will be in her power.

'And massage?' I pleaded.

'Too soft. I'll prepare you a good strong aloe purge.'

This was just banter. She could see I was not malingering. Lunch was bestowed upon me, with the daintiest titbits tenderly passed my way. Wine was warmed. My boots were eased off and replaced with slippers. A steaming bowl of pine oil was prepared for me to breathe under a napkin. A message was sent to the Saepta to inform Anacrites I had retired hurt and was being kept at home. Like a pupil granted a day off school, I felt better at once.

'You can't go out to dinner tonight—'

'I have to.' Playing the dutiful patient under the napkin, I called out the story of the dead ostrich and the Sacred Geese.

'That's terrible. Imagine the furore if the geese had been killed instead. Marcus, the last thing Vespasian needs at this juncture is the public imagination inflamed by a bad omen.'

From all I had heard, Vespasian was himself pretty superstitious; it went with being country born. I popped out of the inhalent tent and was firmly pushed back under again. 'Don't worry,' I coughed as the aromatic heat enveloped me. 'I warned the custodian to keep his mouth shut—'

'Keep breathing.' Thanks, darling!

'Vespasian need never know.'

Helena sounded crisp: 'Saturninus should be challenged, however. He must be behind poisoning the sacks of corn, as revenge for Calliopus freeing his leopardess.'

'It wouldn't have been in anyone's interest to kill Juno's geese.'

'No. So the threat of unwanted imperial attention might help cool the quarrel. I'll go to dinner with Saturninus tonight and warn him—'

'Either we cry off – or we both go.'

'Well then; I'll do the talking.' All my life women who reckoned they knew what was good for me had been telling me that.

I nodded, as best I could in my position, crouched over the inhalant bowl, for once grateful not to have to take control. I could trust Helena to say the right thing and to ask the right questions.

Bored, I came up for air, only to wish myself hidden again. We had a visitor: Smaractus must have been watching to see if I came home for lunch. The fact that he had allowed me long enough to eat it and to mellow warned me that his mission must be serious.

'Is there a funny smell here, Falco?' He must have caught a whiff of the goose dung Nux had wallowed in.

'Well, it's either something nasty the landlord ought to clear away – or it's the landlord himself. What do you want? I'm ill; make it quick.'

'They say you're involved with the new amphitheatre opening.'

Blowing my nose, I made no reply.

Smaractus squirmed with ingratiating oiliness. Now I really felt sick. 'I wondered if there was any chance of you putting in a word for me, Falco?'

'Olympus! I must be delirious.'

'No, you heard him,' said Helena.

I was about to tell him to jump in the Tiber wearing lead-soled boots, when loyalty to Lenia prevailed. I wanted to get her off my back, for one thing. 'It would be a pleasure.' With luck it just sounded as though a sore throat made me croak, not reluctance to utter those charming words. 'I'll make a bargain, Smaractus. Sign the release for the dowry and divorce Lenia, then I'll see what I can do. If not, well you know my position; as an old friend, I promised to help her sort out her affairs. She would never forgive me if I did more for you than for her.'

He was furious. 'I'll see her in Hades first.'

'I'll draw you a map of how to find the Styx. It's your decision. Your outfit is hardly on the list for the opening ceremony. Your gladiators' school is struggling—'

'Only struggling to expand, Falco!'

'Think about my terms then. There will be fabulous pickings when the amphitheatre opens. But a man has to act on his principles—' Smaractus wouldn't recognise a principle if it walked up on six legs and bit the end of his nose.

I buried my head under the napkin and lost myself in soothing steam. I heard a growl, but I did not investigate. Lenia would soon tell me if he did anything – useful or otherwise.

Various other visitors tried to bother me that afternoon, but by then I was tucked up in bed with the dog warming my feet and the bedroom door firmly closed. As I dozed I was vaguely aware of Helena's voice dismissing the intruders. One sounded like Anacrites. Then I heard my young nephew Gaius, no doubt being bribed to look after Julia for us that night. Another, I was more sorry to hear, could have been my old pal Petronius, but he too was sent away. I found out later he had brought me some wine, his favourite remedy for colds as it was for everything. There are doctors who agree with him. Mind you, there are doctors who will agree anything. Plenty of dead patients could testify to that.

Eventually, just when I felt happy to stay where I was for the rest of the week, Helena roused me and brought me a basin of hot water to wash. I made a cursory effort with a sponge and comb, then pulled on several under-tunics and finally the new russet garment. It was so pristine it was just waiting to have a really purple sauce accidentally spilled down it. It felt too bulky, and the sleeves resisted free movement. Whereas my old green number had sat on me like a second skin, in this one I was constantly aware of itchy cloth and folds I wasn't expecting. It smelt of fullers' chemicals too.

Helena Justina made herself deaf to my muttering. Once I was ready – as ready as I was prepared to make myself – I lay on the bed and watched glumly as she quietly dressed her hair. Before she left her father's house to live with me, maids would have curled her long soft locks with hot tongs, but now she had to comb, wind and spear her hair herself. She had become adept with the fine knobbed pins; she made no complaint. Then she peered into a blurry bronze hand mirror, trying to apply wineless rouge and lupinseed powder by the dim light of a small oil lamp. At that point she did start muttering to herself. December was a poor month for beautification. The fine eye-work with colours drawn from green glass flasks on silver spatulas entailed bending close to the rectangular mirror set into her jewel casket, and even that caused explosions of frustration. I heaved myself upright and refilled the lamp for her, not that it seemed to help. And I was in her way, apparently.

According to Helena she was not really bothering. That would be why this took over an hour.

Just when I was comfortable and nodding off again, she pronounced herself ready to escort me to dinner. She was now tastefully bedecked in pale green, with her amber necklace and wooden-soled slippers, topped off by a thick winter wrap that hung around her rather alluringly. She made a graceful contrast to me in my tortuous russet.

'You look very smart, Marcus.' I sighed. 'I've borrowed my parents' litter so you won't be exposed to the weather. It's a cold evening though—' As if the new tunic were not trouble enough, then she hit me with the ultimate embarrassment: 'You could wear your Gallic coat!'

Bought in Lower Germany in a rash moment, this was a sturdy, shapeless, warm felt robe. It had wide sewn-on sleeves that stuck out at right angles and a ludicrous pointed hood. It was intended to be storm-proof; stylishness had not been part of its make up. I had sworn never to be seen in my home city wearing anything so crude. But I must have been really sick that night: despite all protests, Helena somehow swaddled me in my Gallic coat, fastening the toggles under my chin as if I was three years old.

Now I knew I should have stayed in bed. I had planned to waylay Saturninus with my sophistication. Instead, I arrived at his smart house, bundling out of a borrowed litter with a runny nose, fevered eyes, and looking like some little hunchbacked Celtic forest god. What made me most furious was that I realised Helena Justina was laughing at me.

XXVIII

Saturninus and his wife lived near the Quirinal Hill. Every room in their house had been painted about three months before by professional fresco artists. The couple owned a large quantity of silver furniture, which they scattered with bright cushions in compelling shades. The neat legs of the couches and side-tables buried themselves in luxurious fur rugs – some still with the heads on. I just managed to avoid stuffing my left foot into a dead panther's dentistry.

As I was led in and divested of my outer garments, I gathered the wife was called Euphrasia. She and her husband came civilly to welcome us the moment we arrived. She was an extremely handsome woman, about thirty, darker-skinned than him, with a generous mouth, and gorgeous, gentle eyes.

She led us to a warm dining room decorated in rich red and black. Folding doors led into a colonnaded garden which Saturninus said they used for meals in summer. He showed us briefly; there was a sparkling grotto made from coloured glass and seashells at the far end. With kindly expressions of concern for my health, he brought us back in and had me placed near a brazier.

We were the only guests. Apparently their idea of entertaining was to keep the party intimate. Well, that fitted with what I had been told about the night they dined with ex-praetor Urtica.

I tried to remember I was here to work, though in fact the house was so comfortable and my hosts so easygoing that I found I was starting to forget. I had instinctively distrusted Saturninus, yet I was helpless in less than half an hour.

Luckily Helena stayed alert. Once we had talked of this and that, while eating this and that in generous, highly spiced portions, and while I was trying to stop my nose running after the spices, she weighed straight in: 'So tell me what your background is. How did you come to Rome?'

Saturninus stretched his wide frame on his couch. He seemed characteristically relaxed. He was in a grey tunic almost as new as mine, with gold torque bracelets on his upper arms, his fingers glittering with heavy seal rings. 'I came over from Tripolitania – oh, about twenty years ago. I was freeborn and favoured in life. My family was well off, cultured, leaders of the local community. We had land, though like most people not enough of it—'

'This was where? What's your home town?' Helena believed most people were over-keen to impart their life histories, and as a rule she made a point of not asking them. But when she did, she was unstoppable.

'Lepcis Magna.'

'That's one of the three cities that the province takes its name from?'

'Right. The others are Oea and Sabratha. Of course *I* will tell you Lepcis is the most significant.'

'Of course.' Helena had been speaking in a bright, enquiring voice as if making casual conversation, though as a rather nosy guest. The lanista talked with ease and confidence. I believed his claim that in Lepcis his family were people of substance. But that left a large question mark. Helena smiled: 'I don't mean to be impertinent, but when a man from a good background ends up as a lanista, there must be a story behind it.'

Saturninus thought about it. I noticed Euphrasia was watching him. They seemed a companionable couple, but like many wives she viewed her partner with a faint veil of amusement, as though he didn't fool her. I also thought the gentle eyes could be deceptive.

Her husband shrugged. If he had fought in the arena, he had based his life on taking up challenges. I reckon he knew Helena was no easy touch, and perhaps the risk of giving away too much appealed to him. 'I left home claiming I was off to become important in Rome.'

'And so you were too proud to go back before you made your name?' Helena and he were like old friends laughing together sympathetically over the faults of one of them. Saturninus was pretending to be honest; Helena pretended to go along with it.

'Rome was something of a shock,' Saturninus admitted. 'I had money and education. In that respect I could match any youth of my age from the great senatorial families – but I was a provincial and debarred from political life at a high level. I could have engaged in trade – imports and exports – but it was not my style; well, I might as well have stayed in Lepcis and done that. The other alternative was to become some sort of dreary poet, like a Spaniard begging for favours at court—' Euphrasia snorted at this suggestion; Helena smiled; Saturninus acknowledged them. 'All the time I saw beer-swilling lanks from Gallic tribes being admitted to the Senate with full honours, while Tripolitanians did not rate the same distinction.'

'They will,' I assured him. Vespasian had once been governor of Africa; he would extend the senatorial franchise once he thought of it. Previous emperors had done so for provinces they knew well (hence the long-bearded senatorial Gauls Saturninus so despised, who had been championed by loopy old Claudius). In fact, if Vespasian hadn't had the idea yet of doing something for Africa, I could nudge him along with a report. Anything to look helpful to the government. And Vespasian would like it, being a cheap measure.

'Too late for me!' Saturninus was right; he was too old – and in a vile profession.

'So you decided to beat the system?' asked Helena quietly.

'I was young and hotheaded. Of course I was the type who had to take on the world in the hardest way available.'

170

'You became a gladiator.'

'And a good one,' he boasted pleasantly.

'Am I right that willing volunteers have greater status?'

'You still have to win your fights, lady. Otherwise you have all the status of a corpse being dragged out with hooks.'

Helena looked down at her sweetmeat bowl.

'When I won my wooden sword, it gave me a kind of bitter pleasure to become a lanista,' Saturninus went on after a moment. 'Senators were allowed to maintain troupes of gladiators; for them it was just an exotic hobby. I used the profession for real. And it worked; it gave me all the status I wanted in the end.'

This man was an intriguing mixture of ambition and cynicism. He still looked as much like a gladiator as any slave sold into that life, yet he enjoyed his present luxuries quite naturally. Before he joined the fight business, he had grown up in Tripolitania being served his food by respectful minions and receiving it in elegant tableware. His wife Euphrasia ordered in the courses at dinner with an imperious wave; she too was fully at ease with their lifestyle. She wore a huge necklace with rows of twisted wires and copper disks, including fiery carbuncles; it looked both exotic and antique, and was perhaps inherited.

'Yours is a typical Roman story,' I said. 'The rules say you belong where your money places you. But unless your name is Cornelius or Claudius, and your family once owned a house at the base of the Palatine inside the Walls of Romulus, then you have to manoeuvre your way to a place. New men need to push hard to gain acceptance. But it can be done.'

'With respect, Saturninus,' Helena joined in, 'it's not entirely to do with being provincial. Someone like Marcus has just as hard a battle.'

I shrugged. 'The Senate may be closed to many of us, but so what? Who needs the Senate? Who wants the bother of it, frankly? Anyone can move wherever he wants, if he has the staying power. You prove the point,

Saturninus. You fought your way up, literally. Now you dine with city magistrates.' He showed no reaction as I alluded to Pomponius Urtica. 'You lack nothing of luxury or social position' – I decided not to mention power, though he must have that too – 'even though your occupation is sordid.'

Saturninus gave me a wry grin. 'The lowest possible element – both pimps and butchers. We procure men, but as dead meat.'

'Is that how you see it?'

I had thought his mood dark, but Saturninus was thoroughly enjoying the conversation. 'What do you want me to say, Falco? Pretend I supply my men as some religious act? Human sacrifice, a blood payment to appease the gods?'

'Human sacrifice has always been illegal for Romans.'

'Yet that's how it all started,' Helena demurred. 'Pairs of gladiators were matched during funeral games held by the great families. It was a rite, perhaps intended to confer immortality on their dead by the shedding of blood. Even though gladiators fought in the Cattle Market Forum, it was still portrayed as a private ceremony.'

'And that's where everything differs nowadays!' Saturninus leant forwards, shaking his forefinger. 'Now holding a private bout is disallowed.' He was right: the motive would be suspect. I wondered if this had particular relevance. Had there been some private bout recently? Or had somebody at least tried to commission one?

'That's the political element,' I said. 'Now combats are given to bribe the mob during elections – or to glorify the Emperor. The praetors get a look in once a year in December, but otherwise, only the Emperor may offer Games to the public. A private display would be regarded as shocking and self-indulgent – and in effect treasonous. The Emperor would certainly view any man who commissioned one as hostile to him.'

Saturninus knew how to listen completely impassively.

But I felt I was close to some truth. Were we still debating Pomponius Urtica, perhaps?

'Without the ceremony, it would just be a lust for blood,' said Helena.

'Why?' Euphrasia, the elegant wife, made a rare contribution: 'Is it more cruel to shed blood in a private situation than before a huge crowd?'

'The arena enshrines a national ritual,' said Helena. 'I do think it's cruel, and I am not alone. But gladiatorial games set the rhythm of life in Rome, along with the chariot races, the *naumachia*, and theatrical dramas.'

'And many combats are a formal punishment for criminals,' I pointed out.

Helena winced. 'That's the cruellest part — when prisoners fight, naked and unprotected, each knowing that if he prevails against one opponent he will only be kept in the arena and made to fight another, one who is fresh as well as desperate.'

She and I had had this argument before. 'But you don't even enjoy watching the professionals, whose swordplay is a matter of skill,' I said.

'No. Though that's not as bad as what happens to the criminals.'

'It's supposed to be redeeming for them. Their shame is denounced by the crowd; the statues of gods are veiled so they shall not see the proclamation of the condemned men's crimes; and justice is seen to be done.'

Helena still shook her head. 'It ought to make the crowd feel ashamed to partake in the event.'

'Don't you want criminals punished?'

'I find what happens too routine; that's why I dislike it.'

'It's for the public good,' I disagreed.

'At least they are being seen to pay a penalty,' Euphrasia put in.

'If you don't think it's humane,' I wrangled with Helena, 'what else do you think we should do with a monster like Thurius? He put unknown numbers of women through horrendous experiences, killed and dismembered them. Simply to fine him, or send him into exile, would be intolerable. And unlike a private citizen, he can't be ordered to fall on his sword when he is apprehended and disgraced; he's not conditioned to do it – and anyway, he's a slave; he's not allowed a sword unless he's confined in the arena and is fighting as a punishment.'

Helena shook her head. 'I know that prisoners being condemned to die in public is supposed to warn others. I know it's vengeance for the public. I just don't want to be there.'

Saturninus leant towards her. He had been listening in silence while we argued. 'If the state orders an execution, should it not be carried out openly?'

'Perhaps,' Helena agreed. 'But the arena uses punishment as a form of entertainment. That's sinking to the criminals' level.'

'There is some difference,' the lanista explained. 'To extinguish life in the arena, by the swipe of a lion's paw or with the sword, should be quick and fairly efficient. You called it routine – but to me that is what makes it permissible. It's neutral – dispassionate. It's not the same as torture; it's nothing like this criminal Thurius deliberately inflicting prolonged pain, and gloating over his victims' suffering.'

His wife biffed him with one graceful hand. 'Now you're going to tell us about the nobility of a gladiator's death.'

He was blunt. 'No. That's waste; it costs money; every time I have to see it I feel sick. If it's one of mine who dies, I'm angry too.'

'Now you're talking about your expensively trained professionals, not condemned men,' I smiled. 'So you'd like to see fights where they all walk away? Just a display of skill?'

'Nothing wrong with skill! But I like what the crowd likes, Marcus Didius.'

'Always the pragmatist?'

'Always the businessman. There is a demand; I provide what is wanted. If I did not do the job, someone else would.'

The traditional excuse from suppliers of vice! That was why lanistae were called pimps. Since I had eaten at his table, I refrained from saying it. I was tainted too.

Euphrasia liked to stir things, apparently; she had a provocative streak: 'I think you two guests have a big disagreement about cruelty and humanity!'

We lived as man and wife; by definition our disagreements were never sophisticated.

Helena probably resented a near stranger commenting on our relationship. 'Marcus and I both agree that an accusation of cruelty is the worst insult you can offer anyone. Cruel emperors are damned in the public memory and removed from the record. And of course "humanity" is a Latin word – a Roman invention.' For an unsnobbish woman she could lay on a superior air like honey on a cinnamon plait.

'And how do Romans define their wonderful humanity?' asked Euphrasia satirically.

'Kindness,' I supplied. 'Restraint. Education. A civilised attitude towards all people.'

'Even slaves?'

'Even lanistae,' I said drily.

'Oh even them!' Euphrasia glanced sideways at her husband wickedly.

'I want vicious criminals punished,' I said. 'Watching it gives me no personal pleasure, but it does seem right to be a witness. I don't feel I lack humanity – though I do concede, I am glad to live with a girl who has a fuller share of it.'

Euphrasia was still harping: 'And so you are eager to see Thurius fed to a lion?'

'Certainly.' I half turned on my elbow to look squarely at her husband. 'Which brings us rather neatly to the particular lion who had been booked to do the job.'

For a brief instant our host let his guard slip and his

displeasure show. It was evident that Saturninus did not wish to discuss what had happened to Leonidas.

XXIX

Euphrasia knew she had said the wrong thing: Leonidas was a closed subject, though she may not have been told why. Without turning a hair, she waved the servants to clear away the desert course. Four or five discreet waiting staff moved in on silently padding feet to lift out the tables, complete with their litter and used bowls; these slaves conveniently passed in front of our couches, causing a break in the conversation. It gave Saturninus time to recover his composure. The dark furrow on his brow cleared.

He was never going to be easy when cornered, however. 'What,' he asked me directly, 'does Calliopus say happened?'

He was too clever to be finessed. 'Some of his bestiarii released Leonidas during a prank at the barracks, allegedly. The lion played up and ended the night with a spear in him. The ringleader is supposed to be a certain Iddibal.'

'Iddibal?' Saturninus' curiosity sounded genuine.

'A young bestiarius in the Calliopus troupe. He looks like nothing special – though he may be running wild. He has some woman openly chasing after him.'

Saturninus was silent for a second. Was that because he knew Iddibal had had nothing to do with the Leonidas incident? Then he spoke, as if closing the matter, or trying to: 'Calliopus ought to know what happens in his own yard, Falco.'

'Oh I reckon he knows all right!'

'That sounds as if you suspect something else happened, Falco,' Euphrasia interjected. Her husband shot her another irritated look. She had a mercurial way of being all tact one minute, then turning wilful on him.

I cleared my throat. I was starting to feel weary, and would have preferred to shelve this. Helena reached over and squeezed my hand. 'Marcus Didius is an informer; of course he believes all he is told!'

Euphrasia laughed, perhaps more than the irony demanded.

'Is it true,' Helena then asked Saturninus, 'that you and Calliopus are serious rivals?'

'Best of friends,' he lied valiantly.

'Somebody said you had quarrelled when in partnership?'

'Oh we have had a few skirmishes. He's a typical Oean – a devious buffoon. Mind you, he would probably say, trust a Lepcis man to insult him!'

'Is he married?' Helena asked Euphrasia.

'To Artemisia.'

'I see her as somewhat downtrodden.' I revived and joined in again. 'My partner and I unearthed signs that Calliopus has a mistress – and as a result he's currently supposed to be involved in a huge quarrel with his wife about his after-hours activities.'

'Artemisia is a nice woman,' Euphrasia declared firmly.

Helena scowled. 'Poor thing then! Do you know her well, Euphrasia?'

'Not well.' Euphrasia grinned. 'She is from Oea, after all, and I am a good Lepcis citizen. I see her at the baths sometimes. She wasn't there today; somebody said she has gone to their villa at Surrentum.'

'For Saturnalia?' Helena arched her fine eyebrows in astonishment. Surrentum has the best views in Italy and in summer is delightful. December can be bleak up on any seaside cliff, however. I did hope that the work of Falco & Partner had not caused the poor woman's exile.

'Her husband thinks Artemisia is in need of sea air,' Euphrasia jeered; Helena tutted angrily at the unfairness of men.

Saturninus and I exchanged self-righteous male glances.

'Do your skirmishes with your old partner,' I asked him bluntly, 'include the escapade with your leopardess at the Saepta yesterday? I heard that Calliopus' men were at the scene.'

'Oh he was behind it,' Saturninus agreed. Well, there was no point in his denying it.

'Any firm evidence?'

'Of course not.'

'And what can you tell me about a sack of grain that found its way off the Arx today and turned out to be poisonous?'

'I know nothing and can tell you nothing, Falco.' Well, I expected that.

'I'm glad you aren't taking the credit. If the Sacred Geese of Juno had guzzled any of the poison, Rome would face a national crisis.'

'Shocking,' he said impassively.

'Calliopus seems to be the regular recipient of sacks that have "fallen off the back of a cart".'

Saturninus was not in the least put out. 'Roadside thieves nip things off when carts slow down at crossroads, Falco.'

'Yes, it's an old dodge. And a better sounding explanation than that the supplier allowed a regular fiddle to owners of menagerie animals.'

'Oh not us. We buy our feed at cost, through proper channels.'

'Well, I certainly recommend that for the next few months! Do your "proper channels" include the Granary of the Galbae?'

'I believe we get better terms from the Granary of the Lollii.'

'Very astute. Incidentally, Calliopus lost a fine male ostrich who ate some of the bad corn.'

'I'm desolate for him.'

Helena had noticed that I was flagging again: 'Calliopus does seem to have rather bad luck with his menagerie. Or perhaps not. Think about when he first lost his lion: the story of a prank on the yard is clearly untrue. Evidence shows that Leonidas had been taken from his cage and transported elsewhere. Calliopus is either very stupid indeed to believe what he alleges Iddibal did – or he knows the real truth and is foolishly trying to delude Marcus Didius.'

'Why would Calliopus do that?' asked Euphrasia, wide-eyed and giggling.

'The easy solution, the one we are supposed to believe, is that Calliopus has decided to exact his own revenge for his lion's death and he doesn't want interference.'

'And is there a complicated solution, Helena?'

I was secretly watching Saturninus, but he managed to look merely polite.

'One explanation,' Helena decided, 'would be that Calliopus was fully aware of what was planned that night.' For all the interest he showed, Saturninus could have been listening to her describing a new Greek novel.

'Why would he want his lion killed?' Euphrasia scoffed.

'I don't imagine he did. Whatever murky business was in hand, Leonidas probably died by accident.'

'When Calliopus saw the body, his reactions seemed genuine,' I confirmed. In fact his anger and surprise had been the only sure signals he evinced that day. 'But I'm damned certain he knew all along that Leonidas was being taken away in the night.'

The way Saturninus was now staring fixedly at his fingernails marked a change in him. What had given him pause? That Calliopus knew of the plan? No, he had heard Helena say so without a flicker of reaction. *I reckon he knew Leonidas was being taken away* ... Was the key word 'Leonidas'? I remembered a couple of puzzles I had seen at the menagerie: the name board for Leonidas stored in another part of the building, and the second lion being first hidden away then returned to the main corridor as if that was his usual place.

'My opinion,' I submitted crisply, 'is that Leonidas was a substitute.'

'A substitute?' Even Helena was surprised.

'Calliopus owns a second lion, a new one just imported. I think *Draco* was supposed to have gone on the mystery tour that night.'

Saturninus remained silent. This could all be nothing to do with him. Or he might be in the thick of it.

'I think,' I said, 'Calliopus for some reason had Draco and Leonidas secretly switched.'

Saturninus finally looked up. 'It would be very dangerous,' he said slowly, 'if someone was expecting a freshly captured wild animal, to send them a trained man-eater instead.'

I returned his stare levelly. 'The recipients would be on watch for the wrong set of behaviour?' He made no reply. 'The man-eater might be mishandled. Imagine the scene: Leonidas had been accustomed to making journeys in a small travelling cage, and he knew what to expect at the end of it: the arena – and men for him to eat. He was hungry that night; his keeper told me so. On being released from the cage, strangers might unwittingly give him signals that set off his training. He normally looked quiet, even friendly, but once he thought he was supposed to attack he would go for whoever he saw – perhaps even kill them.'

'When he started rampaging, people would panic,' Helena said.

'Anyone who was armed,' I went on, 'would have to try to kill the lion. A gladiator, for instance.'

Finally Saturninus made a slight gesture with his hand. It merely said my suggestion was feasible. It did not say he had ever seen it happen. He would never confess that.

I still had no certain knowledge why Leonidas had been taken from his cage that night, where he went, or who was with him on his journey and at its violent aftermath. But I was convinced that I had just worked out how he came to die.

XXX

Did it matter?

I toyed with a bunch of grape stems that had been mislaid among the lushly fringed spread on my feeding-couch. Was I eccentric to care? Was my obsession with Leonidas unhealthy and pointless? Or was I right, and the noble beast's fate should be as significant to a civilised man as any unexplained killing of a fellow human being?

When Saturninus said that sending a man-eater in place of an untrained lion was dangerous, for a rare moment he had failed to keep his voice calm. Was he remembering the killing? And if he was present, was he in any way responsible for the whole sinister farce? He had already claimed he and Euphrasia had dined with the ex-praetor Urtica that night. I thought him easily the sort of man who knows that the best lies are closest to the truth; the truth could be not that Saturninus possessed a respectable alibi, but far worse: that poor Leonidas had also been the praetor's guest.

Pomponius Urtica had a new, 'wild' girlfriend; he might want to impress her. He was keen on the Circus; he was close to the lanistae. Saturninus for one seemed to view Urtica as a contact with useful influence. The man's status could be about to evaporate, however. If he had used his house for a private display, he was open to blackmail. If it were ever made known that he had commisssioned death for domestic entertainment, then he would be destroyed politically.

Saturninus would of course cover up for him. This could be it: first he had indulged the man by secretly arranging some sort of combat. Then, when the display went wrong, Saturninus had boldly made the best of it. By saving the magistrate's reputation, he would acquire a patron with a permanent debt.

I was beginning to understand. One aspect I saw immediately was that anyone who threatened to expose the people involved was courting danger. Urtica was politically powerful. Saturninus kept a troupe of trained killers. He had been a gladiator himself; if crossed, he looked as if he could still avenge himself quite efficiently.

Across the space where the tables had been, now an expanse of newly swept geometric mosaic tiles, Helena Justina had observed me brooding. She held my gaze until my mood lightened, then she smiled quietly. I was feeling the strain of my cold. I would have liked to be taken home, but it was still too early to retire. Hospitality held us in its relentless grip.

Saturninus had been giving his attention to a bowl of nuts. Now he looked up suddenly and, as people do when you want to be left alone to snuffle, he insisted on making me share his vivacity. 'So, Falco! The word is you're making my old partner Calliopus hop!'

This was the last subject I wanted to discuss. I applied the necessary discreet smile. 'That's privileged information.'

'I bet he's cheating the Censor to Hades and back.'

'He has employed an accountant with flair.'

'But you're thwarting them?'

My irritation was hard to check. 'Saturninus, you're too intelligent to think you can give me dinner then expect me to leak secrets.'

I knew better than to discuss my report with anyone, even Calliopus himself. From what I knew of bureaucracy it was perfectly possible for Falco & Partner to substantiate a million-sesterces fraud, yet still to encounter some slimy high-powered bureaucrat who would decide there were policy reasons, or ancient precedents, or issues affecting his own pension, that made him advise his great imperial master to shelve the exposé.

Saturninus never gave up. 'The rumour in the Forum is that Calliopus looks miserable.'

'That,' interrupted Helena Justina calmly, 'will be because his wife has found out about his mistress.' She smoothed the cover of the cushion she was leaning on. 'He must be afraid Artemisia will insist on him following her to Surrentum at this awful time of year.'

'Is that what you would have arranged, Helena?' asked Euphrasia, with a sidelong glance at me.

'No,' said Helena. 'If I was departing Rome because my husband had offended me, I would either leave the notice of divorce propped against his feeding bowl – or he would be right there in the carriage with me so I could tell him what I thought.'

Saturninus seemed honestly puzzled. 'You would do as your husband directed.'

'I doubt it,' said Helena.

Saturninus looked affronted for a moment, as though he were not used to a woman disagreeing with him – though from our observations that evening at table, he was just as used to it as anyone. Then he decided to duck the issue with more nosy questions. 'So! Now Calliopus must await the results of your enquiries!'

I looked him straight in the eye. 'No peace for me and my partner. We're conducting a composite audit, not just random checks.'

'What does that mean?' smiled Saturninus.

I had a stinking cold, but I was nobody's helpless sparring stake. I made it pleasant, since we were dining in his house: 'It means you're next.'

For the rest of the evening we discussed where to buy garlands in December, religion, pepper, and the wilder sidebranches of formal epic poetry. Very nice. I let Helena do the work. She had been brought up to shine in society. A man with his head blocked so he can only breathe through his teeth is entitled to sink down scowling and pretend to be an uneducated Aventine pig.

'Helena Justina is admirably erudite,' Saturninus complimented me. 'And she speaks of pepper as if she owned a whole warehouse!'

She did. I wondered if he had somehow found out. If not, I had no intention of revealing her private wealth.

I had thought Helena might want to ask Saturninus and Euphrasia what they knew about silphium. They came from the right continent, its geographical habitat. But Saturninus was not a man into whose hands she would deliver her younger brother. Justinus was no innocent, but he was a fugitive, therefore vulnerable. It was unlikely Camillus Justinus would ever seek to join a troupe of gladiators – although it was not unknown for the sons of senators to take that course when desperate for cash, or a defiant new life. The thought of our missing lad catching the lanista's eye was creepily suggestive. This was an entrepreneur, a procurer of men. Saturninus would acquire – for any purposes – anyone who seemed useful to him. That was why we were here tonight.

Had I needed proof, it was to come as we were leaving. In the course of what seemed like a harmless chat about how professional poets in Rome have to operate through patronage or starve, I had let slip that I myself wrote for relaxation. Always a mistake. People want to know if your work has been copied up by scrollsellers, or if you have given readings socially. Saying no shrinks your standing; saying yes makes their eyes glaze defensively. Though I mentioned that I sometimes toyed with the idea of hiring a hall to give an evening of my love poems and satires, it was said ruefully. Everyone, including me, was convinced it was a dream.

I spoke from the clear assumption that self-respect debarred me from toadying to some wealthier man as his client. I would never consent to be a mere commodity, and I wasn't the type to enjoy being grateful. Saturninus lived in a different world and seemed unaware of my attitude: 'That's an attractive idea, Falco! I always hankered to expand into something more cultured – I'll invest in your venue with pleasure—'

I let it slide past me as if I had become too feverish to respond. This had seemed a long evening; it was time to go. I needed to be safely back in our litter before I lost my temper. Our host was an entrepreneur all right: the bastard was openly trying to procure me.

XXXI

I was bilious all night. It led to a severe outbreak of prejudice. Helena told me that houses which present visitors with a sparkling surface generally have old gravy crusting the cauldrons. The more refined the soirée, the more certain to be rats under the cooking bench. Well, something had polluted my guts.

'Poison!'

'Oh Marcus, don't exaggerate.'

'The ostrich, the Sacred Geese of Juno – and now me.'

'You have a bad cold, and you've eaten strange food tonight.'

'In circumstances where indigestion was inevitable.'

I climbed back into bed, where Helena patiently held me in her arms, stroking my hot forehead. 'I found our hosts curiously likable,' she told me, trying not to yawn too much. 'So, are you going to tell me what made you so irascible?'

'I was rude?'

'You're an informer.'

'You mean I was *very* rude?'

'Perhaps a little tetchy and suspicious.' She was laughing.

'That's because the only people who invite us out are even lower in society – and even they only do it when they want something.'

'Saturninus was pretty obvious,' Helena agreed. 'Probing him in return was like trying to poke a hole in an iron bar with a dandelion stem.'

'I did pry something out of him.' I told Helena my

theory about the death of Leonidas having taken place at Urtica's house.

She listened in silence, then remained still for some moments, testing what I had said for herself and considering the implications. 'Was it Saturninus himself who speared the lion?'

'I would say not. He has always admitted he took Rumex with him — besides, the anonymous message to Anacrites specifically blamed Rumex.'

'Even if Rumex killed the poor beast, Saturninus must take responsibility. He organised the party. Who do you think sent the message?'

'It could have been Calliopus, but I still believe he wants this hushed up. For one thing, it gives him a hold over Saturninus — and *he* wants to keep it to himself too. It's good blackmail material. The pet praetor will be in big trouble if it ever gets out that he had a gladiator performing in his house — not to mention causing the death of a Circus man-eater, who was perhaps stolen at the time.'

'But you said Calliopus knew of the escapade in advance.'

'Yes, but he wasn't intended to know.'

Exhausted, I lay prone while Helena pondered. 'If the story gets out, Calliopus will disclaim all connection.' Her breath tickled my forehead. Wonderful. 'He can't have been directly involved — the lion's death did genuinely disconcert both Calliopus and his keeper.'

'Yes; neither Calliopus nor Buxus had been aware that Leonidas was dead until he was found the next morning in his cage.'

'So we can rule out Calliopus also being at this unsavoury party at the ex-praetor's house. Marcus, it was odd though that the keeper failed to hear the lion being taken away and returned. Maybe Buxus had been bribed by Saturninus to let him remove an animal — Draco, supposedly. But instead, maybe Buxus was loyal to

Calliopus, told him the plan, and they worked the switch to cause trouble . . .'

I pretended to drift off to sleep, to end the discussion. I did not want Helena to work around to my own fear: that if Saturninus thought he had told me too much, he would decide I was dangerous. I did not know the form if a lanista took out a contract on a human enemy – but I had seen what he could do to somebody's ostrich. I did not want to be found with my head dangling and my legs all limp.

Next morning Helena kept me at home again. Later, she took me to the baths. Glaucus my trainer found the sight of me with my strict female escort a huge joke.

'Can't you blow your own nose now? And Jupiter, Falco, where have you been? I heard you were working with the Circus crowd. I've been expecting you to rush in here claiming to be undercover on some vitally important mission, and demanding to be brought up to scratch to play at gladiators—'

'Glaucus, you know I'm too sensible.' Actually, going undercover in that way might be a good idea – though I could think of somebody I would rather send to the arena: my dear partner Anacrites.

Glaucus used a laugh I didn't care for. 'There's an even more unpleasant rumour that you're really weazling for the Censors, Falco, but I don't want to hear your excuse about that.'

I pottered off to see his barber, a sleek fellow who took off two days' growth with an expression as if he were cleaning a drain. His expertise with a Spanish razor was the envy of the Forum, and the fee Glaucus charged for him matched his skill. Helena calmly paid. The barber took her money as if he was mortally offended to see a man fall into feminine clutches. He had a way of smiling that was not much better than his master's laugh. I did my best to sneeze all over him.

We went home. I started shivering, and volunteered to go to bed again. I slept soundly for hours, then awoke much refreshed. The baby was asleep or absorbed in her own little world. The dog was just asleep. When Helena came to peek at me, she saw me awake and snuggled up beside me to be sociable.

It was a quiet afternoon, too cold outside for much active street life. Most of the time neither voices nor hoofbeats sounded down in Fountain Court, and our bedroom had an interior aspect so noises from further away could hardly penetrate. The basket-weaver in the shop downstairs had already locked up for a few weeks and gone to the country to enjoy Saturnalia; not that Ennianus or his customers ever made much disturbance.

Lying in bed was soothing, though I had had enough sleep. I did not yet want to start thinking about work, although I wanted to think about something. These few snatched moments with Helena posed a suitable challenge. Pretty soon I had her giggling as I set out to demonstrate that the parts of me that were not befuddled by my cold were even livelier than usual.

Winter does have some advantages.

An hour later I was soundly asleep again, when the world began waking up. The light was fading into dusk; all the Aventine bad people were banging their doors and leaving home to cause trouble. Young boys who ought to have been going home came kicking balls against apartment walls with all the force of seige engines. Dogs barked. Pans rattled on griddles. From overcrowded homes all around us the familiar scent of very old cooking oil, infused with burnt fragments of garlic, began to waft skywards.

Our baby started crying as if she thought she had been abandoned for ever. I stirred. Helena left me and went to Julia, just as a visitor arrived. For a few moments Helena managed to fend him off, but then she opened the door a crack and put round her head. She had one hand pushing in a comb to try and right her tangled hairstyle.

'Marcus, if you feel up to it, I think you'll want to come and see Anacrites.'

She knew that even when healthy I never felt up to that confrontation. The restrained way she spoke told me there was something up. Still luxuriating in drowsiness after our lovemaking, I mouthed *you're beautiful!*, to enjoy the sensation of being suggestive out of sight of Anacrites. Helena was keeping him out, as if the rumpled scene of our passion ought to remain private. I nodded to show I would dress and join them.

Helena then said quietly: 'Anacrites has brought some news. Rumex, the gladiator, has been found dead.'

XXXII

We had lost the best part of a day.

'Olympus!' complained Anacrites, as I dragged him in my wake past the Temple of Ceres on my way down from the Aventine. 'What's special about the death of a gladiator, Falco?'

'Don't pretend you can't see it. Why bother to tell me at all, if you think it's a natural occurrence? Jupiter! Rumex was fighting fit, in every sense. I met him. He was as solid as a frontier rampart—'

'Maybe he caught your cold.'

'Rumex would soon scare off a little cold.' I was ready to ignore it myself now. My windpipe was on fire, but I was holding back the cough even though I was agitated and hurrying. Helena had flung my Gallic coat over me, and topped it off with a hat. I would live – unlike the darling of the arena crowds. 'This fever isn't fatal, Anacrites – however much you would like to think so in my case.'

'Don't be unfair—' He tripped on a kerbstone, which made me smile with satisfaction; he had stubbed his toe so hard it would go black and shed the nail. I jumped down the Middle Stairs three at a time and let him follow as best he could.

At the barracks a large crowd had gathered. A tall pair of perfectly matched cypress trees in handsome stone urns had been set either side of the gate. There, a solemn porter was receiving small commemorative tributes with apparently sincere thanks, moving on with discreet efficiency from one donor to the next. The crowd was mainly composed of women, on the whole silent though occasionally emitting thin cries of distress.

While I lay ill, Anacrites had already begun auditing the Saturninus empire; as we walked, he had told me that our work would be taking place not here, but at the office of an untrustworthily helpful accountant whose office was on the other side of town. That had not surprised me. Saturninus knew all the subtle tricks of being difficult. However, our audit gave us a useful right of entry to any of his property. When we ordered them to let us into the barracks, they did.

Inside the gate, out of sight from the street, the mourners' tributes were being stripped open on a table, the valuables removed methodically and the trash dumped in a large bin for later disposal.

I led Anacrites directly around the various courtyards to the cell where Rumex used to live. The minders who had dallied with Maia and Helena were missing. In their place, guarding a heavily locked door, were a couple of beef-ox colleagues of the dead man.

'Sorry about this—' I adopted an expression of faint annoyance as if we were all being inconvenienced. 'I dare say it's nothing to do with us, but when something like this happens while we are conducting a Census enquiry we have to check the scene—'

That was a complete lie.

The slab-chested fellows in leather loincloths were unused to facing devious officials. In fact they were heavily trained to do just what they were told. They sent a lad to see the man who had possession of the key. He thought it was Saturninus asking for him, so he came along meekly. There were a few doubtful glances among the various personnel, but it seemed easiest to let us do what we wanted, then to lock up again quickly and pretend nothing had occurred.

So, by a mixture of our bluff and their inefficiency, we gained entry to the dead man's quarters. It was easy, even after a murder. I did wonder if last night somebody else had used similar tactics.

When we walked in, to our surprise, Rumex was still there.

In this situation there was more chance than usual that Anacrites and I could make our partnership work. We were both professionals. We both recognised an emergency. We had to act as one. If Saturninus were on the premises, he might any minute hear of our arrival and race to intervene. So I glanced at Anacrites, then we moved in together. We needed to scour the place rapidly for clues, taking notes, each serving as witness to what the other found. We had one chance to do this. There could be no mistakes.

We had entered not a tiny cell with a straw pallet, which was all most fighters ever acquired, but a tall room about ten feet square. Its walls, once plain, had been painted in a rich dark red then completely covered with graffiti of arena scenes. Stickmen with swords chased each other, stabbed each other, fell down and stared up in mute appeal at each other. Lively fights were depicted all over the middle ground and upper frieze. Thracians hung their heads and died above the dado; myrmillons were being dragged out lifeless below it while Rhadamanthus, King of the Underworld, supervised in his beaked mask, accompanied by Hermes with his snaky staff.

Rumex had owned a lot of stuff. Armour and weapons would be kept by his master, but he had been laden with gifts. A vibrant Egyptian carpet, which most people would have preserved as a treasured wall-hanging, lay rucked by casual usage on the floor. Apart from the bed, the furniture comprised huge chests, one or two standing open to reveal mounds of tunics, cloaks, and furnishings, all presumably donated by admirers. On a tripod a smaller coffer revealed a jumble of gold chains, armlets and collars. Goblets of exquisite workmanship stood on burnished trays alongside others that were in execrable taste, though stuck with costly gems. Since Saturninus would have extracted the greater percentage of what was dotingly presented to his hero, the original tally must have been enormous. (An appealing prospect for us two as auditors, since it had not been represented in the lanista's accounts.)

The two gladiator guards and the keyman were peering in after us, starting to grow nervous. Anacrites fetched out a note tablet; despite his bored manner, his stylus moved at speed. He was listing the stuff. I nodded and went to the bed, like a curious tourist.

Rumex lay on his back as if he were asleep. He was wearing only a single white tunic, probably an undergarment. One arm, that nearest to me, was slightly bent, as if he might have been leaning up on his elbow but had fallen back as he died. His great head faced towards me as I stood at his bedside. Beneath him was the kind of coverlet under which imperial princesses snuggle up to their lovers. Its rich nap must be tickling the back of his thick neck.

It was the neck that transfixed my attention. Around it lay a heavy gold chain; but not the one with his name on that I had seen him wearing before. The new one was pulled tight across the throat, but at the back of the head it looked looped up, where it would have caught in the hair had the gladiator not been so closely shaven. The chain lying oddly was intriguing enough. Either somebody had tried to remove it – or Rumex had been pulling it on over his head.

That was not what made me draw so sharp a breath. A short trail of congealed blood disfigured the luxurious bedcover beneath the dead man's cheek. It ran from a small wound where Rumex had been stabbed through the throat.

XXXIII

I crooked an eyebrow to Anacrites. He came across and I heard him groan under his breath. With one forefinger he tried gently to pull loose the gold chain, but it held fast under the weight of Rumex' head.

Each of us must have been thinking this through: he was relaxed in bed when he was stabbed; it was quite unexpected. Something was going on with this chain, but the killer chose not to steal the thing. Perhaps horror overcame him. Perhaps he was disturbed at the scene. Perhaps the cost of the chain had seemed a good investment and it was readily abandoned once the gladiator was dead.

The knife was missing. From the size of the wound, it must have a small, slim blade. A handknife, easily concealed. In a city where it was forbidden to go armed, a bauble you could excuse to the vigiles as your domestic fruitknife. A little thing that might even belong to a woman – though whoever struck that blow had used masculine speed, surprise and force. Also perhaps experience.

Anacrites stepped back; so did I. We had made a space that let the two gladiators see the corpse. From their grim exclamations it was the first time.

They knew death. They must have seen their colleagues killed in the ring. Even so, this deceptive scene, with Rumex so obviously at his ease at the moment of his killing, had deeply affected them. At heart they were men. Horrified, pitying, undemonstrative yet stricken. Just like us.

My own mouth felt dry and sour. *The same old dreary*

depression at life being wasted for some barely credible motive and probably by some lowlife who just thought he could get away with it . . . The same anger and indignation . . . Then the same questions to ask: Who saw him last? How did he spend his last evening? Who were his associates?

When had I said that? Over Leonidas.

I played it as carefully as possible. 'Poor fellow. Do you know who first discovered him?'

One of the gladiators was still speechless. The other forced himself to croak, 'His minders this morning.' The man had no neck, with a broad, ruddy, wide-chinned face that in other situations would have been naturally cheerful. He looked overweight, his chest in a fold and his arms chubbier than was ideal. I put him down as a retired survivor, running to seed.

'What's happened to the minders?'

'The boss took them away somewhere.'

'Saturninus himself extracted them?'

'Yes.'

Well that had a neat symmetry. First Calliopus had lost his lion and tried to disguise the circumstances. Now Saturninus had lost his best fighter and it looked as if a cover up had been applied swiftly here too.

'Was he angry that they let someone get to Rumex?' The two new guards exchanged a glance and I had a feeling the old minders had been given a heavy thrashing. It would serve a double purpose: punishment – and making sure they kept their mouths shut.

'I heard about it in the Forum,' Anacrites murmured, staring at the corpse. He managed to sound like anyone stunned by shocking news. A good spy, lacking character himself, he could blend into the background like fine mist blurring the contours of a Celtic glen. 'Everyone was talking about it, though nobody understood what had happened. All sorts of stories were starting to circulate – if anyone asks us, what is supposed to be put out?'

'Died in his sleep,' said the first guard. I smiled wryly.

Typical of Saturninus. Effectively true – yet it gave away nothing.

'You must have been friends with Rumex. Who do you think did it?' I asked. With a creak of leather, the guard shrugged his big shoulders helplessly. 'Do we know if he had visitors last night?'

'Rumex was always having visitors. Nobody kept count.'

'Women, presumably. Don't his minders know who was here?'

The two gladiators exchanged mirthless laughs. I could not tell whether they were commenting on the number of female admirers their dead friend entertained in his room, the uselessness of the clique of slaves surrounding him, or some much more mysterious point. It was clear they did not intend to enlighten me.

'Didn't Saturninus try to find out if any women called on Rumex last night?'

Again that sense of hidden mirth. 'The boss knows better than to ask about Rumex and his women,' I was told in an oblique tone.

Anacrites pulled a fresh cover from one of the overflowing chests and spread it over the corpse with a show of respect. Just before he covered the face, he asked, 'Was this a new chain?'

'Never seen it before.'

Anacrites asked why the body was still lying here, and we heard that the undertaker was expected later that night. There certainly would be a more than decent funeral, paid for by the gladiators' own burial club, to which Rumex had in his lifetime contributed generously. Nobody knew why Saturninus had locked up the body instead of simply sending for funeral arrangers earlier.

I wondered whether he had more urgent business than attending to the formalities. I asked where he was. Gone home, very upset, apparently. At least that gave us a breathing space.

'Tell me,' I mused, 'what do you know about the other

night? When Rumex had to kill that lion?' Snatched glances passed between his two friends. 'It can't matter any more,' I said.

'The boss won't like us talking.'

'I won't tell him.'

'He has a way of finding out.'

'All right; I won't push you. But whatever occurred, it seems to have done for Rumex!'

At that they looked anxiously towards the door. Anacrites smoothly closed it.

In a low, rapid voice the first gladiator said, 'It was that magistrate. He kept nagging the boss to do him a show at his house. Saturninus offered to take our leopardess, but he was set on a lion.'

'Saturninus doesn't own one?' prompted Anacrites.

'His were all used and killed in the last Games; he's waiting for new stock. He tried to get one a few months ago, but Calliopus sneaked off to Puteoli and pipped him.'

'Draco?' I asked.

'Right.'

'I've seen Draco. He's a handsome beast with great spirit – and I know other people who would have liked to be the purchaser.' Thalia had told me she fancied him for her troupe. 'So Saturninus lost out, but he bribed a keeper at Calliopus' menagerie to let him borrow Draco for a night? Do you know about that?'

'Our folks went there and thought they'd picked him up all right. Afterwards we reckoned it was the wrong lion, of course. But they only saw one; the other must have been hidden away.'

'What was Saturninus planning to do with him?'

'A show with the lion tethered in a harness. No real blood; only noise and drama. Not as frightening as it would look. Our keepers would control the lion, while Rumex dressed up in his gear and pretended to fight him. Just a display so the magistrate could get his girlfriend all hotted up.'

'The totsy? Scilla, isn't it? She's juicy stuff? A lively girl?'

'She's a tough one,' our informant agreed. His companion laughed lewdly.

'I follow – so what went wrong that night at Urtica's house? Did they hold the display as planned?'

'Never got started. Our keepers opened up the cage and were meaning to get the harness round the lion—'

'Sounds a tricky manoeuvre.'

'They do it all the time. They use a piece of meat as bait.'

'Sooner them than me. What if the lion or leopard decides today's choice from the cats' caupona will be human arm?'

'We end up with a one-handed keeper,' grinned the second man, the one who hardly spoke. The cultured, sensitive one.

'Nice! And was Rumex used to fighting animals? He wasn't a bestiarius, surely? I thought he normally played a Samnite and was conventionally paired?'

'Right. He didn't want the job, and that's a fact. The boss leant on him.'

'How?'

'Who knows?' Once again, a shifty look passed between the two gladiators. *They* knew how. The old phrase *'nothing to do with us, legate'* went unsaid, but its implied customary addition *'we could tell you things, all right!'* hung in the air. They shared an unspoken pact that they would not tell me. I would put the whole conversation at risk by pushing it.

'We'll have to ask your boss then,' Anacrites said. They deliberately made no comment, as if daring us.

'Let's go back to the ex-praetor's house,' I suggested. 'The lion's cage was opened up, and then what?'

'The keepers wanted to prepare everything quietly but the damned magistrate came on the scene, wetting himself with excitement. He grabbed one of those straw dummies they use to excite the beasts. He started to wave it about. The lion roared and crashed out past the keepers. It was terrible. He leapt straight at Urtica.'

Anacrites gulped. 'Dear gods. Was he hurt?'

The two men said nothing. He must have been. I could find out. That afternoon when I had tried to see him at his Pincian mansion, perhaps Pomponius Urtica had been groaning indoors, recovering from a mauling. At least I knew now what had befallen the torn straw man I had discovered in the workshops at the Calliopus barracks.

'It must have been an awful scene,' Anacrites joined in again.

'Urtica was down, his girlfriend was screaming, none of our team could handle it.'

'Rumex just grabbed a spear and did his best?'

His two friends were silent. Their attitudes seemed different. One had said his piece while the other listened with a slightly sardonic expression. It could be that the second man disapproved of him telling me the tale. Or it could be something else. He might just possibly disagree with the story as it had just been told.

'Then they had to decide what to do with the dead lion?' suggested Anacrites. Again, nothing from them.

'Well,' I countered, 'you can't just shove a Circus lion behind a bush in Caesar's Gardens and hope the men who trim the lawns will just collect him in their clippings cart.'

'So they put him back where he had come from?'

'Obvious thing to do.'

Anacrites and I were doing the talking because the friends of Rumex were apparently no longer prepared to give. I pushed for one last query: 'What caused the trouble originally between Saturninus and Calliopus?'

It seemed a neutral subject, a change of topic, and they agreed to speak again. 'I heard it was an old row about a tally in the *sparsio*,' the first one told the other. The *sparsio* was the free-for-all when vouchers for prizes and even gifts in kind were hurled at the arena crowds as a bounty.

'Back in the old days.' Even the second became less reticent. Only slightly, however.

'Nero stirred up trouble on purpose,' I prompted. 'He liked to watch the public fighting over the tickets. There was as much blood and broken bones up in the terraces as down on the sand.'

'Calliopus and Saturninus had been partners, hadn't they?' Anacrites said. 'So were they watching the Games together? Then did they fall out over a voucher in the scrum?'

'Saturninus grabbed the voucher first, but Calliopus trod on him and snatched it—'

The lottery had always caused havoc around the arena. Nero had enjoyed stirring up those wonderful human talents: greed, hatred and misery. People used to place huge bets too, gambling on the chance of winning a prize, only to lose everything if they failed to grab a ticket. When the tickets were thrown by attendants or launched from the spitting voucher machine, chaos ensued. Holding on to a ticket was the first lottery; getting one for a worthwhile prize was the second game of chance. You could win three fleas, ten gourds – or a fully laden sailing ship. The only drawback was that if you bagged the day's big prize you were compelled to meet the Emperor.

'What was the controversial win?' I asked.

'The special.'

'In cash?'

'Better.'

'The galleon?'

'The villa.'

'Oho! That must be how Calliopus acquired his desirable cliff-top gem at Surrentum.'

'No wonder they fell out then,' said Anacrites. 'Saturninus must have been very unhappy at losing that.' Ever the master of the banal. He and I knew exactly what that villa at Surrentum was now worth. Losing it, Saturninus had been screwed. It lent an extra dimension to Euphrasia's sarcastic interest in why Calliopus had sent his own wife Artemisia there now.

'They've been feuding ever since,' said the chubby gladiator. 'They hate each other's guts.'

'A lesson to all who work in partnership,' I murmured piously, aiming to worry Anacrites.

Unaware of the undercurrents, our informant went on: 'We reckon they would kill one another, if they had the chance.'

I smiled at Anacrites. That was going too far. I would never kill him. Not even though we both knew he had once tried to arrange a fatal accident for me.

We were partners now. Absolutely pals.

It was time to leave.

As we all stirred ourselves, Anacrites suddenly bent forwards as if on an impulse (though nothing he ever did was without some sly calculation). He drew back the coverlet from Rumex' face and gazed down sombrely once more. Trying to prize out one last relevation, he was pretending to feel some ghastly fascination with the stiffening corpse.

Drama had never been my style. I walked quietly from the room.

Anacrites rejoined me without comment, followed by the dead man's two friends, whom I sensed would now guard him in an extremely subdued spirit. Whatever murky business was stirring in the world of the arena, Rumex was free of all pressure and all danger now. That might not be so for his colleagues.

We said our goodbyes, Anacrites and I showing decent regret. The two gladiators saluted us with dignity. Only when I glanced back as we walked off down the corridor did I realise that the scene had afffected them much more than we had understood. The big overweight one was leaning on the wall covering his eyes, obviously weeping. The other had turned away, green in the face, helplessly throwing up.

They were trained to accept bloody massacre in the ring. But for a man to be slain all unprepared in his bed was, for them, a deeply disturbing event.

It had churned me up too. Added to the anger I had first

felt over Leonidas I felt a grim determination to expose whatever sordid business had now caused another death.

XXXIV

I knew what I intended to do. I was uncertain about Anacrites. I should have remembered that although spies often cause death indirectly, and often deliberately order it, they rarely have to look the results in the face. So he surprised me. Outside the barracks gate I paused, ready to tell him to lose himself while I took up the questioning.

He faced me. Those murky, greyish eyes met mine. His expression was grim.

'One each?' he asked.

I pulled out a coin and spun. He got Calliopus; I took Saturninus.

Without conferring we set off separately to interrogate the rival Tripolitanians. I had my normal methods at my disposal; how Anacrites would manage in a real tussle, without a bank of torture irons and a set of pervertedly inventive assistants, was less clear. I suppose somehow I trusted him. Maybe he even had some faith in me.

We met up again at Fountain Court that night. By then it was late. Before we set about comparisons we ate. I had panfried some sliced sausage which I stirred into a bean and leek braise, lightly flavoured with aniseed, which Helena had prepared. Looking quizzical, she accepted my suggestion to lay a spare bowl for Anacrites. As Helena put a wand to a couple of oil lamps, I could see she was touched by his pleasure at being allowed for the first time to join our domestic life.

I winced. The bastard really wanted to be part of the family. He was yearning to be accepted, both at home and at work. What a creep.

Once we reported results, a pattern emerged. Parallel accusations and synchronised unhelpfulness. Saturninus had blamed Calliopus for Rumex' death — a crude act of revenge for his dead lion. Calliopus had denied that; according to him Saturninus had good reason himself to kill off his prize gladiator: Rumex had been having an affair with Euphrasia.

'Euphrasia? Rumex pronged his own lanista's wife?'

'Easy access to the storecupboard,' cracked Anacrites.

It certainly made sense of our conversation with the other two gladiators and their hints about Saturninus not wanting to look too closely at the female admirers who pursued Rumex. Calliopus had put a real bloom on the story, even telling Anacrites that in the days when they briefly worked together, his rival's wife had flaunted herself at *him*. He made her out to be a trollop and Saturninus to be furious, bitter, vindictive, and without doubt prone to violence.

Helena looked dour. She and I had witnessed the supposed adulteress at home, standing up to her husband and teasingly defying his wishes when it suited her. Helena would merely describe that as having an independent streak.

'So is this yet another doe-eyed dame with a bit of brashness in her character, who sleeps with muscle-men for excitement? Or has the beautiful, gentle, utterly unflawed Euphrasia just been slandered appallingly?'

'I'll go and ask her,' announced Helena Justina bluntly. Anacrites and I exchanged a faintly nervous glance.

Meanwhile I told how Saturninus had taken a different tack, making out that Calliopus was an unstable figure nursing ludicrous jealousies. He jumped to mad conclusions. He fired off on outrageous schemes for revenge when nothing had been done to him. His barracks was struggling, he refused to admit it, and — if we believed Saturninus, who explained it most reasonably — Calliopus had lost his grip on reality. He too was portrayed as being capable of murder, naturally.

I had asked Saturninus himself why he had removed the original minders from Rumex and locked up the corpse. He wheeled out a plausible tale that he needed to keep the deceased hero's room secure from looters and trophy hunters while he had a chance to interrogate the men – who were, after all, his slaves – and to punish their slack vigilance. I asked to interview them. They were produced: flogged, subdued, and unable to tell me anything of use.

I then suggested that Saturninus call in the vigiles, since it was a case of unnatural death. He nodded vaguely. When I made it clear I intended to report it myself, he responded at once, sending out a messenger hotfoot to the local guardhouse. As usual, wrongfooting this man was impossible.

As I discussed all this with Anacrites and Helena I was feeling depressed. Deep pessimism descended on me. Bad signs were already there. The feuding Tripolitanians would supply motives for one another until our hair fell out. What they said about each other could be entirely true or just as false; their home town rivalry and their failed business ventures were motives for mutual hatred. Even if neither of them were really involved in the death of Rumex, accusations and counter-accusations would fly.

There were inconsistencies. Calliopus had always struck Anacrites and me as too well-organised to engage in impetuous spite; besides, although his business was smaller than his rival's, we knew he was *not* struggling financially. As for sexual jealousy, in my opinion Saturninus was fully in control of his domestic life, with a long-term wife from his native shore; if they ran into difficulties he seemed more likely to reach an accommodation with Euphrasia than to explode over a fling, even one with a slave.

I think I knew, even that night, where we would end up. The vigiles would discover nothing to link either man to the crime. Neither would we. Nobody else would be implicated in the killing either.

Helena did visit Euphrasia. To our surprise the woman readily admitted having slept with Rumex. She pointed out she was not alone in that. She seemed to regard having first pick of her husband's men as a perk of her position. She said Saturninus did not like it, though however deeply he cared he had no need to stab the gladiator. He could have matched Rumex in a public fight without quarter, a fight to the death – and earned money from it too. Besides, as an ex-fighter himself, his weapon was not the dainty blade that had been used on Rumex but a short sword, the gladium. Saturninus also would have killed with the arena death thrust.

'That's through the neck, of course,' commented Anacrites.

Both lanistae had produced impeccable alibis, Calliopus proving he was at the theatre with his mistress (in his wife Artemisia's absence at the Surrentum holiday home) and Saturninus declaring he had been out to dinner with Euphrasia, which cleared her too. Very gallant. And meticulously convenient – as I had learned to expect.

Alibis were immaterial. Both men owned groups of trained killers. Both knew plenty of murderous types outside their own exercise yards who could be coerced into bad deeds. Both could wield seriously persuasive quantities of cash.

There was one particular suspect to check up on: Calliopus' allegedly rogue bestiarius, Iddibal. I went to interview him. I was told he had been bought out by a rich aunt, and had left Rome.

Now that did smell suspicious. I had seen the supposed 'aunt' with him, so I knew she existed. But as a gladiator, Iddibal was a slave. Apparently he had originally been a free volunteer, but his status had changed when he enlisted. When he signed up, he had sworn the oath of complete submission: to the whip, the branding iron, and death. There was no backing out. No lanista would ever let his men hope for escape. Gladiators were held to their gory trade by the knowledge that their only route to freedom was through death: their own, or those of the men and animals they vanquished for the pleasure of the crowd. Once in, only many victories could bring escape; being bought out was never a possibility.

Anacrites was with me when I put this to Calliopus. We told him he was liable to be drummed out of the guild of lanistae for allowing the unthinkable. He squirmed and said the woman had been very persistent, her offer had been financially attractive, and anyway Iddibal had been regarded as a troublemaker, moody and unpopular, ever since he joined. Calliopus even claimed Iddibal had had a wall-eye.

It was nonsense. Early in our investigation, I remembered seeing Iddibal throwing spears among his colleagues with good humour and a very keen aim. I also remembered one of the keepers telling me that when the crocodile who ate another member of staff was put down in the arena it was done by 'Iddibal and the others'; that sounded as though in the venatio he had been at least one of the pack, if not actually a leader. Calliopus said no; we thought he was lying. Deadlock again.

We managed to trace Iddibal's movements on the night of the Rumex killing. He had gone, along with the so-called aunt and her servant, all the way to Ostia. We should have caught them there, but the party had actually sailed south in December, a suicidal risk. We could not think how they had persuaded a captain to take them at that time of year. The woman who had plucked Iddibal from the barracks must be absolutely loaded. Anacrites solved it: she owned her own ship. More curious still.

We decided Iddibal had run away from a wealthy home, and had now been fetched back by his family. Perhaps his auntie was a real one. He had bunked off from Rome for good, anyway, whether he had in fact gone home to mother, or bunked off with some hot-blooded widow purchasing herself a stud.

'This is sordid,' said Anacrites. 'Trust a spy to be a prude.

One further line remained unexplored: the ex-praetor Urtica. Camillus Verus reckoned that the man had not put in an appearance at the Curia for some time. Even the sensational tales about his love life had died down. Magistrates may retire from politics, but a taste for sleazy behaviour tends to last. Pomponius Urtica *might* just be lying low to let his reputation pick up again – but the mauling theory seemed more likely to be true.

Once again I travelled out to the Pincian, this time determined to gain admittance if I had to wait all day. This time they told me the truth: Pomponius Urtica was at home, but very sick. The porter stated that he had gout. I said he could talk to me in between groans, and I somehow managed to force my way in as far as the antechamber to the great man's bedroom.

While the attendant doctor was consulted, I noted large quantities of medical equipment, including a bronze stand in the encouraging shape of a skeleton, which had three branches for cupping vessels. Those could be used for a variety of ailments, not least to create diversionary bleeding above a wound. Numerous rolls of bandage were neatly stored on a shelf. There was a smell of pitch – used for sealing holes in flesh, of course. A box with a sliding lid had compartments with hinged lids which contained several ground-up medicines. I stole a pinch of one powder that had been nearly used up and checked it later with Thalia, an expert in exotic substances. 'Opobalsamum, I'd say. From Arabia – costs a packet.'

'The patient can afford it. What's opobalsamum used for, Thalia?'

'Wounds, mainly.'

'How does it work?'

'Gives you a warm glow thinking that anything that costs so much must do you good.'

'An efficacious decoction?'

'Give me essence of thyme. Where is he hurt?'

That I could not tell her, for I never saw the man. His doctor barged out from the bedroom, highly annoyed at me being there. He mentioned an ague, then wouldn't discuss the gout story. Servants were called to escort me from the house in a style that only just stopped short of compensatable assault.

I then tried to see Scilla, the ex-praetor's supposedly wild girlfriend. I always enjoy interrogating a woman with a dirty past; it can pose a challenge in several ways. Scilla was not having it. She lived at the praetor's house – and she stayed indoors. As a female way of life it was suspiciously respectable, though I sounded like a cad when I went home and said so.

Thwarted at every turn, Anacrites and I went back to routine enquiries. That meant asking questions of everyone who was known to have been at the barracks the night Rumex was killed, in the hope that someone would remember seeing something unusual. The vigiles were following up the case in parallel with us, though all their enquiries turned up negative too. Eventually they filed the case in their 'No further action' pigeon-hole, and not long afterwards, so did we.

XXXV

Well, don't blame me.

Sometimes there is quite simply nothing to follow up. Life is not a fable, where stock characters seethe with implausible emotions, stock scenes are described in bland language, and every puzzling death is succeeded in regular progression by four clues (one false), three men with crackable alibis, two women with ulterior motives, and a confession which neatly explains every kink in events and which indicts the supposedly least obvious person – a miscreant any alert enquirer could unmask. In real life when an informer runs a case into the ground, he cannot expect a fortuitous knock on the door, bringing *just* the eyewitness he wants, with confirmation of details that our shrewd hero has already deduced and stored in his phenomenal memory. When enquiries run into the ground it is because the case has gone cold. Ask any member of the vigiles: once that happens you may as well go sheep-shearing.

Better still, have a drink in a winebar. There you may possibly strike up a conversation with a man you haven't seen for twenty years, who will spin you an intriguing yarn about a mystery he hopes you can solve for him.

Don't bother: his wife's dead and buried under the acanthus bed; the tortured wag with the haunted eyes who is cadging the house bilgewater off you in this pitiful manner is the bastard who put her there. I can tell you this without even meeting him. It's just a knack. A knack called experience.

People lie. The good ones do it so niftily that however hard you press them you will never catch them out. That presupposes you can even tell which liars you should be pressing. It's pretty hard, when in the real world everyone is at it.

Witnesses are fallible. Even the rare specimens of humanity who honestly want to help may fail to spot the vital scene taking place under their noses, or they misread its significance. Most of them simply forget what they saw.

Draft blackmail letters are never left lying around. Anyway, who needs a draft to say, *Give me the money, or else?*

If footprints turn up in a newly dug asparagus patch, they never belong to anyone with an easily identifiable limp.

Long-term bullied spouses do not devise schemes of fiendish complexity and then trip themselves up over some tiny detail. They just snap, then grab the heaviest household tool available. The sexually jealous boil over equally messily. The financially greedy may plot with some skill how to escape detection, but they tend to walk away with the money and are long gone, using a new identity, before you even start your detective work.

Murderers sometimes, somehow, do manage to approach their victims when no one is looking. They kill in silence, or when nobody notices the gurgles and thumps. They leave the scene unobserved. Then they sometimes keep quiet for ever.

The fact is, many murderers get away with it.

I suppose the trusting among you still believe I am now going to say that Anacrites and I gave up – yet then stumbled by chance upon a clue?

Excuse me. Go back to the start of this scroll and read it again.

XXXVI

Hello. still waiting for an unexpected development?
There was none. It happens. It happens all the time.

XXXVII

Since Falco & Partner were unable to solve who had killed Rumex, we returned to our commission for the Censors. We were not men who became obsessed. I, Marcus Didius Falco, was an ex-army scout and an informer of eight years standing: a professional. Even my partner, who was an idiot, could recognise a dead end. We felt frustrated, but we handled it. After all, we had our fortunes to earn. That always helps maintain a rational attitude.

At the end of December was Saturnalia, my daughter's first. At seven months, Julia Junilla was still too young to understand what was going on. Far from clamouring to be King-for-the-Day, our prim miss hardly noticed the occasion, but Helena and I happily made fools of ourselves arranging presents, food and fun. Julia endured it gravely, already aware that her parents were as crazed as a cheap pot. Since we had no slaves we made Nux take the role of lording it over us; Nux got the hang of being insubordinate very fast.

Saturninus and Calliopus both left Rome, ostensibly for the festival. When neither had returned after several weeks, I made enquiries and discovered both had now gone to Africa, taking their wives. Hunting, it was said. Lying low, we thought. I asked at the Palace if we could head off in pursuit but, unsurprisingly since there was no evidence against either man in the Rumex case, Vespasian sent word that we were to buckle down to our Census work.

'Ow!' said Anacrites. I just got on with it.

For three months we worked harder than either of us

had ever done. We knew these enquiries were a finite goldmine. The Census was supposed to take a year, and it would be difficult to extend much beyond that unlesss we had exceptional grounds. We just made out our report on the evidence we had, and the culprit was told to cough up. This was a job where suspicion alone sufficed. Vespasian wanted the income. If our victim was important it was wise to be able to substantiate our accusations, but in the arena world 'important' was a contradictory term. So we suggested figures, the Censors issued their demands, and most men did not bother to ask if they could appeal. In fact, the grace with which they accepted our findings told us we perhaps even underestimated their degree of fraud. Our consciences, therefore, remained clear.

Of course we did have consciences. And we hardly ever had to bend them into shape.

I received a letter from Camillus Justinus who had reached the city of Oea, thanks to the money I had sent. After some swift exploration, he confirmed that Calliopus had no 'brother', though he did own a thriving business supplying beasts and gladiators for the local Games as well as exporting them; the arena was a highly popular sport in all parts of Tripolitania. Horribly Carthaginian. A religious rite, replacing actual human sacrifice, in honour of the harsh Punic Saturn − not a god to tangle with.

Justinus supplied enough details of the lanista's Tripolitanian landholdings for us to inflate our estimate of unpaid tax in his case by a satisfying whack. In return for these efforts I sent the fugitive lad my drawing of silphium, though no more money. If Justinus wanted to make a fool of himself in Cyrenaïca, nobody was going to blame me.

The day after the letter went off my mother was visiting; as she poked around in her usual fearless way she saw my rough for the sketch.

'You messed that up. It looks like a mildewed chive. It should be more like giant fennel.'

'How do you know, Ma?' I was surprised anyone in the

backstreets of the Aventine would be familiar with silphium.

'People used the chopped stem, like garlic; it wasn't a veg on its own. And the juice was a medicine. Your generation thinks we were all dumbclucks.'

'No, Ma. I just think you lived on short rations and this is a highly-prized luxury.'

'Well, I know silphium. Scaro tried to grow it once.'

My great-uncle Scaro, deceased whilst in pursuit of the perfect false teeth, had been a noble character; a complete liability, in fact. I had dearly loved the crazy experimentalist, but like all Ma's relations out on the Campania, his schemes were ludicrous. I had thought I knew the worst of them. Now I learned he had tried to break into the notoriously well-protected silphium trade. The merchants of Cyrenaïca may have cherished their ancient monopoly, but they reckoned without my family, it seemed.

'He would have been rich, if he'd managed it.'

'Rich and daft,' said Ma.

'Did he obtain seeds?'

'No, he pinched a cutting from somewhere.'

'He was in Cyrenaïca? I never knew that.'

'We all thought he had a girlfriend in Ptolomaïs. Not that Scaro ever admitted it.'

'Dirty old rogue! But he can't have had much hope of a crop.'

'Well your grandfather and his brother were always hunting myths.' Ma said that as if she held Grandpa responsible for some aspects of my own character.

'Did nobody tell them silphium had never been domesticated?'

'Yes, they were told. They reckoned it was worth a try.'

'So Great-Uncle Scaro sailed off like an overweight, slightly deaf Argonaut? All set on plundering the Gardens of the Hesperides? But silphium grows in the mountains – our market garden isn't a hillside in Cyrene! Was Scaro ever able to reproduce the right conditions?'

'What do you think?' answered Ma.

She changed the subject, now taking me to task for renting an office over at the Saepta Julia, too close to Pa's evil influence. Anacrites had obviously pretended that this was my idea, not his. He was a shameless liar; I tried to expose him to Ma, who just accused me of denigrating her precious Anacrites.

There was not much danger of Pa subverting my loyalty. I almost never saw him, which suited me. Working at full stretch, Anacrites and I were hardly ever in the office during the months after New Year. I was rarely at home, either. It was hard. The long hours took their toll on us, and also on Helena. When I saw her, I was too tired to say much or do much, even in bed. Sometimes I fell asleep in my dinner. Once we were making love. (Only once, believe me.)

Like any young couple attempting to get established, we kept telling ourselves the struggle would be worth it, while all the time our dread slowly grew. We felt we would never escape from the drudgery. Our relationship had come under too much strain, just at the time when we should have been enjoying it most sweetly. I became bad-tempered; Helena was run down; the baby started crying all the time. Even the dog gave me her opinion; she made a bed under the table and refused to come out when I was around.

'Thanks, Nux.'

She whined dolefully.

Then things really went wrong. Anacrites and I submitted our first major fees claim to the Palace; unexpectedly, it came back unpaid. There was a query against the percentage we had charged.

I took the scrolls up to the Palatine and demanded an interview with Laeta, the chief clerk who had commissioned us. He now maintained that the amount we were charging was unacceptable. I reminded him it was what he himself had agreed. He refused to acknowledge that and proposed instead to pay us a fraction of what we had expected. I stood there gazing at the bastard, all too well aware that Anacrites and I had no supporting contract document. My original bid existed, the inflated tender I had been so proud of swinging; Laeta had never confirmed in writing his agreement to the terms. I had never thought it mattered, until now.

Contractually, right was on our side. That didn't matter a damn.

To strengthen our case, I mentioned that our work had first been discussed with Vespasian's lady, Antonia Caenis, implying in the most delicate way that I was subject to her patronage. I still had faith in her. Anyway, I was certain she had taken a shine to Helena.

Claudius Laeta managed to disguise his undoubted relish and assume a suitably doleful face: 'It is with regret that I have to inform you Antonia Caenis recently passed away.'

Disaster.

For a moment I did wonder if he might be lying. Senior bureaucrats are adept at misinforming unwelcome suppliants. But not even Laeta, a snake if I ever met one, would compromise his professional standing with a lie that could be so easily checked and disproved. His deceit was always the unquantifiable kind. This had to be true.

I managed to keep my face expressionless. Laeta and I had a history. I was determined not to show him how I felt.

In fact he appeared slightly subdued. I had no doubt that cutting the rate was his idea, yet he seemed daunted by the personal damage to me. He had his own reasons: if he ever wanted to use me in future for off-colour official work, this knock-back would inspire me to new flights of rhetoric in telling him to disappear up his own rear end – and without leaving a clue of thread to find his way out.

Like a true bureaucrat he was keeping options open. He even asked if I wanted to make a formal request for an interview with Vespasian. I said yes please. Laeta then admitted that the old man was currently keeping to himself. Titus might be prevailed upon to look into my problem; he had a sympathetic reputation, and was known to favour me. Domitian's name never even came up; Laeta knew how I felt about him. Possibly he shared my views. He was the kind of smooth senior politician who would regard the young prince's open vindictiveness as unprofessional.

I shook my head. Only Vespasian would do. However, he had just lost his female partner of forty years; I could not intrude. I knew how I would behave if I ever lost Helena Justina. I did not suppose that the grieving Emperor would feel in a mood to approve exceptional payouts to informers (whom he used, but famously despised), even if their rates had been agreed. I did not know for sure that Antonia Caenis had ever spoken to him about me; anyway now was the wrong moment to remind him of her interest.

'I can make you a payment on account,' said Laeta, 'pending formal clarification of your fees.'

I knew what that meant. Payments on account are made to keep you happy. A sop. Payments on account are volunteered when you can be damned sure that is all that you will ever get. Turn down the offer, though, and you go home with nothing at all.

I accepted the stage-payment with the necessary grace, took my signed voucher for the release of the cash, and turned to leave.

'Oh by the way, Falco.' Laeta had one final jab. 'I understand you have been working with Anacrites. Will you tell him that his salary as an intelligence officer on sick-leave will have to be deducted from what we pay to your partnership?'

Dear gods.

Even then the bastard had to have one more go at flaying us. 'Incidentally, Falco, we must be seen to do everything properly. I suppose I ought to ask: have you completed a Census declaration on your own account?'

Without a word, I left.

As I was storming from Laeta's office a clerk rushed after me. 'You're Didius Falco? I've a message from the Bureau of Beaks.'

'The *what?*'

'Joke name! It's where Laeta pensions off incompetents. They're a pokey section who do nothing all day; they have special responsibilities for traditional augury – sacred chickens and the like.'

'What do they want with me?'

'Some query about geese.'

I thanked him for his trouble then continued on my way.

For once I turned away from the Cryptoporticus, my customary route down to the Forum. I was spurning public life. Instead, I worked my way through the complex of pompous old buildings on the crest of the Palatine, out past the Temples of Apollo, Victory and Cybele, to the supposedly unassuming House of Augustus, that miniature palace with every pampering amenity where our first emperor liked to pretend he was just a common man. Devastated by the blow Laeta had delivered, I let myself stand high on the hill's crest above the Circus Maximus, looking across the valley, homeward to the Aventine. I needed to prepare myself. Telling Helena Justina I had worked myself into the ground just for a sack of hay would be hard. Listening to Anacrites whining was even worse to contemplate.

I bared my teeth in a bitter grin. I knew what I had done, and it was a grand old irony. Falco & Partner had spent four months gloating about the draconian powers of audit we could exercise over our poor victims: our authoritarian Census remit, from which there was so famously no appeal.

Now we had been shafted with exactly the same rules.

XXXVIII

To cheer me up, Helena Justina attempted to distract me by using her own money to hire a lecture hall to stage the recital of poetry over which I had been dreaming for as long as she had known me. I spent a long time preparing the best pieces I had written, practising how to recite them, and thinking up witty introductions. As well as advertising in the Forum, I invited all my friends and family.

Nobody came.

XXXIX

A dippy dog called Anethum, the property of Thalia, did his best to cheer me up that spring. He was a big, warm, floppy old thing who rolled the whites of his eyes manically, and who had been trained to act in pantomimes. He could play dead. A useful trick for anyone.

Anethum was making his début as a warm-up act at the Megalesian Games in honour of Cybele. These are a welcome highlight, starting off the theatre season in April when the weather improves, and are preceded by a drawn-out series of dauntingly peculiar Phrygian rites. As usual the whole business had started back in the middle of March with a procession of persons bearing reeds, which are sacred to Attis, the Great Mother's beloved, whom she apparently first discovered lurking in a bed of bullrushes. (A perfectly understandable act if he had any inkling that his future role was to castrate himself with a potsherd while in a crazed frenzy.)

A week later the Sacred Pine tree of Attis, cut at the dead of night, had been borne to the Temple of Cybele on the Palatine and hung up with wool and with violet crowns while the blood of sacrificial animals was splashed about. If you have a sacred pine tree, obviously you like it treated with reverence. This was followed by a street procession of the Priests of Mars, who leapt about vigorously to the accompaniment of sacred trumpets, causing a few stares in our sober city even though they did it every year.

Then, in honour of the wounds Attis inflicted on himself, the chief priest of the cult ritually slashed his own arm with a knife; given the very specific nature of what

Attis had endured, the fact it was only the priest's arm had always caused me great amusement. At the same time, a wild dance was being enacted around the Sacred Pine tree; to keep up his spirits the chief priest flagellated himself and his fellows with a whip hung with knucklebones; the priests' mutilations were later turned into permanent tattoos as a sign of their dedication. There were screams and yells from devotees, faint from fasting and hysterical from the dance.

More bloody rites and solemn liturgies occurred for those who still had the stamina, followed by a day of formal rejoicing and the real start of the great festival. The reward for lasting out the blood and violence was a general carnival. Citizens of all ranks donned improbable masks and disguises. Thus freed from being recognised, they indulged in improbable behaviour too. Shocking. The priests of the cult, who were normally confined to their enclosure on the Palatine on the grounds that they were foreign and frenzied, were now let out for an annual bash. Flutes, drums and trumpets pounded out strange eastern music with unnerving rhythms as they whirled through the streets. The sacred image of the goddess, a silver statue, its head mystically represented by a great black stone from Pessinus, was taken to the Tiber and washed. The sacrificial implements were also cleaned up, then transported home in showers of rose petals.

Alongside the processional elements ran a secret women's orgy, famous for positively Bacchic scenes. Women who ought to know better tried to revive the old traditions, though in the new Flavian mood of respectability they were on to a loser there. 'I can assure you,' Helena assured me gravely, 'after the doors are closed to men, all that really happens is mint tea and gossip.' She then claimed that the rumours of frenetic debauchery were just a confidence trick to cause worry to the male sex, and I believed her, of course.

The Games started three days after the Kalends of April. Once again a procession bore the sacred image through the streets in a chariot, with the priests of the cult singing Greek hymns and collecting coins from the populace. (Always a useful way for people to dispose of out-of-date and foreign small change.) The chief priest took a prominent role; he was supposed to be a eunuch, a fact borne out by his wearing a purple frock, a veil, long hair under an exotic eastern turban with a peaked top and ear-lappets, necklaces, and a portrait of the goddess on his breast, while carrying a basket of fruit to symbolise abundance, plus a bundle of cymbals and flutes. Conch shells boomed alarmingly. It ought to be terribly exotic, a grim cult that should probably be expelled from the city, but for those who wanted to believe that Trojan Aeneas had founded Rome, then Mount Ida was where Aeneas hewed the wood for his ships and the Great Idaean Mother was the mythical mother of our race; Cybele was here to stay. You could see it as a lot more respectable than us all being descended from a pair of murderous twins who had been fostered by a she-wolf.

Once the Games started, we endured several days of earnest drama in the theatres. Then the chariot races took place in the Circus Maximus, with the statue of Cybele enthroned on the spina beside the central obelisk. She had been carried there in the solemn entry procession on a litter placed in a chariot drawn by tame lions. That had depressed me, remembering Leonidas.

By the time of the races I was in an oddly detached mood. The exotic rituals of the Megalesis had reinforced it. Normally one to avoid such festivals, I found myself taking part in the public gawping, yet in a grey spirit. This was Rome. Alongside the archaic mysteries of religion, other more sinister traditions still flourished: unfair patronage, grinding establishment snobbery, and the harsh cult of blighting the aspirations of the little man. Nothing would change.

It was with relief that we had reached the races and gladiatorial displays. That first ceremonial start, with the president of the Games clad in triumphal uniform as he led in the participants through the main gate of the Circus Maximus was always more vital than any of the succeeding summer shows. It heralded a new dawn. Winter was over. The procession trod on a carpet of spring flowers. The open-roofed theatres and circuses would hum with life again. The streets would abound with life by day and night. Competitive arguments would dominate public discussion. The ancillary trades – snack-sellers, betting touts, prostitutes – would flourish. And there was always a chance that the Blues would drive the Greens off the racetrack and come in victorious.

In fact the one bright spot in my life that April was that my team coasted home. It always carried the secondary benefit that any discomfiture of their arch rivals the Greens upset my brother-in-law Famia. That spring the Greens were fielding lousy teams; even the big Cappadocian greys of whom Famia had boasted to me so outrageously on the day the leopardess escaped were actually shipwrecked first time out. In between drowning his sorrows, Famia kept trying to persuade his faction to adopt a radical new purchase strategy, while the Blue teams thundered past them time and again and I enjoyed myself sniggering.

Work was slack. The Census assessments were tailing off, as they had been bound to. To help him forget how Laeta had cruelly axed his sick-pay, Anacrites busied himself tidying up final reports that were already satisfactory; I left him to grumble and tinker. Instead, one fine, bright day when most of Rome was feeling optimistic, I had volunteered to help Thalia present her wonderdog in his first public acting role. It was, of course, unthinkable for a respectable citizen to appear in a stage performance. But I felt gloomy and obstreperous; breaking the rules suited me just fine. I only pushed it to the limit: all I had to do was look after the dog when he was off-stage.

The pantomime was at the Theatre of Marcellus. It took place at the end of the morning, just before everyone transferred to the Circus Maximus for the races and

226

gladiatorial displays which would happen after lunch. This was a temporary measure: the great stone Amphitheatre of Statilius Taurus where gladiators used to perform had been destroyed in Nero's Great Fire ten years ago. The flamboyant new Flavian creation at the end of the Forum had been designated its formal replacement, but while that was being built the Circus Max stood in. Being the wrong shape, it was not entirely successful, so today we had an extra few hours of theatricals.

A lively programme had been advertised for later in the afternoon at the Circus: gladiators, a formal venatio, and to start with an execution of prisoners. One of them, finally, was to be the mass murderer Thurius.

Thurius, in whom I had such an interest, would be despatched by a new trained lion, the property of an importer called Hannobalus who had a curious history: although he was wealthier than anyone else Anacrites and I had investigated, we had been forced to conclude that this man's Census declaration was unimpeachable.

He came from Sabratha, but was otherwise a mystery man. As far as we were ever able to tell, he had told the Censors nothing but the truth – with an insolence that seemed to say he was doing *so* well in his business that deception was beneath him. We never met him; there was nothing in his accounts to make us demand an interview. He seemed to have a complete contempt for cheating – or as Saturninus, Calliopus and all our other subjects for study would call it, the finer points of accountancy. This man had paid an enormous tax bill as casually as if it were a snack-bar tab for two rissoles. His lion was reckoned to be first-rate too.

With my mind on the execution, it was hard to give Thalia's trained dog his due. However, we had planned that if he was a success I would turn the event to my advantage, so I had to concentrate. It was a comedy with a large cast of characters, its frenetic scenes accompanied by Thalia's circus orchestra – a fine ensemble which included the strenuous tones of long trumpets, circular horns, and

Sophrona the sweetly pretty water-organist. As the organ boomed a throbbing crescendo the dog trotted out, with his coat burnished and his tail up. Pretty quickly the audience allowed themselves to be won over by Anethum's appealing personality. He was a charmer, and he knew it. Like every playboy since antiquity, he was utterly brazen; the crowd knew they ought to have seen through him, but they let him get away with it.

At first the dog was merely required to pay attention to the action and behave appropriately. His reactions were good – especially since the ludicrous plot was so hard to follow most people just looked around for drink-sellers. At one point, for reasons I didn't tax myself with, one of the clowns on stage decided to do away with an enemy and supposedly poisoned a loaf. Anethum ate the bread, swallowing it down greedily. He then appeared to shiver, stagger, and nod drowsily as if drugged; finally he collapsed on the ground.

Playing dead, the dog was dragged about and hauled to and fro. When he continued to lie prone, however roughly he was towed across the stage, it looked as if he might really have been killed – a lousy sacrifice to popular taste in drama. Then, on cue, he slowly roused himself, shaking his great head as if waking from a deep, dream-filled sleep. He looked around, and then ran to the right actor, on whom he fawned with doggy joy.

He was such a good performor, his revival had an eerie quality. People were strangely moved. This included the president of the Games. As Thalia and I had known, today's president was not some half-baked praetor but, resplendent in a palm-embroidered triumphal robe, the Emperor himself.

When the play ended (a relief all round, frankly), word came down for the dog's trainer to attend on Vespasian. Thalia bounded off, followed by me on the end of Anethum's lead.

'New career, Falco?' As soon as Vespasian spoke, I knew

I would get nowhere. Straightening up after patting the wonderdog, the old man gave me one of his long cool stares. His broad forehead creased characteristically into a frown.

'At least dog-walking has the benefits of fresh air and exercise — that's better than working for the Censors, sir.'

As they queued to leave the theatre prior to walking around to the Circus, the crowd was making a lot of noise. Nobody was interested in what passed between the Emperor and mere proponents of a speciality act. My hope of achieving a decent life was being destroyed here, yet it attracted little public notice — and even less sympathy from Vespasian himself.

'Problem? Why can't you send in a petition decently?'

'I know what happens to petitions, sir.' Vespasian must be aware how they were deflected by the very clerks who were thwarting me. He knew all about the Palace secretariats. But he also had no truck with people insulting his staff.

I could see Claudius Laeta lurking among the retinue. The urbane bastard was in his best toga, and unconcernedly chomping a packet of dates. He ignored me.

Vespasian sighed. 'What's your gripe, Falco?'

'A difference over fees.'

'Sort it out with the bureau who commissioned you.'

The Emperor turned away. He only paused to signal a slave to bring Thalia a bulging purse in reward for her trained dog's charm and cleverness. Turning back again to salute her as she curtsied, Vespasian blinked a bit at the flutterings of her indecent skirts, then inadvertently caught my eye. He looked as though he was growling under his breath.

I said in a low voice, 'Helena Justina and I would like to offer our sympathies on your great loss, sir.'

I reckoned if Antonia Caenis had ever discussed my case, he would remember what she had said. I left it at that. This was how it had to be: I had made one last throw, and I would not try to pressurise him any more. That would spare him embarrassment. And it would spare me losing my temper in front of the sneering imperial retinue.

Thanking Thalia, I strode off to the Circus Maximus where I joined Helena at our seats in the upper terraces. Down below, they were already carrying in the placards which recorded the appalling deeds of the men who were to be executed. All around the stadium slaves were sweeping the sand smooth ready for the lions and criminals. Attendants were placing veils on the statues, lest the divine effigies be offended by the convicts' shame and the ghastly sights to come. The stakes to which the condemned criminals would be tied had been hammered into place.

The convicts themselves had been dragged in, chained together by the neck. They were huddled near an entrance, being stripped naked by an armour-clad warder. Surly deserters from the army, spindly slaves caught *in flagrante* with their noble mistresses, and a notorious mass murderer: a good haul today. I did not try to identify Thurius. Soon he and the rest would be dragged out and tied to their stakes; then the beasts, whom we could already hear roaring outside, would be loosed to do their work.

Helena Justina was waiting for me, pale and straight-backed. I knew she had come today because of my personal need to see Thurius die; she saw it as her duty to accompany me, though I had not asked her to do it. We shared our significant events. Supporting me, even when she loathed what was about to happen, was a task from which Helena would not flinch. She would hold my hand – and close her eyes.

Suddenly I was overcome by all the frustrations that had darkened my life for so long. I jerked my head. 'Come on.'

'Marcus?'

'We're going home.'

The trumpets were sounding to announce the gluttony of death. Thurius was being dragged out now to be eaten by the big new Sabrathan lion but we would not be watching the spectacle. Helena and I were leaving the Circus. And then we were leaving Rome.

PART TWO

CYRENAÏCA: April, AD74

XL

Cyrenaïca.

To be precise, the harbour at Berenice. Hercules had made his landing at the ancient seaport of Euesperides, but that had silted up since mythical times. At Berenice however, there was still an otherwordly atmosphere: the first thing we saw was a man slowly walking along the foreshore taking a single sheep for a walk.

'Goodness!' I exclaimed to Helena, as we sneaked a second glance to be sure. 'Is he exceptionally kind to animals, or just fattening it up for a festival?'

'Perhaps it's his lover,' she suggested.

'Very Greek!'

Berenice was one of the five significant cities: where Tripolitania had its eponymous Three, Cyrenaïca boasted a Pentapolis. Greeks do like to be part of a League.

Bonded with Crete for administrative purposes, this was a lousily Hellenistic province, and that was already apparent. Instead of a forum they had an agora, always a bad start. As we stood on the wharf, listlessly looking up at the town walls and the lighthouse on its little knoll, taking a holiday somewhere that looked so fixedly towards the East suddenly seemed a bad idea.

'It's traditional to feel depressed when you arrive at a holiday destination,' said Helena. 'You'll calm down.'

'It's also traditional that your qualms will be proved right.'

'So why did you come?'

'I was sick of Rome.'

'Well, now you're just seasick.'

All the same, as Nux chased around our feet desperately

counting us all like a sheepdog, we were at heart an optimistic party. We had left home, hard work, let-downs – and most happily of all for me, we had left Anacrites. With the spring sun warming our faces and the low hiss of a blue sea behind us, now that our feet were on firm dry land, we expected to relax.

Our party consisted of Helena and me, together with the baby – a factor which had caused ructions back at home. My mother was convinced that little Julia would be captured by Carthaginians and made a victim of child sacrifice. Luckily we had my nephew Gaius to guard her; Gaius had been forbidden to come by his own parents (my feeble sister Galla and her appalling absentee husband Lollius), so he ran away from home and followed us. I had dropped a few hints about where we would be lodging at Ostia, to help him catch up safely.

We also had with us my brother-in-law Famia. Normally I would have run the lengths of several stadia wearing full army kit before agreeing to share weeks at sea with him, but if all worked out, it was Famia who would be paying for our transport home: somehow he had persuaded the Greens that since their chariot horses had been performing so abysmally, it was in their interests to send him out here to buy fine new Libyan stock direct from the stud farms. Well, the Greens certainly needed to beef up their teams, as I kept pointedly reminding him.

For the voyage out we had acquired paying-passenger places on a ship bound for Apollonia. This enabled Famia to economise, or to put it another way, he was defrauding his faction of the full ship-hire costs for the journey out. They had told him to select a decent Italian vessel at Ostia for a two-way trip. Instead, he was just going to pick up a one-way packet home. Maia's husband was not essentially dishonest – but Maia had made sure he had no spending money, and he needed it for drink. She herself had declined to accompany us. My mother had told me on the sly that Maia was worn out by trying to hold the family together and had had enough. Taking her husband out of the country was the best service I could offer my sister.

It quickly became obvious that the whole reason for this trip as far as Famia was concerned was getting away from his worried wife so he could booze himself senseless at every opportunity. Well, every holiday party has one tiresome bore; it gives everyone else somebody to avoid.

Landing at this harbour was more in hope than earnest. We were trying to catch up with Camillus Justinus and Claudia Rufina. There had been a vague arrangement that we might be coming out to see them. Extremely vague. Back in the winter when I let Helena first mention the possibility in a letter to them at Carthage, I had been assuming my work for the Censors would prevent me indulging in this treat. Now we were here — but we had no real idea where along the north shore of this huge continent the two fugitives might have ended up.

The last we had heard from them was two months earlier, saying that they were intending to set off from Oea for Cyrenaïca and would be heading here first, because Claudia wanted to see the fabled Gardens of the Hesperides. Very romantic. Various letters which Helena was bringing them from their abandoned relations were likely to shake the dim-witted elopers out of that. The rich seemed to lose their tempers with their heirs in a formidable style. I did not blame Justinus and Claudia for lying low.

Since I was the informer, whenever we arrived at a strange town that might be unfriendly, it fell to me to scout it out. I was used to being pelted with eggs.

I enquired at the local temple. Rather to my surprise, Helena's brother had actually left a message that he had been here, and that he had gone on to Tocra; his note was dated about a month ago. His military efficiency did not quite dispel my fears that we were about to start on a pointless chase all around the Pentapolis. Once they left Berenice, our chances of making a connection with the flitting pair became much more slim. I foresaw handing over frequent emoluments to temple priests.

Our ship was still in harbour. The master had very generously put in here specially to allow us to make enquiries, and after he took on water and supplies he reloaded all our gear while we rounded up Famia (who was already trying to find a cheap drinking house), then we reboarded.

The vessel was virtually empty. In fact the whole situation was curious. Most ships carry cargos in both directions for economic reasons, so whatever this one was supposed to be fetching from Cyrenaïca must be extremely lucrative if there was no need to trade both ways.

The ship's owner had been on board from Rome. He was a large, curly-haired, black-skinned man, well-dressed and of handsome bearing. If he could speak Latin or even Greek he never obliged us with so much as a good morning; when he conversed with the crew it was in an exotic tongue which Helena eventually guessed must be Punic. He kept himself to himself. Neither the captain nor his crew seemed disposed to discuss the owner or his business. That suited us. The man had done us a favour taking us on board at reasonable rates, and even before the kindness of putting in at Berenice we had no wish to cause ructions.

Basically that meant one thing: we had to conceal from Famia that our host was even slightly tinged with a Carthaginian flavour. Romans are in general tolerant of other races – but some harbour one deeply embedded prejudice and it goes back to Hannibal. Famia had the poison in a double dose. There was no reason for it; his family were Aventine lowlife who had never been in the army or come within smelling range of elephants, but Famia was convinced all Carthaginians were gloomy child-eating monsters whose one aim in life was still the destruction of Rome itself, Roman trade, and all Romans, including Famia. My inebriated brother-in-law was likely to be racially abusive at the top of his voice if anything obviously Punic crossed his wavering path.

Well, keeping him away from our ship's owner took my mind off my seasickness.

Tocra was about forty Roman miles further east. By this time I was beginning to regret not taking the advice my father had boomed at me: to travel on a fast transport right out to Egypt, maybe on one of the giant corn vessels, then to work back from Alexandria. Pottering east in little stages was becoming a trial. In fact I decided the whole trip was pointless.

'No, it's not. Even if we never manage to find my brother and Claudia, it's served a purpose,' Helena tried to comfort me. 'Everyone at home will be grateful we tried. Anyway, we are supposed to be enjoying ourselves.'

I pointed out that nothing which involved me and the ocean would ever be real enjoyment.

'You'll be on land soon. Quintus and Claudia probably do need us to find them; their money must be running out. But so long as they are happy, I don't think it matters if we can't bring them home.'

'What does matter is that your father has contributed to our trip – and if he loses his son, his other son's betrothed bride, and then what it costs to fund us on an abortive mission, my name will be so black in the household of the illustrious Camilli at the Capena Gate, that even I won't ever be going home again.'

'Maybe Quintus will have found the silphium.'

'That's a charming thought.'

★

At Tocra the sea became much rougher; I decided that whether or not we encountered the fugitives, it was as far as I could bring myself to sail. This time when we disembarked, we said goodbye. The silent owner of the ship surprised us by coming to shake hands.

Tocra nestled between the sea and the mountains, where the coastal plain narrowed significantly so the inland escarpment – previously out of sight – appeared distantly as rolling hills. The city was not only Greek, but huge and hideously prosperous. Its urban élite lived in palatial peristyle homes built of a very soft local limestone, which quickly weathered in the brisk sea breeze. The lively wind whipped the white horses on the bay; it tossed the flowers and the fig trees behind the high walls of the gardens and caused sheep and goats to bleat in alarm.

Once again there was a message. This time it led us to the bad end of town, for even flourishing Greek-founded seaports have their low dives for visiting sailors and the slappers who attend them. In a seedy backroom in a raucous area, we discovered Claudia Rufina, all alone.

'I stayed behind in case you came.'

Since we had never said definitely that we were coming, that did seem odd.

Claudia was a tall girl in her early twenties, looking much slimmer and even more solemn than I remembered; she had acquired a rather vivid suntan which would have been out of place in good society. She greeted us quietly, seeming sad and introspective. When we knew her in her home province of Baetica and in Rome she had been a walking fortune, well-dressed, manicured, always expensively coiffured, and wearing ranks of bangles and necklaces. Now she was robed in a simple brown tunic and stole, with her hair loosely tied at the nape of her neck. There was little of either the nervous, rather humourless creature who had come to Rome to marry Aelianus, or the minx who had quickly discovered how to giggle with his more outgoing younger brother, then kicked up her heels and ran off on an adventure. That now seemed to have paled.

Without comment, we paid off her shabby landlady and took the girl to the better premises where we ourselves were lodged. Claudia grabbed Julia Junilla from my nephew Gaius and absorbed herself in the baby. Gaius gave me a disgusted look, and stalked out with the dog. I shouted out for him to look for Famia, whom we had lost again.

'So where is Quintus?' Helena asked Claudia curiously.

'He has gone on to Ptolemaïs, continuing his search.'

'No luck so far?' I grinned.

'No,' said Claudia, returning not the slightest flicker of a smile.

Helena exchanged a discreet glance with me, then took the girl off to the local baths lugging large quantities of scented oil and hairwash, in the hope that pampering would restore Claudia's spirits. Hours later they were back, reeking of balsam but no further forward. Claudia remained tortuously polite, refusing to unbend and spill gossip.

We passed her the letters we had brought from the Camilli and from her own grandparents in Spain. She took the scrolls to read in private. On her reappearance she did ask, in a rather strained voice, 'And how is Camillus Aelianus?'

'How do you think he is?' Respect for a bride who bunked off a week before her formal engagement was not my style. 'It's polite of you to ask, but he lost his betrothed – very suddenly. At first he thought you had been kidnapped by a mass murderer, so that was a bad shock. More importantly, he lost your winsome fortune, lass. He's not a happy boy. He has been viciously rude to me, though Helena still thinks I should be kind to him.'

'And what do you think, Marcus Didius?'

'As is my wont, I accept all blame with a tolerant smile.'

'I must have misheard that,' murmured Helena.

'I did not mean him to be hurt,' said Claudia wanly.

'No? Just humiliated, maybe?' If I sounded angry it was probably because I found myself defending Aelianus, whom I disliked. 'Since he's not getting respectably married, he stood down from the Senate elections this year. Now he's twelve months behind his contemporaries. Every time his career comes under scrutiny in future, he'll have to explain that. He will have cause to remember you, Claudia.'

Helena gave the girl a shrewd stare. 'I doubt if that

marriage would have worked. Don't blame yourself, Claudia,' she said. Predictably, Claudia herself did not react.

For a moment I wondered whether we could return Claudia to her snooty betrothed in Rome, and pretend the adventure with Justinus had never occurred. No. I could not be that cruel to either of them. If she now married Aelianus he would never forget what she had done. The public scandal might die down, but he was the type to harbour a deep grudge. Every time they wanted to quarrel he would be burning to drag up the past, while the normal self-righteousness that helps a woman survive being married to a bastard would be lost to Claudia. She had crossed the bridge into enemy territory, and cut off her own retreat. Now the barbarians were just waiting to descend on her.

We changed the subject and made plans for travelling to Ptolemaïs, to join Justinus. There was no way I would take ship again unnecessarily. It was only about twenty-five more miles along the coast, so I hired a couple of carts. Claudia had made some feeble suggestion about going by sea but I cut her short. 'If we start really early and push ourselves, we might force it in a day,' I assured her. 'All it needs is luck and military discipline.' She still looked miserable. 'Trust me,' I cried. The poor girl clearly needed somebody to invest her with spirit. 'All your cares are over, Claudia: I'm in charge now.'

Then I thought I heard Claudia Rufina mutter to herself, 'Oh Juno – another one!'

XLI

Things were getting worse. Ptolemaïs was even breezier and even more Greek. Whereas Tocra just butted out into the Mediterranean, Ptolomaïs actually had the sea lapping on two sides. Although its harbour was more sheltered, furious waves coursed at an angle in the open water, while flying sand stung us as we hacked into town from the west. Our journey had taken us two days, even though I had pressed on as hard as possible. The coast road was dismal. We found no way-station, and were forced to sleep rough overnight. I noticed that Claudia hunched her shoulders and said nothing, as though she had experienced this before.

By now the rolling green and brown hillocks of the Jebel came down almost to the city. Squeezed between the sea and the mountains, this was an offshoot of Cyrene, still further east. There were historic connections with the Egyptian Ptolomies (hence the name) and the neighbourhood was still used as a cattle-ranching area, fattening flocks for rich Egyptians who lacked pastures of their own.

It was a dry old place to have chosen to build; an aqueduct brought in a vital water supply, which was stored in huge cisterns under the forum. Yet again the meticulous Justinus had left word, so once we had struggled into the city centre, and found the right temple, and dug out the under-priest who was in charge of messages from foreigners, it only took us another hour or so to persuade the disinterested Greek-speaking burghers to give us directions to where he was staying. Needless to say, this was not among the well-appointed homes of the local wool and honey magnates, but in a district that smelt of fish-pickle, where the alleys were so narrow the tormenting wind whistled through your teeth as you battled around every corner. Also needless to say, even when we found his billet, Justinus was out.

We left a note ourselves, then waited for the hero to come to us. To cheer us up, I spent more of Helena's father's money on a slap-up fish supper. It was eaten in a subdued mood by tired, dispirited people. I had now acquired the traditional party-leader's role of irritating everyone and pleasing none, whatever I tried to organise.

'So, Claudia, did you ever see the gorgeous Gardens of the Hesperides?'

'No,' said Claudia.

Helena attempted to take a hand. 'Why; what went wrong?'

'We couldn't find them.'

'I thought they were near Berenice?'

'Apparently.'

Claudia's permanent pose of neutrality had slipped for a moment, and we could hear honest rancour growling through. Helena openly tackled the girl: 'You seem rather low. Is anything wrong?'

'Not at all,' said Claudia, putting down the uneaten half of her grilled red mullet for my dog, Nux. Dear gods, I do hate mimsy girls who pick at their food – especially when I have paid through the nose for it. I was never partial to women who seem unable to enjoy themselves; what was more, to have caused a scandal and then to be so unhappy about it seemed an atrocious waste.

Well, we only had to stick it out in snobbish Ptolemaïs for ten days before a message came from Justinus to Claudia saying he was now living in Cyrene, so there was yet another haughty Greek city waiting to despise us if we cared to trek that way.

This time it did seem as if it might just be worth bothering to pack up and transfer ourselves: Famia became very excited because he thought Cyrene was a good source of horses, Helena and I wanted to see the runaways together so we could try to work out what had gone wrong with them, and besides, Justinus' note had a coded tailpiece which we deciphered as, '*I may have found what I was looking for!*'

We had a satirical discussion about whether he had become so intellectual that he meant the secrets of the universe, but – not knowing that I had already arrived in the province – he had also instructed Claudia, '*Send for Falco urgently!*' Since everyone else agreed my presence was hardly necessary at a philosophical symposium, they reckoned I was needed to formally identify a sprig of silphium.

XLII

Meeting Camillus Justinus came as a huge relief. He at least looked the same as always: a tall, spare figure with neat, short hair, dark eyes, and a striking grin. He managed to combine an apparently unassuming air with a hint of inner strength. I knew he was confident, a linguist, a man-manager, courageous and inventive in crises. At twenty-two he should have been setting out on adult responsibilities in Rome: marriage, children, consolidating the patrician career that had once looked so promising. Instead, here he was at the back of beyond on a mad mission, his hopes dashed by snaring his brother's wench, offending his family, her family, and the Emperor – and all, we were beginning to suspect, for nothing.

The depth of Claudia's unhappiness became most fully apparent once we saw them together. Helena and I had taken a small house at Apollonia down on the coast. When the fabled Justinus eventually joined us, his greeting for his sister and me was far more joyous than the restrained smile with which he favoured Claudia.

Before we arrived they had been alone together for four months; inevitably they shared a visible domestic routine, enough to have fooled some people. She knew his favourite foods; he teased her; they often muttered together in a private undertone. There was no resistance when Helena put them sharing a bedroom – yet when she poked her head around the door nosily she came back to whisper that they had made up two different beds. They seemed just about friends – but by no means in love.

Claudia remained expressionless. She ate with us, went to the baths, came to the theatre, played with the baby, all as if she lived in a world of her own. She made no complaint, but she was holding her tongue in a way that condemned all of us.

I took Justinus aside. 'Do I gather you have made a terrible blunder? If so, we can face it, and deal with it, Quintus. In fact, we must do so—'

He looked at me as if what I said was hard to understand. Then he said curtly that he would prefer other people not to interfere in his life. Helena had been receiving much the same reaction when she tried to probe Claudia.

We cracked it almost by accident. Famia, who was still loosely attached to us, had gone into the interior hunting for horses as he was supposed to, so that had relieved us of one strain. He could drink as he pleased so long as there was no direct pressure on me to keep him sober for the sake of my sister and her young family.

I was starting to understand what life back at home must be like for Maia: Famia preferring to be almost always absent, and tiresome when he did appear; Famia constantly raiding the household budget for wine money; Famia proclaiming loud social jollity at unsuitable moments; Famia forcing other people either to share in his relentless habit, or else making them seem tight-arsed if they tried to save him from himself. Maia would be much better off without him – but he was the father of her children, and really too far gone to abandon.

My nephew Gaius had disappeared for a walk on his own. He had always been a free spirit, and although being part of a group like this generally did him good, he scowled with hostility if he was too closely supervised. Helena thought he needed mothering; Gaius was a tyke who had decided otherwise. I preferred not to tether him too tightly. We were settled in Apollonia; he knew his way around and he would come home when he was ready. He had left Julia with us. The baby was happily playing with a stool she had learned to push around the floor, crashing it into the other furniture.

At last, in private, it seemed an occasion to talk about silphium. The prospects of a fortune were vast if Justinus really had rediscovered the plant, and we brought the subject up indirectly, a delicate acknowledgement of the enormous dreams that might be about to be realised for all of us. As usual in families, being indirect only led to a row about something quite different.

Helena and I, Claudia and Justinus, had been partaking of a fairly basic lunch. Somehow the conversation touched on our first landing at Berenice, and although Helena and I carefully avoided any mention of Claudia's thwarted yearning to visit the Gardens of the Hesperides, in discussing our own sea trip a question was asked about how the other pair had endured their sailing from Oea. That was when Justinus came out with his astonishing remark: 'Oh we didn't sail; we came by land.'

It took a moment to sink in. His sister must have been harbouring suspicions already; while I wiped chickpeas off my chin with a napkin, Helena addressed the issue rather tersely: 'You don't mean all the way?'

'Oh yes.' He pretended to be surprised that she had asked.

I glanced at his fellow traveller. Claudia Rufina was pulling grapes individually from a bunch; she ate each one very carefully, then removed the pips from between her front teeth with exquisite good manners, laying them around the rim of a plate in a neat border, equally spaced. She might have been fortune-telling lovers – only her lover was supposed to be the young man sitting here.

'Tell us about it,' I suggested.

Justinus had the grace to grin. 'We had run out of money, for one thing, Marcus Didius.' I shrugged, accepting his slight rebuke that I could have been more generous with financial help. Like a true patrician, he had no real idea how tight my budget was. 'It was my idea – I wanted to emulate Cato.'

'Cato?' enquired Helena, in a frosty tone. I wondered if this was the Cato who always came home from the Senate in time to see his baby bathed. Or perhaps it was the baby, when grown up. At any rate, my darling had stopped approving of him as a model.

'You know – in the wars between Caesar and Pompey he brought his army all around the Bay of the Sirtes and surprised the enemy.' Justinus was showing off his education; I refused to be impressed. Education is not as good as common sense.

'Amazing,' I said. 'They must have been flabbergasted when he first appeared. It's desert all the way, I believe – and am I right, there is no proper road along most of the coast?'

'Afraid not!' conceded Justinus, impossibly cheerful. 'It took Cato thirty days on foot – we had a couple of donkeys, but we needed longer. It was quite a trip.'

'I should think so.'

'Obviously there is a coastal track that the locals use – and we knew it must go all the way, because Cato had marched through successfully. I thought it would be a grand adventure for us to do the same. Well, in the opposite direction of course.'

'Of course.'

'It must have been hard?' suggested Helena, dangerously quietly.

'Not easy,' her younger brother confessed. 'It took absolute dedication and army-style methods.' Well, he had those. Claudia was a delicately reared young lady from a pampered home. Basic training for an heiress consists only of assaults on Greek novels and a gruelling small talk course. Still fired with enthusiasm, Justinus carried on, 'It was five hundred miles of utterly tedious, seemingly endless desert – all dead flat, for week after week.'

'Places to stay?' I asked neutrally.

'Not always. We always had to carry water for several days; sometimes there were cisterns or wells, but we could never be sure in advance. We often camped out. The small settlements were a long way apart.'

'Bandits?'

'We were not sure. They never attacked us.'

'What a relief.'

'Yes. We just had to flog on, expecting the worst. Nothing but a distant glimpse of the blue ribbon of the sea on the left hand side, and the horizon on the right. Bare dry sand, with tufts of scrub. After Marcomades, the land started to roll a bit, but the desert still went on for ever. Sometimes the road meandered inland a little way, but I knew that so long as we sometimes caught a glimmer of the sea on our left, we were still going in the right direction ... We saw a salt flat once.'

'That must have been very exciting!' Helena said crisply. Claudia ate another grape, with no shadow of a smile. The salt flat must be a hideous memory, but she was blotting out the pain. 'I am trying to imagine,' said Helena to her brother, 'what a catastrophe this must have been for Claudia. Expecting only a shipboard romance and starlit happiness. Finding herself instead cast into an endless desert, in fear of her life. A thousand miles from a hairdresser, and in entirely the wrong shoes!'

A brief silence fell. Helena and I were stunned by what the crazy lad had revealed. Perhaps Justinus finally sensed a critical atmosphere. He polished his plate with a piece of bread.

'How long did it take you?' I ventured, still in a neutral tone.

He cleared his throat. 'Over two months!'

'And Claudia Rufina endured all this with you, Quintus?'

'Claudia has been very intrepid.'

Claudia said nothing.

He was off again: 'As you travel east, there tend to be a few datepalms. Eventually there are flocks – goats, sheep, occasionally cows, horses or camels, then towards Berenice, the terrain starts rolling. I'll never forget the experience. The sea and the sky, the way the desert changes colour to a harsher grey as dusk starts falling—'

Very poetic. Claudia still looked ominously unmoved.

The dead weight of her silence spoke of utter misery. I could work out just how much Justinus was omitting of discomfort, thirst, heat, the threat of marauders, the dread of the unknown. Not to mention their personal relationship rapidly falling apart.

'We did it, that's the main thing.' For him, that was clearly true. For Claudia, her life must have been blighted for ever. 'As I said, we could not afford a ship. Had I not driven us on relentlessly, we would be out there still somewhere – probably dead.'

Claudia Rufina stood up suddenly and left the room; in fact, she left the house. We heard the door slam. Upstairs a shutter rattled so hard its catch fell off. Justinus winced, but did not move; I suppose he had already heard plenty from her about how she felt. Unwilling to let a young woman of my party wander a strange city alone in distress, I hauled myself to my feet and followed the girl.

I left Helena Justina starting to explain to her once favourite brother how most people would regard him as guilty of outright cruel stupidity, not to mention unspeakable selfishness.

XLIII

The city of Apollonia lies at the far edge of a flat plateau which runs out to the sea below an upland where the more refined foundation of Cyrene queens it over the whole area. Down on the red-sanded, rock-strewn, fertile plain, the seaport has a location of great beauty, even though it lacks the panoramic views which Cyrene enjoys from the heights above.

Apollonia is a long habitation, fronding the beach so closely that in really rough weather floods crash into the glamorous temples near the water's edge. The handsome peristyle houses of the Hellenistic traders and landowners are for the most part more judiciously set back. Yet even the most gracious of these habitations nestle close to the inner and outer harbours. Those embrace a rich variety of shipping which throngs the slipways at all times of year. Trade is the life of Apollonia. Trade has for centuries made it one of the most prosperous ports, sited within striking distance of Crete, Greece, Egypt and the East – yet as good a jumping off point for Carthage, Rome, and all the eager markets at the west end of the Mediterranean. Even without silphium, the stink of money vies with the salt tang off the sea.

That bright afternoon, Claudia Rufina had walked rapidly past the well-spaced sunlit mansions; they looked grand enough to be civic palaces, though since Cyrenaïca is administered from Crete they were in fact huge, ostentatiously lavish private homes. As usual at the habitations of the vulgarly rich, there was little sign of life. An occasional bodyguard polished the brightwork on a parked chariot, looking bored, or a neat maid walked out silently on some routine errand. Of the wealthy owners we saw nothing; they were collapsed in stodgy siestas, or might even be living elsewhere.

Eventually, at the eastern extremity, past the outer harbour and beyond the town itself, Claudia emerged on a switchback track which obviously led somewhere, so she kept going. I was a short distance behind her; she would have spotted me if she had looked back, though she never did.

It was hot and peaceful, a tranquil stroll through coastal scenery. Even in her girlish sandals Claudia kept up a cracking pace, despite the increasingly rough and informal track. The terrain climbed slightly. She breasted one ridge at the edge of town only to see another rise in the ground just ahead. Wrapping her stole around her more closely, Claudia strode directly to the further ridge, then abruptly disappeared. Nervous, I speeded up. A startled plover rose almost under my boot and headed inland.

The air was clear as I sprang up the slope. To my left, the sea was stunningly blue, with a series of small islands or rocky outcrops near the shore. Breakers thundered in a cute cove, way below. A steep drop had opened before me. I stopped short; I caught my breath.

Cut into the encircling cliff that had once formed a secluded little beach, was the most perfectly sited amphitheatre. It was in a sad condition, crying out for restoration by some high-minded public benefactor. The approach from the city had brought us out right at the top, with immediate access to the upper rows of seats. While I stood aloft like a statue on the roof of a temple, Claudia had climbed down several of the precarious terraces, where she was now seated with her elbows on her knees and her head in her hands, sobbing hysterically.

I let her get her troubles out of her system for a while. I had to think out what to do. She had been treated appallingly by her crass young lover, and must be ready to throw herself at any sympathetic older man who offered her support. The situation could be dangerous.

I stood still, with the wind dragging my hair and my feet planted apart for balance. From up here the oceanic horizon seemed to stretch in a semicircle. The beauty and isolation of the setting caught the heartstrings. If your life was good, then standing here, drenched in sunlight and exhilarated from the long walk over rocky ground, could make you glow with contentment. But if your soul already grieved for some desperate reason, the melancholy tug of sea and sky would be unbearable. For the sunken, shuddering girl below, sitting all on her own where there ought to be a noisy, sun-bleached audience, this heart-stopping theatre provided a desolate scene in which to dwell upon all she had thrown away.

Once she seemed quieter, I climbed down to her. I made enough noise to warn her that I was coming, then I sat alongside on the steep stone blocks. I felt the trapped heat strike up warm through the cloth of my tunic; the edge of the stonework scratched against the back of my thighs. Claudia must have blown her nose and wiped her eyes, though her face was still wet as she stared out over the stage below us to where the breakers were pounding hard on the pale sand of the cove. She came from Corduba, which has a rather marshy river but is well inland; perhaps for her the call of the sea here would be stirringly exotic.

'The noise of the waves must be quite a challenge for performers.' I chose a neutral remark on purpose. I wished Helena was here to do this for me.

I struck a casual pose, with my arms folded and one boot stuck out. I sighed thoughtfully. Claudia remained expressionless. Soothing young women when they are suffering can be hard work. I too stared out at the horizon. 'Cheer up; things can only improve.'

I sensed that further tears were streaming down Claudia's face, as she ignored my advice.

'However bad it looks to you at the moment, you

haven't ruined your life. Nobody suggests going back to Aelianus – but you can face it out and marry someone else, in Rome or Baetica. What do your grandparents suggest?' Primed before I left Rome, I knew they had written to her that they forgave her. (This took the most practical form – permission to draw on their bankers for funds.) She was all they had – always a good position to hold on the board game of life. 'You're an heiress, Claudia. You can afford to make more mistakes than most people. Some men will admire your initiative.' Or her full coffers, anyway.

Claudia still made no response. When I was younger she would have been a challenge, but now I liked my women to have character. It was more fun if they answered back.

'You know, you really must talk to Quintus. Helena and I had a terrible quarrel once. Part of it was that she thought what I had done to make her angry ought to be obvious. I just believed she had given up and dumped me . . . I mean, if it's Quintus you want, Claudia, I'm sure that can be sorted out.'

At last she did turn and look at me.

I carried on bravely. 'He doesn't know. He really does not understand how horrible your journey was for you. He thinks it is sufficient that you shared an exciting experience and both survived it—'

'He knows how I feel,' Claudia said abruptly, as if defending him. Her tone was too dry, however. 'We had a long talk about that.' Her very restraint told me how angry the argument must have been.

'The trouble with Quintus,' I offered cautiously, 'is that he may not feel too sure yet what he wants from life—'

'Oh he told me what he wants!' scoffed Claudia. Her grey eyes blazed as she announced crossly, 'According to him, this is the tale: when he was with you in the forests of Germania Libera, Marcus Didius, he had an encounter with a beautiful and mysterious rebel prophetess, whom he was forced to leave behind but who will haunt him all his life.'

I myself had spent a great deal of effort concealing that

story in his interests once we returned to Rome. Trust bloody Justinus to tell the one person to whom he should never have confessed.

Claudia stood up. Now she sounded even angrier than I expected: 'It's nonsense, of course. Who did he really have an affair with? I hope it wasn't a tavern trollop; he may have caught a disease. Was it some married tribune's wife?'

Everyone in Rome reckoned that Justinus had had a romance with an actress after he came home; apparently Claudia had not heard that one. I cleared my throat nervously. I thought it best to maintain that her beloved had never sought to confide in me.

'Can I help make this easier for you, Claudia?'

'Not really. Thank you for your advice,' she said coldly. Then she turned and climbed back up the steep rows of seats on her way home, still furious, still heartbroken, yet disconcertingly self-assured.

Done it again, Falco. While I had been so busy worrying about comforting the distraught girl, she had simply felt patronised. She did not welcome my well-meant intrusion. She was utterly straightforward, and thought she could manage everything herself.

I knew Helena well enough; I should have expected this: some sad women don't fall into your open arms, they punch you in the eye. I was lucky Claudia Rufina was too shy to kick me as she went past.

After a few moments of grinning ruefully to myself, I went down to shore level, exploring the theatre. I found Gaius and Nux sunbathing on the beach. I joined them and we relaxed; we threw pebbles and picked seaweed to pieces for a while, then we lads peed against the back of the stage to mark our territory, and since we hadn't eaten for a couple of hours we all strolled home.

Helena Justina had obviously had a blazing row with her brother, who had gone out in a huff. Helena herself was tight-lipped and silent, sitting outside in the shade nursing the baby with her back to the house; she was performing a nice impersonation of someone wanting to be left alone, so naturally I went up behind her and made my presence felt. Being rebuffed by one female never put me off trying the next one I met. Helena at least allowed me to embrace her, whether she wanted it or not.

Famia had come in and collapsed; he was now snoring loudly. Claudia had returned and set herself to prepare dinner for everyone else with a martyred air, as if she were the only sensible person in our group.

It was perhaps true, though if she stuck with it, her future would be lonely, hard-working and glum. There was a spark to her sometimes that I knew made Helena think the girl deserved more. Part of the spark, the only hope of redeeming her, was that Claudia did want better for herself.

The upshot was that even when Justinus returned home that night, we deferred our discussion of silphium. But the next day when the atmosphere had quietened down, he told me that he had found what he believed was a plant of it, growing in an isolated spot many miles away. To visit it, we would be obliged to leave the women, since it could only be reached on horseback. That suited him, of course. And I won my permit to travel from Helena because she thought that spending time alone with Justinus would give me a chance to sort out his love life.

I didn't exactly see how that would work. In my opinion, sorting out a fellow's love life requires at least one woman to be present. Still, I was a perfectionist.

XLIV

It was a fine day towards the end of April when Justinus and I approached the scene of his possible find. We were on horseback, a fact I was seriously regretting, for after four days of hard riding we must have travelled nearly a hundred Roman miles. It might have been more appropriate to calculate the distance in Greek *parasangs* since we were in Cyrenaïca, but why bother; it would not have saved my sore backside.

He had brought me over the hills, somewhere not too far from the coast on the eastern bulge of the province, near where you turn left heading for Egypt. I know that's vague. If you think I intend to be more precise about the possible location of a priceless commodity, known only to me and one close associate, you can think again!

There is a legal restriction, in any case. Justinus and I had a brief but brutally tight contract, drawn up for us by Helena before we set out. Maintaining confidentiality about the product we were in business to exploit was its most critical term. Helena Justina had made us both swear to keep silent in perpetuity.

It was a relief that we had got ourselves away from the troubled atmosphere at Apollonia. In fact even Helena and Claudia had decided they needed a change of scene and were to depart for new lodgings; fired by Justinus' description of the refined city of Cyrene, they were heading there. He and I had made the mistake of querying the possible expense, only to have two independent women inform us they both had their own money, and since we were leaving them with only Gaius and the baby for an unknown period of weeks or months, they would make whatever arrangements suited them, thank you very much.

We had promised to return as soon as possible and rescue them from any difficulties they might let themselves be lured into, and they had then described to us a cauldron in which we could boil our heads.

Before we set out, I had chewed on the musty piece of leaf which Justinus produced as a sample. If I had had any choice, instead of galloping off into unknown terrain, exploring the Greek delights of Cyrene would have suited me best too. The so-called silphium was disgusting. Still, nobody eats raw garlic, and I myself had a high disdain for truffles. Owning a world monopoly was the aim. Luxuries only have to be scarce, not nice. Participants' enjoyment is in thinking they have something other people can't acquire or afford. As Vespasian said to Titus about their lucrative urine tax: don't mock the moolay, even if it stinks.

So here I was. Whether Justinus and I were truly galloping off towards endless chests of chinkies, I did doubt.

'Tell me, how did you set about finding this magical herb, Quintus?'

'Well, I had your sketch.'

'That was wrong, I gather. According to my mother I should have drawn you something more like giant fennel.'

'So what does fennel look like?' Justinus asked, apparently serious.

I watched him thoughtfully, as he forged eagerly ahead. He had a good seat on a horse. He had mastered Rome's least favourite mode of transport with the easy grace he applied to everything. Bareheaded, but with a length of cloth around his neck which he could wind over his dark hair when the sun grew stronger, he seemed to fit in here just as easily as I had seen him merge into Germany. His family had been mad to think they could tie him down to the numbing routine and pomposity of the Senate. He was too acute to stomach the low standards of debate. He would hate the hypocrisy. He enjoyed action too much to be penned into the eternal round of slow dinners among elderly bores with winestains down their togas whom he was supposed to court, unworthy patrons who would be jealous of his talents and energy.

He looked back with that daredevil grin. 'It was a missing plant hunt, Marcus Didius. I set about my mission the way you would pursue a missing person. I went to the scene, studied the ground, tried to win the confidence of the locals, and eventually started asking discreet questions: who saw the stuff last, what its habits were, why people thought it had disappeared, and so forth.'

'Don't tell me it's being ransomed by kidnappers.'

'No such luck. We could infiltrate and retrieve it then—'

'With missing persons, I always assume sex is involved somewhere.'

'I'm too young to know about that.'

'You're not so innocent!'

Perhaps sensing I was about to probe the issue with Claudia, the sly lad burbled, 'Anyway, one aspect I had to deal with was that people might not welcome my enquiries.'

'I don't like the sound of this.'

'I can see two difficulties. One: if the story of the silphium being overgrazed by animals is true, whoever owns the greedy flocks will want to continue to pasture them unhindered. I was told the nomad herdsmen actually tore up silphium by the roots to get rid of it.'

'So they definitely won't be pleased to see us,' I agreed.

'Two: the land where this stuff grows is the hereditary property of the tribes who have always lived here. They may well resent strangers appearing and taking an interest. If the plant was to be exploited again, they might want to control it themselves.'

I coaxed my mount past a little bush that was filling him with foolish terror. 'So you think that going after silphium might be quite dangerous?'

'Only if people see us looking, Marcus Didius.'

'You do know how to reassure me.'

'Suppose we really have found silphium again; people must realise what sort of investment it represents. The whole of the economy of Cyrene once depended on this. We will have to reach an accommodation with the landowners.'

'Or pinch a bit and grow it on land of our own.' I was thinking of Great Uncle Scaro. Of course according to Ma, his experimental snippets all fell down and died. Also according to my mother, of course, the family member I most took after was my hopeless great-uncle.

'Could we cultivate silphium in Italy?' Justinus asked.

'It was tried. Many people had a go down the centuries – if they could lay hands on it, which the smart Cyrenians tried to prevent. A relative of mine attempted to take cuttings, without any luck. Seeds might work better, though we'd have to work out whether to plant them when they ripened up or in the green. Be prepared: the whole reason silphium was so rare was that it only grew in the particular conditions here. The prospects for transplanting it or cultivating it elsewhere are bleak.'

'I wouldn't mind acquiring land out here.' Justinus sounded more than pioneering; he had the grim air of a young man who was resolutely turning his back on all he knew.

'The problem with *that*, Quintus, is that even the locals don't have enough fertile soil to go around.' I had done some research. From the time of Tiberius, Roman efforts at administering this province had mainly consisted of sending out surveyors to adjudicate land disputes.

Justinus looked defiant. 'Why don't you say, and anyway, I belong in Rome?'

'You have to decide for yourself where you belong.'

We flogged on past a few hundred more bushes, each one a source of discontent for the fragile horse I had hired. The only good thing about him was that he was easier to quieten than the agitated people I had cast myself among. If this horse had a tricky love life, he was bravely hiding it. Though when I tried to chivy him along, he ignored it just as stubbornly as everybody else did. Frankly, this was a trip where my funds of compassion were starting to run low.

The day we expected to arrive at the plant site was when things livened up unexpectedly. As we trotted along, trying to merge into the landscape to save us having to invent excuses for being there, shouts disturbed the peace. We ignored them, which led to a series of shrill whistles, then hoarse yells, and finally a thunder of hooves.

'Don't run.'

'Nowhere to run to.'

'What are we going to say?'

'I'll leave that to you, Marcus Didius.'

'Oh thanks.'

A group of five or six mounted locals surrounded us, jabbering loudly and waving their arms. They were brandishing long spears, which we eyed with diffidence. Obviously we were for it. We reined in, aiming to be helpful, since there was no alternative.

Communication was minimal. We tried Greek, then Latin. Justinus applied a friendly smile and even attempted Celtic; he knew enough of that to buy hot damson pies, seduce women, and halt wars – but it carried no weight here. Our captors became more angry. I grinned like a man who was confident that the Pax Romana had spread to every corner of all provinces, while I actually swore obscenely in several unpleasant tongues that I had learned at a low moment of my past career.

'What's up, do you think, Quintus?' I asked, leaning on my horse's neck and playing innocent.

'I don't know,' he murmured, this time through his teeth. 'I just have an uncomfortable feeling these may be representatives of the warlike Garamantes!'

'Would those be the famous, very fierce Garamantes whose traditional recreation is to ride out of the desert looking for plunder? The ones who tend to kill anyone who crosses their path?'

'Yes, didn't we fight a war against them recently?'

'I think we did. Can you remember if we won?'

'I believe a commander called Festus chased them back into the desert, cut them off in a cunning manner, and gave them a smart thrashing.'

'Oh good for him. So if these stalwart fellows are some remnant of a raiding party who survived being slaughtered, they will know we are not to be trifled with?'

'Either that,' agreed my phlegmatic young companion, 'or they are hot for revenge and we're in deep shit.'

We kept up the brilliant smiles.

We extended our repertoire by shrugging a lot, as if helpless to grasp what was wanted. That was pretty plain: we had to ride off with these excitable fellows the way they wanted us to go – and we had to do it immediately. Expecting to be robbed and thrown down a ravine, we let ourselves be nudged along with them. We were armed with swords, though they were in our packs, since we had not expected hairy entertainment. As the men jostled us, still loosing off excited shouts which meant nothing to us, we tried to maintain a cool demeanour; meanwhile inside we were growing increasingly alarmed.

'The Garamantes were in Tripolitania,' Justinus decided.

'So these are the friendly Nasamones? Do they like Rome, Quintus Camillus?'

'I'm sure they do, Marcus Didius.'

'Oh good!'

In fact whoever they were, we had not far to go in their lively company. Quite suddenly we came upon a large party of others, and a dramatic scene that made everything clear: we had stumbled unwittingly into the middle of a lion hunt. Far from capturing us, our new friends had been saving us from being speared or eaten alive. We smiled at them a great deal more, while they laughed back merrily.

It was a scene of well-directed mass activity that must have taken weeks – and a lot of money – to organise.

Justinus and I could now appreciate just how unwelcome it must have been to find two bumbling travellers had strayed directly into the hunters' path. There was an army of men involved. Even the semi-permanent camp to which we were taken had a retinue of attendants and several cooks grilling game for lunch on huge fires behind the neatly pitched lines of tents. Even without seeing the rest we deduced there were scores of them.

From a nearby knoll we could see what was happening. Bleating sheep and even cows were confined in several pens to act as bait. The pens were at the end of a huge funnel made from nets, brushwood and torn-up trees, reinforced by rows of overlapping shields. Towards this elaborate snare came the mounted huntsmen and beaters on foot. They must have assembled much earlier, miles out in open country, and were now at the climax of their long drive, gathering closer and forcing their prey into the trap. Towards us came all sorts of creatures: small herds of long-horned gazelle, high-stepping ostriches, a huge, highly desirable lion, and several leopards.

We were offered spears, but preferred to watch. That what happened shortly was routine in North Africa was evidenced by the men who stayed lounging in camp, hardly moved by the excitement, draining the odd goblet in a relaxed way even at the climax of the hunt. Meanwhile their companions had speared some of the animals when things looked dangerous, but wherever possible cages were brought up in a rush and the beasts were caught alive. The hunters worked hard and fast, with a well-practised rhythm. It looked as if the party had been established here for weeks, and were nowhere near finished. From the large quantity of game being captured it could only have one market: the amphitheatre in Rome.

I had an odd *frisson* of recognition: suddenly, during what had passed for a private, pastoral interlude, I had been reminded directly of my forgotten work back home.

After an hour or so the chase quietened down, although the disturbing roars of the newly caged animals and the frightened bleating of the hapless penned flocks who knew they were bait continued to fill the air. Hot and sweaty, the hunters arrived back in camp in a noisy group, some bloodstained, all exhausted. They threw down their long spears and oval shields, while attendants ran to tether their drenched horses. As the thirsty men quaffed huge quantites of drink and boasted about their day's efforts, Justinus and I, each gnawing rather daintily on pieces of spatch-cocked grilled game, were led off looking sheepish so we could meet the man in charge.

He was climbing down from a high-wheeled cart drawn by two mules, which bore a reinforced cage with a sliding door. From within came the unmistakable deep roar of a fierce Libyan lion. The whole cart shook as the beast threatened to burst out of the outrageous confinement, hurling itself against the sides of the cage. Even the head man, who was of no mean size and strength, leapt from his perch hastily, though the cage held fast. Attendants laughed; he laughed with them, perfectly at ease. Covers were flung over the cage so the beast would quieten down in the dark, and extra ropes were lashed on. Then the man turned to inspect us and he realised, as I had done as soon as we approached him, that he and I had met before. It was the owner of the ship which had brought my party from Ostia.

'Hello,' I grinned, though from past experience I did not expect much conversation with him. 'Quintus, how's your Punic?' Justinus was a great one for picking up smatterings. I knew he would not have wasted his visits to Carthage and Oea. 'Would you mind greeting this character and telling him I'm delighted to renew our acquaintance, and that as he can see, I found you in the end?'

The Punic fellow and Justinus exchanged a few remarks, then Justinus turned to me rather nervously while the big dark man watched my reaction with that close attention that meant he was either insulting my grandmother – or had just made some terrible joke.

'He wants me to ask you,' said Justinus, 'what's happened to that drunk you had with you on his ship, the one who hates Carthaginians?'

XLV

Deploring Famia's horrible habits kept the fun going for an hour or two. We managed to get through the rest of the day, and an obligatory night of feasting and very heavy drinking, without being forced to explain too accurately why we were riding in a suspicious manner around the uninhabited parts of Cyrenaïca. Justinus did most of the talking, and luckily his head for wine was worse than mine so he passed out while we were still in control of the situation; he had managed to avoid indiscretions about our search for the silphium. The big Punic character was an entrepreneur. He was energetic and showed a driving ambition. We did not want him to hear our story and decide that harvesting herbs would be easier work for him than hunting Circus beasts.

As it turned out, we need not have worried about disguising our intentions. When we clambered on to our horses next morning, almost unable to stay upright, the man in charge, now our close crony, came to see us off and shared a few more sweet nothings with my companion. As they talked, Justinus seemed to be laughing at something and looking my way. We all exchanged extremely polite salutes and groaned over our thick heads, then we two rode off very gingerly.

'What were you two giggling over?' I said, once we were clear of the camp. 'It looked like our Punic playmate was announcing that he would sell me his daughter – the ugly one, probably.'

'It was worse than that,' sighed Justinus. He waited patiently while I explained to my horse that a tiny clump of bristly bush could not be a crouching leopard because all the leopards for miles around were in the huntsmen's cages. 'I found out, dear Marcus, why he never asked what we are doing here.'

'How come?'

'He thinks he knows.'

'So what's our secret?'

'It's yours. You're Falco — the Emperor's Census examiner.'

'He's heard of me?'

'Your fame has a long reach.'

'And he's an importer of beasts. I should have thought of it.'

'Hanno thinks you are spying on some soon-to-be-hammered defaulter.'

'Hanno?'

'Our lion-hunting host.'

'I'll tell you something else,' I said, grinning over it to some extent. 'Hannobalus is the romanised name of a tycoon from Sabratha who runs a huge animal import business for the Games in Rome. This must be the same man. Quintus, our genial host at the camp last night has already been the subject of a penetrating enquiry by Falco & Partner.'

Justinus went even more pale than he already had been due to his hangover. 'Oh dear gods! Did you hammer *him*?'

'No; he has a brilliant accountant. I had to let him off.'

'That's fortunate.' Justinus had rapidly recovered powers of logical thought, despite his headache. 'If you had imposed too many penalties, last night the excellent Hanno could have fed us to a lion.'

'And no one the wiser! Let's hope he could tell that our meeting was coincidental. He has a host of men, armed to the teeth.'

'And all the time,' mused my gentle companion, 'we two are just two innocent plant-hunters!'

'Speaking of which, I think you're overdue to present me with your fabled little sprout of greenery.'

Later that day, somewhere before — or maybe after — Antipyrgos, Quintus Camillus Justinus, disgraced son of the most noble Camillus Verus, did produce his sprout for me, though it was not little.

'Olympus, it's grown a bit since I found it!' he marvelled, as the monstrous tussock towered alongside him.

I tipped back my head, shading my eyes from the sun as I admired his treasure. The bigger the better. It was leaning a bit, but looked healthy. 'It's not exactly dainty. How in Hades could anything that size ever get lost?'

'Now we've found it again we could guard it with a dragon like the Apples of the Hesperides, but this plant might eat the dragon—'

'It looks as if it could eat us too.'

'So: is that it, Marcus?'

'Oh yes.'

It was silphium all right. There was just this one, the largest plant I had ever come across: not exactly a pot-herb to grow in your window box. The bright green giant had reared itself over six feet high. It was a coarse, bulbous unattractive creature, with strappy leaves pushing up out of one another to form a thick, central stem. Prominent on top of the stout column was one very large sphere of yellow flowers, an allium-like globe of individual bright gold blossoms, with much smaller clusters nodding on long fine pedicels that came from the junctions of leaves lower down the plant.

My horse, which had been so terrified of every other growing piece of greenery, decided to sniff the silphium with unconcealed interest. We gulped, and rushed to tie him up safely out of reach. We took note; this precious plant was attractive to animals.

Justinus and I then adopted the only possible course for two men who had just discovered a fortune growing in the wilds. We sat down, fetched out a flagon we had brought along for this purpose, and drank a frugal draft to destiny.

'What now?' asked Justinus, after we had toasted

ourselves, our future, our silphium plant, and even the horses who brought us to this elevated spot.

'If we had some vinegar we could make a nice jar of silphium marinade to soak lentils in.'

'I'll bring some next time.'

'And some bean flour to stabilise the sap. We could tap the root for resin. We could cut some stem and grate it on a roast—'

'We could slice it up with cheese—'

'If we needed medicine, we have a wonderful ingredient.'

'If our horses needed medicine, we could dose them.'

'It has an abundance of uses.'

'And it will sell for a *huge* amount!'

Chortling, we rolled about in sheer delight. Soon, every apothecary's snailshell of this treasure would pour profits into our banker's chests.

Our hunter friend Hanno from Sabratha had fed us on decent drumsticks last night, but had not gone so far as to send us on our way with a brace of birds to picnic on tonight. All we actually had to eat was army-style baked biscuit. We were tough lads; we travelled in discomfort to prove the point.

I did trim off a little piece of silphium leaf, to see whether the taste I had winced at in Apollonia could be improved upon. In fact fresh silphium seemed even worse than the elderly version that I had tried before. It smelt of dung. In the raw its taste was as disgusting as its smell forewarned.

'There must be some mistake,' decided Justinus, losing heart. 'I was expecting ambrosia.'

'Then you're a romantic. According to Ma, when silphium is cooked the bad taste vanishes – virtually. And your breath afterwards is – more or less – acceptable. But she reckoned it causes unavoidable wind.'

He recovered himself. 'People who will be able to afford this treat, Marcus Didius, won't need to care where they fart.'

'Quite. The rich make their own social rules.'

We farted ourselves, on principle. As Romans we had been granted this privilege by the kind-hearted, conscientious Emperor Claudius. And we were in the open air. Anyway, we were going to be rich. From now on, we could behave objectionably whenever and wherever we liked. Freedom to expel flatulence without comment had always struck me as the main benefit of wealth.

'This plant of ours is flowering,' observed Justinus. His record as an army tribune was impeccable. His approach to logistical problems never failed to be incisive. He could come up with a reasonable order of the day, even when ecstatic and slightly drunk. 'It's April. So when will there be any seeds?'

'I don't know. We may have to sit this out for a few months before they form and ripen. If you see any bees passing, try to entice them over and speed the stripy fellows on to the flowers. Tomorrow when it's light we'll go for a stroll around the jebel and look for a feather. Then I can try tickling up our big boy by hand.' Real horticultural spoiling lay in store for this baby of ours.

'Anything you say, Marcus Didius.'

We rolled ourselves into our blankets and settled down for one last nightcap under the stars. This time I made a toast to Helena. I was missing her. I wanted her to see this plant of ours, growing so sturdily in its natural habitat. I wanted her to know that we had not failed her, and that soon she would be able to enjoy all the comforts she deserved. I even wanted to hear her caustic comments on the coarse green brute that was supposed to make her lover and her little brother rich.

I was still waiting for Justinus to honour Claudia with similar politeness, when I grew tired of keeping my eyes open, and drifted off to sleep.

XLVI

The tinkle-tonkle of retreating goatbells must have woken me.

It was a wonderful morning. We both slept late, even on the bare ground. Well, we had had a hundred-mile ride, a long night of heavy festivities with a wealthy hunting party, great excitement here in secret, and too much to drink again. Besides, with the prospect of an enormous income, all the troubles of our lives were solved.

Perhaps we should have eaten some of our hard rations last night, while we sat up dreaming of the palatial villas we would own one day, our fleets of ships, the glittering jewels with which we would adorn our adoring women-folk, and the huge inheritances we could leave to our expensively educated children (so long as they grovelled enough as we declined into our well-kept old age) . . .

My head ached as if I had a troop of dancing elephants restyling my haircut. Justinus looked grey. Once I had glimpsed the glaring sunlight as it bounced off the rocks, I preferred to keep horizontal, with my eyes closed. He was the poor devil who sat up and looked around.

He let out a tortured groan. Then he yelled. After that he must have jumped up and thrown back his head, as he howled at the top of his voice.

I too was sitting up by then. Part of me already knew what must have happened, because Camillus Justinus was a senator's son so he had been brought up to be nobly undemonstrative. Even if a vintner's cart drove over his toe, Justinus was supposed to ignore his bones cracking but to wear his toga in neat folds like his ancestors, then to speak nicely as he requested the driver to please move along. Yelling at the sky like that could only mean disaster.

It was quite simple. As the star-filled desert night faded to dawn, while we two still dozed like oblivious logs, a group of nomads must have wandered past. They had taken one of our horses (either despising mine, or else leaving us the means to escape alive out of quaint old desert courtesy), and they had stolen all our money. They had robbed us of our flagon, though like us they rejected the biscuit.

Then their flocks of half-starved sheep or goats had devoured the surrounding vegetation. Taking offence at our silphium, before they meandered off on their age-old journey to nowhere, the nomads had yanked out any remaining shreds of our plant.

Our chance of a fortune had gone. There was almost nothing left.

While we stared in dismay, one lone brown goat skipped down from a rock and chewed up the last sun-baked threads of root.

XLVII

To Greeks, Cyrene was a blessed hole in the heavens that had dropped to earth for them to colonise. A foundation at least as old as Rome, the high ridge where the city stands looks so much like Greece itself that the drought-ridden Therans who had been sent forth by the Oracle of Delphi and who were led here by helpful Libyans must have thought they had nodded off and somehow sailed back home again. From the scrubby grey hills where quails abound, there is a stunning vista over the far plain below to the gleaming sea and the ever-thriving port of Apollonia. The deep wooded valleys of the high jebel are as peaceful and mysterious as Delphi itself. And everywhere is filled with the perfumes of wild thyme, dill, lavender, laurel, and small-leaved mint.

This highly aromatic place was not, to be frank, a good place for two dispirited lads who had just failed in their hunt for a lost herb.

Justinus and I had climbed slowly and gloomily up towards the city one sunlit, pine-scented morning, arriving on the Way of the Tombs; it brought us through a haunting necropolis of ancient grey burial houses, some of them free-standing against the hillside, some carved deep into the native rock; some still tended, but a few long deserted so their rectangular entrances with worn architectural features now stood agape and offered homes to deadly, poisonous, horned vipers who liked lurking in the dark.

We paused.

'The choice is, either to keep searching or—'

'Or to be sensible,' Justinus agreed sadly. We both had

to think about that. Good sense beckoned like a one-eyed whore in a tosspots' dive, while we tried to look away primly.

'The choice element only applies to you. I must consider Helena and our child.'

'And you already have a career in Rome.'

'Call it a trade. Being an informer lacks the glorious attributes of a "career": glamour, prospects, security, reputation – cash rewards.'

'Did you earn money working for the Censors?'

'Not as much as I was promised, though more than I had been used to.'

'Enough?'

'Enough to get addicted to it.'

'So will you stay in partnership with Anacrites?'

'Not if I can replace him with somebody I like more.'

'What is he doing now?'

'Wondering where I vanished to, presumably.'

'You didn't tell him you were coming here?'

'He didn't ask,' I grinned.

'But you will continue as a private informer after you go home?'

'It's traditional to say, "that's the only life I know". I also know it stinks, of course, but being a fool is a talent informers revel in. Anyway, I need to work. When I met your sister I set myself the quaint goal of becoming respectable.'

'I understood that you already had the money to qualify for the middle rank. Didn't your father give it to you?'

I surveyed Helena's brother thoughtfully. I had assumed this would be a discussion of his future, yet I was the one being grilled. 'He loaned it. When I was turned down for social promotion by Domitian, I handed the gold back.'

'Did your father ask you for it?'

'No.'

'Would he lend it again?'

'I won't ask him.'

'There's trouble between you?'

'For one thing, giving the money back when he wanted to look magnanimous caused even more strife than asking for help in the first place.'

It was Justinus' turn to grin. 'So you didn't tell your father that you were coming out here either?'

'You're getting the hang of the merry relationships between the fighting Didii.'

'You rub along though, don't you?' As I choked on the suggestion, Justinus gazed across the valley below us, to the far plain and the faint haze where the land met the sea. He was ready for his own family confrontations: 'I ought to go home and explain myself. What do you reckon my relationship with my own father will be like nowadays?'

'That may depend on whether your mother is sitting in the room at the time.'

'And it certainly alters if Aelianus is listening in?'

'Right. The senator loves you – as I am sure your mother does. But your elder brother hates your guts, and who can blame him? Your parents can't ignore his plight.'

'So I'm for punishment?'

'Well, even though dear Aelianus may suggest it, I don't suppose that you'll be sold into slavery! Some administrative posting to a dull place where the climate is dank and the women have bad breath will no doubt be found for you. What are those three blotty dits on the map where nothing ever happens? Oh yes: the tiny triple provinces of the Maritime Alps! Just a couple of snowed-in valleys each, and one very old tribal chief whom they hand around on a rota—'

Justinus growled. I let him brew for a moment. It was clear from his expression and the way he had broached the subject that he had been thinking hard in private.

'How about this?' he suggested diffidently. A big question must be coming. 'If you think it might be suitable: I could come home and work for you until next spring?'

I had half expected it, including the qualifier. Next spring, he would be planning to return here to look for more silphium; maybe that fond dream would evaporate eventually, though I could see it haunting Justinus for years, along with his lost forest prophetess. 'Work for me? As a partner?'

'As a runner, I should think. I have too much to learn, I know that.'

'I like your modesty.' He could bring himself down to street level if he had to. It was too much to hope he could live that low for ever, though, and I was now looking for permanence. 'Within limits, it's an appealing idea.'

'May I ask what the limits are?'

'What do you think?'

He faced the truth with customary bluntness: 'That I don't know how to live rough. I can't talk to the right sort of people. I have no experience to judge situations, no authority – in fact, no hope.'

'Start at the bottom!' I laughed.

'But I do have talents to offer,' he joked in return. 'As you know, I can read a drawing even if it's inaccurate, speak Punic, and blow a military trumpet when required.'

'*Clean, mild-mannered lad with sense of humour seeks position in established firm . . .* I can't offer you houseroom. But can you face a bachelor apartment of the crudest, most inconvenient kind? I should think that by the time we return home my old friend Petronius is bound to have set up with some new woman, so you could be slotted in at Fountain Court.'

'That's where you used to live?' Justinus did sound nervous. He must have heard just how bleak my old apartment was.

'Look, if you want to come in with me, you have to drop out of patrician society. I can't absorb some dandy whose idea of being my runner is scuttling home to his mother every five minutes for a clean tunic.'

'No. I see that.'

'Well, I'll say this: if you really want to live in squalor and work for nothing, with only the occasional beating-up for light relief, I would be prepared to take you on.'

'Thanks.'

'Right. If you want an audition, you can start here: my theory is that when you have a disaster to announce to your womenfolk, you should be plotting a real bummer to hold in reserve. While they start wailing about the lost silphium, they can hear about us going into partnership; then the first problem won't sound so bad . . .'

'So how are you going to tell Helena and Claudia about the silphium?'

'I'm not,' I said. 'You are. You want to work for me, this is what happens: the junior goes in and makes them cry – then I come along looking manly and dependable, and mop up their tears.'

I was joking. I reckoned Helena and Claudia had both thought we were mad to attempt the search for silphium, and neither would be the least surprised if we came back empty-handed.

It took us a long time to find them. The gracious Greek city of Cyrene stretched over a large area, with three different central areas. In the north-east lay the Sanctuary of Apollo, where a sacred spring dashed over a rockface into a laurel-bordered basin; in the north-west stood a mighty Temple of Zeus; in the south-east was the acropolis and the agora plus other characteristics of a large Hellenistic spread, to which had been added all the attributes of a great Roman centre too. This was a vast city with a great many pretensions, a few of them actually deserved.

We searched the civic centre together. There was a large, square handsome forum, enclosed within a walled Doric colonnade, and at its centre instead of the rather prim Augustan-style imperial monuments of modern Roman towns, a brazen Temple of Bacchus (where the priests had no messages for us). None of the Greeks and native Libyans milling happily together at the basilica had heard of Helena and Claudia, for which I suppose we should have been grateful. We made our way out to the

Street of Battus, named for the city's founding king, passed a very small Roman theatre, paused to observe a pair of red-striped snails screwing each other into oblivion on the pavement, saw the Greek theatre with its wide cold seats to accommodate the big bottoms of the sprawling élite.

We moved on to the agora. There we failed again to find our girls, though we had the chance to admire a naval monument composed of ships' prows and rather sweet dolphins, and towered over by Victory, game girl, in her traditional flying robes. Then on to a king's tomb with a particularly elaborate arrangement of basins and drains to catch the blood of the sacrifices killed outside in a smart circular portico. Among the shops were a whole row of perfumiers, scenting the air with the famous attar of Cyrenian roses. Fine: if you had a willing woman to buy it for. I was beginning to think the people we brought with us to Cyrenaïca had all bunked off home. Apart from Famia, no doubt, who would be lying drunk in a gutter somewhere.

The exotic aura was getting us down. The huge city was deeply Greek, with compressed, wide-bellied red Doric columns where we were accustomed to taller, straighter, greyer Travertine in the Ionic or Corinthian mode, and with austere metopes and tripglyphs below plain friezes where we would expect elaborate statuary. There were too many gymnasia and not enough baths. Its mixed, carefree population were all alien to us. There were even lingering traces of the Ptolomies, who once treated Cyrene as an outpost of Egypt. Everyone spoke Greek, which we could do if we had to, though it was a strain for weary travellers. All the inscriptions had Greek for their first, or only, language. The ancient influences made us feel like upstart New Men.

We needed to split up. Justinus would try the Sanctuary of Apollo in the lower town; I would march out to the Temple of Zeus.

I had picked the long straw for once. As I walked through the clear air of the pine woods to the eastern side of the high plateau on which the city had been founded, I had already cheered up. Soon I came upon the Temple. Amongst all the rich endowments in this city of overflowing coffers, the Temple of Zeus had been favoured with an aloof, authoritative location and a most celebrated statue: a copy of the Phidias Zeus at Olympia. In case I never made it to the sanctuary at Olympia, which was one of the Seven Wonders of the World, I would have liked to take a squint at the Cyrenian replica. I knew the legendary forty-foot-high masterpiece showed sublime Zeus enthroned in cedarwood and black marble, himself in ivory with enamelled robes, a solid gold beard, and solid gold hair – some sight. But here at Cyrene my attention was distracted by an even more winsome spectacle than a famous Phidias.

This was a drowsy spot (though beset with pernicious flies). Squat Doric columns supporting a massive architrave and frieze spoke of the Temple's immense age. Descending its front steps between the magisterial columns, perhaps after renewing a message she had left for me, was a tall young woman in a floating white outfit, who stopped looking superior and shrieked with excitement immediately she saw me.

Very nice. Ignoring protocol, she skipped down from the podium and I grabbed her. Excuse me, Zeus. Well, anyone who seduced that many women ought to understand.

Helena did not have to ask what had happened. That saved a long explanation, and stopped me feeling depressed.

She took me to the peaceful house she and Claudia were renting, sat me in a Greek chair with the baby in my arms, sent Gaius out to look for her brother, sent Claudia shopping, then brushed aside the heartbreaking story of our disaster, while she instead amused me with what I had missed.

'Famia is down in Apollonia, very restless now; he has purchased a good collection of horses – well, so he thinks – and he wants to sail home.'

'I'm ready.'

'He needs you to help commission a ship. We received some letters from Rome. I opened yours, in case there was a crisis—'

'You have my full confidence, beloved.'

'Yes, I decided that! Petronius has written. He is back working with the vigiles; his wife won't be reconciled; she has a boyfriend Petro disapproves of; she won't let him see the children. He says he's sorry he missed you reciting your poetry.'

'Sorry as Hades!'

'Lenia is threatening to kill you because you promised to help Smaractus obtain a contract at the new amphitheatre opening—'

'That was so Smaractus would agree her divorce.'

'He still has not signed the documents. Petro must have seen Maia; she's a lot happier without Famia there. Your mother is well, but annoyed at how you abandoned Anacrites; Anacrites had been hanging around looking for you, but Petro has not seen him for a while and there's a rumour he has left town—'

'Usual gossip.' Anacrites leave town? Where would he go? 'I like going on holiday. I get far more of the news that way.'

'And Petronius says you keep being sent urgent messages from the Palatine Bureau of Beaks—'

I smiled lazily. My feet were on elegant black and white mosaics; a fountain splashed refreshingly in the cool, open atrium. Julia Junilla had remembered me well enough to smack me in the ear with a flailing hand, then scream to be put down so she could play with her pig rattle.

'The Sacred Geese again, eh?' Bugger that. I leaned my head back, smiling. 'Anything else?' I had sensed there was more.

'Just a letter from the Emperor.' The old man? Well, that couldn't be important. I let Helena choose whether to tell me about it. Her dark eyes were gentle as she enjoyed herself: 'Your fee has been re-examined, and you are to be paid what you asked.'

I sat up and whistled. '*Io!* – In full?'

'The percentage you wanted.'

'Then I am a substantial citizen . . .' The implications were too great to consider all at once. 'So what does *he* want?'

'There is a note in his own hand to say Vespasian invites you to a formal audience about what happened with the Capitol geese.'

I really would have to deal with that. I was getting bored with being nagged.

'I love you,' I murmured, pulling her close. The white dress she was wearing was extremely attractive, but the best thing about it was the way the sleeve buttons were loose enough to admit wandering hands. In fact, they slipped easily right out of their fastenings . . .

'You'll love me even more,' said Helena, smiling invitingly, 'when I tell you that you even have a new client.'

XLVIII

The usual reason for visiting the Sanctuary of Apollo was to admire its location at the end of the processional way, with dramatic views over the gorgeous valley where the fountain sprang so aesthetically; there people were parted from money by astute acolytes of that excessively wealthy shrine, in return for sprigs of sacred bay and sips of nasty water in clearly unwashed cups. Handsome buildings crowded the sanctuary, donated by the great and good Greeks of the city, who seemed more keen on planting their generous building projects in the best plots than on planning the effect in the general scheme. Anyone who decided to erect a temple simply shouldered up to what was already there. The main thing was to ensure your inscription was big enough.

I reflected ruefully that had Justinus and I been able to exploit Cyrenian silphium, then one day we too would have been installing major new works here as top dogs in the polis. Still, I had always thought 'Falco' looked silly in Greek.

Approaching past the Greek Propylaea, a monumental entrance archway to the main temple area, we had found the sacred waters on our left, carefully directed down through channels cut diagonally in the cliff so that the water ran into a basin where it was out of reach of the public. That stopped cheapskates sampling it for free.

The fountain approach occupied a shallow shelf, below which lay the temples. You could look down and admire the clustered buildings, or move on as we did. Beyond the shrine lay a scented walkway to a high promontory which overlooked the great seaboard plateau. The view was staggering. Some bright architect had thought of hooking an amphitheatre on to the edge of this headland, where the arena perched precariously above a fabulous vista and, in my opinion, was just waiting to fall down into the gulch.

We all climbed up and sat in a row in the centre, farthest from the edge. I was with Helena, Claudia, Justinus, Gaius, the baby, and even Nux, who perched alongside me on the stone bench, waiting for something to happen in the orchestra below. The place was otherwise deserted yet we were hoping to meet someone. This was my personal reason for coming here. Forget the spring water: I had an appointment with my new client.

I was being hired by someone shy, apparently. That made a change. She was female, allegedly respectable, and modestly reluctant to reveal her address. How quaint.

I did know that the address must be temporary, like our own, because she was not Cyrenian. I also believed that a 'woman-of-mystery' act usually meant the only mystery was how such a scandalous woman had managed to keep out of jail. But Helena had warned me to treat this one with respect.

The client was so impressed with my reputation, she had followed me all the way from Rome. That must mean she had more money than sense. No woman who cared to watch her budget would travel across the Mediterranean to see an informer – let alone do so without ascertaining first whether he was willing to work for her. No informer was worth it, though I kept that to myself.

Helena said it was a foregone conclusion I would take the case. But then Helena knew who the client was.

'You ought to tell me.' I wondered if she was being so secretive because the client was a fabulous looker; I decided in that case Helena would have told her to get lost.

'I want to see your face.'

'She won't show up.'

'I think she will,' promised Helena.

Sunlight blazed on the empty theatre. This was another

highly aromatic place, another part of the heavenly Cyrenaïca herb garden. I was munching wild dill seeds. They had a searing, slightly bitter flavour that suited my mood.

We were going home. The decision had been taken, amidst mixed feelings in my party. Gaius, who in Rome spent most of his time fleeing his family, was perversely missing them. We were too nice to him. He needed people to hate. Helena and I had enjoyed our stay, but were ready for a change of scene; a large sum of money was luring me home too, now Vespasian had come good. Justinus had to face his family. Claudia wanted to reconcile herself with hers, and had announced stiffly that she was planning to return to her grandparents in Spain – without Justinus apparently.

That said, I had noticed only the previous evening that Claudia and Justinus chose the same bench at dinner. At one point, their bare arms had lain side by side upon the table, almost touching; the tingle of awareness between them had been all too evident. At least, the girl's stillness spoke of her intensity. What he felt remained veiled. Wise boy.

It was now after midday. We had sat in the theatre for an hour. Long enough to hang around for a client whose motives I doubted, when I had other pressing plans; I needed to go back to Apollonia, to rescue the agitated Famia and help him find a decent horse-transport for the Greens. I made up my mind to shift back to our lodgings, though the tranquil scene deterred me from moving immediately.

Restlessness slowly overcame the rest of my party too. Nobody said it again, but most of us had decided that the client was a wash-out. If we abandoned this business, once we returned to the house all we had to do was pack. The adventure was over for all of us.

Turning to me suddenly, Camillus Justinus said in his low, understated voice, 'If we are sailing west and have control of our own vessel, Marcus, I shall ask you to land me if possible at Berenice again.'

I raised my eyebrows. 'Giving up the idea of working in Rome?'

'No. Just something I want to do first.'

Helena dug me in the ribs. Obediently I folded my hands together and continued to stare out over the theatre, as if I were watching a really gripping performance by a first-class company of actors. I said nothing. Nobody moved.

Justinus then continued, 'Claudia Rufina and I had had a plan which went uncompleted. I still want to look for the Gardens of the Hesperides.'

Claudia drew a sharp breath. It had been *her* dream. She thought that he now meant to go there alone while she returned to Spain, a failed eloper in ignominy, nursing her private grief.

'You might like to join me,' suggested our hero to his furious girl. It was a charming idea to take her after all; I wished I had thought of suggesting it. Still, when he decided to bother, Justinus seemed to be perfectly capable of taking the initiative. Turning to her, he spoke gently and tenderly; it was rather affecting. 'You and I came through a remarkable adventure together. We shall never forget it, you know. It would be a great sorrow if we both had to remember it in future in silence, when we were with other people.'

Claudia looked at him.

'I need you, Claudia,' he announced. I wanted to cheer. He knew just what he was doing. What a lad. Handsome, charming, utterly dependable (as he needed to be, since he was in fact penniless). The girl was desperately in love with him, and at the last minute he had rescued her.

'Thank you, Quintus.' Claudia stood up. She was a tall thing, sturdily built, with a strong, serious face. I had rarely heard her laugh, except back in Rome when she first knew Justinus; she was not laughing now. 'In the circumstances,' said Claudia Rufina pleasantly, 'I think this is the least that you could offer me.'

Helena caught my eye, frowning.

Claudia's voice hardened. 'So you need me?' What he needed was her fortune, and I suddenly had a bad feeling Claudia understood that. 'You know, nobody has ever in my life bothered to consider what *I* need! Excuse me, Quintus: I can see that everyone else will think you have just done something wonderful, but I would prefer to live with a person who really wanted me.'

Before anyone could stop her, Claudia whipped into the nearest aisle and set off down the rows. I already knew her propensity for bursting into and out of amphitheatres on her own. I rose to my feet, just ahead of Justinus, who was still looking stunned. Dear gods, he had done his best, and was now terribly upset. Women can be so insensitive.

Nux plunged off the seat and raced down after the girl, barking excitedly. Helena and I both called out. As Claudia turned down the passageway towards a covered public exit, a woman who had somehow gained access to the arena entered centrally and strode to a dominating position on the oval stage.

She was of medium height and haughty bearing: long neck, lifted angular chin, a foam of brown hair, and watchful eyes that followed Claudia curiously as the girl rushed down the aisle towards her and then stopped. The woman wore rich clothing in subtle shades, with a gleam of silk in the weave. Her light cloak was held on her shoulders by matched brooches, linked by a heavy gold chain. More gold shone at her neck and on her fingers. Long, elegant earrings dangled from her pale ears.

Her voice, calm, aristocratic – and Latin – carried easily from the stage: 'Which of you is Didius Falco?'

If she had brought attendants they must be waiting elsewhere. Her solo appearance had been calculated to shock us. I raised my arm, still distracted. However, I was always perfectly capable of insulting a supplicant: 'Dear gods, do the Cyrenian élite allow women gladiators into their arena?'

'That would be outrageous.' Resplendent in her chic streetwear, the woman surveyed me coolly. She paused slightly, as people do when they know exactly what effect they will cause. 'My name is Scilla.'

Beside me, Helena Justina smiled faintly. She had been right. I would accept this client.

IL

'How did you find me?'

We were strolling back along the warm, dappled path to the Sanctuary. Helena, my discreet chaperone, walked in silence beside me, holding my hand, and lifting her face to the sun as if absorbed in the beauties of the scenery. Gaius had taken the baby and Nux and rushed off home ahead of us. The young lovers, or whatever they turned out to be, had dawdled behind to tell each other firmly how there was nothing more to be said.

'I traced you eventually through your friend Petronius. Before that I spoke to a man called Anacrites. He said he was your partner. I didn't care for him.' Scilla was forthright, a woman who made her own judgements and acted accordingly.

Letting the prospective client get the measure of me, I explained as we walked slowly, 'I used to work with Petronius, whom I trusted absolutely.' Knowing Petro, I did wonder briefly what he had made of my new client when she approached him. His taste ran to more fragile types, however. Scilla was slim, but she had sinewy arms and a firm spring in her step. 'Unhappily, Petronius returned to his career with the vigiles. Now, yes; I work with Anacrites, whom I don't trust at all – so one thing is certain: he won't ever let me down.'

Faced with the traditional wit of the informing fraternity, Scilla merely looked irritated. Well, that's traditional too.

'You have come a long way. So why me?' I asked her mildly.

'You have been involved already in what I need you to do. You came to the house.'

'To see Pomponius Urtica?' For a moment I was transported back to the ex-praetor's luxury villa on the Pincian last December, on those two useless occasions when I endeavoured to interview him after he had been mauled by Calliopus' lion. Had Scilla been in the house, or was she just told about me afterwards? Either way, I knew she lived there, a close member of the praetor's domestic circle. 'I wanted to talk to Pomponius about that accident.'

Her voice grated: 'An accident that ought not to have happened.'

'So I deduced. And how is Pomponius?'

'He died.' Scilla stopped walking. Her face was pale. 'It took until the end of March. His end was prolonged and horribly painful.' Helena and I had paused too, in the shade of a low pine tree. Some of the story must have been relayed to Helena already, but she had left me to hear it in full for myself. Scilla came to the point briskly: 'Falco, you must have worked out that I want you to help me deal with the people responsible.'

I had indeed guessed that.

What I felt unprepared for was this expensive, cultured, educated-sounding woman. According to the gossip in Rome, she was supposed to be a good-time girl. A low-born fright, a freed slave probably. Even if Pomponius had bequeathed her millions, it would have been impossible for a common piece like that to transform herself in a few weeks into a close match for a Chief Vestal Virgin's niece.

She noticed my stare, which I had made no effort to hide. 'Well?'

'I'm trying to make you out. I had heard you had a "wild" reputation.'

'And what does that mean?' she challenged me.

'To be blunt, I expected a slut of tender years, bearing evidence of adventures.'

Scilla remained calm, though clearly gritting her teeth. 'I am a marble importer's daughter. A knight; he had also held important posts in the tax service. My brothers run a thriving architectural fittings business; one is a priest of the imperial cult. So my origins are respectable and I was brought up in comfort, with all the accomplishments that go with it.'

'Then where does the reputation come from?'

'I have one unusual hobby, not relevant to your enquiry.'

My mind raced salaciously. The strange hobby had to be sexual.

The woman set off walking again. This time Helena slipped a hand through her arm, so the two of them strolled along close together while I kicked my own path through the dill bushes. Helena took up the conversation, as if it were more proper for a knight's accomplished daughter to be interviewed by a woman. Personally, I felt Scilla needed no such concession.

'So tell us about you and the ex-praetor? Were you in love?'

'We were going to be married.'

Helena smiled and allowed that to answer the question, though she knew it did not. 'Your first marriage?'

'Yes.'

'Had you lived with your family until then?'

'Yes, of course.'

Helena's question had been a subtle way of probing whether Scilla had had significant lovers beforehand. Scilla was too canny to say. 'And what about the night Pomponius had the lion brought to his house? That was meant as a "treat" for you?'

The expression in Scilla's hazel eyes seemed sad and far away. 'Men can have a queer idea of what is appropriate.'

'True. Some lack imagination,' Helena sympathised. 'Some, of course, know they are being crass and go ahead anyway . . . And you were present when Pomponius was mauled. That must have been a terrible experience.'

Scilla prowled on for a moment in silence. She had a fine, controlled walk, not like the tripping shuffles of most well-bred dames who only leave their houses carried in a litter. Like Helena, she gave the impression that she could route-march through half a dozen markets, spend with panache, and then carry her own purchases home.

'Pomponius behaved foolishly,' she said, without rancour or blame. 'The lion broke free and leapt at him. It surprised the keepers, though we now know why it behaved that way. It had to be put down.'

I frowned. Somebody had told me the girl had reacted hysterically; that would have been understandable, yet she seemed so composed here I could not quite envisage it. Tipping my head to look around Helena, I said, 'Pomponius had been manoeuvring a straw man, I believe. The lion flew at it, mauled him, and then chaos broke out — what happened next?'

'I shouted — as loudly as I could — and I rushed forwards, to frighten the lion away.'

'That took nerve.'

'Did it work?' asked Helena, taken aback, yet assuming control again.

'The lion stopped and escaped into the garden.'

'Rumex — the gladiator— followed it, and did what was necessary?' I prompted.

I thought a shadow crossed Scilla's face. 'Rumex went after the lion,' she agreed quietly.

She seemed to want to end this conversation, understandably. After a moment Helena said, 'I nearly met Rumex once, but it was shortly after the accident and he was being kept apart from the public.'

'You didn't miss much,' Scilla told her, with unexpected force. 'He was a has-been. All his fights were fixed.'

Still, I thought, feeling obliged to defend the poor fellow; he had speared an agitated lion, single-handedly.

Her opinion was inside information. I wondered how Scilla had acquired the knowledge to judge a gladiator's prowess so scathingly. From Pomponius, perhaps.

We had reached the main sanctuary area. Scilla took us

down some steps. I offered a polite hand to Helena, but Scilla seemed well able to keep her balance without assistance.

There was a small enclosure amongst a cluster of temples, including the large Doric shrine to Apollo, with a dramatic open-air altar outside it. Many of the other temples were elderly and small, cramped around the open square in a friendly style. The Hellenistic gods can be less remote than their Roman equivalents.

'So, will you help me, Falco?' Scilla asked.

'To do what?

'I want Saturninus and Calliopus called to account for causing the death of Pomponius.'

I remained silent. Helena commented, 'That may not be easy. Surely you'd have to prove they knew in advance what was likely to happen that night?'

'They are experts with wild animals,' Scilla responded dismissively. 'Saturninus should never have organised a private show. Loosing a wild beast in a domestic environment was stupidity. And Calliopus must have known that by switching the lions he had issued Pomponius with a death sentence.'

As a senator's daughter Helena Justina proposed the establishment solution: 'You and the ex-praetor's family might do best bringing a civil suit for your loss. Perhaps you need a good lawyer.'

Scilla shook her head impatiently. 'Compensation is not enough. It isn't the point either!' She managed to control her voice, then came out with what sounded like a set speech: 'Pomponius was good to me. I won't let him die unchampioned. Plenty of men take an interest in a girl who has a reputation — but you can guess what kind of interest that is. Pomponius was prepared to marry me. He was a decent man.'

'Then forgive me,' said Helena softly. 'I can understand your anger, but other people may assume you only have low motives. Does his death mean you lost the hope of his fortune, for instance?'

Scilla looked haughty and once more continued like someone who had spent a lot of time brooding over her grievance and practising how to defend her anger: 'He had been married before and his children are his main heirs. What I have lost is the chance of a good marriage to a man of status. Apart from my own great sorrow, it is a disappointment to my family. An ex-praetor is a fine match for any equestrian's daughter. He was generous to offer me that, and I held him in high regard for it.'

'You have to grieve for him – but you are still young.' Scilla was, I guess, twenty-five or so. 'Don't let this blight the rest of your life,' Helena warned.

'But,' Scilla returned drily, 'I carry the extra burden of having lost the man I was supposed to marry, in scandalous circumstances. Who will want me now?'

'Yes, I see.' Helena was regarding her thoughtfully. 'So what is Falco supposed to do for you?'

'Help me force those men to admit their crime.'

'What have you done about it so far?' I enquired.

'The men responsible fled Rome. After Pomponius died, it was left to me to take the matter up. He had been suffering for so long his family wanted no more of it. I first consulted the vigiles. They seemed sympathetic.'

'The vigiles are known for their kind attitude to wild girls!' Some of the vigiles I knew ate wild girls as a dessert after lunch.

Scilla accepted the joke bravely – by ignoring it. 'Unfortunately, with the suspects outside Rome, the case was beyond the vigiles' jurisdiction. Then I appealed to the Emperor.'

'Did he refuse you assistance?' asked Helena, sounding indignant.

'Not exactly. My brothers acted as my advocates, of course, though I know they are both embarrassed by the situation. Nonetheless, they put my case well and the Emperor heard them out. The death of a man of such senior rank had to be taken seriously. But Vespasian's attitude was that Pomponius had been at fault in commissioning a private show.'

Helena looked sympathetic. 'Vespasian would want to avoid gossip.'

'Quite. Since the two men have absconded, everything was put into abeyance in the hope public interest dies down. The Emperor would only promise that if Saturninus and Calliopus return to Rome he will re-examine my petition.'

'Knowing that, they won't come back,' sneered Helena.

'Exactly. They are holed up in Lepcis and Oea, their home cities. I could grow old and grey waiting for these larvae to re-emerge.'

'But within the boundaries of the Empire they cannot escape justice!'

Scilla shook her head. 'I could appeal to the governor of Tripolitania, but he won't take stronger action than the Emperor. Saturninus and Calliopus are notable figures, whereas I have no influence. Governors don't respond well to what Falco calls wild girls!'

'So what are you asking Falco to do?'

'I cannot get close to these men. They will not accept representations, or speak to anyone I send. I have to go after them – I have to go to Tripolitania myself. But they are violent people, from a brutal part of society. They are surrounded by trained fighters—'

'Are you frightened, Scilla?' Helena asked.

'I admit I am. They have already threatened my servants. If I go – as I feel I must – I shall feel vulnerable in foreign territory. Having justice on my side would be no consolation if they hurt me – or worse.'

'Marcus—' Helena appealed to me. I had been silent, wondering why I felt so sceptical.

'I can escort you,' I told Scilla. 'But what happens then?'

'Find them, please, and bring them to me, so I can confront them with what they did.'

'That seems a reasonable request,' Helena commented.

I felt obliged to warn the woman: 'I don't recommend

you to plan any big scenes. It has never been proved – let alone proved in court – that either of them has committed a crime.'

'May I not pursue a civil suit as Helena Justina suggested?' asked Scilla meekly. That sounded harmless. Too harmless, from this one.

'Yes; I'm sure we can find lawyers in Lepcis and Oea who will be prepared to argue that Saturninus and Calliopus owe you financial recompense for the loss of your future husband through their negligence.'

'That's all I want,' Scilla agreed.

'All right. I can round them up and subpoena them. The cost should be modest, you'll feel you've taken action, and there may be a chance of winning the case.' Tripolitania was a famously litigious province. Yet I didn't think the issue would necessarily come to court. Both Saturninus and Calliopus could well afford to pay up just to make this woman go away. Her accusations would never hurt them much in my opinion, but they must be an inconvenience. If the lanistae satisfied her complaints and received an indemnity, they would be free to return to Rome. 'Just one question, though. There was an unsolved death connected with all this. Pomponius was killed by the lion, who was killed by Rumex. Rumex himself then died and his killer has never been found. I have to ask: were you in any way involved?'

Scilla gave me a cold stare. I felt like a young lady's music teacher who inadvertently played a bum note after she for her part had completed perfect scales. 'I could kill a man in the right circumstances,' replied Scilla calmly. 'But I have never done it, I can assure you.' Of course not. She was a knight's daughter, and thoroughly respectable.

'Right.' I felt slightly nonplussed.

Obviously I would have to take the job. We made various arrangements – finance, contact points. Then Scilla said she was now going to make an offering at a temple, so Helena and I bade her a polite farewell. I did notice that the temple she went to was entirely appropriate for a woman with her heart set on vengeance, even vengeance in the civil courts: that of the goddess of night and witchcraft, Hecate.

'Identified with Diana,' said Helena, who had also noticed where Scilla went.

'Moonshine?'

'Goddess of hunting was more what I had in mind.'

Helena and I stood beside that lighter haven of culture, the altar of Apollo. There was a faint scent of charred meat which made me hanker for my dinner. 'Well? What do you think?'

A frown creased Helena's broad forehead. 'Something is not quite right.'

'I'm glad you said it.' I had disliked Scilla intensely: too self-assured.

'It may be straightforward,' Helena suggested in her fair way. 'Scilla has been thwarted when she approached the vigiles and the Emperor. She feels there has been an injustice — but what remedy exists? People who lose someone in a tragedy become very angry and flail around looking for a way to relieve their helplessness.'

'That's fine — if they come and employ me.'

'Are you sure you want to do this?'

'I'm sure.'

When Scilla discussed the night that her lover planned to impress her with the show, I had remembered the dead lion, and later the dead gladiator whose murder was never even halfway solved. It stirred up feelings I had left behind when I came out on this sun-bleached holiday interlude. Devoting myself to Justinus — his wild chase after a fortune and his sad troubles with his love life — had taken me far from those winter days of auditing amongst the menageries. Yet the disturbing problem never left me. Now here we were, in ancient Greek Cyrene, facing the same dark undercurrents.

'So,' Helena said, giving me an odd look. 'You are going to Tripolitania.'

'That I am. You need not come.'

'Oh I'll be there!' She spoke rather warmly. 'I have not forgotten, Marcus Didius, that when we first met you were renowned for spending time with notoriously flexible Tripolitanean acrobats.'

I laughed. It was the wrong reaction.

What a girl she was. Four years had passed since I first knew Helena Justina, and in all that time I had never given a thought to the sinuous young rope dancer I had dallied with before her. I could not even recall the dancer's name. But Helena, who had never even met the girl, was still harbouring jealousies.

I kissed her. That too was the wrong thing to do, but anything else would have been worse. 'You had better be there to fight them off,' I said gently. Helena's chin came up in defiance, so then I winked at her. I hadn't done that for a long time. It was one of those cheeky rituals of courtship that get forgotten when you feel sure of someone.

Too sure, perhaps. Helena could still give me the feeling that she was keeping her options open in case she decided I was a bad risk.

I walked with her across the formal temple area to a dramatic feature where water from the Spring of Apollo had been diverted from the upper level down into a formal fountain. A nude male torso – rather small – leaned at an odd angle on the plinth of a slender obelisk; that was set above a layered basin down which sheets of spring water flowed. Helena looked askance at the solitary column, whose significance she seemed to view suspiciously.

'Some sculptor representing his dreams,' she scoffed. 'I bet it makes his girlfriend laugh.'

Below the obelisk ran a fine semicircular podium, terminated by two grand stone lions. In-turned and grimacing fiercely, the lions were long in the body if rather solid in the trunk and legs, with broad heads, attractive whiskers, and meticulously carved curly manes.

For some time I stood looking up at the guardian beasts, thinking about Leonidas.

PART THREE

TRIPOLITANIA: May, AD74

L

Tripolitania.

Among all the bumptious provinces in the Empire, Tripolitania led by a long head. The Three Towns have a history of independence that is positively shocking. The only thing remotely in their favour, in my view, was the fact that they were not Greek.

They were never through and through Carthaginian either. This accounts for their self-willed attitude; when Carthage foundered, they were laughing. First established by Phoenicians, sure enough, and possibly recolonised on later occasions from Carthage itself, nonetheless the three great seashore cities had consistently retained their independent status. When Rome smashed the power of Carthage they could still claim to be sufficiently separate to avoid punishment. While Carthage was torn down, its populace enslaved, its religion banned, its fields sewn with salt, and its aristocracy fined into oblivion, the Three Towns pleaded innocent and claimed immunity. Tripolitania had never had to surrender formally. It had never been made a military zone. It was not colonised by Roman military veterans. Although there were legal circuit visits, it did not even have a regular administrative presence from the office of the governor of Proconsular Africa, under whose jurisdiction this region fell in theory.

Tripolitania was now Punic, going on Roman. With every appearance of sincerity its people were giving themselves Roman town planning, Roman inscriptions and what passed for Roman names. The Three Towns were collectively known as the Emporia, and that summed them up: an international trade centre. It follows that they were all crammed with well-dressed, thriving ethnic millionaires.

My party was clean and civilised, but when we landed at Sabratha we felt like ragged tinkers with no business to be there.

Two points need to be mentioned. First point: Sabratha is the One Town without a harbour. When I say 'landed' I mean our ship beached itself on the strand unexpectedly and very violently with a horrid rending noise. The captain, who had become a close friend of my brother-in-law Famia, was — we discovered after the abrupt landing — nowhere near sober at the time.

Second point: Although we landed at Sabratha, I had given the captain very precise orders to sail somewhere else.

It seemed clear enough to me; it ought to be my decision. I was in charge of our group. What's more, I had found the vessel at Apollonia, I haggled and commissioned her, then I arranged the loading of the splendid Libyan stock Famia had somehow managed to buy for the Greens. Given that I supported the Blues, this was pretty magnanimous. It is true that Famia had actually paid for the ship. In the end, in the crucial matter of winning the captain's confidence, Famia's amphorae were what carried weight. By bargaining hard for the horses he had managed to leave enough Green funds over for a substantial number of amphorae.

Famia wanted to go to Sabratha because he thought horses were brought there from the interior oases by the desert tribes. He had emptied Cyrenaïca, but was still buying. The Greens had always been profligate. And the more horses he bought, the more banker's orders he could cash, releasing more cash for wine.

The significant tribe from the interior was that of the Garamantes, those whose thrashing by the Roman commander Valerius Festus had already been discussed by Justinus and me when we thought they might have captured us. In view of their very recent defeat it was likely that they had ceased trading, at least temporarily. However, from the great oasis of Cydame caravans still wound their way to Sabratha bearing gold, carbuncles, ivory, cloth, leather, dye stuffs, marble, rare woods and slaves, not to mention exotic animals. The town's commercial emblem was an elephant.

I was after men who traded in wild beasts, but elephants did not come into it, thank the gods.

'Famia,' I had said back in Apollonia, speaking slowly and pleasantly, lest I offend or confuse the drunken bastard, 'I need to go to Oea and I need to go to Lepcis. Either will do to start with, though we shall reach Lepcis first. Sabratha is the one place we can leave out.'

'All right, Marcus,' Famia had replied, smiling in that aggravating way all drunks do when they are about to forget everything you have said. As soon as my back was turned the slippery deviant must have begun palling up with the captain, a swine who turned out to be just as bad as Famia.

When I felt the jolt as we scraped up the rocks and sand at Sabratha, I emerged from below where I had been paralysed with seasickness; I had to grip my hands to keep them from squeezing my brother-in-law's throat. Now I knew why the journey had seemed endless. It ought to have been over days before.

It was absolutely pointless trying to remonstrate. I had now realised Famia floated in a state of incurable inebriation, never totally sobering up. His daily intake propelled him into wilder moods or duller troughs, but he never let himself hit the real world. If I belted him into oblivion as I wanted to do, when we returned to Rome he would moan to my sister and then Maia would hate me.

I felt helpless. I had lost some of my natural supporters too. As Justinus had requested, we had left him behind at Berenice. When we put him off, everything between him and Claudia had still seemed set for tragedy. Then, when he had unloaded his meagre luggage and bade farewell to the rest of us on the quayside, he had marched up to the young lady.

'You had better kiss me goodbye then,' we had heard him say to her quietly. Claudia thought twice, then pecked him on the cheek, bouncing off again rapidly.

Army-trained for speedy reactions, Camillus Justinus seized the advantage and got one arm around her. 'No, I meant properly—'

His steadiness pressurised her so Claudia had to do it. He made the kiss last a long time, holding her about as close as possible without actually committing an impropriety. He had the sense to hang on until she gave up resisting and burst into tears. Consoling her as she wept on his shoulder, Justinus signalled that he intended to keep her with him and for us to collect Claudia's belongings. Then he started talking to her in a low voice.

'Jupiter, I've seen what happens when Quintus has a chat with a girl who secretly thinks he's wonderful!'

Helena paused on the way to pack Claudia's luggage for her. She gave me a piercing look. On reflection, I could not remember if I had ever told Helena about her brother disappearing up the tower in the German forest with the prophetess who subsequently left him lovelorn. I saw him come down from the tower later, visibly altered — and it had been easy to guess why. 'Perhaps he's apologising,' Helena suggested caustically.

Claudia, far from passive even when she was crying her heart out, interrupted Justinus with a long, fierce argument, the gist of which I could not catch. He answered, then she tried to hold off from him, striking aggravated blows on his chest with the palms of her hands until he was forced to step back by degrees almost to the edge of the harbour. She could not bring herself to shove him into the water, and they both knew it.

Justinus let Claudia rant at him until she fell silent. He asked a question. She nodded. Still balanced rather precariously on the edge of the quay, they put their arms around each other. I noticed his face was white, as if he knew he was condemning himself to trouble, but perhaps he thought the trouble he already knew about was better than any other sort.

I myself supressed a grin, thinking about the fortune Justinus had just coralled. My nephew Gaius mimed being violently sick into the harbour at the soppy scene he had just witnessed. Helena went and sat by herself in the prow of the ship, stricken by seeing her younger brother adopt a life of his own.

The rest of us re-boarded. We cast off. Justinus called out that they would try to catch us up before we left Lepcis.

I still thought they were doomed. But people had said that about Helena and me. It had given us a good reason to stick it out. Good omens let you down. Bad ones give you something to fight against.

'Sabratha seems a very attractive city,' Helena tried to mollify me as I absorbed the mistake Famia had then landed on us. That was before she found out there was a sanctuary of Tanit, causing her to take a tighter grip on both the baby and my nephew Gaius.

'I'm sure the rumours of child sacrifice are simply designed to give Tanit a notorious aura and increase her authority.'

'Oh yes,' scoffed Helena. Rumours of revolting religious rites can appal the most sensible girls.

'No doubt the reason for all those tiny sarcophagi is that those who revere the Punic gods also love little children dearly.'

'And have the bad luck to lose a lot of them at a very similar age . . . What are we going to do, Marcus?'

Helena was losing her courage. Travellers always hit low moments. Enduring a long journey, only to find at the very moment you expect to arrive that you are actually two hundred miles away from your destination (and have to go backwards) can reduce the bravest soul to despair.

'Let's hope Scilla won't mind me turning up a week

late.' Scilla had insisted on making her own way to Lepcis Magna – an example of the wayward attitude that made me suspicious of her as a client. 'We can either try to persuade Famia to sail back again – or leave him looking at horses' teeth, hope one of them bites him, and book another ship ourselves. While we're here let's look around like tourists,' I offered. It was my responsibility to make available to my family the Empire's rich variety of cultural experience.

'Oh not another lousy foreign forum!' muttered Gaius. 'And I can do without any more funny foreign temples, thanks a lot.'

Like a decent paterfamilias I ignored the boy. His parents dealt with arguments by swiping him: I wished to set him an example of benign tolerance. Gaius had yet to be impressed by that, but I was a patient man.

Like most cities in the narrow hinterland of North Africa, Sabratha had a superb setting right on the waterfront, where there was a strong smell of fish. Houses, shops and baths almost merged with the deep, deep blue ocean. The cheapest of them were built of unclad local stone, which was a reddish limestone of the most porous kind, readily pocketed with holes. The civic centre also played to the sea views. The spacious, airy forum was not only foreign in tinge as Gaius feared, but its main temple – to Liber Pater, a Punic deity he definitely viewed askance – had partly tumbled down in a recent earthquake and was not yet rebuilt. We tried not to think about earthquakes. We had enough problems.

We prowled about like lost souls. At one end of the forum were the Curia, Capitolium and a Temple of Serapis.

'Ooh look, Gaius – another funny foreign shrine.' We climbed its base and sat there, all tired and dispirited.

Gaius amused himself making a rude noise. 'Uncle Marcus, you're not going to be thwarted by that fat bastard Famia?'

'Of course not,' I lied, wondering where I could buy a

spicy meat rissole and whether in this new town it would give me any new kinds of bellyache. I spotted a stall, and fetched fishcakes for all of us. We ate them like disreputable tourists, an experience which left me covered with oil.

'When you eat you get more food on you than Nux,' Helena commented. I wiped my mouth very carefully before I kissed her – a politeness which always reduced her to giggles. She leaned against me wearily. 'I suppose you are just sitting here waiting for a scantily dressed female acrobat to come along.'

'If it's one of my old Tripolitanian girlfriends she'll be a hundred and on crutches by now.'

'That sounds like a good old Tripolitanian lie . . . There is one thing that you could do,' Helena suggested.

'What – gaze around at this splendid, salt-tanged city with its jostling merchants and shippers and landowners, all totally disinterested in me or my problems, then cut my throat?'

Helena patted my knee. 'Hanno comes from Sabratha. Since we are here, why not find out where he lives?'

'Hanno isn't part of my mission for the new client,' I said.

So we all jumped up and made enquiries straightaway.

LI

Unlike the greek stiffs of Cyrene, the easygoing million-aires of Sabratha looked to the western end of the Inner Sea for their profits, which were obviously magnificent. Their thoroughly modern trade was with Sicily, Spain, Gaul, and of course Italy; their prized commodities were not only the exotics brought in from the desert in caravans, but local olive oil, fish-pickle and pottery. The streets of their fine city had become conduits for barter, crowded with shoving groups of many nationalities. It was clear that the old town on the seaboard would not long satisfy the wealthy, and those who were not already planning to expand into a more spacious area would be demanding smarter suburbs in the near future. It was the kind of town that within a couple of generations would become unrecognisable.

For the present, however, those who could afford the best lived east of the forum. In Sabratha the best was palatial. Hanno had a swank mansion with a Hellenistic ground-plan but tiptop Roman decor. From the street door we passed through a small corridor to a courtyard surrounded by columns. A huge room spanned the far side of the yard, where plasterers on a trestle were remodelling a faded fresco of the Four Seasons into Our Master Courageously Hunting: Libyan lions, out-of-scale pan-thers, and a rather surprised spotty snake (with a dado of doves on a fountain and little bunnyrabbits eating shrubs). Swags of deep-dyed curtaining brightened the doorways to side-rooms. Hanno's taste in marble was extraordinary, and the low table where visitors deposited their sun-hats was a huge slab of African hardwood polished so you could check today's deterioration in your pimples while you waited for the steward to report who had arrived.

He was not reporting to Hanno himself; Hanno was out of town. Still hunting, no doubt. His sister would be informed we notables had called. We could not seriously expect her to appear. However she did.

Hanno's sister was a confident, stately, dark-skinned woman in her late forties wearing a bright turquoise robe. Her walk was slow, her head carried high. A granular gold necklace that must have been as long as a hippodrome weighed down a bosom that was naturally formed to act as a platform for the contents of a very select jewel casket. A column of gem-set bangles occupied her left arm; her right was swathed in a multicoloured shawl which she waved about. She was surprisingly cheery as she greeted us. What she said we could not tell, for like her brother she spoke Punic.

More practical and accommodating than Hanno, as soon as she realised the problem, she broke into a broad grin and sent for her interpreter. He was a small, slim, olivine, whiskery slave of eastern extraction in an off-white tunic: large sandals flapping on medium-sized feet, sturdy legs, quick eyes, and a mildly grumbling manner. He was evidently one of the family, his mutterings tolerated with a graceful wave of his mistress' hand.

Refreshments were produced. My companions tucked in; I apologised, especially for young Gaius. Hanno's sister, whose name was Myrrha, chucked Gaius under the chin (not something I would have risked), laughed a lot, and said she knew about boys; she had a nephew too.

I alluded to business in Lepcis and Oea, making a joke of my enforced visit here. We all laughed. The slave passed on my glowing compliments about Hanno, and my regret not to have found him at home. Then the man relayed back various courtesies from Myrrha to us. It was all tastefully polite. I could think of better ways to waste an afternoon.

As a rather forced silence fell in due course, Helena

caught my eye to say we ought to leave. The statuesque Myrrha must have noticed, for she rose in response. Far from thanking the harsh gods of this neighbourhood for her release from an unwanted bunch of foreigners, she then said that Hanno would be calling in at Lepcis Magna, for business reasons – something about hearing the results of a land survey. She, Myrrha, was about to take her own ship up the coast to meet her brother and would be delighted to carry us as well.

I consulted Helena. The interpreter, who seemed to do whatever he felt like, thought this was too boring to translate, so while we were muttering he dived into what Gaius had left on our refreshment tray. Myrrha, who was a stern disciplinarian apparently, gave the slave a piece of her mind. He just stared back defiantly.

Deep in the crannies of my heat- and travel-exhausted brain a memory stirred. I had been half-conscious that this stately, straight-backed female seemed familiar. Suddenly I remembered why. I had seen her before, on an occasion when she had been expounding strong views in that formidable style to someone else. Her mention of owning her own sea-transport also jogged my memory.

The last time I saw her was in Rome. It had been at the exercise yard at Calliopus' barracks on the Portuensis Road. She had been arguing then too – with a handsome young stud I had assumed must be her lover: but Hanno's sister must also be the woman who soon afterwards paid Calliopus for the release of that gladiator – the young bestiarius from Sabratha whom Calliopus had accused of killing Leonidas.

I turned to the slave. 'The nephew Myrrha mentioned – does he have a name?'

'It's Iddibal,' he told me, while the woman I had once refused to believe could be Iddibal's auntie looked on and smiled.

'And he's Hanno's son?'

'Yes of course.'

I said that since his father had done me so many

kindnesses, I would love to meet Hanno's boy some time, and his aunt replied through her offhand interpreter that if we sailed up to Lepcis with her that would be a good opportunity because Iddibal had already gone there to meet up with his papa.

LII

Myrrha's ship was an extremely large, rather elderly transport that we learned had been used in the past for taking beasts to Rome. Like her brother, and sometimes in partnership with him, she engaged in the export of animals for the amphitheatre – though according to her she herself was a shy provincial who never left Sabratha. Because of the language barrier, conversations with her were rare, but once when we happened to have the interpreter to hand I asked, 'The arena's a family occupation? Does your nephew also help Hanno in the wild beast trade?'

Yes, came the reply. Iddibal was in his twenties, a great hunter, and he relished the family business.

'No plans to send him to be polished up in Rome then?'

No, lied Auntie Myrrha blithely; Iddibal was a homeboy. We all smiled and said how wonderful it was, in our restless age, when young men were satisfied with their heritage.

Everything was extremely friendly, though I feared that would not last. Once we reached Lepcis and Myrrha started talking to Hanno and Iddibal, she would find out that I was the Census examiner. They would all realise that I knew Iddibal had worked for Calliopus. The only possible explanation was that he had been infiltrated into the rival establishment incognito – and that he was there to cause trouble. Once they conferred, this powerful family would realise that I knew more about their secret commercial activities than they liked to have revealed. Myrrha would probably be furious. Hanno, I thought, could become very dangerous indeed.

I decided to relax while we were aboard the aunt's ship.

Once we disembarked I would be my own man again. When we were leaving Sabratha I had made Famia promise that as soon as he was tired of horse-buying he would come back to Lepcis and pick us up. Even if he failed to show, when I had sorted out the business Scilla wanted, Helena and I could pay for our own passage home.

Sorting out the business for Scilla had suddenly acquired a new dimension. Allowance was needed for Hanno's influence – especially since according to Calliopus Iddibal had been tied up with whatever happened to Leonidas. Still, I could handle that.

I assumed that Calliopus had never known that Iddibal was a rival's son. Iddibal would never have left the barracks alive otherwise. In retrospect, it looked to me as if the young man might have been sent to Rome by his family specifically to foment a war between Calliopus and Saturninus. Public strife between those two would make them look unsound; when tenders were invited for the new amphitheatre, Hanno would be able to clean up. Even if Pomponius Urtica had lived and had been prepared to back Saturninus with special patronage, the dirty tricks war would have deterred him. Pomponius would not have wanted to stain his own reputation by any association with such goings-on.

Sending in his son to cause provocation would have been a good ploy on Hanno's part, though risky to Iddibal personally. Apart from having to take part in mock hunts in the venatio, discovery would have put him at Calliopus' mercy. And once he signed up, he was stuck. He was trapped for life unless somebody could rescue him. As soon as he had aroused sufficient jealousy between the other two men – by inciting incidents like the escaped leopard and the ostrich poisoning, if nothing worse – then his father must have wanted to extract him as quickly as possible. But in theory that was impossible.

Iddibal could simply have run away. With outside help, it could have been arranged. Anacrites and I had known that his aunt had had money with her in Rome, and at least one servant (her present interpreter, I reckoned), plus a very fast ship waiting on the coast. But since Iddibal had become a gladiator, he was also a slave. That was a legal condition into which he could volunteer to put himself – but from which he could not then choose to withdraw. Only Calliopus could free him. If he ran off, Iddibal would be an outlaw for life.

His aunt must have been a stranger to Calliopus (well, she had told me she was a home-bird), whereas Hanno would certainly have been well-known to him. So Myrrha must have volunteered to go to Rome to help the youth. The question was, especially since she obviously had to pay through the nose for his unorthodox release, how much did his family think Iddibal had achieved by then?

I was in no doubt now that Hanno wanted the two other lanistae to tear each other apart, while he watched from the sidelines and took over their leavings. So against all the odds, my enforced trip to Sabratha had given me a lead. Whatever went on last winter back in Rome, I reckoned Hanno's stirring partially explained how it all blew up.

That made me determined to interview young Iddibal.

LIII

For the safety of my family, I decided that as soon as possible I must shed Myrrha and distance myself from Hanno. The chance to do it occurred unexpectedly; choppy seas forced us to put in at Oea and rest up for half a day.

This was a bonus, offering me a chance to see Calliopus. I set off hotfoot into town and after hours of searching found his house, only to learn he too was away from home. Tripolitanian beast exporters seemed to spend a great deal of time on the hoof.

'A Roman took the master up coast on business,' said a slave.

'Is the mistress here? Her name's Artemisia, isn't it?'

'She went with him.'

'Where have they gone?'

'Lepcis.'

Brilliant. Scilla was paying me to fix meetings for her with both Calliopus and Saturninus. We had expected they would have to be tackled individually – but Calliopus had pre-empted me of his own accord. If he was in Lepcis we could deal with both at once. If only all jobs were this easy. (On the other hand, if Scilla ran into them both in Lepcis before I arrived there, it struck me I might lose my fee.)

'Who was this man your master went with?'

'Don't know.'

'He must have had a name?'

'Romanus.'

Right. I was none the wiser, and irritated as well now. 'What did he say?'

'My master's old partner is to appear in court on a charge; my master has to give evidence.'

This sounded suspiciously close to what I was supposed to arrange myself. The mad thought crossed my mind that 'Romanus' could be Scilla herself in masculine disguise. She had the spirit – but of course, she liked to claim she was respectable. 'What, is Calliopus on a charge too?'

'Just a witness.' That could be a ruse to get him there. 'For or against?'

The slave looked disgusted. 'Against, man! They hate each other. My master would never have gone otherwise.'

What a wonderful scenario. If I had wanted a way to set the two men up, this was the perfect scheme; tell Calliopus he could help prosecute Saturninus. I wished I had thought of it.

So who did? Who was this mysterious character with the summons, and what, if any, was his interest in my case?

I walked back to the harbour. It was dark by now. The breeze that had driven us to shore lashed cold on my face but it was fading. I needed to consider my sudden feelings of uncertainty. The harbour had a long, attractive water-front; I went for a stroll. Approaching me in the opposite direction came a man who looked obviously Roman. Like me he was mooching idly beside the ocean, in a deep, pensive mood.

No one else was about. We must have both reached the point of knowing that our private thoughts were leading nowhere. We both stopped. He looked at me. I looked at him. He was an upright figure, slightly too much flesh, sharp haircut, clean-shaven, bearing himself like a soldier though with too many years out of action to be an army professional.

'Good evening.' He spoke with an unmistakable Basilica Julia accent. The greeting alone told me he was freeborn, patrician, tutor-educated, army-trained, imperially patron-ised and statue-endowed. Wealth, ancestors and senatorial self-confidence yodelled from his vowels.

'Evening, sir.' I made a quiet legionary salute.

Two Romans far from our native city, protocol allowed us to accept this chance of exchanging news from home. It was necessary to introduce ourselves.

'Excuse me, sir. You seem like the proverbial "one of us" – your name is not Romanus, I suppose?'

'Rutilius Gallicus.' He sounded alarmed. Whoops. Titles are a sensitive matter. I had just accused a highly-bred patrician of being a gutter-rat with just one name. Still, the high-bred one was out ambulating a harbour without his guards and flunkies. You could argue he had asked for it.

'Didius Falco,' I returned. Then I hastened to reassure him that I could tell he was a man of rank. 'Are you connected with the provincial governor in some way, sir?'

'Special envoy status. I'm surveying land boundaries.' He grinned, looking eager to astonish me. 'I have heard of you!' My face fell. 'I've a message from Vespasian,' he told me. 'This is obviously of grave national importance: if I see you out here, Didius Falco, I am to instruct you to return to Rome for an interview about the Sacred Geese.'

After I finished laughing, I had to tell him enough for him to realise just what an administrative shambles was involved. He took it well. He was a sensible, down-to-earth type of administrator himself, which must be why some vengeful clerk had sent him out here on a fool's errand to separate the rebellious landowners of Lepcis and Oea.

'I've just been here in Oea to receive representations from the top men.' He sounded low. 'Hopeless. I need to be out of here very fast tomorrow before they realise I'm coming down in favour of Lepcis. The plan is to announce my results at Lepcis, where the happy winners will ensure I'm not torn apart.'

'What's the problem?'

'The towns were up in arms during the civil war. Nothing to do with Vespasian's accession – they just took advantage of the general chaos to fight a private battle over territory. Oea called in the Garamantes to help, and Lepcis was besieged. No doubt about it, Oea caused the trouble, so when I draw the new official lines I'll be hammering them.'

'Lepcis gets the advantage?'

'It had to be one or the other, and Lepcis has the moral right.'

'Time to flee from Oea!' I agreed. 'How are you going?'

'On my ship,' said Rutilius Gallicus. 'If Lepcis is where you're heading, can I offer you a lift?'

On rare occasions you do meet officials who serve some use. Some will even help without having to be greased with a backhander first.

I managed to slide my party and their luggage off Myrrha's old boat while she and her people were at their evening meal. When it was all fixed, I told the interpreter that I had met an official I knew and hooked up with him. Rutilius Gallicus had a fast caravel that would soon outstrip Myrrha's bum-heavy hulk, and to help matters even further his fearless captain slipped anchor and took off by night.

'I know why I'm doing a flit. What's your hurry, Falco?' Rutilius asked curiously. I told him a little of the background to the dirty tricks war. He grasped the point immediately. 'Struggling for dominance. This all runs parallel to the problems I came to adjudicate—' Rutilius was settling in for a lecture, not that I minded. I was at sea; my concentration was fixed on avoiding being ill. He could talk all night so long as it distracted me. We were out on deck, feeling the breeze as we leant on the rail. 'None of the Three Towns has access to enough fertile land. They occupy this coastal strip, with a high jebel protecting them from the desert. It makes a good climate – well, a better one than the arid interior – but they are stuck on a small plain between the mountains and the sea, plus only whatever they can irrigate inland.'

'So what's their economy, sir? I thought they relied on trade?'

'Well they need to produce food, but in addition, Lepcis and Oea are trying to build up an olive oil industry. Africa Proconsularis proper is a grain basket, as I'm sure you know – I heard one estimate that Africa provides a third of all the corn we need in Rome. Here it's not suitable for so much cereal production, but olive trees do thrive and they need very little effort. I can see a time when Tripolitania will outstrip all the traditional outlets – Greece, Italy, Baetica.'

'So where are these olive groves?'

'Inland, a lot of them. The locals have a very refined system of irrigation, and I've calculated on maybe a thousand or more farms totally geared to production of oil – hardly any living quarters, just huge milling equipment. But as I say, there is not enough land, even with careful resource management. Hence the fighting.'

'Oea and Lepcis slogged it out, and Oea brought in the tribes? That was what caused Valerius Festus to pursue the Garamantes back into the desert?'

'Useful move. Lets them know who's in charge. We don't want to have to install a military presence too far south, purely to control nomads in the sand-dunes. Pins down too many troops. Waste of effort and cash.'

'Quite.'

'As for your wild beast merchants, their problem is probably related to the land famine. Families who own too little ground to match their ambitions with produce are hunting the beasts to supplement their incomes.'

'I think they enjoy it and are good at it too. What's driving them at present is the chance to make a huge profit when the new amphitheatre opens.'

'Exactly,' said Rutilius. 'But that's a long-term thing. The Flavian Amphitheatre has a planned construction timetable of what – ten years? I've seen the design drawings. If it comes off, it will be a beautiful thing but simply quarrying the stone out on the Via Tiburtina will take time.'

'They have had to build a whole new road to take the weight of the marble carts.'

'There you are. You don't build one of the new wonders of the world overnight. While these beast suppliers are waiting to cash in, their business is extremely expensive, and since the Statilius Taurus arena burnt down it's one with few immediate rewards. Capture, keeping the creatures, shipping them – all difficult and fiendishly pricey. They want to keep their organisations up to strength because the year the new amphitheatre opens they will be working flat out. But I can tell you, your fellows are all in hock up to their ear lobes, with no hope of balancing their budgets for a long time.'

'They aren't doing too badly!' He didn't know I had seen their census returns. 'Do you know the men I mean, sir?'

'I think so. I have had to meet and greet anyone who is anyone.'

'Not to mention all the lesser dogs who just *think* they're big?'

'You obviously have a feel for government.'

'Vespasian has been known to use me as an *ad hoc* diplomat.'

Rutilius paused. 'I know,' he said. So he had been briefed. That was curious.

'And I was involved with the Census,' I told him.

He pretended to gulp. 'Oh you're *that* Falco!' I was certain he already knew. 'I hope you're not out here to investigate me?'

'Why?' I put to him in a light tone. 'Is there something on your conscience?'

Rutilius left the personal question unanswered, implying he was innocent. 'Is that how you worked? Offering people a chance to come clean, in return for a fair deal?'

'Eventually. We had to hammer a few subjects, but once word went around most chose to negotiate a settlement before we even started. These Tripolitanian beast importers formed our first caseload.'

'Who were "we"?'

'I worked in partnership.'

I fell silent, thinking how pleasant it was, not to have to think about Anacrites.

Then Rutilius, whose information had already surprised me, said something even more curious: 'Someone else asked me about the beast importers recently.'

'Who was that?'

'I presume you know, since you mentioned him.'

'You've lost me.'

'When we first met you asked if "Romanus" was my name.'

'Somebody in Oea mentioned him. Have you encountered this person?'

'Once. He asked for an interview.'

'Who is he? What's he like?'

Rutilius frowned. 'He didn't really explain himself, and I could not decide what to make of him.'

'So what was his story?'

'Well, that was the odd thing. After he had gone I realised he had never said what it was all about. He had got into my office with a general air of authority. He just wanted to know what I could tell him about a group of lanistae who had attracted interest.'

'Interest from whom?'

'He never said. My feeling was, he was some sort of commercial informer.'

'So were his questions specific?'

'No. In fact I couldn't see why I had let myself be bothered to speak to him, so I gave him a couple of addresses and got rid of him.'

'Whose addresses?'

'Well, since we were in Lepcis at the time, your fellow Saturninus was one.'

This all sounded suspiciously like some agent of Hanno's hard at work. That could well explain why Hanno was coming to Lepcis, 'on business' as Myrrha had put it. She had mentioned the land survey, but maybe he wanted to reconnoitre with this new provocateur. Suppose Hanno had arranged to have Calliopus lured to Lepcis on some trumped up legal excuse – and was intending a showdown with both rivals?

Whatever the truth of it, Scilla's wish to meet both men together could now be put in hand – with Hanno himself also available. It certainly looked as if Lepcis was the place to be.

'And did you see "Romanus" again?' I asked Rutilius.

'No. Though I wanted to, because of my errand for Vespasian. After he left, one of my clerks told me he had been asking if they had seen anything of you.'

LIV

Lepcis Magna did have a harbour. Arriving by sea from Oea, we had sailed past the slight promontory where the civic centre is handsomely sited, out towards a stadium which we could see right on the water's edge, then we turned back slightly into the port with a clear run. The harbour entrance seemed a bit narrow, but once that was negotiated we found ourselves in a lagoon at the end of a wadi, protected by various islands and rocks. One day someone with a great deal of money might come along and provide proper moles, wharfs and maybe a lighthouse, though it would be a substantial project and it was hard to imagine what kind of influential big nut would think it worth the bother.

Things could not have worked out better: I wanted to interview Iddibal, and since he was waiting for his father he was out on the quayside looking at ships coming in. I had been told he was in Lepcis, though he was not expecting me. I was down the gangplank and able to back him into a winebar before he even remembered who I was.

Rutilius Gallicus was taking Helena and the rest of my party to the large house he lived in. That was one great advantage of having a girlfriend whose father was a senator; every time we met another senator abroad, the new one felt obliged to be polite in case Camillus Verus was someone he ought to cultivate. Helena's father did know Vespasian well. That was always useful to mention if we needed help, especially in a strange city where I felt we might be heading into a dangerous situation.

'In view of your Sacred Geese connection, I'm

delighted to offer hospitality and protection!' Rutilius was presumably joking; I smiled as if I had every idea what he meant about the holy honkers, then left him to arrange transport for our baggage while I dealt with the bestiarius.

Iddibal was much as I remembered him – strong, youthful and well-proportioned – though not of course wearing a gladiator's bare chest and bindings; instead he had on a long-sleeved, brightly coloured African-style tunic and a small round cap. Now he was a free man he had adorned himself with bracelets and baubles. He looked healthy and fit. He showed a slight unease at meeting me again, though not as much as he ought to, and not as much as he was going to experience once I tackled him.

'Falco,' I reminded him courteously. I knew that unlike his father and aunt, he could understand and speak Latin; the next generation. Iddibal's sons would probably move to Rome. Well, they would unless he ended up with a capital conviction as a result of what we discussed now. 'I've met your father on a couple of occasions, since I saw you in Rome. Your aunt too.'

On this basis we pretended to be happy social acquaintances, and I bought us both a drink. It was a small one; I was in informing mode. We sat outside, gazing at the dramatic blue sea. Iddibal must have sensed he was in trouble; he left his beaker undrunk, simply twirling it on the table nervously. He stopped himself asking what I wanted, so I let him guess for quite a long period.

'We can do this the easy way,' I said suddenly, 'or I can have you placed under arrest.'

The young man thought about leaping up and making a run for it. I remained motionless. He would see sense. There was nowhere to go. His father was due; he had to stay in Lepcis. I doubted he knew the town well. Where could he hide? Besides, he had no idea what I had just accused him of. For all he knew it was a mad mistake, and he should just try to laugh it off.

'What is the charge?' he decided to croak.

'Rumex was killed. It was the night before you bolted with your aunt's kind help.'

At once Iddibal gave a quiet laugh, almost to himself. He seemed relieved. 'Rumex? I knew of Rumex; he was famous. I never even met the man.'

'You both worked in the arena.'

'For different lanistae — and in different skills. The venatio hunters and the fighters don't mix.'

He looked at me. I gazed back, with a calm appearance that was meant to suggest I had an open mind. 'Calliopus is coming to Lepcis, did you know?'

He had not been aware of it.

'Who's Romanus?' I demanded.

'Never heard of him.' It sounded genuine. If 'Romanus' did work for his father, Hanno must be keeping whatever he was now planning to himself.

'You're not safe in this city,' I warned. However good Iddibal was with a hunting spear, he was at risk when surrounded by enemies on their home ground. Saturninus probably had just as good a reason to turn on him as Calliopus. 'Iddibal, I know you were in Rome to cause trouble between your father's rivals. I imagine neither of them has yet realised what you were up to. I bet they don't even know you are Hanno's son — or that Hanno is quietly destroying them while they fight among themselves.'

'You intend to tell them?' Iddibal demanded proudly.

'I just want to find out what happened. I have a client with an interest in some of it — though perhaps not in what you did. So tell me how far your involvement extended.'

'I'll admit nothing.'

'Foolish.' I drained my drink with an air of finality and banged down the cup.

The sudden action unsettled him. 'What do you want to know?' This young man was tough in some ways, but inexperienced in being interrogated. Fellows with well-known, very wealthy fathers don't have to put up with being stopped and searched by the local watch. He wouldn't have lasted an hour on the Aventine. He had not learned how to bluff, let alone how to lie.

'You stirred up Calliopus to various acts of sabotage? I don't suppose you had to inspire Saturninus; he would simply respond to the other man's stupidity. When did it all start?'

'As soon as I signed up. About six months before I first saw you.'

'How did you play it?'

'When Calliopus was moaning about Saturninus, which he often did, I would suggest ways to get back at him. We made his men drunk just before fights. We sent presents to his gladiators, that purported to come from women – then we reported the items as stolen. The vigiles turned over Saturninus' premises; we then vanished and there was nobody to press the charge. It did no harm; it just caused inconvenience.'

'Especially for the vigiles!'

'Well, them! Who cares?'

'You should do – if you're an honest man.' That was over-pious, but it worried Iddibal. 'What else?'

'When things hotted up, some of us went to Saturninus' cages and let out his leopardess.'

'Then in return, the ostrich was poisoned – after which Rumex was killed. A hit for Saturninus, then one for Calliopus – and since you were thinking up the other incidents, the finger of suspicion falls on you for Rumex too. But the serious trouble started with the dead lion. Are you implicated in what happened to Leonidas?'

'No.'

'Calliopus always said you were.'

'No.'

'You'd better tell me what happened.'

'Buxus told Calliopus that Saturninus had made an approach to borrow a lion. Calliopus himself thought up working a switch. All the rest of us were told to take early nights and stay in our cells.'

'I bet you all peeked! What exactly went on that night?'

Iddibal smiled and confessed, 'Buxus was supposed to pretend he never heard a thing. He was bribed by Saturninus to lie low – Buxus and Calliopus split the cash, I think. Saturninus sent his men, who had been told where to find the spare key to the menagerie.'

'Under Mercury's hat?'

Iddibal raised his eyebrows. 'How do you know that?'

'Never mind. The borrowers had been told they were getting Draco, the wild lion, but Leonidas was put in Draco's cage instead. So it all went wrong, and he ended up dead. Did you look out later when the corpse was being returned?'

'No. I heard them at it, but that was hours afterwards and I was in bed. In fact they woke me up. Saturninus' men were hopeless; they made far too much noise. If we hadn't already known what was going on, the alarm would have been raised. Next day, when we knew the lion was dead and they had been panicking, we could understand their clumsiness. At the time we all grinned to ourselves at how inept they were, then we rolled over and went back to sleep.'

'I don't suppose Saturninus and his people got much rest,' I said.

'Calliopus thought Saturninus had killed Leonidas deliberately. Did he?' asked Iddibal.

'Almost certainly not – though I don't suppose he cared when it happened. His main concern was how it looked for him if news got out that he had arranged a private show. It had to be hushed up, especially in view of an ex-praetor being hurt. Pomponius was very badly mauled; in fact, he's now dead.'

'So are you investigating this officially?' Iddibal asked, seeming worried. He must realise an ex-praetor's death would not go overlooked.

'People close to the ex-praetor have appealed to the Emperor. They want compensation. Whoever is held responsible could face a hefty financial penalty.' That made

Iddibal wince. 'Why did Calliopus keep blaming you afterwards?'

He shrugged. 'It was a ploy.'

'How?'

'Partly to make it look like internal business, when you kept poking about.'

'Try another excuse – and make it a better one.'

'Also, to explain to the others why he let my aunt buy me out.'

'So why did he allow that?'

Iddibal looked annoyed. Either he was an extremely good actor, or it was for real. 'She paid a huge amount. Why else?'

I signalled a waiter who brought us more wine. Iddibal condescended to drink his first beaker, obviously feeling he needed it. When the waiter had gone back inside I asked quietly, 'Why don't you just tell me the truth? That Calliopus wanted to escalate the war with Saturninus, so he asked you to kill Rumex?'

'Yes, he did ask.' I was astonished that Iddibal admitted it.

'And?'

'I refused to do it. I'm not mad.' I was inclined to believe him. Had he accepted the job and carried out the gladiator's murder, Iddibal would not have told me he was ever approached.

'Someone did it.'

'Not me.'

'You will have to prove that, Iddibal.'

'How can I? I knew nothing about Rumex being dead until you told me just now. You say it was the night before I left Rome? I was in the barracks all evening – until my aunt came with my manumission; then I went straight to Ostia with her. Fast,' he explained insistently, 'in case there was any comeback from Calliopus. Until Aunt Myrrha came, I was doing normal things, casual things. Other people will have seen me there, but they work for Calliopus. If you start stirring and he learns I was working for Papa, he'll be furious; then none of his staff will give me an alibi.'

Panic had gripped him, but being intelligent, he at once started to work out his defence. 'Can you prove it was me? Of course not. Nobody can have seen me, since I was not the killer. Can there be any other evidence? What weapon was used?'

'A small knife.'

'A hunting knife?'

'I would say not actually.'

'You don't have it?'

'By the time I saw the corpse, the knife was missing.' It was possible Saturninus had removed it, though there was no obvious reason why he should. Anacrites and I had asked him; Saturninus had told us the weapon had never been found. We saw no reason to disbelieve him. 'The general view is that the killer took the knife away with him.'

'Any other evidence?' Iddibal was cheering up.

'No.'

'So I'm in the clear.'

'No. You are a suspect. You were working incognito, which you admit was in order to cause trouble. You left Rome hastily straight after the murder. You have just told me Calliopus did ask you to kill Rumex. This is certainly enough for me to hand you to an enquiring magistrate.'

He took a deep breath. 'It looks bad.' I liked his honesty. 'Are you arresting me?'

'Not yet.'

'I want to talk to my father.'

'He is expected, I'm told. What's he coming for?'

'A meeting.'

'With whom?'

'Saturninus, primarily.'

'What about?'

'They do talk.'

'Regularly?'

'Not often.'

'Saturninus is pretty gregarious?'

'He likes to have a lot of dealings with a lot of men.'

'He can live on good terms with his rivals?'

'He can live with anyone.'

'Unlike Calliopus?'

'No. That one prefers to go into a corner and brood.'

'He'll be brooding rather heavily if he finds out who you are!'

'He's not supposed to find out.'

'If you had known Calliopus would be coming—'

'I wouldn't be here.'

'So what now?'

'When my father's ship arrives, I shall skip aboard it and lie low until we leave.'

'Back to Sabratha?'

'That's where we live.'

'Don't be smart with me. How much did your aunt pay for your release from slavery?'

'I don't know the amount. She told me it was a high price. I didn't nag her for the details; I felt responsible.'

'Why? Was going under cover your idea?'

'No. We were all in on it. The plan had been for me to do a moonlit flit, but in the end I wanted to be bought out properly. I cannot be a runaway; it would make me a hostage for the rest of my life.'

'Why did Calliopus pick you as a person to ask to kill Rumex?'

'A bribe. My aunt had already been to see him, and he knew I wanted to leave. If I killed Rumex, he said I could have my release in return.' Iddibal looked embarrassed. 'I have to admit, even my aunt thought I should do it. Obviously it would have saved her a great deal of money.'

'Assuming you were not caught! When I was auditing Calliopus, I saw you and Myrrha arguing one night. Was that about killing Rumex?'

'Yes.'

'So she asked you to do what Calliopus wanted, and according to you, you refused.'

Iddibal wanted to protest, but he recognised I was goading him. Hunting was a game he knew. 'Yes, I refused,' he reiterated quietly, keeping his cool.

'Nice Aunt Myrrha then agreed after all to find the money, and she found so much that Calliopus released you on the spot. Has this situation caused you any difficulties with your family since you came home?'

'No. My aunt and father have been very good about it. We are a close and happy family.' Iddibal stared at the ground, suddenly subdued. 'I wish I had never got into all this.'

'It must have seemed like a brilliant adventure.'

'True.'

'You don't realise how complicated and dark that sort of adventure will become.'

'True again.'

I quite liked him. I didn't know whether I could believe him, but he was not sly, nor did he feign outrage when I asked him fair questions. And he had not tried to run away.

Of course running away was not Iddibal's style. We had established that he preferred to be bought out. No doubt if I ever found any grounds to take him before a magistrate, the close happy family would rally round again and buy him out of that too. I had the inexorable feeling that I was wasting my time even trying to progress against these folks.

I told Iddibal I was staying with the special envoy who was surveying land. That had a nice official ring. I gave the young man a long, hard look, then issued the usual wonderful warning about not leaving town without telling me first.

He was young enough to assure me earnestly that, of course, he would do no such thing. He was naïve enough to look as if he really meant what he said.

LV

The air was hot and dry. I walked to the north shore and up to the forum. Whereas the principal building materials in Cyrenaïca had been red-toned, Tripolitanian cities were gold and grey. Lepcis Magna hugged the coast so closely that when I entered the forum I could still hear the sea, surging against low white sand-dunes behind me. There should have been bustle that would have masked the noise of the surf, but the place was dead.

The civic centre must date from the very beginning of the Empire, for the main temple was dedicated to Rome and Augustus. It stood in a cramped row with those of Liber Pater and Hercules – an old-fashioned, very provincial set to site so prominently. Perhaps this was not the real heart of Lepcis, however; the forum seemed to have been placed where it would be by-passed by those in the know. I looked across the square flagstones to the basilica and curia. Nothing doing. For one of the world's great commercial entrepôts, this was a sleepy hole. I then crossed the sun-baked open space and enquired at the basilica if they had any upcoming case in which Saturninus was involved? No. Calliopus of Oea? No. Did they know of a subpoena-deliverer called Romanus? No, again.

The main temple, now opposite me as I emerged, had reassuringly familiar slim, smooth Ionic columns, though even they had been given odd little floral sprigs between the volutes. I walked back to it and checked for messages: none. I left word myself of where I was staying, in case either Scilla or Justinus turned up. I wanted to leave another message for somebody, but not here.

I retraced my steps down the silent side-street between

the temples and took the road into town. This was busier. Keeping to the shade on the left-hand side as it climbed slightly away from the shore, I passed or was passed by various laden mules and cheerful children pushing mountainously piled handcarts. Lock-up shops and modest dwellings lined the streets, which were laid out in a neat enough grid. Activity was increasing the farther I walked. Eventually I came to the theatre, and near it the market area where at last the hum was all I had expected in one of the great cities of the Emporia.

The main provisions market boasted two elegant pavilions, one round and drum-shaped with arches, one octagonal with a Corinthian colonnade – possibly built by different benefactors who had independent views on effect. On a long-winded inscription, however, a certain Tapepius Rufus claimed responsibility for the whole edifice; maybe he had quarrelled with his architect halfway.

Beneath the kiosks' shade every kind of sale was being conducted on flat-topped stone tables, with the emphasis on domestic trade. Peas, lentils and other pulses were piled in dry heaps; figs and dates were set out on fruit stalls; both raw almonds and cakes made from almonds and honey were temptingly available. There were fish. There were cereals. It was the wrong time of year for grapes, but I saw vineleaves, both ready-stuffed or strung together in brine to take home and stuff as you chose. Butchers, advertising with crude pictures of cows, pigs, camels and goats, were honing their knives on a lion-footed bench in the weights and measures corner, while the weights and measures inspectors craned their necks over a hot game of draughts scratched on the ground.

Two streets away another Lepcis millionaire had built another commercial enclosure, this one with a dedication to Venus of Chalcis, where it looked as if large export contracts were being organised by evil, toothless, leather-skinned old negotiators who had no time to eat and no inclination to shave. No doubt this was the exchange for big business: olive oil, fish sauce, mass market pottery and wild beasts, plus the exotics that came in from the nomads: heavy baulks of ivory, negro slaves, gemstones, and strange wild birds and animals. I found a banker who would honour my letter of introduction. Immediately I had funds on my person, a tout tried to sell me an elephant.

Seeing a lone male of foreign origin, persons enquired very helpfully whether I had need of a brothel. I smiled and refused. Some then went so far as to recommend their own sisters as clean, willing and available.

I returned to the main market. There I found a pillar with some free doodling space and scratched up:

ROMANUS: SEE FALCO AT THE HOUSE OF RUTILIUS

If you sound as if you know people, sometimes they believe it is true. Besides, by now I had a disconcerting feeling that Romanus must indeed be an old acquaintance. If so, it was bad news.

I went to a bathhouse to test the local atmosphere. I got myself shaved, just as badly as anywhere else in the Empire. The theatre was another Tapepius Rufus bequest, elegant in style and positioned with stunning views over the sea. I looked at the programme: not much happening there. No point, since the big draw in Lepcis was the coming end-of-harvest Games in the arena outside town. Those were advertising that ever popular programme, 'to be announced', though I noticed they were to be presided over by my host, the visiting Roman dignitary, Rutilius Gallicus. I wondered if anyone had told him about that yet.

I had done enough for a first scout around. It was time to resume contact with my family before they became tetchy being polite to the envoy, while I was out enjoying myself.

I followed the directions Rutilius had given me to the lavish maritime villa some local personage had made available to him (no doubt hoping to court popularity for Lepcis when the surveyor was apportioning land). The set-up seemed secure. In case of trouble over his report, Rutilius had been assigned a squad of military bodyguards; he had also brought his own small domestic staff. All he needed for his own comfort now were a few politically neutral house guests he could talk to, and we had provided those.

I told him he had to wave the white napkin at the Games; he groaned.

For the next few days I spent my working time trying to pin down the three lanistae I was studying. Saturninus was the easiest to locate. After all, he lived here. Rutilius gave me his address and I marked the house. Saturninus himself appeared the first day I was on watch outside. It was a shock to have come right across the dolphin-filled Mediterranean to find myself scrutinising a suspect I last encountered months before in Rome.

He looked the same, but wearing loose, bright nomad robes – stylishly in keeping with his home province. Short, muscular, broken-nosed, balding, confident, urbane. Beringed to the point that I felt an austere Roman distrust of him. Still, I had always recoiled from his entrepreneurial attitude. He was not my type. That did not necessarily make him a criminal.

He swanned past without noticing me. I was lying in the road with a big hat over my eyes, near a tethered donkey that I pretended was in my charge. I was doing my best not to fall asleep, though sloth was beckoning. At least now that my subject had made his move I had to bestir myself and follow him.

He came and went: forum (briefly); market (longer); baths (longer still); his local gladiatorial barracks (an interminable stay). Whenever he moved around in public places he made himself available to men of substance. He mingled. He laughed and chatted. He leant down and spoke to little boys who were out with their fathers. He diced idly; he dallied coarsely with waitresses. He sat at tavern tables watching the world go by, so the passing world could come across and greet him like an uncle who had presents to hand out.

Presumably at his barracks he trained fighters just as he had done in Rome, though on a more limited scale. The outlets here were hardly the same as the great imperial festivals. But his men would appear at the next Lepcis Games. That might be worth watching.

Calliopus took longer to weed out. It was Helena who found him eventually; she heard his wife mentioned by name at the women's baths. Artemisia had never met my lass, so she would not recognise her; Helena took a chance that it was the right person and followed her home.

'She is quite young, slim, absolutely beautiful.'

'Sounds like one of my old girlfriends,' I commented. Very foolishly.

Later, (in fact quite a long time later as I then had some domestic repair work to attend to), I watched the rented apartment that Helena had identified and saw Calliopus go out for his own ablutions that afternoon. Another old face: wide nose, flappy ears, thin, neat, crinkle-haired.

He and his wife led a much quieter life than the Saturninus ménage, presumably because in Lepcis they knew nobody. They sat out in the sun, went for meals in local chop houses, shopped gently. They gave the impression they were waiting for someone or something. I thought Calliopus looked worried, but then he had always been the tall, lanky kind who bit his nails over things others take in their stride.

The young wife was stunning, though desperately quiet.

I had sent Gaius down to the harbour to watch for when Hanno arrived. His ship now rode at anchor next to that of his sister Myrrha amongst the teeming merchant vessels in the lagoon. Iddibal had been glimpsed aboard. Hanno and Myrrha made occasional expeditions to the market, leading a colourful parade of their staff. The insubordinate interpreter who had conversed on my behalf was with them.

Hanno did a great deal of business in the Chalcidicum. It looked as if he was a tough haggler. Sometimes harsh words were exchanged, and although it usually ended amicably with slapped palms sealing the contract, I reckoned Hanno was not popular.

So they were all here. None of the three men appeared to make any attempt to meet the others.

We had Saturninus and Calliopus, just as Scilla had wanted, and I could offer her Hanno, together with the news that his machinations had stirred up the stupid rivalry that caused the death of Pomponius. My only problem was, Scilla herself had still not appeared. She had insisted on coming to Lepcis in her own way and in her own time. After my long detour to Sabratha, thanks to Famia, I had expected her to have arrived here ahead of me. If so, there was no sign of her.

This was tricky. I could not guarantee that any of the parties would remain here long. I suspected that in view of their professional interest Hanno and Calliopus were just hanging on for the Games. I was loth to make contact with any of them on Scilla's behalf until she showed. I would certainly not initiate the court case she had talked about. I had known enough clients; I was prepared now for the single-minded Scilla to set me up in a difficult situation, then vanish without trace. Without paying me either, of course.

I had not forgotten that in my capacity as Census auditor I had made both Calliopus and Saturninus pay huge tax bills. They must both loathe me. I was none too keen on loafing around in their home province, just waiting for them to notice me, remember the financial pain I had caused, and decide to have me thrashed.

Famia had not bothered to follow us here as I had asked him to. What a surprise.

'I've had enough of this,' I told Helena. 'If Scilla hasn't

presented herself here by the end of the Games, we'll pack up and go home. You and I have our own lives to lead.'

'Besides,' she laughed, 'you have been recalled to talk about those geese.'

'Never mind the bloody birds. Vespasian has agreed to pay me a delightful amount for the Census and I want to start enjoying it.'

'You'll have to face Anacrites.'

'No trouble. He earned a packet too. He should have no complaints. Anyway, he ought to be fit again by now; he can go back to his old post.'

'Ah, but he really liked working with you, Marcus! It's been the high spot of his life.'

I growled. 'You're a tease – and Anacrites is dumped.'

'Are you really going to let my brother work with you if he comes to Rome?'

'A privilege. I always liked Quintus.'

'I'm glad. I had an idea, Marcus. I talked about it to Claudia while she and I were waiting for you two to come back from your silphium jaunt, but it was when things between her and Quintus were so strained. That's why I never mentioned it ...' She tailed off, which was not Helena's style.

'What idea?' I asked suspiciously.

'If Quintus and Claudia ever get married, Claudia and I should buy a shared house for us all to live in.'

'I shall have enough money for you and I to live in comfort,' I retorted stiffly.

'Quintus won't.'

'That's his fault.'

Helena sighed.

'Sharing only leads to arguments,' I said.

'I had in mind,' Helena proposed, 'a house that would be big enough to seem like different properties. Separate wings – but common areas where Claudia and I could sit and mutter together when you and Quintus had gone out.'

'If you want to moan about me, darling, you shall be given the right facilities!'

'Well, what do you think?'

'I think—' Inspiration hit me. 'I had better not commit myself to anything until I discover what the bother is about these Sacred Geese.'

'Chicken!' quipped Helena.

Things might have turned very awkward but just then one of our host's staff – who all seemed wary of my group – nervously announced that Helena had a visitor. Jumpy, for the reasons I have outlined, I asked tersely who it was. Assuming I was a stern paterfamilias who expected to vet his poor wife's every move (what a clown!), the slave told me with great diffidence that it was only a woman, one Euphrasia, wife to Saturninus, a principle figure in Lepcis social life. Helena Justina placed her feet neatly on a kickstool, folded her hands over her girdle, then looked at me meekly and enquiringly. I gravely granted permission for her to accept this call. Helena thanked me for my forbearance, addressing me in a gentle voice, while her huge brown eyes flashed sheer wickedness.

I whipped outside the room where she was sitting, and hid myself where I could overhear.

LVI

'My dear, how delightful!'

'What an unexpected privilege!'

'How do you come to be here?'

'How did you realise that I was?'

'My husband spotted some message scrawled up at the market about Falco being in this house – are you aware that my husband and I live in this city?'

'Well, I must have known – how thrilling! We have been having a terrible time – Falco has dragged me everywhere in Africa.'

'Official business?'

'Oh Euphrasia, I don't ask!'

I choked, as Helena pretended to be a downtrodden, weary, excluded wife. If Euphrasia remembered the dinner party we attended, she cannot have been fooled.

'Is it to do with his Census work?' Euphrasia was intending to press the point, however hard Helena feigned disinterest.

I peeked through a doorcrack. Helena had her back to me, which was fortunate as it prevented any danger that one of us would start giggling. Euphrasia, resplendent in glowing stripes of scarlet and purple, a triumph of rich murex dyes, lolled in a long cane chair. She looked relaxed, though those handsome eyes were sharp and she displayed an inner tension that intrigued me. I wondered if Saturninus had sent her here, or whether he even knew that she had come.

Refreshments were sent for. Then the baby was sent for too. Julia Junilla let herself be passed around, kissed, pinched and tickled, had her little tunic straightened, had her fine wisps of hair ruffled, then when she was placed on a floor-rug she produced a bravura display of crawling and playing with dolls. Instead of screaming with disgust she hiccuped cutely. My daughter was a star.

'The darling! How old is she?'

'Not quite one.' Julia's birthday was ten days away; another reason to try to reach home beforehand and placate her two doting grandmothers.

'She's charming – and so intelligent!'

'Takes after her father,' said Helena, knowing I would be listening. I half expected her to go on with a few teasing insults, but she was probably preoccupied with wondering about the reason for Euphrasia's call.

'And how is dear Falco?'

'When I ever get to see him, he seems his usual self – deep in causes and schemes as usual.' Even from my hiding place I thought Euphrasia's eyes narrowed. Helena would be close enough to tell for sure. 'And how are you and your husband, Euphrasia?'

'Oh much happier. We had to get away from Rome, you know, Helena. All that squabbling and double dealing was too much.' That comment would include the domestic after-effects of Euphrasia's affair with Rumex, no doubt. 'The atmosphere in the provinces is far more pleasant; we may stay here permanently now—'

Helena was reclining gracefully in a similar chair to her guest. I could see one of her bare arms dangling casually. Its familiar smooth curve raised the hairs on my neck as I thought about tracing my finger along her skin in the way that made her arch her back and laugh . . . 'Can your husband run his business from Tripolitania?'

'Oh yes. Anyway, I want him to retire.' Women always say that, though not many are prepared to put up with cutting back on the housekeeping. 'He's done enough. So what brings Falco to Lepcis Magna?'

Helena finally took pity: 'He's working for a private client.'

'Anyone I know?'

'Oh nothing terribly exciting. It's just a commission for a woman who needs help to bring a lawsuit, I believe.'

'It seems a long way for you to come.'

'We were out here for family reasons,' Helena replied reassuringly.

Euphrasia ignored that. 'I'm fascinated . . . however would your husband find a client in a strange province? Did he advertise?'

'Not at all.' Helena was perfectly calm, in marked contrast to the other woman's obvious edginess. 'We were on holiday. The client found us. She was somebody who had heard of Falco in Rome.'

Euphrasia could no longer bear the suspense and came out with her question bluntly: 'He's not working for that hard trout who was involved with Pomponius Urtica?'

'Do you mean Scilla?' asked Helena innocently.

'I know she wants to cause trouble,' Euphrasia said, backing off slightly and becoming more offhand again. 'She has been harassing my husband. I dare say she's been on at Calliopus too. We know he's in Lepcis,' Euphrasia continued, now speaking bitterly. 'With that wife of his, I hear. Artemisia has a lot to answer for!'

'Why would that be?' asked Helena, in quiet astonishment. As far as we knew, all Artemisia had done was to let herself be married to Calliopus, a man who reckoned that being wealthy meant owning a full set of everything – including a mistress called Saccarina in Borealis Street. Euphrasia's accusatory tone seemed uncalled for. Mind you, I had now seen that Artemisia was young and beautiful, which many another woman would find unforgivable.

'Oh never mind her,' Euphrasia said dismissively. 'If Artemisia takes chances, Calliopus puts her right with his fist. If you ask me,' she leant forward, looking earnest, 'Scilla's the who intends to cause serious trouble. She's the maggot to watch.'

'I quite liked her,' Helena commented, resisting Euphrasia's condemnation.

'You're too tolerant. She's trying to force a confrontation with my husband and Calliopus. We're certain she's persuaded that dreadful man Hanno to back her.'

'She had a terrible experience when the lion attacked her lover,' Helena remonstrated gently. 'I'm sure it wasn't her fault. I don't believe she ever asked for a private display in her honour. It seems to have been her fiancé's idea; she disapproved of it. He made a misjudgment, a typical male error. It's very sad for Scilla that Pomponius died that way.'

'You know quite a lot about her then?' Euphrasia asked narrowly.

'She approached me first. Falco was off on a jaunt with my brother, so in a way I vetted her. As I say, I did feel for her. Some compensation for her loss would seem to be desirable.'

There was a short silence.

'I was there of course,' Euphrasia barked.

'Where, Euphrasia?' Helena may not have grasped immediately what she meant. I could tell she soon remembered that Saturninus had told me the four evening diners at the intended private show had been Pomponius and Scilla, plus himself – and also his wife. We should have asked Euphrasia for her version before this.

'At Pomponius' house. When the lion got loose.'

'You saw what happened then?' Helena replied quietly.

'Oh yes. I shan't say any more; my husband would be furious. It was agreed that nothing would be said. Pomponius wanted it that way.'

'I don't understand.'

'Naturally, it was to protect her. Scilla, I mean. Pomponius was loyal, you have to give him that. When he realised he was dying, he was more insistent than ever. She had enough of a reputation without all Rome hearing about the lion incident!'

'Well, Pomponius is dead now—'

'Stupid man!' Euphrasia snarled. 'Don't ask me about it,' she repeated. 'But Scilla could tell you. Before you start feeling sorry for that little madam, Helena Justina, you should make her admit the truth. Ask Scilla,' commanded Euphrasia resoundingly, 'who *really* killed that lion!'

She swept to her feet. As she did so, she must have disturbed something, a small golden creature which darted along a skirting not far from where the baby was inspecting her own pink little toes on the floor.

'Is that a mouse?' Helena gasped.

'No, a scorpion.'

I walked into the room, like a husband just returning from a morning on the quayside. Keeping up the charade, I let my face register all the right things: surprise at seeing Euphrasia, alarm at Helena's set white face, rapid reaction to the emergency.

I scooped up the baby; passed her to Helena; moved Helena out of the way; pushed past Euphrasia. I seized a vase and dropped it over the scorpion. Helena had closed her eyes, rigid with shock.

'Helena once had a bad scorpion sting,' I explained tersely.

I shepherded them all from the room then went back to deal with the scuttling thing. After I had battered it to pieces, taking revenge for what the other had done to the precious girl I loved, I sat on my haunches in private for a moment, remembering how Helena nearly died.

I went out to find her. Holding her and Julia, hushing them, even I trembled.

'It's all right, Marcus.'

'We'll go home.'

'No; it's all right.'

When we had settled down again, we realised that in the panic Euphrasia had taken her chance to avoid awkward questions; she had slipped away.

We could not ask my client what Euphrasia had meant, because Scilla still failed to appear.

Then, out of the blue next day, the elusive Scilla wrote to me. The letter was found on the doorstep in the morning, so there was no messenger to trace. It appeared she was now in Lepcis, though as usual, she was coy about her address.

She confessed that when she arrived here (which must have been some time ago) after she failed to find me she had hired someone else. She did not specify Romanus, though I reckoned it was him. He had managed to contact the two men for her, and there were plans for a settlement. I could send a bill to the house of Pomponius Urtica in Rome to cover any expenses I myself had incurred so far. My services were no longer required.

Paid off, eh?

Not me, Scilla. My clients were always losing heart and backing away; it was a hazard of the job. The mud they stirred up often took them by surprise and caused a rethink. It was not worth pressurising them once they lost the initial impetus.

Nor, when a case had once attracted my interest was I ever in the habit of allowing myself to abandon it. I would stop work when I chose. Which meant, when I had satisfied my own curiosity.

LVII

The night before the Games, Rutilius and I took a quiet walk out to the amphitheatre.

We crossed the wadi by the harbour, then hiked along the beach, alternately hopping on rocky outcrops and sinking into soft white sand.

'This is hard going,' Rutilius complained, stretching his calf muscles. 'I'll arrange transport tomorrow. Will Helena want to come?'

I picked up a piece of cuttlefish. 'Yes, sir. She says she's afraid I may end up in the arena fighting somebody.'

'Is it likely?' He sounded shocked.

'I'm not stupid.' Playing at gladiators meant permanent disgrace, with legal penalties.

All three lanistae were bound to attend the Games. I was expecting some sort of showdown; Helena Justina knew that. There was no point trying to hide it from her; she was far too sensitive. I was prepared for anything. So, therefore, was Helena.

'The work you get involved in can be dangerous?' Rutilius asked. 'So what might be in store for us tomorrow, may I ask?'

'Sir, I don't know. Nothing, maybe.'

Perhaps, but I was not alone in suspecting a crisis; this trip to reconnoitre the layout had been his idea. He looked calm, but I reckoned Rutilius Gallicus, special envoy of Vespasian, was as keyed up as me.

He had his own troubles. He had surveyed the land between Lepcis and Oea and was ready to announce results. 'I'm just the latest sucker in a traditional line,' he told me as we approached the stadium, which we came to first. 'Boundaries have been a source of bitter contention for a long time. There was a famous event when Carthage and Cyrenaïca were in dispute. Two pairs of brothers set out simultaneously running from Lepcis and Cyrene. Where they met was the new border; unfortunately the Greeks of Cyrene accused the two brothers from Lepcis of cheating. To prove their innocence they demanded to be buried alive.'

'Olympus! Did it happen?'

'It did. There's a grand old commemorative arch over the roadway to this day . . . I have felt, Falco, the same fate may be waiting to ambush me!'

'Rome, sir, will applaud your sacrifice.'

'Oh good. That will make it all worthwhile.'

I liked him. The men Vespasian chose to establish order in the Empire were of a dry, down-to-earth type. They got on with the job, fairly and quickly, undeterred by incipient unpopularity.

'It's a good province,' he said. 'I'm not the first to come out to Africa Proconsularis and feel a tug. The place attracts strong loyalty.'

'It's Mediterranean. Warm; honest; cheerful. Nicely exotic, yet still smacks of home.'

'Needs a good sorting,' Rutilius exclaimed.

'Helena is compiling a set of recommendations that she wants to hand in to the Emperor.'

'Really? Did he ask you to do that?' Rutilius sounded surprised again.

I grinned. 'He didn't ask. That won't stop Helena Justina ensuring he's told. And she is covering Cyrenaïca where we were first. She has listed everything from restoring the amphitheatre at Apollonia to rebuilding the earthquake-damaged temple in the forum at Sabratha. She likes to be comprehensive. She's tackled the fight business as well. When they open the new Flavian Amphitheatre, Helena thinks it should all come under state control: everything from gladiatorial training to the import of beasts. The legions should supervise provincial collection of wild animals. Imperial agents should be in control.' I happened to know Helena had had the wonderful idea of suggesting that Anacrites should be put in charge of presenting the position papers on new policy. It would be a ten-year job – and would certainly keep him away from me.

'That all?' asked Rutilius drily.

'No, sir. To complete the picture, she recommends that chief men from Africa be admitted to the Senate, as has already happened with other provinces.'

'Great gods. It's all good stuff – but do you seriously expect Vespasian to accept this from a woman?'

'No, sir. I'll sign the report. He'll think it's from me.' That was no better to a man like Rutilius. I was an Aventine pleb, hardly decent material for the Emperor's inner cabinet.

'You make suggestions like these every time you go abroad?'

'If there seems anything to recommend.'

'And it all gets put into effect?'

'Oh no!' I laughed, reassuring him that the world he knew was not turning upside down. 'You know what happens up on the Palatine: the scroll is simply filed away. But maybe in twenty years time or so, some of the items that Helena thought important will float to the top of an agenda in some short-of-work secretariat.'

Rutilius shook his head in disbelief.

We had reached the stadium. It lay parallel to the shore, swept by brisk sea breezes, one of the finest locations possible. It looked a good course, and a well-used one apparently.

We walked slowly across the racetrack. At present the low evening sun and the sound of the sea at our backs gave the place a peaceful air, though when the whole town came out here to fill the rows of seats, the atmosphere would be totally different. 'Tomorrow, in the amphi-theatre, at this show I have to supervise—' Rutilius paused.

'The show you've been stuck with,' I grinned.

'Which I will be honoured to preside over!' he sighed. 'Under my auspices anyway, they are planning a pro-gramme of paired gladiators. As far as I can see, nothing exceptional. That's preceded by a criminal execution, some halfwit blasphemer getting his due *ad bestias*.'

'A capital crime? Doesn't that need the approval of the governor, sir?'

'The case caused a bit of a crisis. I got drawn in, and it was expedient to say I hold the governor's remit while I'm here. It all blew up this morning, and on top of the land survey it was set to cause a riot. We already have too many people from the rival cities in town at present – things could get ugly tomorrow.'

'So what's the capital case?'

'Totally unacceptable. Some lout passing through drank himself into a stupor, then woke up in the forum and started insulting the local gods. Terribly embarrassing. Attempts were made to restrain him, but he just started bollocking Hannibal and all his descendants at the top of his voice. He was whacked on the head, rescued from the mob, and dragged before the nearest person in authority – I found myself in that unfortunate role. It was an issue, of course: Rome's attitude to the Punic element. I had no choice. So tomorrow there's dinner for the lions.'

'Has a beast been provided?'

'Saturninus just happened to have one,' replied Rutilius.

'I had better warn Helena.'

'Not keen? Neither am I. Ask her to shut her eyes and endure it, if she will. She'll be sitting in my party, right in full view; things have to look good. They say it's a fierce animal; the business should be swift.'

We had now come to a covered walkway that linked the stadium to the arena. The light was fading but we took a chance and marched briskly through a tall, arched corridor. It was probably just intended for pedestrians, though it offered possibilities for joint presentations using both venues. The scope and placing of their auditoria suggested the people of Lepcis had a sophisticated love of being entertained, and demanded a high standard.

Emerging into the amphitheatre, a gracious elipse cut into a hillside, we found workers hard at it, consolidating and raking the white sand on the arena floor. Tomorrow the pristine results of their careful labours would be violently scuffed up and blood-soaked. After a look, I consulted Rutilius, then we set out to climb the rows of seats. Somebody on the top level called my name.

'Who's that, Falco?'

'Wonderful! It's Camillus Justinus, Helena's younger brother. He has been looking for the Gardens of the Hesperides to impress his lady-love – I had hoped he might catch up with us.'

'I've heard of him,' said Rutilius, puffing as we speeded up our climb. 'Didn't he cause some trouble, running off with a young woman?'

'He might have got away with stealing the girl, sir – but he ran off with her money too, and there was a lot of it. I'm taking him home to be spanked.'

'Quite right.'

Having formally assumed a proper attitude, the envoy joined me in greeting Justinus with great friendliness.

We found a way we could return to town along the top of the dunes, to avoid the beach. The first unfamiliar African stars winked overhead as we marched along, exchanging news.

'Everything all right with Claudia?'

'Why shouldn't it be?' Justinus had the grace to grin. 'I've seen Famia's horse transport in the lagoon today, Marcus, though no sign of him.'

'He'll be in a wineshop. Well, it sounds as though we're all set to sail home then.'

Briefly I toyed with the idea of forgetting the Games, finding Famia, and slipping off straightaway. I was ready to see Rome again. Julia's first birthday ought to be celebrated at home. And anyway, why should we stay? I had no client employing me.

Justinus provided the answer: 'Have you heard the rumour running wild? There's a needle-match planned for tomorrow's Games. Saturninus, Calliopus, and Hanno have agreed to arrange a special three-sided bout.'

'What! How's that?'

'It's all rather mysterious, but I heard that each is putting up a gladiator for a fight to the death. It will be the final event — something to make the rival groups from the different towns really yell their heads off.'

The tingle I had felt all day increased. 'Hades! That sounds as if this could degenerate into an occasion when the amphitheatre erupts.'

'You haven't heard the best. The part that will interest you, Marcus, is that this bout is supposed to settle a legal claim. There's an unusual twist — whichever lanista owns the last man left alive has agreed to pay compensation to a certain Scilla in a suit she has against them all.'

'Io! That means they'll want to lose, surely?'

Justinus laughed. 'All three of them are supposed to be putting up some complete no-hoper so it turns into a comedy. The fighters won't want to die — but for once their lanistae will be trying to persuade them to go down.'

'Oh very colourful.'

'From what I heard in the market place, there is a curious interest in the deadbeats.'

'Do they have names?' asked Rutilius, just beating me to it.

'None that I heard. All sorts of rumours are flying — freaks with two heads each are the favourite suggestion. Fascinating, eh?'

'Sounds enough to crank up interest,' I said.

'It's high,' Justinus confirmed. 'Large bets being taken, perfectly openly.'

'This is it then,' I said. I was speaking to no one in

particular, though both of my companions must have known just what I meant.

Somewhere in Lepcis that night menagerie keepers would be starving a lion.

Somewhere too, gladiators of various qualities were enjoying the traditional lavish eve-of-fight meal. It was their privilege – and could be their curse. It was often the clincher when the following day dawned; they would be tempted to enjoy all they could, since it might be their last chance. But indulge too much, and that would count against them in the ring.

On the way back through town Justinus and I did make a feeble attempt to get into the main local training school – the Saturninus spread – with a view to inspecting the men at their feast. Members of the public were being barred. We thought it best not to make an issue. For one thing, I reckoned any special combatants would be shut away somewhere secret.

I spent an uneasy night. To save Helena worrying, I pretended to sleep perfectly peacefully. All the time, thoughts churned in my head. I was damned sure whatever happened, this special bout the three lanistae had planned was not intended to be fair. Each of them would be going into it with his own evil plans.

From the president's box it would be impossible to intervene in any emergency. Justinus and I had racked our brains wondering how we could overcome that. The only useful place to be was out in the ring – but I had had to promise Helena I would not in any circumstances go out there to fight.

LVIII

A blaze of sunlight swathed the arena from the first hour. Slowly the stone seats and the brilliant white sand on the arena floor began to warm up. As the crowd started to assemble, the sound of the ocean was lost, though we could still smell it on the salty air that dried our faces and made our hair stiff and lank.

Justinus and I had gone early. Rutilius would arrive much later, ceremonially. We thought we were prompt yet other people had beaten us to it, though the atmosphere remained relaxed. Even at that stage, however, the holiday mood had extra tension caused by the presence of contingents from Oea and Sabratha.

Admission was free, but the ticket-men were in place, ready to hand out the tokens which assigned places in the various tiers and wedges of seats. Cushions for the front row seats were being unladen from mules. Smoke rose lazily from fires on the beach where hot titbits were being cooked by food-sellers. Wineskins and amphorae had been brought in large quantities. Snack-sellers were hoping for a lucrative day.

Country dwellers, drawn by the spectacle and the chance of making sales of their produce and crafts, had turned up on horses and the occasional camel, and were squatting on the beach. Some had even pitched long, dark, desert tents. And keen folk from town were meandering up the shore and along other paths even as we ourselves arrived, looking for friends to greet or betting touts to haggle with. Playbills appeared; we got hold of one, but apart from the professional fighters who were listed by name and fighting style, the special bout was only described as a 'combat of three novices'.

After the first arrivals had strolled up, some still eating their breakfasts, the influx suddenly increased and the atmosphere pulsated. The citizens of Lepcis were now pouring forth, some dressed in white in the formal Roman manner (as we were), others robed in brilliant colours. Women in their best finery, bejewelled, incredibly coiffed, saucily veiled or lurking under parasols, were carried here in litters or forced to walk by frugal husbands. Children scampered free or clung shyly to parents. Men wandered about making contacts, perhaps with male business acquaintances, perhaps even with forward women who ought not to have been available. Ushers finally appeared – far too late to make much impact, though no one seemed to care.

The rows of seats were filling fast. Cheeks, foreheads and bald pates were already shining up and reddening in the sun. Bare-armed beauties would look like lobsters this evening. An elderly man was carried off on a stretcher, overcome before the event even started. A fine haze of unguents, perspiration, fried squid and garlic gently assaulted our nostrils.

The hum of noise rose, then fell off expectantly. Rutilius Gallicus arrived.

Toga-clad and wearing a wreath to which he must be officially entitled, he took his seat, received with warm applause. The citizens of Lepcis were well aware he had given them territorial preference over Sabratha, and particularly Oea. There were a few jeers, presumably from the visitors, immediately swamped by another surge of appreciation from the victorious Lepcitanians.

Justinus and I slipped into our seats beside Claudia and Helena. We had the best view available. Rutilius had extended his favour to allow us, as his house guests, to share his plot like equals. This put us in prime position – with cushions – among the three front rows of the nobility, priests and dignitaries who were enthroned on their hereditary wide marble seats. Behind us the massed crowds craned their necks from the plain benches that would give them stiff buttocks and backache by the end of the day.

I spotted Euphrasia amongst the elegantly turned out

town councillors and their wives. She looked extremely expensive in a grand set of gold hardwear and near-sheer indigo drapes. To my surprise she had Artemisia, Calliopus' handsome young wife, on her left and the expansive shape of Hanno's sister Myrrha on her right. Any public display of close affinity usually masks an intended coup. So that looked good news. The three lanistae were presumably off somewhere preparing their gladiators. I wondered where Scilla was. I could not believe she would not be observing today's activity; especially as the special bout was so important for her compensation claim.

Rutilius had to leave his seat again. A parade of statues of local gods, crudely disguised under the names of Roman ones, heralded a few brisk religious formalities. He took part with suitable gravity, slitting open a chicken so its entrails could be surveyed. His manner was quiet and extremely efficient as he then pronounced the omens good and the procedures all in order. This enabled the Games to start.

Immediately preparations rushed ahead for the execution of the man caught raving against the gods yesterday. Veils were now wrapped discreetly around syncretised Jupiter Ammon and around Milk'ashtart and Shadrapa, ancient eastern deities who apparently passed themselves off as Punic variants of Hercules and Liber Pater or Bacchus. A huge chorus of booing went up as an armed guard dragged in the criminal. His crimes were posted up, though without the dignity of naming him – assuming anyone had even bothered to find out who this ranting foreigner was. He was shaven-headed and filthy. The man had been beaten up last night in prison, without doubt. He hung limply in the arms of his captors, either unconscious from the beating or still drunk. Both maybe.

'He's way out of it. That's a relief.'

Barely glancing at the slumped figure, I turned to talk to Helena. She sat, purse-lipped, with her hands clasped in her lap and with downcast eyes. I heard the trundling noise as a low-wheeled platform was brought. The victim, stripped naked, was being tied to a stake on this conveyance, which had a shin-high guard shaped like a low chariot front. Every move brought a new surge of angry noise from the crowd. I dropped one hand reassuringly over Helena's clenched fists.

'Soon be over,' muttered Rutilius, soothing her like a surgeon while maintaining his smile for the crowd.

The little cart was pushed out into the ring. Attendants poked it forwards with long poles. From nowhere a lion had been released. Needing little encouragement it ran out towards the man at the stake. Helena closed her eyes. The animal seemed to hesitate. At the roar from the crowd, the prisoner finally revived, raised his head, saw the lion and shrieked. The hysterical voice caught my attention, shockingly familiar.

A sea-breeze dragged at the veil covering one of the statues, causing it to flutter free. The attendants pushed the cart closer to the lion. The lion took a closer interest. One of the guards cracked a whip. The prisoner looked up at the statue of Shadrapa, then yelled defiantly, 'Stuff your Carthaginian gods — and stuff bloody one-eyed Hannibal!'

The lion leapt on him.

I was on my feet. I now knew his voice, his Aventine intonation, the shape of his head, his stupidity, his raving prejudice — everything. There was nothing I could do. I could never have reached him. He was too far away. There was no way to get there. A thirteen-foot-high smooth-sided marble barrier kept wild beasts from invading the audience and kept spectators out of the ring. The whole crowd rose in a standing ovation, shouting out their indignation at the blasphemy and their approval of the kill. Seconds later the lion was tearing the man to pieces, while I fell back holding my head in my hands.

'Oh dear gods . . . Oh no, oh no!'

'Falco?'

'It's my brother-in-law.'

Famia was dead.

LIX

Guilt and dread were beginning their inexorable descent on me as I shoved my way to the backstage area. What was left of Famia's bloody corpse had been dragged out, still hanging from the cart. The sated lion had been retrieved with the customary efficiency; with its jowls dripping red, it was already caged, and about to be whisked away down the covered tunnel. After an execution beasts were removed from sight very speedily. I heard somebody laugh. The amphitheatre staff were in happy mood.

Gagging, I made a family claim for the body, though there would be little to cremate at a funeral.

Rutilius had warned me to be careful what I said. His caution was unnecessary. Famia's appalling outcry still rang in my ears. I would do what was proper here for my own people at home, though probably no one would thank me. I had no wish to add to the insult that had been offered locally.

How could I ever explain this to Maia — my favourite sister — and her nice, well-brought-up children? Marius, who wanted to teach rhetoric. Ancus, with the big ears and the shy smile. Rhea, the pretty, funny one. Little Cloelia, who had never seen her father for what he was and who doggedly worshipped him. I knew what they would think. I thought it too. He came out here with me. Without me, he would never have left Rome. It was my fault.

'Marcus.' Camillus Justinus was at my shoulder now. 'Anything to do?'

'Don't look.'

'Right.' Utterly sensible like most of his family, he

gripped me by the arm and wheeled me away from where I had stood rooted to the spot. I heard him speaking in a low voice to whoever was in charge. Money changed hands. Helena or Claudia must have given him a purse. Arrangements were concluded. The remains were to go to an undertaker. What was needed would be done.

What was needed should have happened a long time ago. Famia should have been dried out. Neither his wife nor I had had the time nor the will to do it. Maia was long past trying.

Well, that burden was over now. But I knew the tragedy had hardly started yet.

I wanted to go.

I would have to extricate Helena. Leaving the presidential seats was bad form. Two of us had already abandoned Rutilius very publicly. He might not be too displeased, knowing the circumstances, though the crowd certainly would. In Rome showing disinterest in the expensive bloodshed of the arena caused the kind of unpopularity that even Emperors feared.

'We have to go back, Marcus.' Justinus spoke quietly and calmly, the approved way of dealing with a man in shock. 'Apart from our diplomatic duty, we don't want to get crucified!'

'I don't need you looking after me.'

'I wouldn't dare suggest it. But we owe it to Rutilius to respect appearances.'

'Rutilius condemned him.'

'Rutilius had no choice.'

'True.' I was a fair man. My brother-in-law had just been mauled to death in front of me, but I knew the rules: cheer loudly, and say he asked for it. 'Even if Rutilius had known the man was related to me, insulting Hannibal in his home province isn't allowed. Blaspheming the gods like that would have got him flogged even at home ... Don't worry. I shall return looking shifty, like a man who has just had to run out after being taken short.'

'Tact,' agreed Justinus, walking me steadily back to my seat. 'Wonderful feature of civic life. Dear gods, now don't let anybody offer us a friendly dip in their honeyed nuts . . .'

Although we meant to do the right thing, we were forestalled in rejoining the happy crowd. As we passed the end of the tunnel nearest the amphitheatre, we realised the next phase of the Games had now begun. The bloody sand had been raked clean; the tracks made by the cart as it was dragged out had been smoothed over. The huge doors were open and the procession of gladiators was entering the ring. They passed right in front of us, and we felt drawn to follow them as far as the great rectangular gateway through which they all marched.

It was a sight of mingled grandeur and bad taste, as always. Fed, exercised and honed to a high pitch of fitness, the huge men who fought professionally strode out, to be greeted by a tremendous roar. Trumpets and horns were blasting away. The fighters were dressed ceremonially, each in a gold-embroidered cloth-of-purple Greek military cloak. Oiled, and showing off their muscles, they strutted forth in order of the programme. Their names were hailed. They acknowledged this arrogantly with upheld arms, turning to either side of the crowd, buoyed up by a surge of energy.

They made a stately circuit, showing themselves to every portion of the audience. They were attended by their lanistae, all in crisp white tunics striped over the shoulders with narrow coloured braid, and bearing long staves. Amongst them I spotted Saturninus, parading to roars from the locals. Attendants came on, carrying salvers on which large purses of prize money bulged. The slaves who raked and brushed the sand attempted a ragged goose-step in a shaky line, holding their implements on their shoulders like ceremonial spears; others led on the horses which would be used in mounted combats, manes burnished and harnesses glittering with enamel disks.

Finally in walked an eerie figure portraying the mystical judge of the Underworld, Rhadamanthus, in a tight sombre tunic, long supple boots, and the sinister beaked mask of a bird; he was followed by his hard-hearted crony, Hermes Psycopompus – the black messenger with the fiercely heated snaky staff, a branding iron with which he would prod the inert, to discover whether they were really dead, simply unconscious – or feigning.

Crowded in the doorway with a group of arena staff, Justinus and I could see Rutilius on his feet as he supervised the drawing of lots. Fighters of equal experience would be pitted against one another, but that still left the actual draw at each level; this now took place. Some of the pairings were popular and drew enthusiastic cheers; others produced good-humoured groans. Eventually the programme was all settled, and the weapons to be used were presented formally to the president. Inspecting the swords, Rutilius took his time. This improved the mood of the crowd even further because it showed he knew what he was about; he even rejected one or two after testing their edges.

All through these formalities, the fighters in the ring were showing off. Their warm-up consisted of straightforward muscle exercises with plenty of grunts and knee bends, plus feats of balance and tricks with javelins. One or two hurled their shields aloft and caught them spectacularly. All made great play of feinting and parrying with practice weapons, some lost in total private concentration, others miming attacks on each other, playing up real or imagined enmities. A few egotistical amateurs from the crowd went down to the arena and joined them, wanting to look big.

When the weapons had been approved, attendants carried them from the president's tribunal to be distributed. The warm-up ended. More trumpets blared. The procession formed again as all those who were not in the first bout made to leave. The gladiators marched around the whole elipse once more, this time deafening the president with the time-honoured shout: 'Those about to die salute you!'

Rutilius acknowledged them. He looked tired.

Out came most of the gladiators again through the great doorway. We stepped aside hastily. They were heavy and huge-thighed, not men to be trampled by. Behind them someone bawled the formal incitement to the first pair: 'Approach!'

The hum of noise subsided. A Thracian and a myrmillon in a fish-crested helmet circled each other warily. The long day's professional slaughter had begun.

Justinus and I turned away, still intending to resume our seats. Then, coming from the tunnel, we saw a young man, running fast.

'That's Hanno's son. It's Iddibal.'

Stung into action, I was the first to waylay him and demand what was wrong. Iddibal seemed hysterical. 'It's Auntie Myrrha! She's been attacked—'

My heart lurched. Things were starting to happen. 'Show us!' I commanded him. Then Justinus and I took him by an arm each and pretty well dragged him to where he had found his injured aunt.

LX

We shouted for a doctor, but as soon as we examined her we reckoned Myrrha was done for. Justinus exchanged a look with me, discreetly shaking his head. We pulled Iddibal away to the side of the tunnel on the pretext of allowing the medical staff space.

'What was your aunt doing here?' I could not remember seeing Myrrha leave her seat. My last sighting had been with Euphrasia, looking like any substantial matron stuck there for the day, with a packet of dates in her well beringed hand and a large white kerchief shading her pinned and rolled hair.

Staring over my shoulder to where Myrrha lay, Iddibal trembled. We had found the woman lying against the wall of the tunnel near its far exit at the stadium end. She had made no sound since we reached her. There was blood soaking her robe and now spreading on the sandy floor. Somebody had slashed her right across the throat; she must have seen the attack coming and had tried to fend it off. Her hands and arms were cut too. There was even a knife scratch on one cheek. Judging from a long trail of bloodspots, she had staggered out here, coming from the stadium, wrapping her marine blue stole around her wounded throat in an attempt to staunch the blood.

Now she was fading fast, though Iddibal had not accepted it. I knew Myrrha would never recover consciousness.

'Why was she here?' I urged him a second time.

'Our novice fighter is being armed in the stadium.'

'Why the stadium?'

'For secrecy.'

Justinus touched my arm and went to take a look.

'Who's your fighter?' The frightened nephew had gone limp on me. 'Who, Iddibal?'

'Just a slave.'

'Whose slave?'

'One of her own that Aunt Myrrha had taken a dislike to. Nobody. Just a nobody.'

I pulled Iddibal more upright and rammed him back against the wall. Then I loosened my hold on him, to seem more friendly. He was dressed in holiday style, even more colourful than the last time I saw him. A long tunic in shades of green and saffron. A wide belt around it. A couple of finger rings and a gold chain.

'That's a nice chain, Iddibal.' Its workmanship looked familiar. 'Any others at home?'

Bemused and troubled, he answered numbly, 'It's not my favourite. I lost that when all this began . . .'

'When and how?'

'In Rome.'

'Where, Iddibal?'

'I left my best clothes with my aunt when I signed on with Calliopus—' He was still straining to look past me to where a doctor was crouched over his aunt. 'After I was manumitted, I found the chain was gone.'

'What did your aunt say?'

'She had to assume somebody had stolen it. In fact, the slave we're putting up today was the only suspect; Aunt Myrrha told that to father and me last night when she suggested him for the bout—'

'Theft sounds a good reason to get rid of him, yes.' I bet Myrrha had had another motive. I had a filthy feeling about this so-called thief, and what Myrrha really knew about her nephew's chain. I tugged at the one Iddibal was now wearing. 'Same style as this, was it? The one you lost in Rome?'

'Similar.'

'I may have seen it once.'

At that Iddibal roused himself. He must have interpreted my ominous tone. 'Who had it?'

'Somebody gave it to Rumex, the night he was killed.'

He seemed astonished. 'How can that be?'

The doctor attending Myrrha stood up. 'She's gone,' he called. Iddibal abandoned me and rushed over to the corpse. The doctor was holding out an object he had found among Myrrha's clothing; since the nephew was grief-stricken the man gave it to me. It was a small knife, with a bone handle and straight blade, such as a domestic slave might use for sharpening styli.

'Seen this before, Iddibal?'

'I don't know. I don't care – for heaven's sake, Falco – leave me alone!'

Justinus came back.

'Marcus.' He stepped close to talk privately. 'They have an area where their novice is being hidden from the public. I insisted they let me see him; he's nothing much. Sitting quietly in his armour, inside a small tent.'

'Alone?'

'Yes. But Myrrha went in to speak to him a short time ago. The attendants are outside, playing dice, and took no notice – he was her slave, apparently. They saw Myrrha leave, heading fast towards the tunnel with her head wrapped up. They thought no more about it.'

'Did you mention that she had been hurt?'

'No.'

'What's the name of their gladiator?'

'Fidelis, they say.'

'I thought it might be!'

Iddibal looked up. Tear-stained and haggard yet no longer so distraught, he rose from his knees beside the stricken figure of his aunt. 'That's his knife,' he told me, rediscovering himself. 'Fidelis was her interpreter.'

My voice must have been grim: 'A man of that name ran errands as a messenger in Rome. I have an idea your aunt then used him for something very serious. Iddibal, you aren't going to like this but you'll have to face up to it:

I don't believe Myrrha ever paid over any money for your release from Calliopus.'

'What?'

'When she heard from you that Calliopus wanted Rumex dead, she offered to do the job you had refused. I think she used Fidelis. He took your lost chain to the Saturninus barracks, to offer as a supposed gift. Rumex let him bring it close, then as he put it on he was stabbed in the throat. Unlike Myrrha who must have been wary today, Rumex was caught off guard. On that occasion the slave was able to kill neatly and take his weapon home.'

'I don't believe it,' said Iddibal. People never do. Then they think things through.

'Myrrha must have decided Fidelis knew too much,' Justinus followed up gently. 'So she planned to have him killed in the arena today to silence him.'

'Perhaps once he killed Rumex, Fidelis became too cocky,' I suggested, remembering his attitude when we met them at Sabratha.

'For some stupid reason, she visited him — perhaps to apologise.' Justinus was a nice lad. I thought it more likely that Myrrha had been taunting the condemned slave. 'He stabbed her, and she must have been too shocked to call for help—'

'Impossible to do so,' I said. 'She had set him up to kill Rumex; she was guilty too. She needed to keep that secret.'

So, fatally wounded, though perhaps unaware of just how grave her condition was, Myrrha had proudly walked away. She collapsed. Now she was dead.

I was all set to visit Fidelis myself and interrogate the bastard. But Fidelis would keep. He had nothing to tell me, really; I was now sure I knew exactly what he had done, and how he was now being made to pay for his faithful service to Myrrha. From the way Justinus described him sitting quietly, it sounded as though Fidelis himself understood that discovery had come and was resigned to his fate. He was a slave. If he died in the arena, that was only where a trial judge would send him anyway.

I had something else to think about. Somebody walked out towards us and stopped on seeing the body. A female voice exclaimed in cultured but callous tones, 'What – Myrrha dead? My word, it looks as if we're set to have a bloody day. What fun!'

Then, Scilla, my ex-client, deigned to recognise me.

'I want a word with you, Falco! What have you done to my agent?'

'I thought *I* was your agent.'

Scilla shrugged her shoulders under a full-length purple cloak. 'You failed to put in an appearance so I found someone else to do my work.'

'Romanus?'

'That's just an alias.'

'I thought so. So who is he?'

She blinked, and avoided telling me. 'The point is – *where* is he, Falco? I sent him to see Calliopus last night and he's vanished.'

I had little sympathy. 'Better ask Calliopus then.'

She smiled, far too coyly for my liking. 'I might do that later!'

Then Scilla turned on her heel and loped off towards the amphitheatre. Her mass of brown hair was today tightly plaited. The cloak she was clutching around her covered the rest of her outfit, but as she walked away from us she released her hold and let it billow out dramatically. When the garment swung loose, I noticed she was bare-legged and wearing boots.

LXI

I told the arena staff to move Myrrha's body out of sight as discreetly as they could. Justinus and I started to walk slowly back to the arena, taking Iddibal with us.

'Iddibal, who set up the special mystery bout your father's holding with the others later? Was it Scilla?'

'Yes. She had met Papa when he was hunting in Cyrenaïca. He was interested in her feud with the other lanistae.'

'I bet he was! Does Scilla realise that Hanno has been actively involved in stirring up trouble between Saturninus and Calliopus in Rome?'

'How could she?'

'Your father keeps his machinations quiet, but she has an enquiry agent working for her.'

'You?'

'No. I don't know who he is.' Well, that was my official line.

Scilla was up to no good here, planning new mischief. Iddibal thought so too, and perhaps troubled by his father's involvement with her, he decided to warn me: 'Scilla has convinced Saturninus and Calliopus that this bout is a way to settle her legal claim – but Papa is certain it's a blind. She's hoping to use the occasion to get back at them in some more dramatic way.'

We had reached the arena approach. In the past few minutes Saturninus and his men had set up an enclosure. Like Hanno with Fidelis in the stadium, he was keeping his chosen fighter from public view; portable screens had been erected. Around them a large group of his men now stood looking ugly – easy enough, for they were brutal types. We glimpsed Saturninus himself ducking behind the screens – with Scilla at his side.

'Hello!' I muttered.

'Surely not?' said Justinus, but like me he must have noticed her boots a few minutes earlier.

'She has a wild reputation – for a dubious hobby.'

'And we've just found out what it is?'

'Scilla is a girl who wants to play at being one of the boys. What do you say, Iddibal?'

He was showing professional distaste. 'There always are women who like to shock society by attending a training palaestra. If she's taking part as one of the novice fighters, that's very bad form—'

'And it makes a nonsense of her pretence that this bout is a legal device.'

'It's a fight to the death,' scoffed Justinus in disgust. 'She'll get herself killed!'

I wondered who she was hoping to finish off at the same time.

Just then, the great door swung open. The noise of the crowd roared out, then a man's body was pulled through towards us by a horse, using a rope and a savage hook. Rhadamanthus escorted the dead gladiator from the ring; Hermes must have touched him with the hot caduceus, leaving a livid red mark on his upper arm.

The Lord of the Underworld pushed up his beaked mask and swore in Latin with a heavy Punic accent; someone handed him a small cup of wine. Hermes scratched his leg dopily. Close to, they were an uncouth pair of roughnecks. Off-duty shellfish-catchers, by the looks and smell of them.

'Justus,' said Hermes, noticing our interest and nodding at the prone Thracian who was being unhooked. A small round shield was thrown out of the ring after him. His curved scimitar followed; Rhadamanthus kicked it so it lay with the shield.

'Hopeless.' One of the thin, seedy slaves who raked the sand decided we needed a commentary. There is always some spark wanting to say what's going on when you can see that perfectly well for yourself. 'No class. Only lasted a couple of strokes. Waste of everyone's time.'

I had had an idea. I turned to the man with the beak. 'Want a break? Cool off – enjoy your drink.'

'No peace for the King of the Dead!' Rhadamanthus laughed.

'You could send in an understudy – nip inside the tunnel with me, and swap clothes. Give me your mallet for the rest of the morning, and I'll make it worth your while.'

'You don't want this job,' Rhadamanthus tried to warn me, really earnest in his wish to spare me a tedious experience. He clung to the ceremonial mallet with which he claimed the dead. 'Nobody loves you. You get no credit, and it's damned hot in the gear.'

Justinus thought I was being stupid, so he weighed in to supervise. 'Helena said you were not to fight.'

'Who me? I'll just be the jolly fellow who counts out the dead.' I had a feeling we were about to see rather a lot of them.

'I'm not happy about what you're proposing, Marcus.'

'Learn to like it. Getting into trouble is the way Falco & Partner operate. How about this, Rhadamanthus? Suppose you and the mighty Hermes sit offside with a flagon during the special bout, and let my partner and me go out to officiate for that one, masked and anonymous?'

'Will there be any comeback?'

'Why should there be?'

First we returned to our seats, taking Iddibal; that would keep him from telling his father what Fidelis had done. The slave was doomed now, for one murder or another. I wanted to see what had been engineered for him in the ring.

We had to sit through the remaining professional bouts. There were more of these than we had realised, though not all ended in a fatality. My mind was racing; I hardly paid any attention to the fights. At Lepcis Magna the full

371

range was offered, but I had lost any enthusiasm I had ever felt.

In their red apron-like loincloths and wide belts, gladiators came and went that morning. Myrmillons with fish-topped helmets and Gallic arms tussled against Thracians; secutors ran light-footed after unarmoured, unhelmeted retarii, who turned in mid-flight like startled birds and disabled their pursuers, wielding their tridents with the tiny pronged heads, not much bigger than kitchen toasting-forks but capable of dealing horrific injuries to a man whose sword arm had been tied up in a flung net. Gladiators fought two-handed with a pair of swords; fought from chariots; fought from horseback with light hunting spears; even fought with lassos. A hoplomachus, covered by a full body-height shield, was booed for remaining too static, his regular swipes from behind his protection bored the crowd; they preferred faster action, though the fighters themselves knew it was best to conserve as much strength as possible. They were likely to be overcome by the heat and tiredness just as much as by their opponents. With blood and sweat making their grip slide, or blinding them, they had to struggle on, just hoping the other man was equally unfortunate and that they could both be sent off in a draw.

Most escaped alive. It was too expensive to lose them. The lanistae dancing around them crying encouragement were also watching keenly to ensure no one was killed unnecessarily. The choreographed movements became almost an elaborate joke, with the crowd sometimes jeering sarcastically, in the full knowledge that they were witnessing the proverbial 'fix'. Only the betting touts could lose by that – and they somehow knew enough to avoid bankruptcy.

Eventually we reached the mock-comic partnership of two men in fully enclosed helmets. This was the last of the professional pairings. While they blundered about blind, swiping at one another ineffectually, Justinus and I rose from our seats again.

'What are you up to?'

'Nothing, dear heart.'

That was him, bluffing Claudia. Helena had simply glared at me, too wise even to ask.

As I stood waiting for Justinus to move first, I happened to glance over to where Euphrasia sat, with Calliopus' gorgeous young wife Artemisia. They made a strange contrast. Euphrasia in her flashy, diaphanous robe, looked every inch a daredevil who would have had an affair with Rumex. Young Artemisia was covered up to the neck and even half veiled: just as a husband might want her to be turned out. Not many very beautiful girls would stand for it.

I turned back to Iddibal, who sat hunched beside Helena, hardly aware of what was happening around him. 'Iddibal, *why* was Calliopus so determined to have Rumex despatched – surely it was not just part of the dirty tricks war?'

The young man shook his head. 'No; Calliopus hated Rumex.'

I wondered now if Artemisia had been sent to the villa at Surrentum in December not just to stop her nagging about her husband's mistress, but actually as a punishment. Helena caught my drift; I guessed she too was remembering how Euphrasia had said to her that Calliopus' wife had a lot to answer for and that he probably hit her. Helena exclaimed in a low voice, 'Calliopus is a desperately jealous man, a brooder and a plotter, a completely unforgiving type. Can it be that Artemisia was one of the women involved with Rumex?'

'They had an affair,' confirmed Iddibal with a slight shrug, as though everyone knew as much. 'Calliopus was after Rumex from a purely personal motive. It had nothing to do with business.'

My eyes met Helena's and we both sighed: a crime of passion, after all.

I looked again at where Artemisia sat so quiet and subdued, just like a woman whose husband had badly beaten her. Bruising could well explain the long sleeves and high neckline – not to mention her cowed attitude. Her face and figure were breathtaking, though her eyes were vacant. I wondered whether that had always been the case, or whether her spirit had been knocked out of her. Whatever trouble she had caused, Artemisia was without question one of the victims now.

Justinus and I reached the amphitheatre's main entrance again. We waited for our cronies to come out to work their exchange with us.

In the ring, the two groping andabates were still slowly circling. Fully protected by armoured links of mail, the blind combatants had been trained to manoeuvre like sponge-divers in deep water, each step or gesture taken with immense care, all the while keyed up for any sound that would locate the man opposite. They could only defeat him by swiping through the links of his mailsuit – hard enough to achieve even if they had been able to see. I always expected them to survive unharmed, yet time and again one triumphed, whacking apart the metal segments to destroy a limb or pierce an organ.

It happened that day, as usual. The blind fighters were chosen for being swift on their feet and dexterous, yet immensely strong. Once one did hit home, it was generally a good blow. The thwack resounded all over the arena, heard even in the highest seats from where the combatants looked like tiny toys. As soon as he had found his mark, he would strike hard again repeatedly. So Rhadamanthus was soon tapping a corpse with his mallet, and once again the dead meat was towed out.

We changed clothes with Rhadamanthus and Hermes very quickly.

'Shamble a bit or we'll be spotted as fakes,' I advised Justinus. Then I took charge of the long-handled Etruscan mallet and he solemnly grasped the caduceus, which came with a small boy holding a brazier in which the snaky stick was heated up for use.

The heat off the sand swamped us, as we waited for the rakemen to smooth a clear path for our entry. The soft boots I had had to wear were springy even on the loose surface. The beaked mask made it difficult to see; my vision was impeded sideways and I had to get used to moving my head round physically if I needed to look left or right. We were bound to be spotted by Helena and Claudia; Hermes goes unmasked so we knew they would recognise Justinus immediately.

There was a short interval before the special event. Justinus and I paced around the ring, accustoming ourselves to the space and atmosphere. Nobody bothered us, or took any notice at all.

Vigorous trumpets announced the next set. A herald proclaimed the terms: 'Three; fighting severally and without repricve.' Exultant cheers. There was no mention that the victor's lanista had to pay Scilla's lawsuit – though everybody knew. What they might not know was that Scilla had decided to take a hand in the fight herself. But in an already crammed and exotic programme, here was something a touch different. Because the three lanistae came from different Tripolitanian towns, a huge murmur went up and the atmosphere sizzled with rivalry.

Justinus and I stationed ourselves together at the side of the arena while the combatants marched in and their names were at last announced.

First, the Sabratha contingent. No surprises there. Hanno led in Fidelis. This was the undersized, unappealing slave I had encountered at Myrrha's house, now dressed up for his execution like a retiarius. It was a fatal role for an untrained man and from his expression he knew it. He wore the red loincloth, cinched around his scrawny frame by a heavy belt. He was completely unarmed except for one leather sleeve reinforced with narrow metal plates on his left arm; it was finished with a tall, solid shoulder-piece, the weight of which threatened to buckle him. He had on the same large sandals he always wore. He carried the net in an untidy clump, as if he knew it was pointless; he gripped the trident so nervously his knuckles were white.

Next the party representing Oea. Calliopus, tall, thin and glowering with tension brought in his man.

'Romanus!' cried the herald. That was a surprise.

I stared at the fellow closely. Age indeterminate, height ordinary, legs medium, chest nothing. He was to fight as a secutor. At least this meant he had some protection – a half-cylindrical greave on his left shin, a leather armguard and a long rectangular shield, decorated with crude stars and circles; his weapon was a short sword, which he did hold as if somebody had taught him what to do with steel. The traditional crested helmet, with two eyeholes in a solid front, hid his face from view eerily.

Scilla had said she sent her agent to see Calliopus. Had he seized the man and compelled him to fight? Romanus walked quietly; he seemed a willing contender. If he was some kind of agent, whatever was he thinking of getting himself into this?

Finally Saturninus, the local trainer; clearly a popular character. Even before the herald's announcement, the crowd gasped. The champion he brought would be regarded as outrageous; it was a woman.

'Scilla!'

Escorting her, Saturninus made a wide, self-mocking gesture as if saying that under pressure he had allowed her to defend her cause herself. There were cynical laughs in reply. The local crowd leered, while the smaller contingents from Oea and Sabratha mocked the Lepcis champion.

Instead of just a loincloth she wore a short tunic for decency, with a normal gladiator's swordbelt hugging her waist. Boots. Two shinguards. A round buckler and curved sickle-shaped sword – she was assuming the role of a Thracian. Her helmet, customised perhaps, looked light but strong, with a grille she had opened so the crowd could see her face as she strutted in proudly.

Her big moment. It was unlikely she had ever appeared

in an arena previously, though bouts between women did happen. They were greeted with a mixture of scandalised contempt and prurience. Women who attended gymnasia to exercise were held in the lowest regard in Rome. No wonder Pomponius had wanted to keep any further taint of unsuitable behaviour away from his betrothed after Leonidas died. He would have tried to excuse her passion as a misguided hobby – though he had still wanted to impress her by staging that fatal private show. At least now I could see why he had thought it would appeal to her. One aspect of this brutal muddle at last made sense.

When women did fight in the arena, they were always put against other women. To the Roman mind that was bad enough. Nobody would even contemplate pitting a female against men. Still, at least one of Scilla's opponents today was a slave and 'Romanus' must surely be of low origin to have ended up here. But she had damned herself; even if she could survive the fighting, she was now socially untouchable. As to the fight, every man present would tell you, she stood no chance.

Suddenly, worrying alarums rang. There was no time to pursue the thought that raced through my mind, however. The fight was about to start.

'Approach!'

The three gladiators, such as they were, took up three points of a triangle at first. This was fighting severally – that is, not in fixed pairs. Unless their lanistae allowed two of them to co-operate and together batter the third, that meant one would probably stand back while two others fought each other first.

So it transpired. I had expected a long period of prowling around, while all three hoped to be the last in action, saving their strength. Instead, the woman chose her mark. She began at once: Scilla snapped shut the grille of her helmet and took on Fidelis.

He was always the victim figure, likely to be attacked hard by both the others early on. Unarmed, he had no alternative but to run. First, he fled across the arena to the far end. Scilla pursued him yet held back from attack; she was toying with the slave. Doomed by Myrrha, nobody had given him any advice. He had no idea how to deal with the netman's equipment. The dangerous skills that would normally make such a match an equal combat were cruelly denied him.

He did not want to die, though. Since he must, he decided it would be with a flourish. He swung at Scilla with the net, and somehow managed a half-decent sweep, even clinging on to the cord that surrounded the bulk of his net. He had cast it over one of her shoulders – unfortunately for him the wrong one; instead of her sword arm he had hampered her left side, tangling up her shield. Scilla just let it fall. Sufficient free play remained for the weight of the round shield to drag the net off her. It caught once on her belt but she shook herself violently and it fell free. Fidelis lost his hold on the cord. She was then facing Fidelis unprotected, and his trident had a longer reach than her curved sword, but she showed no fear. She skated rapidly backwards, yet she was laughing – still taunting him. Her confidence was astonishing.

He advanced, with an awkward, unattractive lope. She retreated further back, towards us. She was deft on her feet; he was clumsy. He plunged the trident at her, missing badly. She swept her sword at it, but somehow he snatched it back. She skipped several strides backwards again – then stopped abruptly. Fidelis had run in too close. The head of his trident passed by her harmlessly. Left-handed, Scilla fearlessly grabbed the shaft and pulled towards herself hard. She jerked her sword into Fidelis with a vicious blow. He fell at once.

Scilla stepped away, her blade dripping blood.

Fidelis was clearly still alive. Hanno and Saturninus, who had been sidelined, neither attempting to encourage their fighters with the usual prancing around, now raced up to inspect the damage. Fidelis was raising an arm, one finger up. It was the standard appeal to the crowd for mercy. In a fight without quarter this should not be allowed.

Some of the unruly audience began to drum their heels and give the thumbs up sign, themselves appealing to the president to grant Fidelis his life.

Rutilius stood up. He must have thought fast. He signalled that he passed the judgement to Hanno, as the lanista whose man was down. Hanno swept an arm viciously sideways, indicating death.

With a coolness that made people gasp, Scilla at once stepped forwards and delivered a death blow straight at the base of the prone man's neck. Fidelis had never been trained as real gladiators were to take the force without flinching; yet he had no time to disgrace himself. A murmur of real shock ran around the crowd.

A brief glance passed between Scilla and Saturninus. According to the secret agenda of this combat, Fidelis had always been intended to die. From his intimacy with the Pomponius ménage, Saturninus probably knew that Scilla had been trained to fight. But he cannot have been expecting that she would prove quite so efficient and merciless. Or did he?

Ask Scilla who really killed that lion! Euphrasia had urged Helena. Dear gods. Of course! Saturninus already knew what I now finally realised.

Scilla herself had said Rumex had been decrepit; all his fights, she claimed, were fixed. Such a man would not even have tried to tackle the beast when Leonidas broke loose. As he fatally mauled her lover, Scilla had yelled at him to make him leave his prey. Then, I had no doubt at all, it was Scilla who had grabbed a spear and followed the lion into the garden. She had speared Leonidas herself.

LXII

A short trumpet blast warned all those present that the rites of the dead must be followed. Justinus and I paced out across the sand to where Fidelis lay. Everyone stood back.

He was done for. Justinus touched him only lightly with the caduceus, though even then the waft of burnt human flesh was off-putting. I struck Fidelis soundly with my mallet, claiming his soul for Hades. We followed as he was taken from the arena, stretchered off this time. Apparently since these three combatants were not professionals they were to be accorded gentler treatment than the toughs we had seen dragged away previously. I felt a wry pride that under my auspices as the Judge of the Underworld, the ceremonies were more civilised.

As soon as we had seen out the corpse we turned back from the doorway into the arena. I had a bad taste, sickened by the merciless behaviour Scilla had exhibited. This was more than a legitimate quest for vengeance. The woman had no sense of proportion, as well as no sense of shame.

Justinus signalled the protagonists to recommence. Scilla was already under attack. While she had been preening for the crowd, Romanus, whoever he was, had had the nous to interpose himself so she was cut off from her buckler where it still lay tangled in the net. I saw him kick it further towards the barrier. He was on guard, well positioned – head up, eyes no doubt watchful behind his helmet vizor, sword point at the correct height, big shield held close to the body. A textbook stance – or trying too hard, perhaps.

Scilla pulled back her shoulders and crouched, on the

alert. This new situation clearly posed a far bigger challenge than Fidelis. She looked eager, completely unafraid.

Hanno retired slightly now that his champion was dead. I wondered what he was thinking. Did he already know what Scilla was planning? Calliopus had moved forward to support Romanus, who ignored the lanista stalwartly.

The crowd had become menacing. There were rival chants from small groups of troublemakers. A lot of people were on their feet, in a frenzy at the sight of a woman fighting against a man. The wall of noise seemed almost physical.

The two fighters exchanged a few feints. It was very programmed: they looked like novices in their first lesson, practising at their trainer's command. Scilla tried fighting back harder. Her sword flirted rapidly, several times crashing on her opponent's shield. He parried compe-tently, standing his ground. Suddenly Scilla rushed him, then performed an astonishing summersault. Being of female weight and so lightly armoured, she was able to flip over acrobatically as most gladiators never could. She passed Romanus, and retrieved her shield, wheedling it with one hand until it came free from the net in which Fidelis had caught it.

At once, she turned and pursued Romanus in the classic Thracian style – holding the small shield at chin height, horizontally, while the sharp sickle-shaped blade of her sword was poised at hip level. Scilla's sword whipped back and forth as she pressed forwards. Fierce shaking move-ments of the shield sought to disconcert her opponent. Saturninus, showing real or feigned enthusiasm as her lanista, ululated excitedly. The crowd joined in with more satirical cries.

Romanus fought back with some ability, though I had no great hopes of him. The girl was fiercely driven, surely not just by her desire for revenge for Pomponius – but by some extra urge to make a big display of feminine prowess. I did not believe she would be satisfied with the death of

Fidelis, someone else's slave. I doubted that her fight with Romanus was personal either.

Who was this Romanus? Did Scilla herself know? If he was her agent, who had lured Calliopus here from Oea, how had he let himself be made Calliopus' booby today? Had Calliopus taken against him over the story about a court summons to denounce Saturninus, then had he imprisoned the messenger, and used threats to force him to fulfil this role today?

I had a horrible feeling I knew why 'Romanus' was in the arena. I even felt I should find a way to get him out of his predicament. There was no way I could do it.

They battled for longer than I had thought possible. Scilla took a wound to one calf. It bled profusely; it must have hurt too, but she refused to acknowledge it. Romanus was acting ruffled now. In the helmet with the solid faceguard it was impossible to gauge his expression, but he was moving more jerkily. Scilla appeared to have boundless energy. He was carrying a greater weight of arms and must be feeling the heat. At one point they drifted apart by accident and he had a chance to catch his breath for a second. I noticed him shake his head, like a swimmer with water in his ears. If sweat ran down behind the eyeholes, inside his helmet, he would be fighting blind.

Something about him was increasingly familiar.

They rejoined battle. It was a sharp, angry exchange this time. He pressed her back across the sand. When on form he showed greater strength, but sustaining it for more than short bursts seemed to defeat him. She seemed to have more experience and technical skill. The crowd fell almost silent, gripped with awe and anticipation. Suddenly Romanus stumbled. One foot slid from under him; he was on his back. He must have twisted his leg; he could not rise. He had managed to support himself one-handed, with his elbow bent. Scilla let out a shrill crow of triumph. Standing over him, she turned to the crowd again, arms high, sword poised. She was about to deliver the death blow again.

There was uproar. Calliopus ran to his man. Scilla whipped around towards where Romanus lay, her eyes still on the tiers of seats where now everyone was on their feet, and bellowing their lungs out. With a furious blow, the woman struck. She had not looked – or so it seemed. A man cried out. A man then died. But instead of Romanus, it was Calliopus.

As before, Scilla leapt back, holding her sword aloft in victory. That she had killed the wrong man made no difference to her. I saw Saturninus move; he knew he would be her next target.

'That was deliberate!' Justinus gasped.

Then he gasped again. People in the crowd shrieked. As the woman wheeled away triumphantly, Romanus astonished them: he launched himself upright from ground level, and stood on his feet again.

It was a move I knew. Glaucus called it 'Trainer's Cheat'. He did it when a pupil grew too cocky and was sure he had won a practice fight. My trainer would wait until his pupil turned away, then jump up, clinch an arm around his throat, and lay the edge of his own blade hard against the idiot's throat.

That was exactly what Romanus did. Only he was not using a wooden practice sword – and he did not stop. He cut deep with all his strength, and almost severed Scilla's neck.

LXIII

Romanus laid her down, then he stepped back. There was blood everywhere.

I was already striding out across the sand, Justinus at my heels. With medical detachment we claimed Calliopus for Hades, then repeated the procedure for the girl.

It ought to be all over. With Scilla dead, her claim for compensation fell. But despite the unrelenting parade of death already placed before them, the crowd were baying for more. For one thing, the big bets today would have been on all three novices ending up dead. Besides, the rivalry between supporters from the three towns had flared into jeers of abuse. The noise became appalling; it was terrifying too.

Saturninus, the grim professional, did not hesitate: he raised an arm, palm flat. The crowd began to drum their heels and shout in unison. Saturninus picked up the long stave which he had been using in his professional role; he brandished and then broke it. After that he pulled off over his head the uniform white tunic that all lanistae wore in the ring. Then he pointed to Romanus as if telling him to wait where he was. The gesture was plain. He was taking on the task: Saturninus was intending to fight Romanus and give the crowd one final thrill.

To renewed, better-tempered applause, Saturninus was already walking off to arm himself. Of all the three lanistae, he had the most direct experience – a professional ex-gladiator who had survived to win his freedom. Here, he was the local hero too, with most of the crowd behind him. Romanus stood no chance.

The crowd reseated themselves amidst a loud hum of

discussion. There had to be a short unprogrammed intermission while Saturninus armed. Justinus and I wheeled slowly around as the latest corpses were removed.

'Clean the ring,' I called, summoning the rakemen. This was not in the remit of the beaked Rhadamanthus, but as always a command spoken with authority got results.

Officials had surrounded Romanus; he was being given a waterflask.

First I walked over to Hanno, followed by Justinus. Hanno was standing aloof, no longer needed for the action since Fidelis died, yet still formally part of the show.

'It's Didius Falco.' From behind the beaked mask Hanno recognised my voice, I think, though he made no sign. I said to Justinus, 'Translate for me, Hermes! Tell him, I know he colluded with Scilla to arrange this fight. Calliopus is dead; if Romanus now kills Saturninus, Hanno will have his heart's desire.'

Hanno looked annoyed when we spoke to him, but he replied and Justinus translated back to me: 'I just push an idea along, here and there.'

'Oh yes. Nothing illegal.'

'If other people do the work, that is for their consciences.'

'Time to learn Latin. You will be going to Rome far more often now.'

'Why do you think that?'

'When the new amphitheatre opens.'

'Yes,' Hanno agreed, smiling. 'That is quite likely.'

I felt annoyed by his complacency. Justinus was still doggedly translating as I changed tack: 'Do you know why your sister wanted Fidelis dead?'

'He had stolen from my son.'

'No – tell him, Quintus. Myrrha had Fidelis kill Rumex. What's very neat is that before he was marched out here to be silenced, Fidelis had killed Myrrha too.'

Justinus made the statement in Punic, then had no need to translate how Hanno reacted. He was deeply shocked.

He stared hard at us as if to see if what we had said could be trusted, then he strode from the arena.

Yes, I thought. When the great new amphitheatre opened, the businessman from Sabratha would still clean up financially – but today he had been stopped in his stride for a moment. That could only be healthy for him and his son.

Saturninus must be returning; there was an expectant hum.

Time was running out. Romanus was now standing alone. As I approached, he spoke to me: 'Falco!' croaked a desperate voice from out of my nightmares. 'Falco; it's me!'

'You bastard,' I answered, without any surprise. 'How did you get Glaucus to accept you at the gym? If there's one person I don't want to see at my private bathhouse, frankly – Anacrites – it's you!'

The men sweeping the final marks from the sand worked around us.

Behind the owl-eyed helmet, I now detected Anacrites' familiar pale grey irises. 'Aren't you going to ask what I'm doing here?'

'I can guess that.' I was furious. 'When I left you in Rome, you decided that you would solve my case – that's the case you had said we should abandon. You were contacted by Scilla. Either you said no at first, or she took against you and went to Cyrene to hire me instead. You came out to Tripolitania of your own accord—'

'Falco, we are a partnership!'

I felt sick. 'I was already hired by the woman; you were trying to compete! You met Scilla again in Lepcis, helped her lure Calliopus here – and now you have killed her. That was not very sensible; she'll never pay her bill! And however did you end up fighting, you fool?'

'Calliopus saw through my disguise. He had me set upon and imprisoned. He said I could either be killed straightaway and dumped in a gutter, or I could fight today and at least stand a chance – Falco, how can I get out of this?'

'Too late, you idiot. Anacrites, when they brought you into the ring you should have appealed to Rutilius. You're a free man, sold into the arena against your will – why go along with it?'

'Scilla had told me she was going to fight for Saturninus. I guessed she intended to somehow try to kill both him and Calliopus. I thought if I was out here, I might be able to intervene – Falco,' said Anacrites plaintively, 'I thought that it was what you would do yourself.'

Dear gods. The madman wanted to be me.

The crowd was baying for the final contest. There was no way I could rescue him, even assuming I wanted to.

'I can't help you,' I told him. 'It's now you against Saturninus and if you try to back out, Lepcis Magna will riot.'

He was being brave, damn him: 'Ah well, I enjoyed working with you, partner.'

I tried to find a joke in return. 'You'll have to trust in the old stories – all the fights are fixed—'

'And the referee is blind!'

I turned on my heel. Justinus followed me. I took two strides then turned back with one final desperate quip. 'If you get wounded, remember Thalia's performing dog: lie still and play dead.'

To my horror Anacrites then held out his hand to me. He would be killed here in a few minutes; I had no alternative. I shook hands, just like a partner wishing him good luck. A partner who knew no luck in the world could possibly help him now.

Saturninus had prepared himself with a professional's efficiency. Over his embroidered loincloth, his belt was a wide, champion's effort. He wore one greave, an arm-protector, and a curved, rectangular shield. His helmet was a pair to that worn by Anacrites. His bare chest and limbs looked oiled. He swept out across the arena, visibly fresh. An expert. The local man. Undefeatable.

I stared up at the massed faces, twenty-five or so rows of them. The crowd was murmuring feverishly. Then silence fell.

I expected it to be short. It was nearly so short most people missed it. Saturninus took up his guard. Anacrites was facing him, though probably not yet concentrating. With a loud yell, a heavy stamp forwards, and a powerful swordstroke, Saturninus struck Anacrites' own sword from his hand. Now, Anacrites was not even armed.

Anacrites went straight in. Even Saturninus must have been startled. Anacrites plunged forwards and pushed his opponent, shield against shield. Good try. Almost an army move. Saturninus may not have expected this, but he reached around and stabbed inwards. Anacrites dragged himself sideways away from the blow but kept close, so they wheeled. Carried on by the momentum and still locked together, they continued to push each other in a wild stumbling circle while Saturninus hacked with his sword. Anacrites was already covered in Scilla's blood, but new streams of his own were flowing. I could hardly bear to watch.

Anacrites fell. He at once raised his finger, appealing for compassion. Saturninus stepped back, looking contemptuous. In the crowd I saw a few thumbs up and fluttering white handkerchiefs, though nowhere near enough. I dared not look at Rutilius. Saturninus took his own decision; in the time-honoured move, he bent to hoick up his opponent's helmet by the chin, exposing his throat. He was about to give Anacrites the death blow.

Suddenly Saturninus reeled back. His sword fell to the sand. He had recoiled from Anacrites and was bent forwards, clutching his stomach. Blood welled between his fingers. I could not see the weapon, but I recognised his action – familiar to anyone who has seen a tavern brawl. He had been stabbed in the bowels with a knife.

Anacrites was the Chief Spy. No one should have expected a clean fight.

Saturninus made a desperate effort. He stumbled forwards, caught up his sword again, then fell on to Anacrites. The sword seemed to go in somewhere, but the knife found another target too. They both lay still.

There was uproar again, but even the crowd had seen enough by now. Justinus and I walked out to the corpses as steadily as we could. We pulled them apart. There was no sign of life. I found the knife Anacrites had used and managed to slide it up my sleeve unseen. We made a show of performing a formal inspection, then I tapped both bodies briskly with the mallet and signalled for bearers. Saturninus was afforded the honour of a stretcher. 'Romanus', as a stranger, was towed from the ring face up and feet first, with the back of his helmet dragging on the bloody sand. The only way he could have left was as a corpse. Had he survived the fight, the outraged crowd would have torn him apart.

LXIV

After the necessary salutes to the president, I set off for the great doorway, with Justinus close behind me. The hubbub continued in the arena as we walked outside.

We surveyed the grim row of bloody bodies. I pushed up the beaked mask I wore, feeling as if my legs would give way.

Justinus looked at me sombrely. 'Your partnerships seem to get wound up rather roughly.'

'He brought it on himself. Always consult your colleague – who will dissuade you from sheer stupidity.'

I forced myself to walk over to the line of carcasses. Groaning at the effort, I knelt down. More gently than he would have expected, I released the helmet from Anacrites and laid it to one side. His face was as white as the time I found him with a smashed head, as close to dying as anybody could have been and yet survive.

'I shall have to tell my mother about this. We'd better make sure he's really gone this time. Hermes—' Justinus stepped forwards with the snaky staff. 'Right; give him a quick shove somewhere with your hot caduceus.'

A pair of pale grey eyes opened, very wide. As Justinus knelt down to touch the 'corpse', a resounding yell of terror rose to the Tripolitanian skies.

I smiled to myself resignedly. Anacrites was still alive.